PENGUIN BOOKS

FATHER UNKNOWN

Lesley Pearse's previous novels are *Georgia, Tara, Charity, Ellie, Camellia, Rosie, Charlie, Never Look Back* and *Trust Me*, the last four of which are also published by Penguin. She was born in Rochester, Kent, but has now lived in Bristol for over twenty-five years. She has three daughters.

Father Unknown

Lesley Pearse

PENGUIN BOOKS

PENGUIN BOOKS

Published by the Penguin Group
Penguin Books Ltd, 80 Strand, London WC2R 0RL, England
Penguin Putnam Inc., 375 Hudson Street, New York, New York 10014, USA
Penguin Books Australia Ltd, 250 Camberwell Road,
Camberwell, Victoria 3124, Australia
Penguin Books Canada Ltd, 10 Alcorn Avenue, Toronto, Ontario, Canada M4V 3B2
Penguin Books India (P) Ltd, 11 Community Centre,
Panchsheel Park, New Delhi – 110 017, India
Penguin Books (NZ) Ltd, Cnr Rosedale and Airborne Roads,
Albany, Auckland, New Zealand
Penguin Books (South Africa) (Pty) Ltd, 24 Sturdee Avenue,
Rosebank 2196, South Africa

Penguin Books Ltd, Registered Offices: 80 Strand, London WC2R 0RL, England

www.penguin.com

First published 2002
3

Set in 10/11.5pt Linotype Palatino
Printed in England by Clays Ltd, St Ives plc

To my sister Selena with my love and deepest respect. We may have been flung together as children and had to accept what we couldn't change. But you became a true sister of the heart, and that's what counts. I wish you all the happiness you deserve.

Chapter One

'Come here and hold my hand, darling. I hate to sound melodramatic, but I think I'm on the way out.'

Daisy was just leaving the bedroom as she had thought her mother was sound asleep. Hearing these words, she wheeled round in shock and dismay.

Lorna Buchan had cancer. She had fought it bravely for over two years with radiotherapy, a mastectomy and countless alternative treatments, always believing she would get better. But two months ago she had been told by her specialist that the cancer had spread throughout her body. She had resigned herself to this and refused any further hospital treatment, because she wanted to spend her last weeks at home with her husband and children.

Daisy was beside her mother's bed in a trice. 'I'll call the doctor,' she said, her heart pounding with fear.

Lorna smiled up weakly at her daughter. 'No, darling, there's no point. I'm not in any pain and I feel really calm. Just sit with me.'

Daisy was appalled – she couldn't just sit there and watch her mother die without doing something. Yet to argue with her now seemed awful too. So with her free hand she gently stroked her mother's head, while she considered what she should do.

Lorna had lost her lovely honey-blonde hair after the radiotherapy, and the new growth was white and as soft as a baby's. Her face was gaunt because she had lost so

1

much weight and even her blue eyes had faded to a pale duck-egg colour.

It wasn't fair, Daisy thought, that her mother should be singled out for this. She was only fifty and she'd been such a striking, robust woman, always fashionably dressed, known to everyone for her vivacious and warm personality. She was the sort of indomitable woman who could tirelessly supervise a school fête, then at the end of a day which would have exhausted anyone else, invite all the helpers home for an impromptu party. She would still be dancing and laughing as her guests finally left. Yet miraculously by breakfast the following day the whole house would be tidied and cleaned as if nothing had gone on there.

'I *must* call Daddy,' Daisy said after a few moments' thought.

'Certainly not,' Lorna said surprisingly firmly. 'He has an important meeting this afternoon and I don't want him rushing home through the traffic in a panic.'

'But I must do something. Let me call the college and get the twins home.'

'No, not them either, they'll be home soon anyway.'

Daisy had given up her job a month before when her mother became too ill to be left at home alone. This was not an act of martyrdom – Daisy loathed her job, just as she had loathed practically every one she'd ever had, and there had been dozens. Housekeeping and caring for her mother was something she liked and was good at, and she used to think that she could handle any situation or emergency. Yet she knew she couldn't handle this one alone.

'I've got to phone the doctor at least,' she said resolutely.

Lorna turned her head away in a stubborn attempt to try to dissuade her. Daisy picked up the phone by the bed regardless and quickly phoned the surgery to tell them she needed a doctor immediately.

'That wasn't necessary, I only need you here,' Lorna

2

said weakly, as Daisy put the phone down. 'Besides, there's something I want to talk to you about.'

'I will get a real career,' Daisy said quickly, assuming that this was what was on her mother's mind. She was twenty-five and she knew her parents despaired because she was feckless and lacking in ambition. 'I thought I might join the police force.'

Lorna smiled. 'You'd be hopeless at that, you don't like taking orders and you're so soft you'd be bringing all the villains home for tea.'

'So is it Joel, then?' Daisy asked.

Joel was her policeman boyfriend of a year's standing, the longest she'd ever gone out with any man. Her parents approved of him, and she thought perhaps her mother was going to urge her to marry him.

'No, not Joel either, you are perfectly well able to make your own mind up about him. I wanted to talk about your real mother.'

Daisy looked at her mother in horror, 'I don't want to talk about her now,' she said.

'Well, I do,' Lorna said. 'What's more, I want you to find her when I've gone. I think it will help you.'

Her words made tears well up in Daisy's eyes. 'Nothing and nobody will ever replace you,' she said passionately. 'You are my *real* mother. I don't want anyone else.'

She had known she was adopted since she was a tiny child. Lorna and John had told her that she was extra special because they had chosen her, while ordinary parents got no choice at all. Even when she was five and the twins were born – a miracle because Lorna had been told she was sterile – nothing changed. Daisy never felt her parents loved them more, in fact she imagined they'd got Tom and Lucy just to please her. Not once in her twenty-five years had Daisy shown any interest in her birth mother. She knew she was a Buchan, whoever she was born to.

'You might think that way now, Dizzie,' Lorna used the

3

family nickname lovingly, 'but I know from experience that a death in the family can bring up so many unexpected emotions and questions. I believe finding her would help you through all that.'

Daisy didn't know what to say. Lorna wasn't one to make a suggestion like this without having thought long and hard about it. Since she knew she was dying she had organized everything, from her funeral service to filling the freezer with ready-cooked meals. There was nothing morbid about any of her arrangements, she'd been this way all her life, always thinking ahead, making life easier and more comfortable for her family. Yet Daisy couldn't imagine why her mother thought that finding a woman who had given her child away so many years ago would help her grief.

She stared out at the view of the back garden and there, as everywhere in the house, was more evidence of Lorna's planning and patience. It was beautiful, the herbaceous border just coming into its full glory, a bank of blue, pink and mauve plants. Honeysuckle had all but covered the roof of the old Wendy house where Daisy and the twins had spent many happy hours as children. Yet Lorna hadn't led it slide into decay or removed it once there were no children to use it. Each spring she planted flowers in its window-boxes and cleaned it out. Daisy knew that if she were to go in there now, she'd find the little pots and pans, the chairs and table all still arranged carefully.

Of course Lorna had hoped that one day there would be grandchildren playing in it, and Daisy's eyes filled with tears as she was reminded that her mother wouldn't be there to play her part in weddings and babies' birth and upbringing.

'I'll look for her if you really want me to,' Daisy said, keeping her face turned to the window so her mother wouldn't see her tears. 'But whatever she's like, she'll never take your place.'

'Come and lie down with me,' Lorna said.

Daisy remembered that her mother had always been able to sense tears or unhappiness even from a distance, and so she did what she was told and snuggled up beside her.

Her parents' bed had always been a special place. She and the twins had used it like a trampoline, pretended it was a boat, a desert island and a hospital. They had opened their stockings here on Christmas mornings, been tucked in here when they were ill, climbed in during the night when they had bad dreams, and as a teenager Daisy had often lain beside her mother and confided all her fears and dreams. But it was the more recent memories that Daisy thought of now as she put her arm around her mother: Sunday mornings when Dad had gone out with Fred, their West Highland terrier, or evenings when he was down in his study working. Then she'd come in here and end up baring her soul, about Joel, her anxiety that she'd never find a job she really liked, and her friends.

Most of Daisy's friends said they couldn't tell their mother anything important. Yet she had only to lie here, her mother tucked under the covers beside her, and she could talk about things that were unimaginable outside this room.

'I used to bring you into bed with me here when you were a baby,' Lorna said, turning her head on the pillow to face Daisy. 'I used to lie and marvel at how perfect you were, and how lucky I was to be given you. You may be a grown women of twenty-five now, but I still think that way.'

She caught hold of one of Daisy's corkscrew curls and wound it round her finger. 'You were bald at first, and I always expected your hair to be fair and straight when it finally grew. I never expected a curly red-head.' She laughed softly, and her hand moved to caress Daisy's cheek. 'You are so beautiful, Dizzie, funny, generous and big-hearted too. I'm so very proud of you. That's why I want you to find your real mother, so she can share my joy and see for herself that I took good care of you.'

5

As always, Lorna had struck right at the heart of the matter, giving Daisy a reason to do so that she would never have thought of. But she still couldn't promise, she knew that no other woman would ever measure up to Lorna as a mother.

'Do you remember when I had chicken-pox?' she asked, changing the subject because it was just too heavy for her.

'Mmm,' Lorna replied as if she was sleepy.

'I painted on some of the spots with felt tips,' Daisy admitted. 'Did you know?'

'Of course I did,' Lorna replied, her voice hardly more than a whisper. 'Daddy and I laughed about it. We thought you might grow up to be an actress. You always liked to make things more dramatic than they really were.'

'I love you, Mum,' Daisy whispered.

Lorna murmured something about making absolutely certain of her feelings towards Joel before committing herself to marrying him, and then appeared to be dropping off to sleep.

Daisy lay there beside her for several minutes, but as she wriggled towards the edge of the bed to get up and phone her father, Lorna opened her eyes again. 'Say goodbye to Daddy and the twins for me, tell them I love them,' she said in a faint, croaky voice.

Daisy was instantly alarmed by the weakness in her mother's voice. 'They'll be home soon,' she said. 'You can tell them yourself.'

There was no response to her words, not a fluttering of Lorna's eyelids, nor any movement around her lips.

'Oh no,' Daisy gasped. In horror she knelt up on the bed, putting her ear to her mother's heart, but she could hear nothing. She held her wrist but could feel no pulse either. 'Mummy, no,' she cried out, looking down at Lorna's pale blue eyes, which were open and seemed to be focused on something in the far distance.

Her head told her that her mother was dead, yet she

couldn't believe it could come so suddenly, without some warning or a cry of pain.

It was so quiet that she could hear bees buzzing and birds singing in the garden. It was the kind of warm, sunny day that Lorna would once have spent gardening, or washing bedding so she could hang it out to dry. She had always been so practical and predictable, her days governed by a strict routine which was only altered by weather conditions. Daisy had sneered at this once; it seemed so mind-blowingly dull. Yet in the last few weeks she'd come to enjoy routine herself, found a sense of achievement in doing mundane but important tasks. She'd come to believe she had finally grown up.

But she didn't feel grown-up now. She felt as helpless as a five-year-old, kneeling there on the bed, tears running down her cheeks, not knowing what she had to do.

The shrill ring of the door-bell reverberated right through the house, and Fred began to bark. Daisy rushed out of the room and down the stairs, willing it to be the doctor. It was, and he took one look at her distraught expression and went straight on up to the bedroom.

At eight that same evening, Daisy went to her room, taking Fred with her. She shut the door and lay on her bed sobbing. Fred snuggled up beside her, gently licking at her face as if he understood how she felt.

The last few hours had been so strange and bewildering that Daisy felt as if her whole world had caved in. There was nothing normal to hang on to and the silence was eerie. But worst of all was the way her family were behaving.

The doctor was still here when Dad arrived home unexpectedly early. He said he was driving to his meeting when he had a feeling something was wrong, so he'd come straight home. Yet even though he had responded to a seemingly irrational impulse, he didn't react in any way when the doctor told him that his wife had passed away only minutes before. He just stood in the hall looking blankly at him.

He continued to behave oddly, kind of stiff and distant. He didn't attempt to go upstairs to see Lorna, but politely asked the doctor whether he would like tea or coffee. Daisy desperately needed comfort, a hug, to be asked about her mother's final moments and given some reassurance she'd done all the right things, but she got none of those. The twins seemed to be important to Dad, though, for no sooner had he seen the doctor out than he telephoned the college and asked the principal to send them home immediately.

The death certificate was on the kitchen table. John picked it up, read it, then finally went upstairs to see Lorna. Daisy heard the bedroom door shut with a very final click, and she suddenly felt completely isolated.

John was still in the bedroom when Lucy and Tom came home. They had their mother's fair hair and blue eyes in common, but the similarity ended there. Lucy had her mother's rather stocky build, but her face was set in an almost permanent scowl. Tom was tall and slender like their father and normally had a wide grin.

They were red-faced and panting from running. 'Is Mum worse?' they asked in unison.

Daisy burst into tears then. 'She died a little while ago,' she blurted out. 'Dad's up there with her now.'

Tom immediately came over to Daisy to embrace her. He leaned over till his face was on her shoulder and Daisy could hear him crying softly. But to her astonishment Lucy rounded on her.

'Was Dad here when she died?' she asked accusingly.

'No,' Daisy sobbed. 'Just me. Dad came home while the doctor was here.'

'Why didn't you get hold of us?' Lucy demanded, her blue eyes cold and suspicious.

Daisy was in no mood to give lengthy explanations. 'It all happened so fast. She told me she thought her time had come, and I asked if she wanted me to phone the college and Dad, but she said I wasn't to. She didn't want me to phone the doctor either, but I did anyway. He came just a couple of minutes after she died.'

'You should have phoned us, you had no right to prevent us from being here,' Lucy snapped, then, bursting into loud hiccuping sobs, she ran upstairs. Tom broke away from Daisy, made a sort of grimace, and quickly followed his twin.

The three of them remained upstairs for over an hour, and Daisy got the distinct impression she wasn't wanted there with them. It didn't make any sense, she had never been treated differently before, never felt she was different in any way, and it hurt to think they didn't know her grief was every bit as great as theirs.

She sat in the kitchen with only Fred for company, and she was still there crying on her own when Dad came downstairs much later. He spoke sharply to her, saying there were things which had to be done, one of which was calling an undertaker to take the body away. Daisy was well aware of that, but she thought he could have spared some time first to ask her how she was, and talk through what had happened.

Not knowing what else to do, Daisy began preparing the evening meal, but Dad just said he didn't understand how she could think of her stomach at such a time. Yet he and the twins ate the meal later and she was the only one who couldn't eat anything. After the undertakers had called and taken Lorna away, she was left to clear up the kitchen while they all went into the sitting-room together, and she wasn't asked to join them.

Joel had been very sympathetic when she phoned him, but he was on duty and couldn't come round. He said she mustn't take anything to heart as most people behaved a little strangely when they were in shock.

Now Daisy was alone in her room where reminders of her mother sprang painfully out at her: the many teddybears in leotards, one for every gymnastic competition she'd ever taken part in during her teens; the blue frilly dressing-gown Lorna'd made her last year hanging on the door; the beautifully arranged and framed montage of photographs which she had lovingly put together because she said she couldn't stand any more sticky fixers spoiling the wallpaper.

Had Mum known it was going to be like this once she was gone? Was it only Mum who had been holding everyone together as a family, knowing it would collapse without her? That seemed impossible, but then why had she been so anxious for Daisy to find her real mother?

Daisy pulled Fred tighter into her arms, leaned her head against his fur and sobbed. At least he hadn't deserted her.

A soft tap on the bedroom door startled her. She sat up and quickly mopped her face. 'Come in,' she said, expecting it to be Tom as he often came in to talk to her late at night. But to her surprise it was her father.

He stood in the doorway for a second just looking at her, perhaps noting her red-rimmed eyes. He was a consultant in a company of surveyors who specialized in ancient listed properties, and he often joked that he was becoming like one himself, for his brown hair was speckled with grey and his once lean body was getting flabby. But in fact he was still remarkably young-looking, and handsome for a man in his late fifties; he was fit because he still played badminton and went sailing when he could. But his brown eyes looked heavy now, and Daisy didn't think she had ever seen him look so miserable or uncertain.

'We should talk,' he said softly. 'I'm sorry, Dizzie, I was so wrapped up in myself earlier, I didn't think what it must have been like for you.'

The nickname had started with the twins when they were babies and couldn't say Daisy properly, but it had remained in use because of her nature. Compared with her father and the twins, who were academically minded,

Daisy was dizzy, she flitted from interest to interest, never mastering any of them. If she read a book it was always a light, racy one, and she liked comedy, dancing, skating and gymnastics, anything fast-moving and visual. Yet one of her greatest attributes was her ability to forgive and forget too, and as soon as she saw her father was hurting, she forgot her own bruised feelings.

'It's okay, Daddy,' she said. 'Come on in.'

He perched on the edge of the bed and petted Fred as he asked her a few questions about what had happened. Daisy explained how Lorna had insisted she wasn't to call him or the twins.

'Just like her,' he said sadly, fondling Fred's ears. 'I suppose I couldn't have got back any quicker anyway. But I wasn't prepared for it to be so sudden, Daisy. Last night she seemed so well.'

'And she was fine when I helped her into the bath this morning,' Daisy said, leaning against her father's side. 'She was talking about planting some new chrysanthemums for the autumn. I went in to see her later and I thought she was asleep, that's when she said she thought it was the end and she wanted me to hold her hand.'

Daisy broke down then, and her father pulled her into his arms. 'She's going to leave such a big hole in all our lives,' he said sorrowfully. 'We would have been married thirty years next month, and I always supposed we'd grow old together.'

She felt better now he was holding her and behaving the way he normally did, and they talked for some little while about who they ought to tell right now, and who could wait until tomorrow.

'I'm dreading having to repeat it again and again,' he said wearily, running his fingers through his hair. 'But as there's no need for a post-mortem, the funeral can be quite soon.'

'I could phone some people for you,' Daisy offered.

'No,' he sighed, 'I must do it. Her friends would be hurt

to be told by anyone but me. But tell me, Daisy, what did you two talk about before it happened?'

She hadn't intended to tell him about any of that, not for a while, but now she had no choice.

Her father grimaced. 'She had been saying that to me for some time,' he said. 'You know how she was, Daisy, she wanted to make everyone happy, tie up all the loose ends. You know her own mother died when she was only nine, and her father remarried a couple of years later. She didn't get on with her stepmother and I think her father took the line of least resistance and refused to talk to Lorna about her mother. That left her with a lot of unanswered questions. I suppose she thought you felt the same.'

'I don't,' Daisy said stoutly. 'I'm not the least bit interested in my birth mother. I've got everything I want in this family, even if Lucy is nasty sometimes.'

'She's just a bit jealous of you,' he said soothingly. 'I think she has the idea that your mum favoured you. It will pass.'

'I hope so, Daddy,' Daisy said in a small voice. 'She's got Tom after all, they do everything together. I'm the one out on a limb.'

'Neither of them will be going back to college until after the funeral, so we'll all have time to talk and get things off our chests,' he said as he got up off the bed. 'But I'd better start making those phone calls, and I think maybe you should get into bed. It's been a very harrowing day.'

Daisy did fall asleep quite quickly, but she woke later and switched on the light to see it was only two in the morning. Unable to get back to sleep, she went downstairs to warm some milk.

Daisy had left home many times in the past, to share a flat with friends, to live in a bed-sitter on her own, and once with a boy she wanted to marry, but however much she craved complete freedom, this house and her mother had always drawn her back. It was a spacious Victorian family house, with large bay windows, beautiful leaded lights and all the best features of that period. Lorna and John hadn't changed it much. The dining-room floor had been stripped and varnished a few years ago, the kitchen had been extended and modernized, but as Lorna and John had always loved Victoriana, comfortable velvet couches, sumptuous William Morris prints and well-polished wood, it was probably very close to how the original designer had intended it to look.

Most of their neighbours were wealthy people now, but it hadn't been that way when Daisy was small. In those days Bedford Park was very much a middle-class family area and almost everyone had three or four children. They went in and out of each other's houses, stayed overnight, played and went to school together. Their parents had all been friends too, and Lorna was the one who kept it all going, organizing coffee mornings, supper parties and events in the garden during the summer.

But one by one the old friends left, their arms twisted by the ridiculously high offers for their properties. The new people had nannies for their children and sent them to private school. The women had no time for coffee mornings.

Daisy went into the sitting-room and sat down at her mother's writing desk. On it was the list of people her father had to phone. Judging by the ticks beside some of the names, he'd got about half-way through it.

She turned in the chair, looking around her, and felt a pang of unbearable sadness that she would never again see Mum sitting here writing letters, sewing or reading. It was a cluttered room, with many books, pictures, photographs and ornaments – Lorna could never part with anything which had sentimental value. And everything had remained, from small glass animals bought by Daisy, Tom and Lucy for various birthdays or Mother's Day, to an ugly elephant's foot made into a stool which Lorna had been given by her grandfather. It was an awesome task to clean and dust this room alone, and Daisy really didn't know how they would all manage when the time came for her to go back to work again.

Part of Daisy's problem with work was that she really preferred domestic work to anything else. She was sublimely happy cooking, cleaning and gardening; she didn't take kindly to office or shop work with the petty rules and regulations. This made her something of an oddity among her friends who were real Nineties yuppies, bent on making money and buying their own houses. She had no ambition or qualifications – she hadn't done very well at school. All she really wanted was exactly what her parents had; a strong, loving marriage and a couple of children. But to admit that to anyone these days was like admitting to cannibalism.

That too was part of the problem with Lucy. For today's hostility was nothing new, she was always sniping at Daisy, saying she was aimless, dopey and out of touch with the real world. And in some ways Lucy was right. If Daisy was sent out to buy something, she often forgot what it was. Her love life had always been tangled and dramatic, she was emotional, generous, a spendthrift and very impulsive.

Lucy, on the other hand, was very bright. She had nine GCSEs and three 'A' levels and was studying economics. She chose her boyfriends carefully, managed to live on her allowance, and never forgot anything. Yet oddly it was none of these things which had caused the rift between them. That had started through Daisy's ability at gymnastics, and perhaps a bit of bad timing on her part showing it off. She had been something of a star in gymnastics at junior school, and won many competitions, but by the time she was fourteen she was tired of competing and only did it for fun.

Lucy could play both the piano and clarinet very well, something Daisy deeply admired because she knew she would never have the patience to learn. One summer afternoon about six years ago, the whole family was sitting out in the garden, and Lucy was playing the piano in the dining-room with the French windows open so they could hear her.

Daisy didn't really know why she did it – perhaps, as Lucy said, it was because she hated her sister getting attention. As Lucy broke into a particularly stirring piece of music, Daisy went up to the kitchen door and proceeded to do a series of back-flips right down the garden, and came back up it again walking on her hands.

Tom and her parents cheered, interrupting the piano recital. There was a loud clonk as Lucy angrily crashed the piano lid down and shouted out something like, 'You'd better get a job in a circus, that's all you're good for' before flouncing upstairs in a sulk.

Daisy apologized later, but Lucy didn't come round and it was as though that day set a kind of standard which could not be changed. Open warfare became the norm, and Lucy used any way she could find to discredit or belittle Daisy.

It didn't help that Lucy suddenly sprouted up to five feet nine, got more than her fair share of spots and had to wear size fourteen clothes. Daisy couldn't help being slender, only five feet five and rarely bothered by spots, but Lucy behaved as if she thought a wicked fairy had cast a spell over her which was meant for Daisy.

Time and again she accused Daisy of being anorexic. She would hide her favourite clothes and relentlessly point out how stupid she was. Daisy was aware that she had often made the situation worse by yelling abuse at Lucy, calling her a fat swot and offering her medicated facial cleansers for her spots, and she was ashamed of this now. But Lucy had worn her down, spying on her, going through her room when she was out and generally getting up her nose.

When Daisy moved into her first bed-sitter, they did get

on better when she came home on visits. But as soon as she moved back, it all started again. By this time she was twenty-one and a little more sympathetic, so she tried to win Lucy over by asking her to come to the pictures or go out shopping with her. Yet Lucy seemed set on being disagreeable, and more often than not these trips out ended in a slanging match.

As Daisy wandered into the kitchen, Fred looked up from his basket and wagged his tail, clearly hoping he was going to be taken out for a walk. 'No walkies,' Daisy said, leaning down to pat him, 'it's the middle of the night.' She poured herself some milk, wishing now that she'd confided in Mum about Lucy – perhaps she would have had some good advice on how to deal with her. But it had always been just a private thing between the two girls; they'd never let it show in front of their parents.

'I just won't rise to it in future,' she said to herself, putting the mug of milk into the microwave and feeling guilty at the many fights they'd had when their parents weren't around. 'We have to be adults now.'

It was a very warm night, and Daisy got her cigarettes from her handbag and went out into the garden to smoke one, Fred padding softly behind her.

She had never smoked in front of her parents, it just didn't seem right to as they were non-smokers. Mostly she only smoked when she went out with friends, but the garden was a place where she enjoyed having a cigarette, it felt deliciously illicit. Joel didn't approve of smoking, and of course Lucy thought it was the pits. But Tom indulged, and they often had a cigarette together out here in the evenings.

Daisy sat on the swing seat and Fred jumped up beside her. She lit a cigarette and gently swung to and fro in the darkness, thinking about Joel and wondering if he would be able to get time off for the funeral.

Suddenly Fred let out a low growl, and Daisy looked round to see Tom coming down the garden in his pyjamas.

'Hi!' she whispered, not wanting to wake anyone else. 'Couldn't you sleep either?'

He shook his head. 'I can't really get my head round it, Dizzie. She seemed so well when I said goodbye in the morning.'

Daisy gave him a cigarette, and he sat next to her on the swing. Despite being like Lucy in looks, Tom had a very different temperament. He was equally clever, but he liked to act dumb. He was far more thoughtful and considerate than his twin, and more generous with his time, affections and money. He was popular with both his tutors and the other students, he was good at sport, passionate about rock music, and he had a great sense of humour.

They talked for a while about how they felt about their mother, and Tom began to cry. 'I didn't know it would hurt this much,' he whispered. 'I thought I'd be almost glad when it happened because she wouldn't have any more pain. But I'm angry, Dizzie, I keep thinking, why her? Look at all the useless, pathetic people there are! Why don't they get it?'

Daisy instinctively knew he didn't expect her to give him any answers, he was just getting it off his chest. So she held him and let him cry, suddenly aware that she would have to take her mother's place in the family now, for he and Lucy were going to be lost for a while without Lorna.

Neither of them had ever left home, they'd been in the same class since infants' school, they'd chosen a college in West London rather than going away to university, and their closeness had sheltered them from loneliness, bullying and all the many other little things that affect other children. Daisy could remember envying them when they were tiny. Before they could speak properly they used a kind of secret language which she didn't understand. They often slept in the same bed and they shared everything.

Yet Mum had always been equally important to them.

Wherever she went in the house, they followed. Even as twenty-year-olds this link had never really been severed – they had never wanted to go out at night as much as Daisy did at their age, they were just as happy at home.

'Everything will be all right,' she assured Tom. 'We'll still be a family, we'll keep the house and garden up together. I'll still be here.'

'You aren't going to move out then?' he said, wiping his eyes with the back of his hand. 'Lucy said she reckoned you'd be off like a rocket.'

'Now, why would she think that?' Daisy asked.

He shrugged. 'I don't know really. But she heard Mum and Dad talking a while back, you know, about how Dad was going to manage when Mum had gone. Dad said he thought he'd probably sell this house and get somewhere smaller and more manageable because he couldn't expect you to stay and look after it forever.'

Daisy thought about that for a minute. 'I don't suppose I would want to stay forever. I might get married, and so might you and Lucy. It would be more sensible for Dad to have somewhere smaller. But I can't think why Lucy thinks I'd run off immediately.'

'Because Mum's left each of us some money,' he said. 'Lucy and I don't get ours till we're twenty-one, but you'll get yours straight away.'

Daisy felt a stab of anger towards her sister. She hadn't known she was going to be left anything, and it should have been a nice surprise, but it was just like Lucy to use it as a weapon.

'Well, Lucy's wrong for once. I will not be off like a rocket, money or no money, so you can tell her that from me,' Daisy said resolutely. 'Mum would want me to stay here until everyone's settled down again, and I shall. Now, we'd better go back to bed, there will be an awful lot to do later today.'

It rained on the day of the funeral, the kind of soft rain

Lorna had always liked because it nurtured her garden. A great many people came – relatives, many of them distant ones, old friends and neighbours – and the flowers filled the courtyard outside the crematorium.

The service seemed so short to Daisy, and although the words the vicar spoke about Lorna were lovely, somehow he had seemed to miss the real gist of what she was all about. Perhaps Daisy shouldn't have aired this view later back at the house, but many of the neighbours from the time when she and the twins were small had come back for a drink, and they were all discussing the things they loved most about Lorna.

'I would have liked him to say how her greatest gift was to be able to chew the fat with people,' Daisy said. 'Do you know what I mean? She didn't just advise people when they had a problem, she'd sit them down, give them a cup of tea, and talk the whole thing through with them.'

Almost every one of Lorna's closest friends of many years nodded in agreement. One of them went on to talk about how Lorna had supported and consoled her on a daily basis when her husband had left her. She said Lorna was far better than a trained counsellor, because she had the ability to make you laugh even when you were in the depths of despair.

Another old friend, whom Daisy and the twins had always called Auntie Madge, a hearty woman of some sixteen stone who had called in at least once a week for as long as they could remember, spoke up then.

'You've inherited that gift, Daisy,' she said approvingly. 'Don't you ever lose it either, it's a great talent to have.'

Lucy, who was sitting on one of the couches with her best friend, Alice, hadn't appeared to be listening to any of this conversation. Yet even though Daisy had her back to her, she felt her sister stiffen and a kind of chill come into the room.

Later, after all the visitors had gone, Daisy was emptying

out the dishwasher to reload it with more dirty crockery and glasses, when Lucy came into the kitchen, stood by the door and folded her arms. She was wearing a very crumpled long black dress and a pair of Doc Marten boots. It was her usual style; Lucy professed to be a feminist and believed that women who dressed up in glamorous clothes and made up their faces were air-heads. Yet Lorna had hated those boots more than anything, and even Tom had urged her to look pretty and conventional for this one special day, because it would have pleased her mother. Lucy had taken no notice, and John, who was very shaky this morning, hadn't taken her to task about it when perhaps he should have.

'Something wrong?' Daisy inquired. Tom had gone upstairs with Dad to sort out some papers, and the house was very quiet.

'You haven't inherited anything from Mum, how could you when you aren't her flesh and blood?' Lucy said, her voice tight with anger.

Daisy wanted to say something nasty in reply, but knew that today wasn't the right day for a row. 'Auntie Madge was only using it as a figure of speech,' she said with a shrug. 'Everyone in the room today knew perfectly well I was adopted, but you do also inherit things from people through being around them so long.'

'So how come you haven't picked up any brains then?'

'Oh, come on, Lucy,' Daisy said impatiently. 'Don't be nasty today of all days. I might be tempted to ask why you haven't inherited any of our mother's sense of timing or diplomacy.'

She thought that would be enough for her sister to flounce off to her room, but instead Lucy flew at Daisy, clasped a handful of her hair, and hit her right in the face with her fist.

'How's that for timing?' she shrieked like a madwoman. 'I've been watching you all day, sucking up to all those boring old neighbours. Letting them know that you looked

20

after Mum, like you were the only one in the family that cared. The only reason you were here was because you got the sack from your last job.'

Daisy's nose felt as if it was on fire, and blood spurted down her face and dripped on to her dress. She was too stunned to attempt to hit Lucy back, and besides, she knew she was no match for her younger sister when she was this angry.

'I didn't suck up to anyone,' she said, trying not to cry. 'I was just being polite because they were Mum's friends and many of them had come a long way today. And for your information I got the sack from that last job because I kept having to take time off work when Mum was so ill. I don't remember you ever offering to drive her to the hospital for her checkups, or to help her have a bath, or anything if it comes to that.'

Lucy took another menacing step towards her, so Daisy picked up a French cook's knife, which was lying on the work surface. 'Touch me again and I'll stick this in you,' she hissed at her.

'Why don't you fuck off and shack up with your pig boyfriend?' Lucy snarled at her, but keeping her distance. 'You aren't wanted here. Mum might have put up with you, but that was only because she felt she had to. Dad, Tom and I all despise you. All you are is the cuckoo in the nest.'

'Better a cuckoo than an old crow,' Daisy retorted. 'Look at the state of you, like an advert for War on Want! You keep telling me how brainy you are, but only a complete idiot would dress like that for her mother's funeral. How do you think Dad felt seeing you looking like that? If he despised anyone today, it was you.'

She went to walk past her sister, still holding the knife in her hand, but as she brushed against her in the doorway, Lucy grabbed her hair again and tipped her head back. The knife was in Daisy's right hand, and as she moved to defend herself it caught Lucy's arm.

Bellowing like a stuck pig, Lucy let go of Daisy and went rushing out into the hall and up the stairs. 'She stabbed me, she stabbed me,' she screamed at the top of her voice. 'Dad, come quickly, Daisy's freaked out.'

Daisy grabbed a wad of kitchen paper to try to stop the blood flowing from her nose all over her and on to the floor. Then she heard Dad and Tom clattering down the stairs, demanding to know what was going on. The bottom of the stairway wasn't visible from the kitchen as the hallway was L-shaped, so as Daisy held the kitchen roll to her nose, she couldn't see her father and Tom with Lucy who was hysterical, shrieking as if she'd been the victim of an entirely unprovoked attack. Daisy was just about to make her way out there and say her piece when she suddenly felt faint and slumped down on to a kitchen chair.

'Stop screaming and sit down,' Dad said to Lucy, but his voice grew fainter as he led Lucy into the sitting-room to examine her arm.

Tom came out into the kitchen. He stopped short when he saw Daisy with blood all over her. 'What's been going on?' he asked.

'She punched me for nothing,' Daisy said weakly. 'Have I really stabbed her? I didn't mean to, I only picked up the knife because she was going to hit me again. She grabbed me by the hair as I walked past her.'

'Dad's looking at it now,' he said. 'What's the matter with you two? Isn't it enough that Mum's dead without this?'

It was unusual for Tom to be critical, normally everything washed over him. He was a calm person, who liked to take a back seat.

'She started it,' Daisy insisted. 'If she walked into the knife then it serves her right, she told me to fuck off and shack up with Joel, she said you all despise me.'

'I'm going to have to take Lucy to the hospital to get this wound looked at,' Dad shouted from the hall. 'I'll talk to you when I get back, Daisy,' he added ominously, and the front door slammed as he left.

'I didn't mean to hurt her.' Daisy looked up at Tom, pleading to be believed. 'She's such a bitch, Tom. I bet she's telling Dad a whole load of lies right now.'

It wasn't clear if Tom believed her or not, but he got some ice from the fridge and held it against Daisy's nose until the bleeding stopped.

As Daisy sat there she told him exactly what had happened and why, but Tom still seemed to think she was mainly to blame. 'Why didn't you just refuse to get into an argument?' he said, his normally sunny face contorted with anxiety. 'You know what she can be like.'

'I can't take insults like that and say nothing,' Daisy said wearily. 'Nobody could. Can't you imagine how hurtful it is to be told I'm a cuckoo in the nest here? Am I, Tom? Is it true what she said, that you and Dad despise me?'

'Of course not,' he said, shaking his head. 'Lucy was just jealous because you were in the limelight today, everyone admiring the cakes and flans you made, saying how nice you'd kept the house and what a comfort it must have been to Mum to have you looking after her. She was hurt that she didn't get any compliments.'

'Well, she didn't do anything to get them,' Daisy retorted. 'It wasn't that I wanted to do it all alone. She wouldn't help me, if you remember. I'm every bit as upset as anyone else at losing Mum, but I couldn't stay moping in my room, someone had to prepare things.'

Tom gave her the same despairing look she'd often seen on her father's face. Dad was a person who didn't like confrontation, or being asked to take sides. 'Your nose is badly swollen,' he said, and it sounded like a pretext to get off the subject of his sister. 'I'll get you some brandy, and maybe you'd better go to bed.'

There was nothing Daisy wanted more than to sleep. She'd been up since six that morning preparing the food and she was totally drained now. 'Okay, but will you explain my side of it to Dad when they get back?' she asked.

He nodded.

'Perhaps it would be best if I moved out,' she said.

He looked at her for a moment without replying.

'You think that's the answer, don't you?' she said, tears starting up again.

'I don't know, Daisy,' he said wearily, running his fingers distractedly through his hair. 'But I know I'm sick of being piggy-in-the-middle.'

Chapter Two

Daisy woke as Fred jumped on to her bed to lick her face.

'Don't,' she said sleepily, pulling the duvet up to cover herself. But Fred burrowed his nose under it to find her, and she was suddenly wide awake and remembering the events of the night before.

She had heard Dad and Lucy come back from the hospital at about half past ten, but they went into the sitting-room with Tom and shut the door behind them. Someone must have come up later to see if she was asleep, otherwise Fred wouldn't have been able to get into her room this morning, but she hadn't heard them. She wondered if it had been her father wanting to get to the bottom of what happened with the knife.

She touched her nose gingerly. It felt very sore, so she reached out for a mirror on her bedside table, at the same time noticing it was only seven o'clock.

Her nose was badly swollen, and there was bruising under both her eyes, but although it made her look gross, at least it was evidence that Lucy wasn't blameless. Joel had said he was going to come round in the evening and take her out for a quiet meal, but she didn't think they'd be going anywhere now, not with her looking as if she'd been in a road accident.

She lay down again and tried to get back to sleep, but her mind kept churning over the previous day's events. She was ashamed that such an important day had been trivialized by her and Lucy fighting, wishing she'd walked away and ignored her sister when she started the argument. If Joel hadn't had to return to work straight after the funeral, she doubted anything would have happened. Lucy was never nasty in front of him.

Yet she'd called him a pig. Was that just to rile Daisy, or did she secretly hate him too?

Daisy sighed deeply. One of the things she liked best about Joel was the fact that he got on with everyone. After so many years of having boyfriends no one approved off, it felt good to be with someone who was admired and respected. Trust Lucy to undermine the one thing Daisy was sure of.

She closed her eyes and remembered when she first met Joel at a wine bar in Hammersmith over a year ago. She had noticed the big man wearing a tight black tee-shirt and jeans sitting at the next table to her and her girlfriends. In fact she'd whispered to them that he looked like a sex bomb. After a few drinks she'd knocked her handbag on to the floor, and the contents, much of it embarrassing, had spilled all over the place. He'd leapt up to help her pick everything up and had teased her about having a spanner and a screw-driver, asking her if they were burglary tools.

At the time she was sharing a flat with some girlfriends just across the road from the wine bar and she'd often voiced her opinion that it was impossible to find a man who was solvent, kind, reliable, trustworthy and sexy. Yet Joel turned out to be all those things and more. He made her laugh, he was strong and fit, and he was charmingly old-fashioned too.

Joel believed in real courtship. He bought her flowers the first time he took her out, and didn't try to get her into bed until their third date. Yet once they did go to bed, they were never out of it. In all her relationships with men she'd never known such utter bliss.

Maybe it was as well that they had all that wild passion then, because it had come to a somewhat abrupt end. First Joel got accepted by Hendon Police Academy, then she'd moved home again because her mum was ill, and they'd had precious few opportunities lately for anything more than a quick snog.

'Do you want to marry him?' she asked herself, recalling how her mother had said she must be absolutely sure. A year ago she would have had no hesitation in answering yes to that question, but Joel's new career and Mum's illness had changed the relationship. She loved him just as much, but they never had time for fun any more. They were almost like an old married couple, meeting for a chat and a cup of tea, except even old married couples lived together and had opportunities for sex.

Of course, she was jumping the gun anyway. Joel talked loosely about getting married in a vague, well-into-the-future sort of way, but he'd never actually proposed. She supposed that if she asked him if she could move into his flat with him he'd agree, but did she really want that?

She just didn't know. He worked such long, odd hours, she hadn't even got a job, and leaving here just because of Lucy could be a serious mistake. But then she was an expert on serious mistakes, she seemed to have made them all. Looking back, she could see she had lived her life as though she was a piece of driftwood, being tossed this way and that by the boyfriends she'd had, never really making decisions for herself.

She should have gone into catering or hotel management work when she left school at sixteen, because she had a flair for cooking and was good with people. But the boyfriend she had at the time didn't want her to work unsocial hours. Looking back, that was a joke because he didn't work at all, and all they ever did was stay in his grubby bed-sitter, watching TV and making love. To add insult to injury, he ditched her for a nurse, and nurses' hours couldn't be more unsocial.

Daisy's next serious love affair was with a car parts salesman. He lived in Leicester, and she stayed with him in his hotel room whenever he was in London overnight. As she always had to make herself available for him, she couldn't start a night-school course then. Later she discovered he was married with three children, and it took her a long time to get over that betrayal.

So it went on. Work was just something she did for money, her main concern was pleasing the current man in her life. There had been quite lengthy periods without a man, of course, but then her mind was always full of where to find the next one, never thinking she should take some time out and discover what she really wanted for herself.

Daisy compared herself to some of her friends for a moment. Cathy was in computers, Sarah was a financial adviser, and Trudy worked for a travel agent. What was it about each of them that made them so ambitious and hard-working?

It was true they'd all done better than her at school and had furthered their education with various training courses, yet the one thing which the other three shared, which she realized she had overlooked before, was that they didn't come from backgrounds like hers.

She suddenly understood why they often teased her. Trudy came from a council flat in Hammersmith, the other two were estranged from their parents and had been living alone since they were eighteen. None of them had ever had either the material things Daisy had or the benefits of intelligent, loving and supporting parents. So it wasn't really surprising that they were hungry for the good things in life, and unlike Daisy knew the only way they were going to get them was through their own hard work.

Ashamed of herself, she got up and pulled on jeans and a tee-shirt to take Fred out. As she walked down towards Turnham Green with Fred pulling on the lead to get to the grass, her thoughts turned from herself to Lucy. She wondered how badly cut her sister's arm was, and if they could make it up today.

The sky was a sullen grey and it looked as though it was going to rain later. But walking with Fred lifted her spirits slightly, for the way he ran around enthusiastically sniffing every last tree, post or seat was amusing. He too had been very confused for the last few days. He kept going up to her parents' bedroom and looking through the door as if he expected to see Mum there. While Lorna had been in bed during the day, he'd got into the habit of going up there to keep her company, even though prior to her illness the bedrooms were out of bounds. Now Dad kept chasing him off downstairs again, and poor Fred must be wondering what they'd done with Mum, Daisy thought, for he'd been very much her dog.

That was another problem: what would they do about Fred when Daisy went back to work? It was hardly fair on him to be shut indoors alone all day when he wasn't used to it.

Daisy was out much longer than usual as Fred kept running off when she tried to put him back on the lead. As she opened the front door her father was coming down the stairs, already dressed in casual trousers and a sweat-shirt.

He frowned when he saw her. 'I think we'd better talk,' he said sharply.

Daisy put the kettle on and began laying the kitchen table for breakfast. 'Don't bother with that,' he said impatiently. 'I want to know what on earth you thought you were doing sticking a knife in Lucy.'

'I didn't stick it in her,' she said indignantly, and went on to explain that Lucy had only herself to blame as she'd grabbed hold of her hair.

'I know all that,' he said impatiently. 'Tom told me. But how could you even think of threatening your sister with a knife?'

'Because she did this to me for no reason whatsoever,' Daisy said, tapping her nose. 'She was like a madwoman. I picked up the knife so she'd back off. You should have heard the things she said!'

'That's no excuse,' he insisted. 'Lucy had just been to

her mother's funeral, for God's sake, she was upset. Surely you could have seen she couldn't be rational?'

'It was my mother's funeral too, and so was I upset.' Daisy's voice rose high with hurt. 'It seems to me you share Lucy's opinion that I'm just a cuckoo in the nest and have no rights or feelings,' she said, her eyes filling with tears.

'Of course I don't, but you are five years older than her and I expect some restraint from you,' he said, his face flushed with irritation. 'I can't be doing with any more fireworks between you two.'

Daisy didn't have restraint, she tended to be bull-headed, charging in when she should have stopped to think. She was so hurt because Dad seemed to be putting all the blame on to her that she struck out, 'Well, thanks a bunch, Dad, for taking into consideration that it was me who took care of Mum for all these weeks. Lucy didn't care enough for her when she was alive to even wash her hair for her. It was me too who got everything together in the last few days, with no help from Lucy.' She paused to take a breath and saw no sympathy on her father's face, only irritation.

'I'll clear off now and find somewhere else to live,' she added. 'Then maybe you'll see what a selfish little bugger Lucy really is.'

She turned and ran out of the kitchen and up to her bedroom, tears streaming down her face. She hastily threw some things into an overnight bag and within minutes she was slamming the front door behind her and running to her car. Surprisingly, as it usually took a while to decide to go, her old VW Beetle started first time and she took off in the direction of Acton and Joel's flat.

Joel had been in the navy before she met him, and he'd bought this place when he came back to London. He had been very reluctant for Daisy to see it when they first met, and she understood why when he did eventually take her there. It was a poky two-bedroom flat on the second floor of a small, run-down council block. Its only attribute was that it was cheap. Joel had no furniture other than a bed, a fridge and a cooker, not even curtains at the windows.

He had done a great deal more to the flat while he was waiting to start his police training. He'd decorated and put down carpets, and it was quite cosy inside now, but the mucky communal concrete staircases and landings made it a very depressing-looking place to live.

Daisy let herself in with her own key, as she didn't expect Joel to be there. To her amazement he came into the hall, wearing only his boxer shorts, just as she was closing the door behind her.

'What on earth!' he exclaimed in surprise, and at that she burst into tears.

Joel was big, six feet two of hard-packed muscle, with brown hair cut as short as a squaddie's and a thick neck. Yet he had a surprisingly boyish face, pinkish-toned skin, long dark eyelashes and a soft, full mouth. But then, he was a man of many opposing attributes. He looked tough, yet he could be so gentle; he played rugby, yet he liked poetry. He would drive his car with heavy-metal rock playing full blast, yet at home he liked to listen to classical music.

Daisy told him all that had happened and he took her into the bedroom, sat her down on his unmade bed and went to make her a cup of tea.

As always, his flat was like a tip. Every time Daisy came round here she cleaned it up and put his clothes away, but it was always a mess the next time she called. He used the ironing board for everything. Right now his boots were sitting on it, as he'd been cleaning them. Quite often she'd seen empty takeaway cartons on it, but rarely an iron. Yet strangely, Joel was very fastidious. His fingernails were always clean, he smelled of soap and water, he didn't even have smelly feet like most men she knew.

'I don't think you should have run off like that,' he said

sternly when he came back with her tea. 'Your dad is facing the biggest crisis he's ever known, and he can't cope with you and Lucy squabbling.'

'It was all her,' Daisy said indignantly. 'I want to be friends, she doesn't. She hates me.'

Joel looked anxious. 'I wish I could stay with you for a bit and talk about it, but I've got to go to work now,' he said, going over to the chair where his uniform was hanging. 'I won't be back till six either. You are welcome to stay here, but I don't think it's the right thing to do.'

'Well, thanks for being so understanding. I thought you'd be on my side,' Daisy snapped at him.

'Of course I'm on your side,' he assured her. 'Lucy's a jealous little cow, I've seen that dozens of times. I suppose it's all just surfaced because of what's happened.'

'What's she got to be jealous of me for?'

Joel laughed, his brown eyes twinkling. 'Look in the mirror, Daisy. You're lovely and she's quite ordinary, you sparkle, she's like a flat beer. All she's got is her superior intellect, but I don't suppose that gives her much comfort.'

He kissed her lingeringly before he left, whispering that tonight they'd make up for lost time. 'Put your feet up and relax,' he said. 'Part of the trouble is that you've been overwrought for a long time. But I have some special magic to put that right.'

Daisy didn't relax, she couldn't in such a messy place. She put clean linen on the bed, washed the mountain of dirty dishes, then cleaned the flat throughout.

She was just sitting down with a cup of tea, intending to watch the Friday afternoon film later, when the doorbell rang. Joel said the only callers he ever had were people selling things from catalogues, so she expected it to be one of them.

It was a shock to open the door and find her father standing there.

'May I come in?' he asked.

'How did you know where I was?' Daisy asked.

He smiled wryly. 'I hardly need to be Brain of Britain to work that one out. Don't worry, I'm not going to drag you home if you want to stay here. But I couldn't let you go without telling you I love you and hope you'll reconsider.'

That took the wind right out of her sails. She had spent the morning imagining he was glad she'd gone.

He came in and sat down in the living-room while Daisy made him some coffee. 'It's very neat and tidy,' he said, looking round the room approvingly. 'Joel's a bit of a wonder all round.'

'I just finished cleaning it,' she admitted. 'I'm glad you didn't come earlier, you might not have been so impressed.'

'Actually, I like people to have faults.' He smiled faintly. 'It makes them human. Mine is that I want everything to run smoothly, but don't know how to arrange that myself. Lucy's is that she's riddled with jealousy, and Tom's is that he tries very hard not to take sides. Yours, Daisy, is that you are far too impetuous. Now, are we going to find a way so that we can all live together without any more fights? I feel so wretched without Lorna, and I know you do too, and it's only together that we'll feel a bit better.'

Daisy looked down at her hands and said nothing. There was nothing she *could* say. Lucy had been out of order, they both knew that.

'We can't manage without you,' Dad went on. 'None of us is good at cooking or housekeeping. We need time and a bit of training all round before we'll be able to cope on our own. I know that sounds as if I only want you as a housekeeper, but I'm sure you know that isn't the way it is.'

Daisy had never seen herself as a Cinderella type. Long before Mum became ill she'd always helped around the house and cooked meals because she liked to. She could see the logic in what Dad had said, and in her heart of hearts she wanted to go back home. She also knew it wasn't right to put more strain on her father now while he was grieving.

'But I can't come back unless Lucy changes a bit,' she said. 'I can't live with her always sniping at me.'

'She isn't only jealous, she's also burdened with guilt,' he answered. 'She knows she should have done more for her mother in the past months, she admitted it last night. The less she did, the more you had to do, and so it went on, round and round, screwing her up even more.'

'Well, can't we forget all that and start again?' Daisy said.

'That statement, my darling Dizzie, is precisely the fundamental difference between you two girls. You could do that, wipe the slate clean and start again. Lucy can't. Her whole nature is completely opposite to yours. She sees everything in black and white, no shades of grey. She compartmentalizes her life – college work in one box, home life in another, social life in another, and so on. You throw her because you are fluid, adapting to circumstances, and you don't just see shades of grey, you see the whole rainbow.'

'Do I?' Daisy said in surprise.

He chuckled. 'That wasn't the best analogy in the world, but it's the best I can come up with for now. Both of you have great strengths. Lucy has determination, ambition and a keen analytical mind. You have warmth, compassion and a wonderful sense of fun.'

'I sometimes wish I had Lucy's strengths,' Daisy said sadly.

'She wishes she had yours too,' he answered, leaning towards her and taking her hand in his. 'But the one thing she wished she had, above all else, was the easy, comfortable relationship you had with your mother. She told me last night that she would hear you laughing and talking together and she hated that she couldn't do it. She couldn't tell her mother that she loved her either. I think she imagines that if she'd got back to the house before she died, she could have said it.'

'I see,' Daisy said thoughtfully, suddenly understanding why Lucy flew at her that day. 'But she's daft, Mum knew everything about all of us. She accepted us all as we were.'

'Lucy will see that in time too,' he said soothingly. 'So my suggestion is that you stay here with Joel over the weekend, then come home again on Monday. Tom and Lucy will be back at college, and you can look for a job again. I'll have to try and find a cleaning lady fairly soon. It isn't fair to expect you to do everything for evermore.'

'What does Lucy say about this plan?'

'Well, she was in her compartmentalization mood again this morning.' He smiled wryly. 'She was terrified she'd be expected to cook, clean and do her college work, so she'll be relieved. As for Tom and me, we just want you back where you belong.'

That was enough for Daisy. She moved over to sit beside her father and hugged him. 'Okay, I'll come back on Monday morning. I'd do anything to try and keep you from feeling sad.'

'That comes in waves,' he said. 'One minute I'm glad she was released from all the pain, the next I'd sell my soul to the devil to have her back. I keep getting these images of her around the house, sometimes they are so clear I really think she's there. Maybe I'll feel better once I get back to work.'

'What's that?' Daisy said, suddenly noticing he had brought a bag with him.

He grinned. 'Actually it's for you. I thought it might be a good time for you to go through it. It's a box of stuff all relating to you, from when you were a baby. Your mum made one for each of you, she religiously added stuff whenever she thought something important had happened. I daresay there'll be a letter in there for you too, you know how organized she was.'

Daisy unzipped the bag. Inside was an oblong tin box,

like a large cash-box with a handle on the top, only it had been decorated with a montage of pictures and varnished over.

'Here's the key,' Dad said, standing up and taking it from his pocket. 'I'll be off now. I've got to get Fred some dog food and buy some bread.'

After Daisy had seen her father out she took the box on to her knee and studied it. She thought she knew every single thing that was in her parents' house, they'd never been one for keeping things secret, but she'd never seen this box before, and that made it even more exciting.

All the pictures on the outside were of her, family snaps cut up and stuck on at random. She wondered exactly when Mum had finished it. Some of the pictures were only a year old, so it must have been quite recently, and there was no room for any more so she must have finished it off knowing her end was near. Daisy opened the box gingerly, not sure what to expect. Her eyes filled with tears at what she saw.

There were newspaper cuttings about her gymnastics wins, school reports, an essay she'd written about her family, pieces of artwork she couldn't remember doing, a needle case she'd made for her mother one Christmas. There were her first teeth, sealed in a little plastic bag, a photograph of her with no front teeth, and a class photograph from when she left junior school. So much stuff, important to nobody but her, and she was overwhelmed by the knowledge that it had all been collected with such love and care.

Between the pictures, cuttings and miscellaneous items were many little notes written by her mother. Some were humorous reports on incidents, like the time she fell into a pond on a school outing and had to be brought back with a teacher's gloves on her feet, or when she starred as Dorothy in the school production of *The Wizard of Oz*.

Daisy laughed at many of these, for it was an adult view

on occasions she'd almost forgotten, and an insight into how Lorna viewed her daughter's character. But some were serious, and showed her just how worried her mother had been on many occasions.

One such note was written at the time Daisy was seeing Kevin. He was the boy who dissuaded her against hotel or catering work when she was sixteen.

I feel so powerless and frightened for her, her mother had written. *I keep asking myself am I just a snob that I can't bear to think of my baby being with such an uncouth lout? I'm tortured with fear that she will get pregnant, and that will lead to a lifetime of misery for her. I wish I were brave enough to just lock her in her room so she can't see him, but of course I know that will only make her keener on him. So I pretend to if not approve, at least seem resigned to it. I even try and act as if I like Kevin on the rare occasions he comes here. I'm sure every mother believes her daughter is the most beautiful, talented child in the world, and wants nothing less than a prince for her. But I'd be happy to settle for just a good man for my Daisy, one who would take care of her, treat her with love and respect. I wouldn't mind at all if he were just an ordinary working man.*

Daisy felt choked up as she read this, for she had never realized her mother felt so strongly. She remembered how understanding she had been when Kevin finally ditched her, she had listened to Daisy raging about him, yet not once had she ever said that she was well rid of him.

Daisy shuddered herself now when she thought about Kevin, but how wise Mum had been to keep her own counsel. Daisy might very well have gone out and found an identical replacement for him if she had known how much her mother had despised him. Girls are like that at sixteen.

There were notes about Harry, the married man, too. Her mother had suspected he was married all along, and she spoke of her fear that Daisy's heart would be broken. Again, when it was over, the only thing Mum had said on the subject that stood out in Daisy's mind was that no woman should take happiness at another's expense.

There was no real order in the box, it seemed as if her mother had often gone through it, read things and put them back. Sometimes there was a note on an event when Daisy was five or six, then one right next to it from her twenties. There was a great deal about her early days, problems with feeding, trips to the clinic to get her weighed and vaccinated, even a very funny report on the trials of potty training. But as Daisy got right down to the bottom of the box, she found two sealed envelopes.

Daisy opened the fatter one first, to find it contained her adoption papers, her original birth certificate, two faded black and white photographs and a note from Lorna. She recalled Mum trying to show her this bundle when she was about thirteen. Daisy had refused point-blank to look at the contents. In subsequent years it became something of a joke: Lorna would ask if she was ready to look at them now, and Daisy continued to refuse. She had really wanted to look, at least she had once she was around sixteen, but she had always been afraid her mother would be hurt by her change of heart.

She looked at the birth certificate now and saw that her real name was Catherine Pengelly, her mother's name was Ellen Dorothy and her birth was registered in Bristol. Yet the saddest thing of all was in the space for her father's name – the word *UNKNOWN*, in spidery writing.

Daisy sat looking at it for some time. *Unknown* was such a bleak, chilling word. Did it mean her mother didn't know who the father was? Or had she refused to name him for some reason known only to herself?

Daisy knew that nowadays when a couple weren't married the child could be registered in the father's or the mother's name, and in either case the father had to attend the registration. But perhaps it was different back in the Sixties.

Daisy had always known she was illegitimate, that didn't bother her. Lots of girls she'd grown up with were as well, and besides, her mother would hardly have given her up for adoption if she'd been in a stable relationship. Yet 'Father unknown' had a desolate ring to it, almost a Dickensian workhouse image.

She turned to the photographs and found one of two young girls. They were very alike, both with curly hair just like her own, and probably no more than two years between them. On the back it said, 'Ellen and Josie, 1955. On the farm at Mawnan Smith'.

The other photograph was of herself as a very young baby. She felt it must have been taken while still in hospital as she couldn't have been more than a couple of days old. Bald, as Mum had said, hands waving like two little starfish.

She read the note from Lorna then. It was a series of facts, as if she had hastily written down everything at the time of the adoption, for fear she would forget it, then added a postscript at a much later date.

Ellen Dorothy Pengelly, born 1947. Left parents' farm in Cornwall during pregnancy. Unable to tell parents of her predicament. Refused to give any information about baby's father, other than that he was white, fair-haired, blue-eyed, slim build, athletic and of above-average intelligence.

The adoption society were of the opinion he was a married man.

Worked as a mother's help in Bristol during her pregnancy. Arrangements had been made for her to enter a mother-and-baby home later, but did not go there. Adoption arranged privately, through doctor. Daisy put with foster-mother from hospital while health checks were made. Ellen returned to job in Bristol.

Ellen Pengelly showed great promise at school. She was in the sixth form intending to sit 'A' levels, having achieved eight GCEs in the summer of 1963.

Father Albert Pengelly, farmer. Clare, Ellen's mother, died in 1948 when Ellen was fourteen months old. Albert remarried soon after. Another daughter, Josie May, born 1949.

It was reported that Ellen and Josie were very close, but Ellen had problems with her stepmother.

Postscript, 1971.

I suspect now that Ellen was pressured into giving up Daisy for adoption, perhaps by the family she worked for at the time, in conjunction with the doctor who arranged it.

I feel this because of a letter from Ellen which was forwarded to me by the doctor in Bristol, along with two photographs, one of Daisy taken in hospital, and one of her and Josie at the farm.

Sadly the original letter was accidentally lost, but in it Ellen said she was unable to forget her baby, and she asked me to tell you when you were old enough to understand that she wasn't given any choice in the matter. She asked me to keep these pictures safe until that time too. She added that it was her hope that one day you would meet, so she could explain everything to you.

The tone of Ellen's letter was of someone haunted by the past, deeply regretful, yet appreciative that her daughter had gone to a loving home. It was written beautifully, in clear, neat handwriting, her spelling and grammar proving she was intelligent and thoughtful. Although it is considered inadvisable to enter into any correspondence after an adoption has been made legal, I was so deeply moved that I sent back a reply through the same doctor, enclosing a recent picture of you and details of your progress at school, and your delight in the twins. I told her that I'd made a little story for you about adoption, and that later on when you were old enough to understand fully I would go into it in more depth. I told her too that by giving you to us, she'd blessed us with more joy than she could possibly imagine.

I found it staggering to see the similarities between the picture I sent of you, and the one she sent of herself. Aside from the early Fifties clothes, it could have been the same child.

The doctor's name was Dr Julia Fordham, 7 Pembroke Road, Clifton, Bristol. In 1964 she would have been around forty-five. We met and talked on the telephone several times. She struck me as being a very domineering but good-hearted woman.

Please bear in mind, Daisy, that you cannot judge any of the decisions made on your behalf right back in the early 1960s by present-day standards. Up until 1967/8, unmarried mothers were virtually outcasts. There was little financial help for them, and accommodation would have been difficult to find. The societies which did help them were mostly run by the Church, and in most cases, unless the father was willing to marry the girl, or help came from her family, unmarried mothers had very little choice but to give up their child. The advent of the Pill and the Flower Power era, with its Free Love ethic, changed everything dramatically just a few years later. Social workers moved heaven and earth to help young unmarried mothers, and of course babies put up for adoption were few and far between. So don't judge Ellen harshly, everything I was told about her, and what I gleaned from her letter, points to her being a very decent, sweet girl who was just a victim of circumstance.

Daisy picked up the photograph of the two girls and looked at it more carefully. Mum was right, they were very alike. She thought Ellen's family must have been quite poor, for the girls' dresses looked very shabby.

She then picked up the slimmer envelope and opened it. It enclosed a letter from Mum dated April of this year, and a cheque for six thousand pounds.

Dear Daisy, she read. I always liked to get the last word in, didn't I? As I sit here writing this, preparing to put it in the

41

box with all the other memorabilia that I collected for you over the years, I sincerely hope that the doctors may be wrong in their prognosis, and that in a few years' time we will go through the box together and laugh at its contents.

But if I am unable to share it with you, I hope you will find comfort in it, for it was accumulated with a great deal of love, and my little notes, though a little embarrassing to me now, do show how I felt at the time.

No child was ever loved more than you were. The utter joy your father and I felt when you were handed to us still gives me a lump in the throat now, after all these years. That joy was almost certainly the reason why five years later I managed to conceive the twins, when we had been told that was impossible.

You filled our lives with happiness after many years of disappointment and we were always so proud of you. Stay close to the twins, for the ties of a shared childhood are just as strong as blood lines. I wish you as much joy and happiness in your life as I had in mine, and the only sadness I have is that I won't be around to see my grandchildren. The cheque I've enclosed is a share of the money left to me by my father. He too died without seeing the grandchildren he hoped for, and saving some of it for you, Lucy and Tom was my way of honouring him. So spend it wisely, my darling. A final goodbye is no time for lectures, and I've given you enough of those in the past. So all I can say now is that I love you, and that I shall be watching over you.

My love,
Mummy

Daisy read the letter three times, sobbing uncontrollably. It was so like Mum to have had the foresight to put something in writing that Daisy could hang on to, yet at the time she wrote it and sealed the envelope she must have been so afraid for herself.

What an incredibly brave and honourable woman she was, with such compassion for others, and an indomitable spirit. In the face of such courage and goodness, Daisy knew that now she had to put her own house in order and justify her mother's faith in her.

She picked up the picture of the two little girls again later. Ellen had to be about eight, her half-sister six. They were standing under a tree, arms around each other's shoulders, both smiling. The picture was crackly with age, the feel of it suggested Ellen had kept it close to her for a long time before sending it to Mum. Why send such an old picture? Did it hold some special significance?

Daisy thought about this deeply for some time. Most people would send a recent, flattering picture just of themselves, especially if they were in a position like Ellen's, hoping to make a good impression. Therefore it stood to reason that this picture was very important to her. But why?

Chapter Three

Cornwall, 1955

'You're mad, Ellen Pengelly, just like your mum,' Sally Trevoise screamed out above the tumult of sixty noisy children turned loose into the small playground of Mawnan Smith primary school. 'Go and jump off a cliff like she did.'

Trouble had started between the two eight-year-olds in the classroom a few minutes earlier. They had been painting at easels side by side, when Sally had spoilt Ellen's picture by daubing a large black cross over it. Ellen had retaliated by concealing some blue paint in her hands as the bell rang for playtime, and the moment they got outside she'd grabbed Sally's plaits and smeared the paint on to them.

A sudden hush fell over the playground, all the children as taken aback as Ellen by Sally's statement. Silently they grouped themselves around the two girls, expecting a real fight to start.

But Ellen just stood there staring at Sally, utterly confused by what she'd just heard. Her mother was home on the farm, just as she always was.

Sally's parents owned the grocery shop in the village, and her appearance confirmed that they were rich by local standards. She wore a pleated skirt, and unlike the many cheap ones in the playground that had no depth to the pleats and lost them altogether after a few washes, hers swung with style. Her red hand-knitted cardigan coordinated perfectly with her skirt, and the blouse beneath had a lace-trimmed collar. Her socks were snow-white and knee-length, shoes patent leather bar-straps. She had an air of supreme confidence, along with blonde hair and blue eyes, and few people noticed her mean, narrow lips and tightly pinched nose.

Ellen, by contrast, was a ragamuffin. Her curly red hair rarely saw a good brushing, her grey pinafore dress had a badly sewn patch by the hem, and the jumper beneath it which had once been pale yellow was now matted and a dirty ivory colour. She wore plimsolls on her feet, and knee-socks that hung in festoons around her ankles.

Yet Ellen was popular with both adults and other children, for she had a sweet nature and a sort of glow from within. Her teacher, Mrs Palstow, said she was a rewarding pupil, always enthusiastic and eager to learn. Few people ever really noticed her shabby clothes – she was after all a farmer's daughter, and there weren't many parents in the area who could afford to deck their children out like the Trevoises could.

'You're the one who's mad, Sally,' one of the older girls called out. 'I saw Ellen's mum just this morning, or do you think I saw a ghost?'

Sally puffed out her chest and folded her arms defiantly. 'Don't any of you know?' she asked, her eyes scanning her audience. 'That isn't her real mum; she only got hooked up with Mr Pengelly after Ellen's mum killed herself. She killed her baby too.'

There was a gasp from all the children. Even the boys who had previously carried on with their games of tag and leap-frog came closer, picking up that they were missing something shattering. 'I heard my mum and dad talking about it,' Sally said proudly. 'They said she was mad, and if she hadn't thrown herself off the cliff she would have been taken to the loony bin.'

At this Josie Pengelly, Ellen's younger sister, pushed her way through the crowd. The girls were as alike as two peas in a pod, only two and a half years between them and two inches in height.

'You're a liar!' she exclaimed. 'I'm going to tell my dad what you said and he'll come round and knock your dad out. So there.'

'Shut up, Nosy Josie,' Sally said. 'You don't know anything about this, you weren't even born then. Ellen isn't even your real sister.'

'She is,' Josie screeched at the older girl, running forward to batter her with her fists. 'You're a nasty, lying, stuck-up cow.'

At that point Mrs Palstow appeared in the playground. She had observed something going on from the staff-room window, and remembering that Sally had ruined Ellen's painting, guessed she was taking her revenge. When she saw Sally's blue-stained plaits she decided justice had already been done, so she blew her whistle for the children to return to their classes.

All of them moved into line with the exception of Ellen. She was left standing alone, looking stunned. The rest of the children filed into school but still Ellen remained where she was.

'Go and wash your hands please Ellen,' Mrs Palstow said, assuming the child thought she was in trouble. 'It wasn't very wise to put paint in Sally's hair, I expect her mother will be cross. But I did see what she did to your painting and I shall tell her so.'

Ellen didn't answer but ran towards the school building and disappeared into the cloakroom. Mrs Palstow walked on back to her classroom, her mind now on the story she intended to read to her class.

Ellen stood in the cloakroom, her hands under the running tap but her mind firmly fixed on what Sally had said. She very much wanted to discount it entirely, to laugh in Sally's face, yet she sensed that the other girl had got the story from listening to someone in her parents' grocer's shop. Could it possibly be true?

Her hands became numb from the cold water, but she didn't feel it as she was picturing a woman with a baby in her arms jumping from a cliff top. It couldn't be right; mothers protected their babies. Although she couldn't remember back to when Josie was born, she could recall when she started walking. Mum was always shouting at her to watch her baby sister, and sometimes Ellen got blamed when Josie fell in mud. The confusion of it all made her cry, and with that she grabbed her raincoat from the peg and ran out of the school, across the playground and into the street, leaving the tap still running.

She took the short-cut home across the fields, but it was still a long way and she had a stitch from running long before she got to the stile that took her back on to the road. It was only three weeks into the autumn term, but it was already turning colder, and recently heavy rain had turned the path to mud. At the back of her mind she knew she would be in trouble for leaving school, for not putting on her Wellingtons, and especially for leaving Josie to come home alone. But that seemed far less important than to see her dad to find out if what Sally had said was true.

Beacon Farm, the Pengelly land, stretched for about a mile along the road between Mawnan Smith and Maunporth. But although this might have seemed fair acreage to a passer-by, it wasn't good farming land, for it was a narrow strip, running down to the cliffs and the sea, with no flat fields for crops, and clumps of thick woodland and marshy areas. Only the very committed would have tried to farm it.

But the Pengellys were too committed, or at least too stubborn, to walk away from it. It had been passed down through three generations, and each one of them believed it was better to eke out an existence on their own land than to go cap in hand to anyone else for a job.

Albert, Ellen's father, had finally come to own it when his father died back at the start of the Second World War, and Albert still farmed it in much the same way. He kept cows, chickens and a few sheep, and grew vegetables. Even if he had had the money to buy new modern machinery, it was doubtful that he'd have done so. To him, his ancient tractor and his muscle were enough. When times were hard, he would take himself off to Falmouth and join a fishing boat for a few weeks. That was the way his father, and his grandfather before that, had got by, and Albert knew no other way.

The farmhouse reflected the hand-to-mouth existence of its owners. Situated in a dip and concealed from the road by woodland, it was in a sorry state. The roof sagged, the windows were ill-fitting, and wooden outhouses and extra rooms had been added in a haphazard fashion to the original stone-built two-room cottage. Inside was no better; there were no modern amenities, and the furniture was a motley collection of hand-me-downs.

But however dilapidated the farmhouse was, its setting was idyllic. The front of the house faced the sea, there were wooded hills to either side and before it the land gradually sloped down to a small rocky cove. The view was beautiful, whatever the season. Even in the depths of winter when the sea was dark and menacing and the trees bare of leaves, it had majesty, for the waves would crash over the rocks in the cove and frost stayed glittering on bare branches. Purple and white heather sprang up in crevices, rose-hips and other berries were bright on the bushes. In spring the stream to the right of the house, swollen from snow further inland, would gush down its rocky path to the sea; wild iris, bluebells, primroses and violets grew in profusion on its banks. There were rhododendrons too, huge masses of purple and pink, and as the new lambs skipped around their mothers it became a place of enchantment. By summer the trees made a thick canopy of leaves and welcome shade, the fields were bright with buttercups and the cove was paradise for children.

Now, at the end of September, there were signs of autumn approaching. Dew-sprinkled spiders' webs adorned every bush, Old Man's Beard festooned the hedges, and elderberry bushes were weighed down by their purple berries.

Normally as Ellen came down the narrow footpath through the woods to the farmhouse she would linger, looking out for squirrels, squeezing elderberries between her fingers to stain them purple, and checking the horse-chestnut tree to see the progress of the conkers, but today she didn't even notice her surroundings. She was turning over in her mind what Sally had told her, cutting out everything else. As she finally came to the clearing above the farmhouse and saw her father cutting cabbages down below, she ran towards him at full tilt, tears pouring down her face.

'Whatever's wrong, me handsome?' he said in alarm, lifting her up into his arms to comfort her.

Albert looked like a gypsy, not just because of his torn checked shirt, the knotted handkerchief around his neck and his moleskin trousers. His skin had a leathery texture and deep brown colour, and his long, curly hair flowed out like a flag behind him as he strode around his fields. His hair had once been as bright as his daughter's, for curly, red hair was the Pengelly trademark, but now that he was thirty-seven it was peppered with grey and growing thin. It wasn't known for certain why he never cut it, but some old men in the village claimed it was intended as an insult to his father who had ill-treated him as a child and used to shave his son's head to humiliate him.

Yet no one dared laugh at Albert's long hair, or his tenacity in farming land that yielded so little reward. They even described him as a big man, although in reality he was just five feet eight and quite slender. But perhaps that was because his shoulders were powerful, his fists like sledgehammers, and he had a reputation as a man who was dangerous to cross.

Ellen of course did not see him that way, for he was

affectionate with her and gentle with animals. But then her knowledge of other men was extremely limited for the only ones she knew were other farmers who were as strong and silent as her father.

'Sally Trevoise said my mum was mad and jumped off a cliff,' she blurted out. 'She said she killed her baby too and Josie isn't my sister.'

She felt a sense of relief once she'd got it out and she buried her face in her father's shoulder, expecting him to chuckle and tell her it was nonsense. But instead he said nothing, just held her.

'It's not true, is it?' she asked, not daring to lift her face and look at him.

Albert Pengelly was thunderstruck. A quiet man by nature, only partially educated and scraping a meagre living from his land, he felt he had little to offer anyone. Over the years, the hard life and the bitterness that went with it had made him withdraw into himself even more. He had always known that a day would come when he would have to tell Ellen about her real mother, but he hadn't expected it to come this soon. He silently vowed to get even with Meg Trevoise for her vicious, loose tongue. How could he explain something as complex as his wife's death to an eight-year-old?

'It isn't true, is it, Daddy?' Ellen asked again, this time looking him right in the face, her slender body tense with anxiety. 'That is my mummy indoors, isn't it?' she added, pointing towards the house.

Albert thought for a second. He could lie to her, and maybe for a time she'd believe him, but he knew in his heart it would only be a stay of execution. Better she should hear the truth now, however bad, from him, who at least had no malicious intent.

'Violet is your stepmother,' he said, then, putting the child down on the ground, he took her hand and led her down the path towards the cove, well away from the house. 'I married her after your mother died.'

50

'So my real mummy did kill herself then?' Ellen said in a small voice. 'Why? Didn't she care about me?'

Albert had never been able to agree with the coroner's opinion that Clare took her and her infant child's lives when the balance of her mind was disturbed.

'I reckon she just fell from the cliff,' he said.

'Why did she take her baby up there?' Ellen asked, looking up at him with wide brown eyes so like his own. 'Was it in a pram? Was I there too?'

Albert sighed. He could see Ellen wasn't going to be satisfied unless she had a more detailed explanation. But he wasn't good with words, and he was scared he might let slip things a child should never know.

'No, you were with me. Your mum just went for a walk with the babby in her arms. When she didn't come back I went to look for her. But look here, Ellen,' he said gruffly. 'you got to believe what I tell you, not blather from those who don't know.'

'But you didn't tell me Violet wasn't my real mummy,' she said, beginning to cry again. 'So it's true that Josie isn't my real sister too?'

'Josie's your half-sister,' he said curtly for emotional scenes acutely embarrassed him. 'She were born after I married Violet. I couldn't 'ave told you afore. You was too little.'

Ellen sensed he wasn't going to say any more. It wasn't anywhere near enough for her; she had a million more questions buzzing around in her head. But she knew that if she continued to question him he would only get angry.

'Where's Josie?' he asked, confirming that he considered the matter closed.

'Still at school,' she admitted, and looked up at him fearfully. It was her job to get Josie to and from school safely, and Mum was going to be angry with her.

They had reached the little cove now, and the tide was in, throwing the waves up against the rocks, covering the small stretch of sand that she and Josie played on at low tide. They always considered this was their own beach and resented anyone coming there, but in fact there was a footpath right along the cliffs almost from Falmouth to Mawnan Smith and then on down to the Helford estuary. In summer holidaymakers sometimes used it, even having the cheek to come up to the farmhouse and ask for a drink of water.

Some of the other farms in the area had these people to stay with them as paying guests. The Trevoises had a caravan in the field behind their shop that they rented out, and had often suggested to Mr Pengelly that he should let people pitch tents on his land down by the cove, but he wouldn't. He hated the holidaymakers – they left the gates open and let the animals out, left their picnic rubbish about and sometimes even started fires. He said Cornwall belonged to the Cornish, and if he had his way he wouldn't even allow them into the county just to look, let alone stay.

'Reckon you'd best go back to meet Josie,' Albert said, putting his hand on Ellen's shoulder. 'I'll go back in and square it with your mum.'

Ellen glanced at the steep cliffs on either side of the cove and wondered where it was her real mother had met her death, what her name was, what she looked like, but she didn't dare ask. Her father had that set to his mouth that he always got when something was wrong. If anyone pestered him when he was like that, they were asking for trouble.

Josie was just climbing over the stile on the other side of the road as Ellen came along.

'Why did you run out of school?' she asked indignantly. 'Mrs Palstow was very worried.'

'Mind your own business,' Ellen said. She knew if she told Josie why, she'd tell everyone at school the following day.

'Mummy will be cross with you,' Josie retorted.

It was only then as they walked the rest of the way home

together that a sudden thought struck Ellen. Mum always seemed to be cross with her, she expected her to look after Josie all the time, do chores and run messages. It had never crossed Ellen's mind before that there might be a special reason for this, but in the light of what she'd found out today, it had to be because she didn't like her as much as Josie.

'Sally was talking rubbish, wasn't she?' Josie said suddenly, interrupting Ellen's thoughts. 'I am your sister, aren't I?'

Once again Ellen was thrown into confusion. She couldn't repeat what her father had told her, he wouldn't like it. 'Ask Mummy if you want to know anything,' she said sharply. 'She knows everything and I don't.'

Violet Pengelly watched the girls coming down the path through the woods from the small kitchen window at the back of the house. But instead of feeling anxious about Ellen, she was furious with her.

Anger seethed inside Violet constantly, a result of being overlooked and used too often, yet she rarely had any convenient outlet for this anger. She had now; she was convinced her stepchild had wilfully stirred up the events of seven years ago, and in doing so would bring down shame on her and her own daughter's characters.

Reason wasn't in Violet's nature. She was a bovine, unimaginative type, who never thought things through logically. It didn't occur to her that it would be distressing for an eight-year-old to be told in a playground that the woman she called Mummy was not her true mother, and that her own mother had killed both herself and her baby. Violet felt that Ellen's only reaction to hearing she had a stepmother should be gratitude.

It wasn't often that she dared voice what she thought to Albert, but the long-suppressed anger had spilt over when he told her what had happened at the school that day. To her shock and further hurt, he slapped her round the face and said she was inhuman. Was it inhuman to expect a child to be grateful to the woman who had stepped in to feed and care for her when there was no one else? And what had Violet herself got out of it? She was treated like a servant, slighted continually, and worst of all, she saw daily that Albert cared far more for Ellen than Josie.

Josie was the only light in Violet's life. Through her pretty child she had a small ray of hope that one day she might be released from digging potatoes, feeding chickens and milking cows. Had it not been for this hope, Violet might have been tempted to follow Clare Pengelly's example and throw herself off a cliff too, and with greater reason. Clare had had everything that had been denied to Violet. She had been beautiful, from a rich family, well educated and on top of that loved and adored by Albert. Violet hated the woman, even though she had never met her, for if she had been given one-tenth of what Clare had, she certainly wouldn't be living in a tumbledown cottage, working herself into an early grave for such a cold-hearted man as Albert.

Violet was born in Helston, the eldest of six children. Their father had been a tin miner, but the mine closed soon after Violet's birth and he was never in regular work again. Life in Cornwall was bleak for all working-class people during the Twenties and Thirties, but for the tin miners it was especially bad, with many families being forced into the workhouse. Violet's father managed to keep them from that, but her mother was a weak, humourless woman who whined continually, and each time a new baby was born she found even more to grumble about. Violet was a plain child with lank, mousy hair, crooked teeth and a slight cast in one eye, and it was she who took the brunt of her mother's misery, unable even to go to school regularly as she was kept at home to help with the younger children. As a result she was labelled 'slow' because she could barely read or write.

At fourteen she was packed off to Plymouth to work as a live-in kitchen maid in a hotel. The work was hard, but she was well fed for the first time in her life, didn't have to share a bed with anyone and no longer had to listen to her mother's complaints. Plymouth, with its naval dockyard, big shops and cinemas, was a great deal more exciting than Helston, so despite feeling she'd been cast off from her family, overall she felt she'd got a good deal.

For three years, however, she could only view the city's attractions from a distance, like a child looking into a toy-shop window, for she had no friends to explore it with. The other girls she worked with were all older, quicker, prettier, and had more personality than she did, and she was too timid even to try to make friends with any of them.

Everything changed though when she was seventeen and war broke out. The more sophisticated older girls left the hotel for more promising war work, and other young country girls more like Violet took their places. Emboldened by suddenly finding herself one or two rungs ahead of them up the ladder of experience, she was able to overcome her timidity and before long she was joining them in going to dances on her evenings off.

Violet felt as though she'd come out of a cocoon to find herself putting on a pretty frock and makeup and being swirled around in a man's arms under glittering lights. Even though she hadn't metamorphosed into anything approaching a beauty, she appeared to have something special because she was always in demand with the sailors. It never occurred to her that this popularity was purely due to the shortage of available girls, or that the men might be telling her they loved her in order to get her into bed. She believed it when they said they'd write and come back for her, and when no letter arrived she comforted herself with a new man, always convinced that this time it would end in marriage.

By the time the war ended in 1945 she was twenty-three and disillusioned. Dozens of girls she'd worked with over the years had left to get married, or were engaged. The few that weren't had moved on to better jobs, but Violet still worked in the kitchen, and she was growing fat now as well as being plain. Yet the real horror was finally to realize she had spent the war being used by men. She had a reputation for being easy, and they laughed at her behind her back.

Times had been hard during the war with the bombing, the food rationing and the shortages of everything, though the hotel had always been bustling with the service wives, officers and businessmen who came to stay there. But by the New Year of '46 it was growing alarmingly quiet – it was apparent that few people had any desire to stay in a city-centre hotel, especially one which had grown very shabby.

Violet was one of the first of the staff to be given notice, despite her being one of the most long-standing and reliable girls. Hurt and unable to go home to Helston, she took a series of badly paid jobs in cafés and restaurants. After six months of utter misery, working like a slave by day and going home to a lonely room at night, she decided Plymouth had nothing to offer her, and took the train to Falmouth to try her luck there.

She felt better back in Cornwall. There weren't the flocks of attractive and lively single girls there had been in Plymouth to remind her of her shortcomings, and her easy reputation had been left behind there too. After the madness of war, families wanted holidays somewhere pretty and quaint, so the hotels and pubs were thriving and Violet found a job in a harbour pub with guest-rooms above. She did all the donkeywork from cleaning, laundry and cooking, to serving behind the bar, and while not exactly happy, she was resigned to it.

In 1948, after being in Falmouth for over two years, she heard the shocking news of Clare Pengelly's suicide. Violet had been interested in Albert Pengelly right from the first time she met him in the pub. He stood out with his long curly red hair and his lean, muscular body, and like many women she found him very attractive and sexy. Although they did no more than pass the time of day, she was curious about him, and eager to listen to the story of the scandal that had rocked Falmouth in 1944.

Clare's father was a leading London barrister by the name of Rupert Soames. He had five children, Clare being the only daughter. Although their permanent home was in London, they had a second palatial one in Swanpool, just outside Falmouth, which they used for holidays. At the outset of war the London house was closed, and Mrs Soames, with the children and the governess, moved down to Cornwall for safety.

The locals said that the mother and governess were unable to control the three oldest children, of whom Clare, then aged fourteen, was one. They roamed around the countryside and Falmouth harbour getting into mischief, until eventually their father clamped down and sent the two boys to a boarding school. But Clare was never curbed, and from being a tomboy she became an equally wild young lady who was over-indulged and full of silly, romantic ideas about Cornwall, particularly the fishermen and farmers. Violet had heard that she wrote poetry and painted water-colours and would often be seen sitting on a stool in the harbour painting picturesque scenes.

It was the Soameses' gardener who brought the news of Clare announcing her love affair with Albert to her parents. A terrible row ensued. Mr Soames said he would disown Clare if she continued with this folly, and Mrs Soames had hysterics. But Clare wouldn't back down and told them that if they didn't agree to the marriage she would go and live in sin with Albert anyway.

Everyone in Falmouth was agog. Albert was ten years older than Clare, his farmhouse was falling down, and it seemed unbelievable that a gently brought-up girl destined for a society marriage could possibly fall for such a brutish working-class man.

When the wedding went ahead at Mawnan Smith church it was assumed Clare must be pregnant – certainly her family showed their disapproval by not being there. But if she was pregnant, she must have lost the child later, because Ellen wasn't born until early 1947, some two and half years after the much talked about wedding. Violet could remember her birth well, for it was the first time Albert actually spoke to her. He enthused rapturously about his little daughter and said he was the happiest man in Cornwall.

It was just a year later that the second child, a boy, was born, but that time Albert didn't come into the bar to celebrate. There was gossip though; other neighbouring farmers said Clare was acting strangely, that they thought she regretted giving up her family and all the luxury she'd been used to, for Albert. Then came the appalling news that she'd jumped off the cliff with her baby son in her arms, leaving Ellen who was only about fourteen months old.

Violet took the bus out to Mawnan Smith to see Albert. She told other people she was worried about how he was coping with a baby and the farm to look after, but it wasn't really a compassionate urge. Albert intrigued her, he had a farm, which to her meant money, and she knew he was unlikely to turn her away when he was grief-stricken.

He *was* grief-stricken too, confused, frightened and finding it impossible to cope with his loss, the farm and little Ellen too. So Violet offered to stay and help him, and within a week she was sharing his bed.

When she looked back, Violet often wondered why she didn't see how it would turn out right from the start. Albert was always indifferent to her, the farmhouse was even more primitive than the one she'd lived in as a child, there was no money, and farming wasn't the easy life she'd imagined.

But she did grow fond of Ellen, for she was a happy baby and easy to take care of. Then, when she discovered that she too was expecting a child, her first feelings were ones of utter amazement, for after all those men she'd been with in Plymouth, without once missing, she'd begun to believe she was infertile.

Albert agreed to marry her, but he made it quite clear that he considered it only a marriage of convenience, and she knew he compared her unfavourably with Clare. All Violet could hope for was that this would change when their own child was born, and that he would grow to love her.

But Clare's ghost would not go away. Violet felt her presence constantly. Albert took her paintings off the parlour wall and burned them, tore up her poetry and gave away her clothes, but she was still there, if only in Albert's heart. It was as if she even entered the room at the moment of Josie's birth too, and prevented Violet's baby from having any of her mother's characteristics, for even at a few days old it was plain that she was going to look exactly like Ellen.

Violet was glad enough that her child was so obviously a Pengelly, with the trademark curly red hair. It made life simpler; newcomers to the area had no reason to guess she wasn't the first and only Mrs Pengelly. Gradually the gossip about them faded and died. Maybe this was only because people knew Albert was not a man to upset, but Violet liked to think it was because they approved of her. Yet as the two girls grew older and their characters began to form, Violet often felt a sharp stab of jealousy towards Ellen because she was clever. Josie might not have inherited her mother's lank hair, or the cast in her eye, but she seemed far slower than her half-sister. It was also Ellen that people were drawn to, not Josie.

Violet could put up with playing second fiddle to a dead woman, but she was not going to let Ellen overshadow her daughter.

As the two girls walked into the farmhouse, Violet flew at Ellen and slapped her hard across the face. 'How dare you leave Josie to come home alone?' she shouted at her. 'Anything could have happened to her.'

Ellen burst into tears. Dad wasn't there, but she knew he must have told her mum what had happened today, otherwise she wouldn't have known Josie had had to come most of the way home on her own. So why wasn't she being kind?

'I couldn't help it,' Ellen sobbed. 'I had to leave school to ask Daddy if it was true. I didn't think about Josie.'

'I didn't mind coming home on my own,' Josie piped up. She didn't understand what was going on at all, and she didn't like seeing her sister slapped. 'Don't be cross with her, Mummy!'

But instead of calming her mother down Josie's words seemed to rile her even more. 'Get upstairs,' she yelled at Josie, flapping at her with a towel as though she was a chicken that had run into the kitchen.

As Josie ran upstairs, Violet rounded on Ellen again. 'Now, look here, madam,' she said, her pale fat face contorted with spite, 'I took care of you when no one else would. I've dearly suffered for you and your damned mother. But one more word of this business again to anyone, especially your father, and I'll skin you alive. You got that?'

Ellen had. With those few words she knew without any doubt that this woman she'd believed to be her mother didn't care about her at all.

Chapter Four

1963

'What are you going to do then, Ellen?' Josie asked.

It was a Sunday afternoon in June and very warm. The two girls were sitting on a rock down on the beach in the little cove, and the subject under discussion was Ellen's future education.

'I dunno,' Ellen said, wriggling her toes in a rock pool in front of her. 'Half of me wants to go back to school in September if my "O" levels are good enough and sit some "A"s, but the other half wants to earn some money.'

'You don't want to work on the farm then?' Josie asked.

Ellen wondered if Josie had been ordered to ask her that by their mother.

At sixteen and fourteen, the girls were still remarkably alike. One of their neighbours had described them as 'two chocolate-box beauties'. Tangled hair was a thing of the past; they both took great care of their auburn curls, and protected their complexions with cream for fear they would end up with their father's leathery skin. With their identical smouldering dark brown eyes, wide, well-shaped mouths, perfect teeth and slender but shapely figures, they were often mistaken for each other when apart. But when they were together the differences were immediately obvious.

Josie was a giggler and a chatterbox, lacking any powers of concentration. A moody girl, she veered between sullenness and wild excitability, quick to take umbrage at any criticism and always believing she knew best about everything.

Ellen was far more intelligent, a studious, thoughtful girl who preferred to listen rather than talk. People liked her for her genuine interest in them, her quiet yet proud demeanour. She was a girl who won trust and admiration and locals often commented on how well she'd grown up.

Ellen's quietness had developed after she learned the truth about her real mother. It wasn't so much the shock of her discovery that upset her as her stepmother's reaction to her distress. Young as Ellen was, she had recognized that the woman had no real affection for her, and so she stayed out of trouble by being quiet and obedient.

By the time Ellen got to her teens she had come to see that her stepmother's problem with her was jealousy. She wanted Josie to shine brightest, to be the one everyone loved and admired. So Ellen obliged her in this, pushing her younger sister forward, doing and saying nothing to antagonize their mother, keeping out of her way as much as possible and suppressing her opinions.

It would have been far harder had she not had an ally in her father – he seemed to sense when she wanted to talk and would ask her to help him with a task. Although not a talker himself, he liked to hear her opinions and how she was doing at school. When she won a place at the grammar school in Falmouth he had beamed from ear to ear, and said that was 'handsome', which was enough to override her stepmother's sarcasm. The happiest times for Ellen were when she was helping him around the farm, and if it hadn't been for her stepmother, she would have gladly spent the rest of her life working with him. But of course she couldn't admit that to Josie for fear of her telling Violet.

'Work on the farm!' she exclaimed, and raised her eyebrows as if the idea was too outlandish to contemplate. 'Not on your nelly!'

It hurt to deny her real passion. She was a true country

girl at heart, happiest being outside, feeling the wind, rain or sunshine on her face and watching things grow. She loved the animals, growing vegetables, even driving the tractor and milking. She had inherited not only the Pengelly looks but also their feeling for the land. Ellen had the education they had all lacked, and she knew she could learn how to make the farm far more productive.

She thought about enrolling at an agricultural college and coming back to work with her father, but she knew it was a pipe-dream. Violet's hostility towards her had grown even greater when Josie failed to get a place at the grammar school. She would see Ellen deciding to work with her father as a plot to oust Josie from her share of her inheritance when Albert died. In her blackest moods Violet often made caustic remarks along those lines.

It didn't make any sense to Ellen. Josie hadn't got the slightest interest in farming, all her dreams were of escaping to London and becoming a model. She hated the outdoors, unless it was hot like today and she could work on her sun-tan. Besides, Ellen was so close to her sister that even if her father did leave her the farm one day, she would see Josie got her share.

The love and deep friendship the two girls shared was the buffer that protected them from the often bitter hatred that raged between their parents. Josie felt her father didn't love her, Ellen was barely tolerated by their mother. Yet when they were alone together all this disappeared. They were equals, loving each other's company, playmates, sisters and friends, and they did their best to ignore the shortcomings of their parents.

'I don't know how you can even think of spending another two years at school,' Josie said, getting down into the rock pool and splashing some water at Ellen. 'I'm going to leave as soon as I'm fifteen.'

Ellen splashed water back at her sister. 'And what are you going to do as a job, work in Woolworths?' She said this lightly, not intending to hurt her sister for her lack of academic ability. Josie was after all netball captain and swimming champion at her school. 'Why don't you ask if you can do a secretarial course? You'd like that and you'd be able to get a good office job if you got some qualifications.'

Josie pulled a face. 'I'm sick of learning, I want to have some fun and some money of my own. It's a good job we live so far away from all my friends. I'd die if they saw how I'm dressed at home.'

On this subject they were both in full agreement. They had no nice clothes. Monday to Friday they both went off to their respective schools in their uniforms and looked much like everyone else. But at weekends and in the holidays they were too embarrassed to visit friends or have a day out in Falmouth. They looked like a couple of refugees in their home-made frocks and their sturdy, sensible shoes.

The farm was doing better now than it had been when they were little, as their father got a great deal more money for his vegetables and the animals when he sold them at the market. But the extra cash went on improvements to the house and farm. Electricity had been put in five years ago. The barn had to have a new roof, and when the old tractor had conked out for good, that had to be replaced. The girls were delighted when just a year before, a real bathroom complete with inside lavatory was installed, but that wiped out any hope of clothes or other luxuries. Ellen accepted this better than Josie, as she rarely wanted to go anywhere in public. But for Josie it was a major issue – she thought it was all because her father was miserly.

'You're so pretty that no one notices what you wear,' Ellen said, trying to make her feel better. 'You look far more stunning in those shorts than in anything Sally Trevoise wears.'

Sally was still a thorn in Ellen's side. All through junior school she had belittled her, and then to Ellen's horror she got a place at the grammar school too. As they were in the same class and travelled home on the same school bus, she couldn't avoid her. Sally swanned around the village like Lady Muck in the latest fashions from London. On Sunday at church she'd been wearing a pink sheath dress with a matching jacket that both Ellen and Josie would have died for. The only consolation was that Sally had grown fat, and had bad acne, probably as the result of stuffing her face with sweets in her parents' shop, so she didn't look that good in the dress and jacket.

Josie looked down at her legs, which were long, slender and brown, and although the khaki shorts were boy's ones, handed down by a neighbour some years ago, they fitted to perfection. 'Have you seen Sally's legs? They're like bottles,' she giggled.

They kept up a litany of things that were wrong with Sally for some minutes, until they were both giggling helplessly.

'She's got a boyfriend now,' Ellen said eventually, suddenly remembering she hadn't told Josie this yet. 'He works in a shoe shop in Falmouth, and he's got as much acne as her.'

'I expect they give it to each other when they're snogging.' Josie giggled again. 'Imagine if they get married and have kids! What'll they look like?'

Josie suddenly fell silent and a shadow crossed her face. Ellen knew she was embarrassed because of what they'd overheard a few days earlier.

'Are you thinking about what Mum said?' Ellen asked. 'Nothing she says hurts me any more.'

They had been in bed with all the windows open because it was such a warm night, and when their parents began rowing they couldn't help but hear. It had started about money; Mum was saying she couldn't see what was wrong with turning the lower field into a camping site this summer. That way she could get a washing-machine and a television.

Dad said he wasn't going to have people tramping all

over his land just so she could sit on her fat arse in a chair all night watching TV. Then it got even worse, with Mum screeching that he was mean and selfish and surely after all she did during the day she warranted some entertainment in the evenings when he went off to the pub?

Dad retorted that she didn't help on the farm at all and she was too lazy even to clean the house properly, and of course Mum retaliated.

'Being lazy is better than being mad,' she screamed at him. 'God help that brat upstairs, she's got a double dose of it from both you and her mother. She'll end up in the loony bin.'

It sounded as if their father must have struck Violet, because she screamed, and he went out slamming the door behind him. The girls had just lain silently in their beds, neither of them daring to speak, for to have done so would have forced them to take sides and very likely fall out.

'They are always on at each other,' Josie said sadly. 'She says evil things about him, and he's just as bad. That's the real reason I want to leave school. To get enough money so I can get right away. The only thing I'd miss is you.'

Ellen felt a surge of sympathy for her sister, for she could see that in some ways her situation was very much worse than her own. Ellen knew that her father would never oppose any decision she made. He would be pleased if she stayed on at school, delighted if she went to college after that. But even if she said she wanted to leave school now and take off for London, he wouldn't try to stop her.

But Violet clung to Josie like a blood-sucking leech. She grilled her daily about school and her friends and she expected far more of her daughter than Josie could ever hope to attain. Sometimes Ellen could almost see her sister sagging under the weight of her mother's ambitions for her. Yet the worst of it was that Josie knew what was behind it. Violet didn't want her to be successful just so she'd have a better life. The woman was banking on her daughter rescuing her from the farm and her unhappy marriage and giving her a life of ease.

'We'll stick together no matter what,' Ellen assured her. 'Don't rush into leaving school next year and take a dead-end job, Josie. You'll be sorry later.'

Josie gave her a long and thoughtful look. 'I wish I had your patience,' she said wistfully. 'I want pretty clothes, a boyfriend, and freedom to do what I like and go where I like. And I want it all now!'

Ellen smiled. 'Do you remember when you wanted a doll's pram so badly?'

Josie grinned. It was when she was five, she had talked about nothing else, kept on and on about it. 'What's that got to do with what I want now?' she asked.

'You got the doll's pram in the end,' Ellen reminded her. 'But you only played with it a few times and then you lost interest. Sometimes dreaming about something is better than really having it. Just dream for now and wait and see what happens.'

'You're weird sometimes,' Josie giggled. 'What do you dream about?'

'Much the same as you,' Ellen replied. She couldn't admit that her only dream was that one day her stepmother would find she'd had enough of her husband and the farm and leave for good, so that Ellen would be free to run it with her father.

A yell from the farmhouse prevented any further speculation about their future.

'That's Mum,' Josie said gloomily. 'We'd better go and see what she wants.'

As they walked up the steep path through the lower field they could see their mother standing hands on hips by the garden fence. Even from a distance they could see she was het-up about something.

Violet was forty-one now, but she looked far older. She had put on several stones in weight in the last two or three years, and her bitterness showed in the deep scowl lines around her mouth. The girls were used to her bad teeth and the cast in her eye, but it was her slatternly appearance that embarrassed them most. Violet wore the same shabby, shapeless dress day after day regardless of how dirty it was, rarely washed her hair, and she always smelled of sweat. She had slept alone now for over a year. Dad had moved into the tiny spare bedroom when she was ill once, and he'd never moved back. Josie was always trying to encourage her to smarten herself up, but her suggestions fell on deaf ears.

As far as Ellen at least could see, the only good thing about the woman was that she was an excellent cook. But then food was the only thing aside from Josie that interested Violet, and she ate constantly. Josie would often defend her, reminding Ellen that as a child she had very little to eat, and that she was sad because she hadn't had any more children.

But Ellen couldn't feel any real sympathy for her stepmother. A great many of their neighbours had been brought up in terrible poverty, yet they didn't stuff themselves all the time. She thought that if Violet made herself more attractive to her husband, she might have had more children too.

'Where have you two been?' Violet shouted as the girls came nearer.

'Only down at the beach, Mum,' Josie shouted back cheerfully. 'What's wrong?'

'I've had a telegram,' she said. 'My mother's very ill and I have to go to Helston immediately. You, Ellen, go up to the village and ask Mr Peters if he can take me, tell him it's an emergency. Josie, you'd better come inside with me and help me pack some things.'

The girls looked at each other in surprise. They had been taken to Helston to see this grandmother only once, around six years ago. She was very old, nasty to everyone, and her house was smelly and dark. They had both been convinced she was a witch. To their knowledge their mother hadn't had any contact with her since that day.

'Don't just stand there,' Violet roared at Ellen. 'Go now, and quickly.'

Ellen didn't ask why she didn't get Dad to take her in the old truck, or even where he was, because the thought of a couple of days without her stepmother was too wonderful to delay her. She sped up the track on to the road, ran the half-mile without stopping once, then climbed over the stile to the footpath that led across the fields to Mawnan Smith.

Mr Peters lived in a pretty little cottage right in the centre of the village. He had moved down here from Exeter when he retired as a schoolmaster. He wasn't a real taxi driver, but he supplemented his pension by ferrying local people about at a much lower cost than the taxi firms in Falmouth charged.

He was weeding his front garden as Ellen ran up the road. She liked him, as he was one of the few adults in the village who was really interesting. He was tall and thin, and wore his customary summer outfit of baggy knee-length shorts, a rather loud-patterned shirt and a battered straw hat.

'Could you possibly take Mum to Helston? Our grandmother's very ill,' Ellen blurted out breathlessly for she had a stitch in her side.

He dropped his gardening fork and smiled. 'Now, which one are you? Ellen or Josie?' he asked.

'Ellen of course,' she said, grinning at him because he always teased her with the same thing. Josie never bothered to speak to Mr Peters, whereas Ellen went out of her way to talk to him.

'Of course,' he said, tipping his hat back and smiling broadly. 'You are the one with brains as well as beauty. How did the exams go?'

'Pretty good,' she admitted. 'But I won't get the results for a while. Can you take Mum?'

'Of course I will,' he said, though he didn't look exactly

pleased at the prospect, and Ellen hoped Josie might persuade Violet to have a wash and change her dress before they went. 'Come on in and have a cold drink, my dear, while I wash my hands and explain to Mrs Peters. You look very hot and bothered.'

Ellen followed him into the cottage and looked about her eagerly. She loved it when Mr Peters invited her in, for it was the prettiest little house she'd ever seen. So many books and pictures, lovely rugs on the floor, and beautiful shiny old furniture. She wished she could wave a magic wand and make Beacon farmhouse like it.

Mr Peters went out through the French windows to speak to his wife who was sitting in the garden in a deckchair doing some embroidery. She turned her head as he spoke to her and called out for Ellen to join her.

Ellen admired Mrs Peters almost as much as she admired her husband, even though she didn't know her as well. She was younger than him, and had the kind of style Ellen saw as 'knitting-pattern models'. She went in for neat costumes, with pearls at her neck, and her greying hair was fixed up in a bun. Ellen had been very impressed when she had run into her out walking in the fields. She had been wearing pale blue slacks and a checked coat that matched perfectly. Ellen had decided that day that when she was over fifty she would make sure she didn't slop about in nasty old dark clothes, but be as well groomed as Mrs Peters.

'So your grandmother's very ill,' Mrs Peters said, her soft voice full of sympathy. 'Is she very old?'

Mr Peters brought Ellen a glass of lemonade, then disappeared again.

'I've only seen her once,' Ellen said, sipping the drink and looking around the garden which was even nicer than the front one, with dozens of rose-bushes in full bloom. 'She looked very old then.'

'How are you girls going to manage if your mother stays there for a while?' Mrs Peters asked.

'We'll be fine,' Ellen said, trying not to look too happy about it. 'We can both cook and I always help Dad around the farm anyway.'

'If you need any help, you come to me,' Mrs Peters said, and she reached out her hand and patted Ellen's knee as if trying to say she understood how it was for her.

Ellen often felt this wordless understanding from people in the village. She guessed that everyone knew about her real mother, and perhaps if she was brave enough to ask they could tell her a great deal more than her father had. But it seemed so disloyal to him to ask about her, and anyway he'd be furious if he found out.

Yet the Peters were people she *could* ask. Just to see the loving way they treated each other and the way they always helped anyone in the village if they could, was enough to know they could be trusted never to pass on what was said to anyone.

'That's very kind of you, Mrs Peters,' she said. 'I just love coming here, your house and garden are so beautiful.'

'Bless you, dear.' Mrs Peters beamed. 'But with your looks and brains I don't doubt for a moment that you'll end up somewhere even nicer. If you wish for something hard enough it comes, you know.'

That night in bed Ellen thought of Mrs Peters' remark again. She had wished for her stepmother to go away, and she had, so perhaps her other wishes would come true too.

She had been driven back to the farm by Mr Peters, and she was pleased to see that Josie had managed to tidy their mother up. Violet was still barking out instructions to them when she left, one of which was to explain to their father where she'd gone and that she might be away for some days.

Dad grinned broadly when Ellen relayed this to him. He didn't even bother to ask why his wife hadn't come and found him to tell him herself. It turned out to be quite the jolliest evening they'd had in a long time; they had their tea sitting outside in the sunshine, then Josie washed up while Ellen helped Dad with the milking and getting the chickens in. Then to their surprise Dad suggested they played cards, something he never did. When it was bedtime he kissed both girls and said they weren't to worry about anything as they'd all manage fine. Josie looked so delighted Ellen thought she might burst.

A note arrived from their mother three days later, just as the girls were leaving to catch the school bus. Dad read it and put it down on the table. 'Her mother's had a stroke, and she'll be staying for some time, as she can't do anything for herself,' he said. 'She says Josie is to join her there.'

Josie looked at Ellen in absolute horror.

Ellen thought quickly. It was one thing to get shot of her stepmother for a few weeks, quite another to lose Josie too. She remembered how nasty the old woman's house was. Josie would be miserable there. 'She can't go, Dad, she's got the end of term exams to sit, and the teachers won't like it if she misses them,' she said quickly.

There was utter silence as they waited for Dad to reply. He scratched his head, read the letter again, then rolled up a cigarette and looked at Josie thoughtfully.

'Don't you want to go?'

She shook her head furiously. 'Please don't make me, Dad,' she pleaded. 'I want to stay here with you and Ellen.'

'Fair enough,' he said, but his expression gave nothing away. 'You go off to school and I'll post a letter back sometime today.'

Josie leapt to her feet; they would have to run to catch the bus. 'Thank you, Dad,' she said, hesitating at the door, 'but don't say I didn't want to go, it might hurt her feelings.'

They never did find out if their mother's feelings were hurt. She sent another letter back a few days later, but their father didn't disclose the contents. All he said was that they had better both write to her, and not forget to ask after the old lady's health.

Both girls were equally happy that their mother was staying away indefinitely. For Ellen it was heaven not to have to put up with her sarcasm and criticism, and Josie could escape the endless questions.

It seemed as though all the clouds had rolled away. The weather was hot and sunny, Dad was much nicer to Josie, and she reciprocated by helping out on the farm, which she didn't usually do. Ellen knew she wouldn't get her 'O' level results until August, but the headmistress called her into her study on the last day of school and gave her a pep talk about not thinking of leaving because she was sure she'd passed all her exams and she was clever enough to go on to university. That decided Ellen once and for all. Two more years of school was a long time, but she thought it would be worth it in the end.

Everyone was let out of school early that day, so Ellen decided to walk home. As she got to Swanpool beach, she saw that the beach kiosk was advertising for part-time staff. They needed two girls for three days a week right through till the end of August. So Ellen suggested her sister could work with her, and to her delight the owner agreed, never even asking if Josie was over fifteen.

When Ellen got home and told Josie the good news, they were both wildly excited. Even their father laughed with them and told them to clear off to the beach to give him some peace.

It was baking hot, so they were only too eager to strip off their uniforms, and ran down to the cove in their swimming costumes, screaming with laughter. As Ellen lay on her back floating in the water, she couldn't remember ever being so happy before. The thought of six whole weeks of holiday, a job and money to spend was wonderful. Everything seemed magical that afternoon, the sea was a calm clear blue, with a heat haze shimmering over the rocks. She and Josie played childish games, ducking under the water and grabbing each other's legs, climbing on each other's backs and having wild water fights. Later they lay on the baking sand with their toes just in the water, and for the first time ever they revealed to each other how they felt about their parents.

'It's Mum who spoils everything,' Josie admitted. 'I used to think it was because Dad was mean to her, but now she's gone I can see who really starts it all.'

'She can't help it, I suppose,' Ellen said. She was so happy that old grievances had disappeared. 'I don't think she was ever cut out to be a farmer's wife. I reckon she must have married him thinking she could change the way he lived.'

'She told me a while ago that she still feels the ghost of your mother around,' Josie said, and giggled. 'Does he ever talk to you about her?'

'No, never,' Ellen said and told Josie what was said between them the day she found out Violet was her step-mother. 'I don't even know where she is buried.'

'Don't you?' Josie said in surprise. 'She's in the grave-yard by the church. Not right in the churchyard, just outside. Mum said she couldn't be buried in consecrated ground because she took her own life.'

'Why didn't you tell me before?' Ellen asked. It stung to think of anyone being put into unhallowed ground, and even more that her younger sister knew this, but she hadn't been told.

'Mum said I wasn't to, and I didn't dare,' Josie said, looking a little shamefaced. 'I'm sorry, but I thought you would have found out by now.'

'Don't let Mum get in between us any more,' Ellen suggested. 'I'm sure that's why Dad is mean to you some-times, because he knows Mum's mean to me. If we stand together maybe it will stop for good.'

Josie nodded agreement. 'Don't you wish we had a

normal mum and dad, lived in an ordinary house and stuff?'

Ellen had wished that countless times in the past, especially in the days when they had no electricity and only an outside lavatory. She would look at the modern houses in Falmouth with their neat gardens and white nets at the window and ache for the comforts other children took for granted. Yet another part of her knew she and Josie had some things lots of kids would die for – this beach, the animals, woods and cliffs. Those other kids might have televisions, record-players and a home that was always clean and tidy, but that might be very dull sometimes.

'Sometimes, but we haven't got ordinary parents, so there's not much point in wishing for them. Josie, we'll set the world alight, you and I – , you'll be a famous model and I'll be – ' She stopped short, suddenly aware she didn't really know what she wanted to be.

'What are you going to be?' Josie asked, sensing her sister hadn't got a clear picture.

'I don't know, maybe a teacher or something like that.'

'You won't get it if you don't want it bad enough,' Josie said. 'I go to sleep every night imagining myself modelling on a catwalk.'

They lapsed into companionable silence then, letting the sun's rays toast their skin. But Ellen was a little disturbed to find she hadn't got any clear idea about what she wanted to do with her life. It was as if she couldn't see further ahead than just going back to school in September to be in the sixth form.

They walked back to the farmhouse later, their arms linked, singing the Gerry and the Pacemakers' song 'I Like It' at the top of their lungs.

Suddenly Josie broke off and prodded Ellen. 'There's a car. Who's that?'

'I don't know,' Ellen said, looking at the light grey saloon on the farm track down from the road. 'I've never seen it before.'

Curious, they began to run, but stopped short just outside the fence around the front garden as they saw their mother at the open front door.

'Oh no,' Ellen gasped.

Josie said nothing, but her face had blanched.

'So this is what you do all day while I'm away,' Mum shouted as they came in through the gate. 'Off swimming. Clothes left all over the floor. Beds not made. Come on in at once and go upstairs to put something decent on. It's a good job I came back to get Josie. I knew I couldn't trust you two to take care of her.'

With that the girls saw their father was in the kitchen, looking tense. Another man was there too; he was short and stout, wearing a dark suit.

'Hello, Mum,' Josie said nervously. 'How's grandma?'

'Very sick,' Mum said tersely. 'And this is your Uncle Brian. I had to ask him to drive me over and get you, because it was clear to me you need supervision.'

'Violet, they've both been fine,' Dad said, his voice tight with anger. 'They broke up from school today and it's hot. Why shouldn't they go swimming?'

'Upstairs now.' Violet pointed to the stairs and kept her hand up as if intending to clout them both as they passed her. 'Get your clothes together, Josie, we'll be leaving in a few minutes. I've kept Brian waiting for long enough.'

Upstairs the girls wriggled out of their wet swimming costumes and into their clothes. 'I can't go with her, I'll just die there,' Josie whispered. 'What shall I do?'

Ellen was horrified too. They had their new job to start on Monday, and there were all the other plans they'd made. She couldn't bear the thought of being separated, but it would be much worse for Josie.

'I'll try and get Dad to stop her,' Ellen said hurriedly.

But as they went back downstairs again, Ellen realized that Mum and her brother had already been here for some time, and that their dad had already told Mum about the job, because she began ranting about it.

'No daughter of mine is going to work in a beach kiosk,' she shouted. 'Whatever are you thinking of, Albert? Her place is with her mother and grandmother.'

'Don't make her go.' Ellen was so anxious she forgot Violet hated the sound of her voice. 'She'll be miserable in Helston and there's nothing wrong with working at the beach. Most of the other people working there are students.'

'Miserable with her mother?' Violet screeched, her usually pallid face flushed with anger. 'I'm giving her a chance to meet her real relatives, her aunts, uncles and cousins. You might be happy to spend the rest of your life mucking out cow sheds like your father, but I have much bigger plans for *my* daughter.'

'Josie's my daughter too and I say she stays here where she belongs,' Albert snapped at her. 'Your bloody relatives in Helston have never given a damn about you, why should they suddenly care about Josie?' He caught hold of both the girls' arms and bundled them outside, telling them to make themselves scarce.

'Look here, woman,' he shouted as he went back in, 'I know what this is all about. You want to parade Josie round like a prize trophy, I expect she's the first real beauty ever to enter your bloody family. Well, you aren't going to make her miserable doing that. Or turn her head with all that praise. Get on back to your bloody mother, get whatever kicks you can out of being her nurse, but I'll be buggered if Josie's got to watch it.'

The two girls clung to each other outside, both scared now, for when their father was angry enough to string more than a few words together, he could do anything.

'Violet has a right to have her daughter with her,' Brian chimed in, his tone measured as if trying to calm down his sister and brother-in-law.

'You stay out of this,' Albert warned him. 'I say Josie stays here, so get in that car and go.'

'I don't trust you with Josie,' Violet suddenly yelled out. 'I wouldn't put it past you to interfere with her.'

'What did you say?' Albert roared out, and the girls clung even tighter to each other, looking at the door of the house expecting to see a body come flying out of it. 'I always knew you were a dirty-minded cow, but that's sickening. Get out now!'

The girls ran for the woods behind the house, but from behind them they heard the sharp crack of a slap. Violet screamed, then they heard what sounded like the two men fighting for there were crashing noises as if furniture was being overturned.

'What am I going to do?' Josie asked. Her face drained of all colour.

'I don't know,' Ellen replied. Her father was so strong she was afraid he would seriously hurt Violet's brother, and that might lead to criminal charges. Yet what had really thrown her was her stepmother saying she wouldn't put it past Dad to interfere with Josie. She knew exactly what that meant – only a few months ago a man from Padstow had been sent to prison for raping his daughter, and everyone in the neighbourhood had talked about it for weeks.

'Would Dad really do that to me?' Josie asked pitifully, beginning to cry.

'Of course he wouldn't,' Ellen retorted. 'She just wants to get her brother on her side. She deserves a good thumping for being so evil.'

Josie didn't reply, but began to walk back towards the farmhouse, leaving Ellen all too aware that she'd lost all the new ground she'd made with her sister in the past few weeks, and once again her wretched stepmother had triumphed by pushing a wedge between them.

Ellen stayed in the woods for a few more minutes, wishing she hadn't spoken out. Then, realizing her father might need someone on his side, she went back too.

Uncle Brian was slumped in one of the chairs outside

the house, holding a bloody handkerchief to his mouth. There was no sign of Dad, but she could hear Josie and Mum opening and closing drawers upstairs.

Horrified, Ellen ran over to the barn and found her father sitting on a box, nursing bruised knuckles. 'Is she leaving you for good?' Ellen asked. While she was only too glad to see the back of her stepmother, she didn't feel the same way about Josie.

'I couldn't be that lucky,' he said dourly. 'She'll be back, but she'll have ruined Josie by then.'

'Don't let her take her,' Ellen implored him.

He looked up at her with troubled dark eyes. 'I can't stop her,' he said, his voice cracking. 'I tried to, but by bringing her brother here and making me mad enough to hit both of them, I've hung myself.'

Ellen realized he meant that if her stepmother did take legal proceedings, the law would be on her side. 'Please go and speak to Josie before Mum takes her away,' she pleaded. 'Don't let her go thinking you don't care.'

When he didn't move or speak, Ellen took that as a refusal and she turned and left the barn. Her stepmother was putting some bags into the boot of the car, her brother was already in the driving seat and Josie was just coming out of the house, her face streaked with tears.

'Dad and I don't want you to go,' Ellen said, catching hold of both her sister's arms. 'We want you here.'

Josie pulled away from her. 'Don't make it any worse,' she said, sniffing and rubbing her eyes.

'Get in the car, Josie,' her mother called out.

'Don't hate Dad and me for this,' Ellen said in a whisper, not wanting her stepmother to hear. 'Remember what we promised each other today, that we wouldn't let her come between us any more.'

Josie just shrugged. Ellen couldn't tell if that was agreement or her way of saying she didn't care any more. She got in the back of the grey car and it roared off up the track. She didn't even turn to wave.

Chapter Five

As Albert came into the kitchen for his breakfast, Ellen put the bacon and eggs she'd cooked for him on the table.

'Where's yours? he asked.

'I'm not hungry,' she said. 'I'll just have a cup of tea.'

It was early August. Josie had been gone for two weeks now, and as it promised to be another hot, sunny day Ellen knew it would be very busy down at the beach kiosk.

'What's up?' Albert asked. He thought his daughter looked a bit peaky and she usually ate a hearty breakfast. 'Don't like the job?'

'The job's fine,' she said, but her voice held the weariness she felt. 'I'm just missing Josie, that's all.'

She half expected him to snap at her, but he didn't. 'Me too, the place isn't the same without her,' he said, glancing at the empty chair. 'I'd feel better if I knew she was enjoying herself, but Helston's not much of a place, and her mother will keep on at her.'

Albert got on with his breakfast and Ellen poured them both a cup of tea. It was in the evenings that she missed Josie the most, they seemed so long and lonely. She did chores to fill the time, but when she saw Josie's empty bed before she went to sleep she often felt like crying.

'Will Mum bring her back when school starts again?' she asked.

Albert mopped up the egg yolk with a slice of bread. 'I reckon that will depend on which place gives her the better deal.'

'What do you mean by a better deal?'

Albert sniffed. 'Vi's one of those people who don't go

80

much on loyalty, duty or even love. She looks out for herself. Always has.'

'But you must have loved each other when you got married,' Ellen said.

He didn't answer for a moment or two, and Ellen could see he was mulling over the question in his mind. Eventually he looked at her. 'I guess you're old enough to know the truth. She just turned up here when your mother died, looking for the main chance,' he said bitterly. 'I scarcely knew her; she was just a barmaid in the pub in Falmouth. She said she'd got to worrying about how I was going to cope with you and the farm.' He paused for a moment and took a gulp of tea. 'I weren't coping, I hardly knew what time of day it was, so I let her feed and change you, clean the house and that. She stayed, gave up her job, just moved in on me.'

This was a surprise to Ellen. Despite her father's coldness to Violet, the closeness in her age and Josie's made her suppose it must have been a love match at the beginning. 'But why did you let her stay?' she asked.

He grimaced. 'I hope's you never get in a position that you understand that one,' he said. 'I was mad with grief; your mother meant everything in the world to me, you see. I didn't care much whether I lived or died, or if the farm failed. But you were here, fourteen months old, just starting to walk. However bad I felt, I knew you'd got to be taken care of.'

'So she stayed for me?'

He half smiled at that question. 'I liked to think she did back then, heaven knows I gave her no reason to think I wanted her. But it was the farm and security she was after. You see, it was spring when she came here first, I guess she looked around, saw how pretty it was, and thought she'd fallen on her feet. I was a fool letting her into my bed, can't think now what got into me, next thing I know she's expecting Josie.'

Ellen was embarrassed to think of her father having sex,

81

and also shocked because he was usually a very moral man. 'So you had to marry her then?'

'Had to, it was the proper thing to do,' he said gloomily. 'I couldn't kick her out carrying my babby, and I was beholden to her for taking care of you.'

'Oh Dad,' Ellen sighed, feeling a little responsible herself. 'But what kind of "deal" might she find in Helston? I don't know what you mean.'

'I reckon she thinks her family will see her right,' he said with a tight little laugh. 'All her brothers and sisters have done all right for theyselves. That Brian, he's got his own business, he owns property; one of her sisters is married to a doctor. But none of them wants to look after their mother, and Vi was the answer to their prayers, I reckon. You can bet when she got there she laid it on thick about missing Josie, and that's why Brian drove her over here to get her. He saw me at my worst.'

To Ellen's knowledge, Brian had never met her father until that day, so he must have been shocked at the violent scene that ensued. 'So you think she might play on her brothers' and sisters' sympathy about that?'

'I expect she's already told 'em I was a bad 'un.' He grinned sheepishly. 'Now they's going to believe it, and maybe they think Josie's in danger from me an' all. So one of 'em's bound to take her in.'

All at once Ellen could see what he was getting at, and it made her see red. It was despicable that a mother should imply that her husband had interfered with her daughter or that Josie was unloved, just so she could get what she wanted.

Ellen didn't much care about adults gossiping about her father, but she did care about the effect it would have on Josie. If those relatives of hers started fussing around her, buying her nice clothes, giving her treats, maybe she'd even start to believe her mother's claims.

'Surely you can't just let her get away with it?' she asked.

Albert made a hopeless gesture with his hands. 'I can't do nought. Vi won't give Josie any letters from you or me. If I went there they wouldn't let me get near her. If I tried to get her back through the courts, I'd lose. Everything's stacked against me.'

'I can't really believe Josie will forget us that easily,' Ellen said hopefully.

'Don't bank on that, me handsome,' he said getting up from the table. 'She's her ma's daughter in many ways. She don't love the farm like you do, and she's been taught from a babby that I've got no time for her. But you'd better hurry along now or you'll be late for your job. I'll clear up here.'

Ellen got up from the table and went over to her father, putting her arms around him and leaning into his chest. She knew now he did love Josie, because she could see he was every bit as sad as she was and blaming himself for how things had turned out. She wished she could tell him she loved him, but she knew he was always embarrassed by what he called 'slop'.

He hugged her tightly, then nudged her away from him. 'Off to work now, it's payday, isn't it?'

Ellen nodded.

'Well, spend it all on yerself,' he suggested. 'It's about time you had a few treats. Don't rush home to get my dinner either. Get yerself out with yer friends, maybe go to the pictures.'

When Ellen went into her bedroom to get a cardigan, she stopped for a moment and picked up the picture of her and Josie which she kept by her bed. It was a very old one, she was eight, Josie six, but it was a special one, for a real photographer had taken it for the local newspaper. He had called with a journalist in the summer of 1955 because they were doing an article about local farmers. The photographer had said how pretty she and Josie were and asked to take their picture. He sent them each a copy of it later.

To Ellen it was a happy memory of the time before she knew about her real mother, when her world was just the farm and her family. But looking at it now, alone without Josie, she felt an unbearable pang of sorrow. She sensed that this separation was going to change them both, and nothing would ever be the same again.

It was very busy in the kiosk that day. The other girl who usually worked with Ellen hadn't shown up, and Swanpool beach was more crowded than she'd ever seen it. As Ellen served a continual stream of customers with ice-creams and trays of tea, she was glad to have something to take her mind off Josie and her mother.

Holidaymakers fascinated Ellen. Their different accents, the way they acted with their children, was like a glimpse into another world. She and Josie had never been taken to a beach for the day. If they went down to the little cove, it was always alone – the most their mother did was give them dire warnings of the dangers of going in too deep. They had taught themselves to swim, just as they'd learned to ride bikes, do leap-frog and hand-stands or climb rocks, by trying together on their own. A picnic to them was nothing more than an apple and Ellen couldn't possibly imagine Mum and Dad sitting on the sand doling out cups of tea from a Thermos, or paddling with them and making sandcastles the way these parents did.

But it was the places these people came from that intrigued her more than anything else. As she'd never been further than Truro, big cities like London, Bristol and Birmingham were a mystery. She thought they must be very dirty, noisy and full of mean people because the tourists were always remarking on the Cornish clean air, the pretty countryside, and how friendly people were down here.

Ellen grabbed any opportunity to talk to the holiday-makers. She told them about places of interest to visit and often sympathized when they complained about the guest-houses or camping sites they were staying at.

She would have liked to talk to girls and boys of her own age, and get their views on city life, but she was wary of them. When they were in groups they often mimicked her Cornish accent; they seemed to think she was simple because she couldn't tell them about dance-halls or pubs.

She lived too far out of Falmouth to know what went on there at night, and so did most of her friends from school. She knew of course that there were Saturday night dances in village halls all over Cornwall, but she suspected that sophisticated teenagers wouldn't want to go to one of those.

Maybe it was only because she was lonely without Josie that she started wishing she had a boyfriend. Her experience in that direction didn't go beyond a couple of kisses on the school bus last Christmas, and they were boys she'd grown up with. She thought it would be nice to have someone special of her own.

This summer might have been so different if Josie had been here with her, she thought. Together they could have laughed off the girls who mimicked them and might even have given each other enough confidence to chat and flirt with the boys.

At four that afternoon it was quiet, and Ellen was day-dreaming as she washed up and cleaned the counter in readiness for the kiosk owner arriving at half past to close it down. She didn't notice anyone approaching.

'Hello, gorgeous!' a male voice said suddenly, making her jump.

Ellen blushed furiously, for the man was extraordinarily handsome. He was about twenty-five, tall with blond hair and azure blue eyes, and wearing nothing more than a skimpy pair of black swimming trunks.

'What would you like?' she asked nervously.

'A kiss would be nice,' he said, his wide grin showing perfect white teeth. 'But I suppose they aren't on the menu?'

Ellen giggled, but quickly managed to act as if men said that sort of thing to her all the time. 'There's tea, sandwiches, ice-cream and chocolate, but no kisses,' she replied airily.

He made a glum face. 'Shame. Well, suppose you tell me where you were just now?'

She coloured up again in confusion. 'Just now? I haven't been anywhere.'

'You have, I've been watching you for a while,' he said, leaning his muscular forearms on the counter and looking right into her eyes. 'You were lost in thought.'

Ellen could hardly believe that any man could be interested enough to study her, yet alone someone as gorgeous as he was. 'Oh, I was just thinking about my sister,' she giggled. 'She's away in Helston and I miss her.'

'Is she as pretty as you?' he asked.

Ellen gulped. He was very deeply tanned and she'd never seen such muscles on any man before, except in films. She wished more than ever that Josie was here, she would have been so impressed by him.

'We're very alike,' she said bashfully. 'Lots of people can't tell us apart.'

'Twins?'

Ellen shook her head. 'She's two years younger than me.'

'Can you both dance, do gymnastics or ride horses?' he asked.

It was such an odd question that Ellen forgot her nerves. 'Why on earth would you want to know that?'

'Because if you could, you could have a future in the circus. Two of you very much alike in spangled costumes would be a great draw.'

'I can ride horses, I live on a farm,' she giggled. 'I can do a hand-stand, cartwheels and the Twist. I also make a good cup of tea.'

'Then I'll have one,' he said. 'I'll audition you for the cartwheels later.'

As she poured him a cup of tea, she suddenly remembered the circus had set up just outside Falmouth. 'Are you with the circus?' she asked.

He grinned, showing his perfect teeth. 'Indeed I am,' he said. 'Watch this!'

To her surprise he took a couple of steps away from the kiosk and then, seemingly completely effortlessly, he leapt into the air, turned a back somersault and landed on his feet. Ellen's mouth fell open in shock, and several people who happened to be close by also looked amazed.

He came back to her, not even out of breath, and held out his hand. 'Pierre, one of the Flying Adolphus Brothers,' he said.

'You're French,' she said incredulously, taking his hand to shake it. She thought his accent was from the north of England.

He winked at her. 'No more French than my partners are my brothers, but for our public we put on a little show.' He raised her hand to his lips. '*Tu es très jolie, madame*, may I know your name?'

'Ellen,' she said, and as he kissed her fingertips tingles ran down her spine. 'But I don't think I can run away to the circus, I'm only used to riding old nags, and my gymnastics aren't up to yours.'

'I could train you,' he said, still holding her hand and looking into her eyes. 'I can see you now under the spotlight as you turn the rope for me to climb up to my trapeze, emerald-green spangles, little silver stars in your hair, you would be a sensation.'

Ellen knew this was a joke, but a little part of her wanted to believe it. She had only been to the circus once, on an outing with the Sunday school when she was ten, and she'd never seen anything so wonderful. For weeks afterwards, she and Josie had played circuses. They would put on their swimming costumes, and holding a length of old curtain net as a kind of stole, they would strut around the barn pretending they were trapeze artists.

'There's your tea,' she said to hide her confusion, pushing the mug at him. 'No circus for me, I've got two more years of school yet and then on to college or university. This is just a holiday job.'

'So you have brains along with great beauty,' he said, and his smile was very warm. 'Come and see the circus tonight anyway. I'll give you a free ticket and after the show I'll take you to meet all the acts and see the animals.'

Ellen was astounded. She didn't know if he was asking her for a date, or it was just a free ticket to the show. But whatever his motives, she wanted to go.

'Well?' he said, raising one fair eyebrow questioningly. 'Do you want to come?'

Just one look at his handsome face, his high cheek-bones and wide smiling mouth and she knew she would go willingly to anything as long as it meant seeing him. Yet she knew her father wouldn't approve one little bit.

'I don't know,' she faltered, thinking rapidly. Her father didn't have to know, and anyway he'd told her himself to go out tonight. 'You see, I have to get the last bus home and that leaves Falmouth at half past ten,' she said. 'What time does the show end?'

'In plenty of time to catch the bus,' he said, and reached out and patted her cheek. 'I'm going for a last swim now, it's part of my training. But I'll leave a ticket at the ticket office for you. Just say Pierre said there would be one for you.'

He was gone, striding off down the beach before she could even remind him he hadn't paid for his tea.

Breathless with excitement and nerves, Ellen rushed into the little dress shop in Falmouth minutes before they were due to close, intent on buying the cream dress she'd tried on earlier in the week. Luckily it was still there, and she snatched it up and paid for it, then, running down the high street through the throngs of holidaymakers, she made for Dolcis, which stayed open till half past five, to buy shoes.

There were posters advertising the circus everywhere, and it gave her a thrill to see the Adolphus Brothers pictured on it, flying through the air, while tigers and lions snarled at the ringmaster in a cage below. The evening performance didn't begin until seven-thirty, so once she'd got some shoes she would have plenty of time.

The ladies' room in the Harbourside Café wasn't very well lit, but it had about the only lavatory she knew that had clean towels and hot water, and few people seemed to use it. She stripped off to her bra and pants and before anyone could come in she washed herself quickly, including her feet, then put on her new dress.

If it hadn't been for Pierre she wouldn't have spent her wages on something so impractical. But once she had it on she didn't care about whether she could run or ride a bike in it, or if it had to be washed after every wearing, it was just so lovely. The colour set off her tan, its close cut enhanced her slender figure, and she felt she was an equal to any big-city girl.

By the time she'd brushed out her hair and put on some lipstick, mascara and her new brown sling-backs with pointed toes, she was a completely different girl to the one who'd left the farm at nine o'clock that morning wearing a black shapeless skirt, white blouse and gym shoes, with her hair pulled severely off her face in a pony-tail.

Ellen sighed as she looked at her hair; it was too wild and curly, like something out of a Forties Hollywood film. The fashion was for short, sleek styles at the moment, but even if she had it cut, it still wouldn't behave, so she supposed she was stuck with it. She bundled her old clothes and gym shoes into the shop bag and marched out through the café, avoiding the customers' curious glances.

It was only as Ellen queued at the ticket office that she felt frightened. She would look so silly if Pierre hadn't left a ticket. What would she do? Pay to see the show anyway? What if that made him think she was chasing him?

But the ticket was there; in fact he'd attached a note to it. 'I'll be looking right at you, every smile will be for you alone,' he'd written.

The tingles down her spine began again and combined with the jostling, excited crowd around her, the smell of the animals and the jangling music from a fairground organ, to make her feel quite faint. She couldn't really believe she was daring enough to do this.

Her seat was right at the ringside, a proper plush-covered seat, not like the uncomfortable tiered planks most people had to watch from. There was a souvenir programme too, and among the many pictures of the acts was one of Pierre with his brothers looking wonderful in tight-fitting sky-blue sparkly outfits. She looked around the Big Top nervously, hoping no one she knew was there. She fully intended to tell her father she'd been to the circus, but she couldn't say she went alone. Again she cursed her conspicuous hair and remembered how often in the past it had been her undoing when she'd got up to mischief. But she couldn't see anyone she knew, and the seats were filling up quickly all around her. Then at last the band started to play, and a troupe of acrobats came tumbling into the ring.

Every emotion Ellen had felt as a child seeing her first circus was trebled this time, for now she knew it wasn't just magic that made people able to walk on wires or make big cats jump on to stools, but years of practice. She forgot she was alone, laughed at the clowns, cried at the beauty of the prancing white horses, and cheered with everyone else when the seals balanced balls on their noses.

Then at last the Flying Adolphus Brothers came running into the ring. They all looked so young and handsome in their blue outfits, with short spangly capes around their shoulders, yet Pierre looked the best. To her delight he came straight over to her and bowed low in front of her, before turning a row of cartwheels around the ring.

She watched in awe as he and the other five men tossed off their capes and climbed up ropes to the trapezes. There was a safety net, but it didn't look very strong, and her heart was in her mouth. Up and up they went, right up to the roof of the Big Top, and then one after another they began swinging on the trapeze. It became more terrifying when three of them, Pierre included, hung by their knees and caught their partners by the hands. Then it was his turn to swing and jump and be caught by someone else.

Ellen could hardly bear to watch. Her heart was pounding with fright and yet tears came to her eyes because it was all so beautiful, like a ballet in the air. Each time Pierre was left standing alone on his trapeze he blew her a kiss, and the tingles came back to her spine.

It was almost a relief when the finale came; four of the men gradually made themselves into a human chain, each holding another man's feet. They swung lower and lower until at last the first man dropped into the net, did a somersault and landed safely back in the ring, quickly followed by each of the others. But Pierre and his partner were still up there, and all at once instead of coming down, they were flying through the air again, this time doing double somersaults before catching the opposite trapeze. The crowd cheered, many people standing up and stamping and clapping their approval.

Finally the men came down and picked up their capes, and all six strutted around the ring blowing kisses at the audience. Once again Pierre stopped in front of Ellen and bowed low, then he threw her his cape.

'Is he your boyfriend?' the woman next to her whispered.

'Just a friend,' Ellen whispered back, clutching the cape like a lifesaver.

'You lucky girl,' the woman replied. 'He looks like a god.'

It occurred to Ellen as the Grand Finale began and the

horses and elephants circled the ring with all the different artists and clowns either riding or marching alongside the animals, that when Pierre threw his cape to her, he knew she would have to stay behind to give it back to him. But by now she was swept away into a fantasy world. Let Sally Trevoise go out with a spotty-faced boy from a shoe shop, she was going to have a date with the blond god riding on an elephant.

As everyone made for the way out of the Big Top, Pierre came back through the empty ring wearing a kind of dressing-gown over his performing clothes.

'Come with me,' he said, holding out his hand for her to climb over into the ring too. 'Did you like the show?' he asked.

'It was all wonderful, amazing,' she said. 'But you were truly fantastic. Aren't you scared up there?'

He glanced up and shrugged. 'It's second nature to me now, I never think about it. Now, what would you like to see first?'

'The animals,' she said eagerly. 'Especially the chimp who was with the clowns.'

He led her out through the performers' entrance and Ellen found herself in what seemed a chaotic maze of caravans, lorries, tents and cages. Many of the performers were sitting around smoking and drinking tea, their makeup garish in the fast-fading evening light.

Over to one side, the elephants were tethered to posts by a chain above their feet, the horses were being led into a small fenced paddock on the other, while the seals were in a shallow water tank. But it was the lions and tigers that affected her most, for they were back in their cages and had very little room to move.

'Isn't that a bit cruel?' she asked nervously. They were snarling and roaring and swishing their tails. Close up they didn't look as splendid as they had in the ring; their coats were thin and dull.

'They're used to it,' Pierre said nonchalantly.

The smell of dung was overpowering; Ellen had to cover her nose which made Pierre laugh. 'It's not so glamorous from here, is it?'

He was right. The last of the magic vanished when she saw that the tiny clown dressed as a baby was in fact a rather ugly dwarf, and the girls who had looked so young and beautiful riding the horses in their red satin shorts and waistcoats were in fact plump women of around thirty, slopping around now in dressing-gowns, cigarettes dangling from their lips.

Yet the lack of glamour made it even more fascinating, especially as Pierre was holding her hand, and every now and then he would touch her cheek or hair and whisper that she was beautiful. She saw the caravan he shared with one of the other brothers, Jack, or Jacques as he was billed in the programme. It was tiny, yet very neat and clean, and Pierre told her that all circus people had to be organized for their world was one of discipline and hard work.

'We never get a break from it,' he explained. 'When the show leaves here everything has to be packed away. We might spend two or three days travelling to the next show, then everyone has to pitch in to put up the Big Top, fit the seating and assemble our equipment. When we aren't performing there's practice, advance publicity, mending things that have been broken, and the costumes have to be washed and dried. A couple of days of rain and we're up to our knees in mud, but the show still has to go on, the animals have to be fed and watered, there's no let-up, ever.'

All at once it was quarter past ten, and Ellen knew she must go. She hadn't seen nearly enough, she wanted to talk to the other performers, meet all the Adolphus Brothers, to find out where Pierre came from and how he became a trapeze artist, but there was no time left.

'I shall have to go now,' she said wistfully. 'The bus leaves soon.'

'I wish you didn't have to,' he said, cupping her face in his two hands and looking down into her eyes. 'I knew when I met you at the beach that you were the only girl for me. I'm afraid to let you go now in case you won't come back and see me tomorrow.'

This staggered Ellen. 'You want to see me again?' she whispered, unable to believe anyone as handsome and talented could really want her as his girlfriend.

'Tomorrow, the next day, next week, all the time,' he said.

They were by the caravans; lights were coming on in each of their windows, casting small golden pools of light on the worn grass. Laughter, shouting and music could be heard from every direction, cooking smells mingled with that of the animals, and the sky was studded with stars. It was so exotic, like a foreign country, and very hard to imagine that just beyond the circle of caravans and trucks lay sleepy little Falmouth.

'I'll have to run,' she said, yet she knew that if he begged her to stay she would, regardless of what her father would say.

'One kiss before you go,' he said, and swept her into his arms.

As his lips met hers, she left all her inhibitions behind. Nothing had ever been so sweet, yet so dangerous. Her body seemed to melt into his, and every nerve end tingled.

'Run now, don't miss the bus,' he said, holding her shoulders, his fingers caressing the soft skin on the top of her arms. 'I'd come with you, but I can't dressed like this, can I?'

Ellen giggled. There would be people she knew on the bus home, and she could imagine the gossip in the village shop tomorrow if she was seen with a man in a tight blue spangled costume. 'No, you can't come with me like that. But where shall I meet you tomorrow?'

'There is a matinee. Come for that at two-thirty, we'll

94

go for something to eat afterwards. But run now, you've only five minutes to get to the bus.'

Ellen had to take her shoes off and hitch her dress up, but she was so exhilarated she felt she could have run the whole four miles home if necessary. The people in the queue were boarding the bus as she got there, and being out of breath gave her the perfect excuse to do no more than nod and smile at those she knew.

As the bus sped away she leaned her head against the window and shut her eyes to relive Pierre's kiss. She felt a tightening in her belly, a kind of wonderful yearning feeling all over her. For once she was glad Josie wasn't at home. She didn't want to share this with anyone.

Chapter Six

Ellen worked like fury on Saturday morning. She was up at six and by seven she was out with her father harvesting the potatoes, having already fed the chickens, cooked the breakfast and swept and washed the kitchen floor.

'You're chipper today,' Albert remarked as he got down off the tractor to help her pick up the potatoes he'd just dug up. It was nearly ten now and she'd already filled a dozen large sacks, yet she looked as full of energy as when she first started. 'Any reason?'

Ellen smiled and wiped the sweat from her brow with her forearm, her hands were encrusted with dirt. 'I love doing this, the soil's all warm and crumbly and it smells so good. It's a bit like digging up buried treasure.'

'I never saw it that way,' Albert said, but he smiled because this year's crop was a bumper one. 'I remember all the times I've had to do it when the ground was waterlogged and the spuds so small I could scarcely find them.'

He got the flask of tea from the tractor and they sat down on a couple of upturned crates to pour it. 'Was it very hard farming here when you were my age?' Ellen asked.

'Looking back it were, but I didn't know nothing else,' he said with a shrug. 'I counted myself lucky that I had a hot meal every day, a lot of people were starving during the Thirties.'

'Didn't you ever want to do something else, go somewhere else?' she asked curiously, suddenly aware she knew very little about his past.

'There was only farming, the mines and fishing in those days, unless you were born a gentleman. I suppose if my brothers hadn't beaten me to joining up when the war broke out it might have been different. But one of us had to stay and it fell to me. Our Dick got killed in 1940 over in France, he was just twenty-six, a year older than me, and it knocked the stuffing out of our father. He died a year later so I didn't have any choice but to stay on here.'

'I didn't know you had brothers!' Ellen exclaimed in surprise. 'Where are the others now?'

'There's only Eric, he's two years younger than me. We fell out when mother died and I was left the farm, and he cleared off soon after. Don't know where he is, haven't heard from him since.'

'Why didn't you ever tell me about Dick and Eric?' she asked tentatively. It seemed almost sinister that he'd never spoken of having any brothers before.

Albert shrugged. 'I dunno, reckon as we didn't get along it weren't worth mentioning. I married Clare, your mother, then anyway. She weren't cut out to be a farmer's wife, it's too hard a life for women that ain't born to it. Maybe if I'd been a carpenter, a builder, got us a little house in town, things might've turned out different.'

He was silent then, and Ellen could tell he wouldn't say anything more on the subject.

She thought about what he had said as she drank her tea. A week ago she would have agreed, but meeting Pierre had opened up a different perspective for her. Would she be as smitten with him if he did something ordinary like driving a truck or working on a building site? Maybe part of the attraction of Albert Pengelly for her mother had been this beautiful place, the romantic idea of her man growing their vegetables and milking his cows.

'Maybe,' she said. 'But I think it's just fate, and people fall in love because they just can't help themselves.'

Albert chuckled and tweaked her hair. 'Now, what would my little girl know about that?'

She blushed. 'Only what I've read in books,' she said. 'But I'd better start picking the spuds again. I promised Janet I'd go into town this afternoon to meet her.'

Over breakfast she'd told him she'd gone to the circus last night with Janet, her friend from school, she'd even shown him her new dress and shoes. He seemed pleased she'd been out for once, even said she should do it more often. She hoped he wasn't going to mind that she intended to stay out this evening.

'You'd better stop picking around twelve, the sun's too hot for you to be out much longer,' he said. 'Besides, you've earned a rest, stay in town if you want. I'll be going down the pub tonight anyway.'

Ellen beamed. She hadn't expected it to be that easy!

The matinee was every bit as thrilling as the evening performance, partly because Ellen knew a little about the performers now, and also because there were so many children in the audience. Their gasps and amazement at it all were infectious.

At last Pierre and his brothers came running into the ring, and like the previous night, Pierre came over to her and passed her his cape with a broad smile. When he blew her a kiss before climbing the rope, her insides contracted with memories of the kiss last night. Her eyes never left him as he climbed up and up to the trapezes, she noted his taut buttocks, thigh and arm muscles bulging through the thin fabric of his suit. When he stood on the trapeze and smiled down at his audience, once again she observed his high cheek-bones and his full lips. She wondered if he felt powerful up there, knowing every eye was on him. Would it make him conceited, or did he just see it as a kind of acting?

The only male body she had ever seen naked was her father's and that was a few years ago before they had a bathroom, and he used to have a weekly bath in a tub in the kitchen. She could remember as a little girl being curious as to why he had that dangly thing surrounded by hair, and it wasn't until years later when she saw a stallion mounting a mare that she realized what it was.

She had a very good idea of what Pierre would look like naked; after all, when she met him he was wearing the briefest of swimming trunks. She thought his body was beautiful, and that made her wonder what he'd think of hers. She knew she ought to be ashamed of thinking of such things, yet she couldn't help it. She had once watched her cat Fluff when she was in season; two tom-cats had come to visit her, and Fluff had stretched herself out on the ground and writhed sensuously in front of them, teasing and yet inviting them to take her. That was how Ellen felt now – washing her hair, painting her toenails and putting on her new dress was all part of the preparation. She wanted Pierre to want her.

But it seemed indecent, putting her in the same light as the common, over-made-up girls who hung around street corners in Falmouth and made eyes at any boys who passed.

Like the previous time, Pierre came back into the ring to meet her at the end of the show. But now he pulled her into his arms and kissed her, regardless of the fact that the Big Top was still full of people filing out. Ellen felt a pang of fear that someone she knew might be watching, but that was overridden by her delight in his eagerness to see her.

'You look good enough to eat,' he said, even though she was wearing exactly what she'd worn the previous day. 'Were you in time for the bus? I was worried. I ought to have gone with you.'

'I caught it by the skin of my teeth,' she said with a smile, touched by how gentlemanly he was.

Ellen sat on the doorstep of Pierre's caravan while he changed and took off his makeup. He had suggested catching the ferry to St Mawes across the estuary and having a meal later. As she sat there watching the performers drifting by she imagined telling her friends about Pierre when she got back to school. 'He's a trapeze artist, on our first date he took me to St Mawes for a meal.' They would be so impressed; it sounded so adult and sophisticated.

Pierre came out of the caravan wearing jeans and a white short-sleeved shirt and he looked more handsome than a film star. 'I've never been across the estuary,' he said, taking her hand and leading her out through the maze of caravans. 'But people have told me it's beautiful there.'

'All of Cornwall is lovely,' she said with some pride. 'Where do you come from?'

'I don't really come from anywhere,' he said. 'I was born in Leeds, but my folks were always on the move, the longest I stayed in one place was during the war when they left me with an aunt in Ilkley while they were entertaining the troops.'

'Were they trapeze artists too?' she asked.

'No, my father was a magician, Ma was his assistant. He retired a few years ago now, they've gone back to live in Leeds.'

'So how did you become a trapeze artist then?'

'When the war ended my father got a job in Blackpool, at the Tower. It was a great show, all kinds of different acts. I used to watch the acrobats and the trapeze artists, and before long they were giving me lessons. I guess I was a natural because a couple of years on, a family of trapeze artists invited me to spend the summer with them. I only did the easy things, but they started training me, then every holiday I would join them, and that was that.'

By this time they had arrived at the ferry, and as it was crowded Ellen didn't ask him any more personal questions until they'd reached the other side.

Ellen had only been to St Mawes a couple of times, most

recently the previous summer with Josie. They hadn't thought much of it, it was too small and quiet and the few shops were boring, but when Pierre began admiring the quaint cottages along by the harbour, remarking with real pleasure about the peace and quiet, how clean it was, and how much he'd like to live in such a beautiful place, Ellen found herself looking at it with new eyes.

'Would you really like to live somewhere so sleepy?' she asked, surprised that he could stand and stare at a cottage garden for so long without being bored.

'It's my idea of heaven,' he said dreamily. 'No stink from animals, no mud, no shouting. I'd get a little boat and go out fishing all day, and at night I'd sit in front of a real fire and read.'

'But what about your performing?' she asked in surprise.

He shrugged. 'I can't do that forever. My ambition is to make as much money as I can while I'm still good, then get out. The circus won't be popular forever. Already television has made a difference; we don't always play to packed houses like we used to. The real money today is in cabaret acts in casinos and places like that.'

'Aren't casinos where people go and gamble?' She frowned.

He laughed at her naivety. 'Yes, but some of them are fabulous places, which put on fantastic shows. There's one in Beirut that is spectacular. I met a couple who had just come back from a six-month contract there and they earned enough money to get married and buy themselves a house.'

Ellen's heart quickened. If that was the sort of ambition he had, she was all for it. 'Would you like to be married then?' she asked, and hoped she wasn't blushing.

He put his arms around her and kissed her lightly on the lips. 'If the right girl came along.'

There were times that afternoon when Ellen had to pinch herself to make sure she wasn't dreaming, for everything was so perfect – the hot sun, the sparkling sea, and the thrill of being with such a handsome man. She noticed older people glancing at them walking hand in hand and for the first time in her life she felt as if she was truly beautiful and that the world was at her feet. Pierre was so interesting; he had a view of life quite unlike anyone she'd ever known. He'd been to all the big cities, both in England and on the Continent. He could speak French, Spanish and Italian, and he was well read. He told her he often spent the winter months doing other jobs, mending cars, bricklaying and painting and decorating, there seemed to be no end to his talents. But the thing she liked best about him was his openness. She was used to people who never expressed their feelings, who lived in a narrow world that they didn't want any stranger prying into.

One of her teachers at school had once said that Cornish people were by nature insular and suspicious. At the time Ellen had felt it was a sweeping statement, and hadn't taken it seriously, but through Pierre she could see it was true.

She told him about her conversation with her father that morning, and how she hadn't known until then that he had two brothers. Pierre looked thoughtful for a moment, then said he expected that it was a can of worms her father was afraid to open in case he couldn't get the lid back on it again.

She didn't quite understand what he meant by that, and wanted to ask him to explain, but then Pierre asked her what it was like living on a farm in winter, if she felt cut off and lonely, and if she resented her stepmother. It was good finally to be able to admit that she did resent Violet for causing so much unhappiness, and that she hoped she would never come back. She also told him her feelings about Josie.

'She's always been my best friend, and I miss her so much. I can't bear to think of what it's like for her to be stuck out in Helston with her mother pushing her around.

I'd sooner have her mother back being mean to me and making Dad miserable, than Josie being unhappy.'

'She might not be unhappy,' Pierre said, cuddling her tightly. 'If she's like you say she is, she'd have run away by now if that was the case. I see that kind of thing all the time in the circus, the kids that want a normal life, and the ones who love the oddness of it all. They sort themselves out eventually; nothing their parents do or say makes much difference. She's fourteen, you say, that's old enough to have a mind of her own. You said too she didn't like the farm much, so all she'll miss is you, Ellen. Neither of you will forget the good times you had together, so get on with your own life and let her get on with hers.'

They walked up by the castle and sat on the grass looking at the view of Falmouth across the estuary. 'I wish today could go on and on,' Pierre sighed. 'I don't want to be in the ring again tonight, I'd like to just sit here with you and watch the sun set.'

As they lay on the grass he kissed her long and hard, and the knowledge that they would soon have to go made it all the sweeter. Ellen felt as if she was on fire inside, each passionate kiss only serving to make her hotter still. When he cupped his hand around her breast she moved it away, yet she longed for it to creep back for the feeling was so divine.

But at five they had to go and find somewhere to eat, for Pierre said if he left it any later he wouldn't be able to do his act. He suggested that instead of watching the show yet again, she stayed in his caravan, so he could see more of her.

Ellen smiled to herself when she heard the music for the Adolphus Brothers striking up, and imagined him running into the ring and removing his cape with a swirl.

She was so comfortable, lying on his bunk in the caravan, and she closed her eyes for a moment, remembering how wonderful the afternoon had been: the ferry ride, the talking, kisses and the hand-holding. She had been ravenous when they got into the little café by the harbour, and egg, sausage and chips had never tasted so good. There weren't many people on the return ferry, and he'd cuddled her all the way because the wind felt cold. Then they'd come here to the caravan and he'd made her a cup of tea.

Jack had come in for a while, but he'd taken his costume and makeup and said he'd get dressed somewhere else. It was so companionable with Pierre washing and changing just behind a thin curtain, only a foot away from her head as she lay on the bunk – they carried on with their conversation as if they'd done this together a million times before. It was so strange to see a man putting on makeup. She giggled at what her father would have to say about that. But Pierre had explained that the lights in the Big Top made the performers look pale and ill and it wasn't any different to actors on the stage who did the same.

She could hear the gasps from the audience through the open caravan window, even above the snarling of the lions which were now back in their cages. Pierre had said earlier that he too felt like snarling and roaring sometimes when he had to come back to this caravan, knowing that he'd got to do the same show twice a day for weeks on end.

Ellen dropped off to sleep and was suddenly woken by a noise close by her. She opened her eyes in fright to see Pierre completely naked.

'It's only me,' he said, caressing her cheek. 'I was trying to change quietly so I wouldn't wake you, but I knocked a teaspoon off the shelf.'

Ellen was perturbed at his nudity, but then he'd already told her he couldn't wear anything under his costume, and he was changing to take her to the bus stop later. She averted her eyes and he wrapped a towel round his waist, then sat down on the bunk beside her to take off his makeup.

'Frankie slipped tonight,' he said. 'He's been drinking again. Rolf has taken him over to his caravan.'

Frankie was the oldest man in the troupe; Pierre had told her earlier he drank too much and that none of the other men felt entirely safe when he was catching them.

'Was anyone hurt?' she asked.

'No one but him, luckily it happened when he was solo. He'll have a few bruises tomorrow; it hurts when you hit the net from that height. The trouble is he's done it too many times now. We can't rely on him, I think he'll have to go.'

'How will you manage without him?' she asked.

Pierre turned to her and bent over to kiss her. 'I'm more concerned about how I'm going to manage without you when we have to move on,' he whispered.

Ellen quite forgot that he was naked but for the towel and put her arms round him to draw him closer. One kiss led to another and another and when his hand slid around her back to pull down the zipper on her dress she made no protest.

'You are so lovely,' he murmured as he pushed her dress down and removed her bra. 'I never felt this way about anyone before.'

The sensation of her naked breasts against his bare chest was so thrilling that even though she'd told herself a hundred times today she wouldn't allow him to take any liberties with her, that was forgotten in the heat of the moment. She wasn't prepared for the mind-robbing bliss of him kissing and caressing her breasts, and any thought of protest flew out of the window. All at once her dress was removed entirely, his towel was gone and he was peeling off her knickers hungrily.

'We mustn't,' she murmured, but he stopped her feeble protest with another long kiss. His fingers started probing inside her.

'I love you, Ellen,' he whispered against her neck. 'Let me show you how much.'

Those words removed all her last inhibitions. If he loved her it couldn't be wrong, and if she loved him she must trust him. He guided her hand to his penis as he continued to play with her, and she could hear her own breathing becoming as heavy as his. There were noises from outside the caravan, the big cats still roaring, bursts of laughter and music, but somehow it all made it seem so right and safe. The feelings she'd had earlier in the day when he kissed her were intensified a hundred times over, and she knew now that the aching feeling in her belly had been the dawning of real desire. She marvelled that his fingers and kisses could make her feel so abandoned and beautiful, and as he slipped between her open legs and into her, her need was as great as his.

It hurt a little, and at that moment she wanted to stop him, but his hands were on her buttocks, his mouth over her own. 'You are everything I want,' he whispered. 'My beautiful, sweet Ellen, let yourself go and give yourself to me.'

While it didn't feel as blissful as it had earlier, his pleasure in her seemed more important, and she held on to him, wrapped her legs around his back and let herself be taken willingly.

Suddenly he was still, and she could feel his perspiration already growing cool on his smooth back. She was surprised that was all there was, somehow she'd expected something far more dramatic to happen.

'Do you really love me?' she whispered, all at once aware that she shouldn't have let things go this far.

'Of course I do,' he said sleepily, snuggling down until his head was between her breasts. 'I wish you could stay with me here forever.'

It was then she noticed it had grown dark outside – the light coming through the caravan window was that of a lantern. 'What time is it?' she asked. 'The last bus!'

He leaned up on his elbow and fumbled for an alarm

clock. 'Nearly quarter past ten,' he said. 'Oh shit, I clean forgot about the time.'

In a panic Ellen leapt off the bed and rummaged for her clothes. She felt all sticky down below but she was too embarrassed to ask if she could wash. She couldn't do up her bra, but Pierre did it for her, then zipped up her dress and found her shoes. 'I'll come with you,' he said. 'Don't worry, we'll catch it.'

He was dressed in a trice, and taking her hand led her out of the caravan and through the parked lorries out on to the green.

'Don't come all the way with me,' she gasped breathlessly as they ran together towards the road. 'The bus is always crowded on a Saturday night, and I want to tell my father about you before he gets to hear from someone else.'

He hastily kissed her once more before she ran off to the bus stop, and it wasn't until Ellen was sitting down in the bus that she realized they hadn't made any plans to see each other again.

It was raining hard when she woke up on Sunday morning. Her father had still been out when she got home the previous night, which was lucky because her dress was all creased and her hair was wild, and he might have questioned her. She heard him come in just after she got into bed so she pretended she was asleep when he looked round her door. But she couldn't sleep. She lay there listening to the owls hooting, the rustlings of nocturnal animals around the farm, her father snoring and the wind getting up that eventually brought the first rain in weeks.

Sundays never varied. Her father never did any work other than milking the cows – as soon as that was done he put on his best clothes, took the family to church, then home for a big dinner. In the afternoon he usually dozed in an armchair. This tradition hadn't changed since Violet went away, and even if it had been fine today, Ellen knew her father would never let her go into Falmouth in the afternoon. So she would have to wait until Monday. But that seemed such an age away.

At the morning service in church, Ellen drifted off into thinking about Pierre and her father had to nudge her several times when she forgot responses or remained sitting while everyone else was kneeling.

Had she been wrong to let Pierre make love to her? Did he really love her? Would they get married and live happily ever after? She didn't feel as if she'd done anything bad, just the thought of him made her want to smile. Yet she could see big problems ahead – a circus performer wasn't the kind of husband her father had in mind for her. Albert would be prejudiced before he even met him, and he wasn't going to want her following Pierre around the country like a nomad.

Yet for all that Ellen felt optimistic. Pierre had said himself he wanted to live somewhere quiet, he could do so many things which would be useful on the farm. Maybe once she'd convinced her father she loved this man he'd be prepared to give him a chance.

'You seem in a dream today,' Albert said as they ate their dinner later. 'You've hardly said a word.'

Ellen looked at him and opened her mouth to blurt out that she'd met someone, but the suspicious expression in his eyes stopped her. It was too soon to tell him, he might very well fly off the handle and refuse to let her go out again. She would wait for a few weeks.

'I was thinking about the potatoes,' she lied. 'I've got to work tomorrow, will you be able to pick them on your own?'

'I picked all the ones I'd dug up,' he said. 'It won't hurt the rest to stay in the ground another few days. I think this rain will be gone by tonight anyway.'

Ellen had never minded the quietness of the farm before, but that Sunday afternoon it seemed unbearable. Once her father had dozed off in his chair she went up to her room and sat on the windowsill staring out at the driving rain. Normally the view cheered her, whatever the weather or the season. The woods to either side of the farmhouse were so many different shades of green, the pasture land was usually a mass of wild flowers, and she loved to look at the progress of the crops and welcomed the rain that made them grow more vigorously, But today it just looked miserable. The grazing cows and sheep and the low rainfall had turned the pasture into brown stubble, the section of the potato field which had been turned over by the tractor looked messy. The cove down at the bottom of their land made a sort of V-shape, but today the rocks, sea and sky were all a sullen dark grey.

She turned her back on the view but looking into her room did nothing to cheer her either, for it looked as forlorn as she felt. The window was low down and quite small so except in bright sunshine the room was always a bit gloomy. The furniture was sparse, just the two beds, each covered with a faded pale blue bedspread, a battered old chest of drawers and a few hooks on the wall where she hung her clothes. The bare boards had been painted many years ago, but the paint was peeling off now, the whitewashed walls were dingy, and the posters of the Beatles and Elvis Presley which Josie had pinned up some time ago were crooked.

When Josie was here, Ellen had never given a thought to how shabby and comfortless the room was, but then she hadn't ever felt lonely either when she had Josie for company. All at once the thought of living alone with her father for two more years of school filled her with absolute dread. If she had a record-player, or if there'd been a television downstairs, it might not be quite so bad, but even the radio in the kitchen didn't work very well. In her heart she knew Dad wasn't going to approve of anything about Pierre, not his name, his profession or his age. What on earth was she going to do?

The rain had gone by the following morning and Ellen set off for work in the kiosk feeling optimistic. But although the sun was shining again, it was much cooler than of late, and there weren't anywhere near so many people on the beach. As there weren't many customers Ellen busied herself cleaning all the shelves in the kiosk, but her mind was still on Pierre.

She relived each wonderful moment of their date on Saturday, reminding herself how he'd said he'd never felt this way about any other girl. It would work out, she knew it. Maybe for the time being she would have to keep him secret and just go to see him when he was in another town nearby, but she could live with that.

On the other hand Pierre had said he often spent the winter working in London, so maybe she could go there and get a job. A couple of girls from school had found places in a girls' hostel there; she could go and ask their parents for their address in London. She didn't think her father would object to that, not if she had somewhere safe to move to.

At four-thirty the kiosk owners came to cash up and close down for the day, and still Pierre hadn't come. She was just about to leave, intending to walk over to the circus ground and find Pierre, when her father turned up in his old truck.

'I had to order some seed,' he called out as he walked towards her. 'So I thought I'd time it to give you a lift home. Want an ice-cream?'

Ellen knew by her father's warm smile that this was his idea of a treat for her, and she couldn't hurt his feelings by looking less than delighted. He bought two cornets and he suggested that instead of getting back into the truck they sat on the wall in the sunshine to eat them.

There were more people around now than there had been all day, many couples with young children. Some were laying a picnic on the sand.

'I met your mother here,' Albert said suddenly. 'The

110

beach was fenced off with barbed wire then because it was wartime, but she was sitting on a stool, painting. I stopped to look and we got talking.'

It was very ironic that he should choose today of all days to start telling her things she'd always wanted to know, right here. Yet instead of being pleased, she was frightened Pierre might come along and see them together. She had never before been embarrassed or ashamed of her father, but she was prickling with it now, for in his rough working clothes he didn't look much better than a tramp.

'I never told you before, but she came from a wealthy family,' he went on. 'Her house was up that way.' He pointed to the houses up on the hill beside the lake on the other side of the road. 'I could take you up there now and show it to you.'

'No. Not now. I want to go home,' Ellen said, and she got up and walked towards the truck.

Later that same evening Ellen stood down by the little cove, watching the sun go down, bitterly regretting the way she'd behaved with her father. He didn't say a word all the way home and went straight back to work picking potatoes, but she knew he was very hurt.

Why had she been embarrassed to be seen with her own father? That was so horrible, she'd never been ashamed of him before.

Tears trickled down her cheeks. She felt so mixed up inside, where once everything had been orderly and safe. Was this what love did to people? Made them turn against their own family? Was that what happened to her mother when she married someone her parents didn't approve of?

The saddest thing was that she knew she'd never get the whole story now. Her father had come specially to meet her. It was his way of showing his affection and appreciation. Now he'd been rebuffed she knew he'd stay silent and brooding for weeks. Even an apology wouldn't make any difference. For what reason could she offer for being so rude?

The following morning Ellen didn't have to go to the café, but she got up when her father did and went out to help him with the milking. He merely nodded at her, nothing more, and as she sat on the milking stool, her forehead leaning against the cow's flank while she milked, she shed a few more tears.

After a silent breakfast, Ellen washed up, then went straight to the potato field. Albert was driving the tractor, churning up the remaining rows of potatoes, so she picked up a sack from the pile and began filling it. Two hours later, her back was aching from bending over and she stood up to watch her father. He was working his way down the furrow next to the one she was on, from the opposite end, picking so fast he looked like a machine. Yet for some reason her former pity for him turned to resentment. She had witnessed him shutting Violet out like this many a time, Josie too, and if he wanted to do it to her then she was going to ignore it.

'I think I'll go into town to the library,' she shouted out. 'Would you like some tea before I go?'

'Okay,' he shouted back. 'How many sacks have you filled?'

'Five, and I can't do any more, my back's hurting.'

There was no reply to this, no praise for filling so many, no concern for her back. He could get his own tea, and she wasn't going to feel guilty at leaving him to finish the job while she rode off on her bike to see Pierre.

Ellen didn't have any choice about what to wear to ride to the circus ground. It was a case of her shorts or a very shabby pair of slacks – a dress or skirt would ride up on the bike. The shorts won, they were old too, but they fitted well and her legs were nice and brown. With a sleeveless blouse, plimsolls and her hair tied up in a pony-tail, she didn't look sophisticated as she had in the cream dress, but then she didn't want to look as if she was chasing Pierre.

She forgot about her father on the ride into town. All her thoughts were of seeing Pierre again. She had her swim-suit and a towel in the basket on her bike, along with a library book. She hoped he'd want to go swimming with her.

But as she rode up the hill from Falmouth town, even from a distance she could see the Big Top had been taken down. Trees hid the caravans and trucks, and the hill was too steep to ride all the way up, so she had to get off and push and all the time her heart was fluttering with panic. Surely he wasn't thinking of leaving without seeing her first?

Finally she reached the crest of the hill, the big field spread out in front of her. But there were no trucks, no caravans or sideshows. It was all gone, the ground where the Big Top had stood bald and brown.

In horror she crossed the road and slung her bike down. There was nothing. The paddock fences where the horses had been kept were gone and the site where the caravans and trucks had stood was a patchwork of yellow, squashed grass. There were deep tracks from truck tyres, chewed-up areas of mud from the recent heavy rain, a pile of animal dung and rubbish, empty cans and bottles, sweet wrappers, sticks from candy floss, cigarette packets and even a few discarded programmes, birds picking eagerly at crumbs, and a lone dog sniffing around an overflowing litter-bin.

Ellen stood there, rooted to the spot, her eyes filling with tears as she saw a red balloon bowling along the grass in the light breeze. It seemed to represent her abandonment and soon it would impale itself on something sharp and burst.

Why hadn't he said they would be leaving today? Was it all pretence that he loved her?

On the far side of the field she saw a small pick-up truck

and a man raking up rubbish. She ran over to him, thinking he belonged to the circus, but as she got nearer she saw his overalls were those of the Town Corporation.

'When did they leave?' she asked the man. He was small and stout with a weatherbeaten face.

'Yesterday,' he said. 'Bloody mess they've left, and only me to clear it.'

He had a strong Cornish accent, and a slight speech impediment too. Ellen guessed he was a little simple. 'Do you know where they've gone next?' she asked.

'Dunno, they's like gypsies, in um?'

'But someone must know.' She couldn't hold back her tears now. 'Who owns this field?'

'Dunno,' he said shaking his head. 'Sent me up to clear it, that all I know.'

Ellen walked back to her bike sobbing. She was trembling all over, her mind in a fog, yet even through that she knew she had told Pierre she would be at the kiosk all day Monday. The only possible reason for him not coming to let her know he was leaving was that he didn't care about her.

Chapter Seven

On the second Sunday in September, shortly after one, Ellen was out in the garden picking some mint to go with the lamb for dinner, when she heard a car coming down the track.

Her heart leapt as it had been doing for the whole past month every time she heard such a sound. Could it be Pierre coming looking for her?

Sadly she knew it was unlikely. He wouldn't have left the way he did if he cared. Even if something had happened that day which prevented him from coming down to the kiosk at Swanpool, he could have sent a letter there afterwards. Yet still she continued to hope.

Since the day she found out he'd left town it was as if a black cloud had engulfed her. She didn't want to eat, couldn't sleep, and had no interest in anything. It did no good telling herself that she'd only known Pierre for a short time and that it wouldn't take long to forget him. Her feelings were as raw now as they had been a month ago. What she couldn't understand was why he'd pretended she was special to him. That made no sense to her at all.

It was another warm, sunny day, and she was wearing a new dress she'd made herself. It was just a sleeveless shift style, but a pretty green and white printed cotton. Mrs Peters had prompted this. About three weeks ago she'd stopped Ellen in the village to speak to her and seemed to sense something was wrong, for she took her into her house for a cup of tea. Ellen gave the impression she was just desperately lonely without Josie, so Mrs Peters suggested she took up dressmaking as a distraction and offered to give her a hand if she got stuck.

Since that day Ellen had been a regular visitor at the Peters' cottage. She used the excuse that she needed advice with her sewing, but in reality she felt comforted by Mavis Peters' motherly ways, and it helped take her mind off Pierre. This morning at church Mrs Peters had told her she had a length of navy-blue wool she didn't need, which would make a nice winter dress. She suggested that if Ellen came round the following evening, they could cut it out together. So Ellen had come home from church feeling a little more cheerful than of late, and the shoulder of lamb she'd left cooking slowly in the oven smelled wonderful. Now they had a visitor, and maybe that would turn out to be another nice surprise. Albert came out into the garden then; he too had heard the car. As it came into view, they both gasped in shock. It was a taxi. Violet was sitting in the front seat with the driver and Josie was in the back.

'Well I never!' Albert exclaimed, for he had heard nothing from Violet since the day she took Josie away.

Ellen ran to the car on winged feet and yanked the door open. 'Josie!' she yelled. 'It's so good to see you. You can't imagine how much I've missed you!'

But it was immediately obvious that something was badly wrong. Josie didn't return Ellen's joyful greeting, she slunk out of the car like a whipped dog, and Violet had a face like a bag of hammers. The driver took the bags out of the boot, put them on the ground, and was back in the driving seat and turning the car round so fast that it was clear that he sensed trouble.

'How's yer mother?' Albert said with icy politeness.

'She died ten days ago,' Violet said curtly. 'So we came back.'

'I'm sorry,' Albert said, perhaps thinking sorrow was the only reason for Violet's grim expression. 'You should have let me know.'

Ellen looked round at her family. She wasn't surprised

by Violet's starchiness, that was her all over. But she couldn't imagine what was wrong with Josie, she looked so sullen. She was wearing a lovely pale blue dress and white sandals on her feet, but her eyes were cold, her mouth pinched and angry. As for her father, he just looked plain bewildered.

'We were just about to have our dinner. I'd better put some more vegetables on for you,' Ellen said, hoping to sound really welcoming and defuse the situation. 'But first I'll help Josie unpack her things.'

Ellen picked up both the bags and walked into the house, Josie following her. Their parents remained outside. 'You've made my day coming home,' Ellen said to her sister as they went up the stairs. 'But tell me what's wrong. Aren't you pleased to be home?'

'No, I'm not.' Josie flounced into their bedroom and flung herself down on her bed. 'Mum's evil. You can't imagine how horrible she's been to me and everyone else. I hate her; I don't want to live in this crumby place either. Look at this room, Ellen! Don't you think we deserve something better?'

This was a shock to Ellen for Josie had never complained before. 'I suppose we could paint it ourselves,' she suggested. 'But what's happened to make you like this?'

'I can't say now, she'll go for me if she hears me telling you anything,' Josie said, looking fearfully over her shoulder towards the door. 'You go on downstairs and do the vegetables. I'll unpack my things. I don't want my new clothes spoiled.'

Ellen couldn't bear to leave it like that. She sat down on the bed beside her sister and took her hand in hers. 'Whatever's happened between you and Mum hasn't got anything to do with us,' she reminded her. 'I love you, Josie, I missed you like hell. Don't be mean to me.'

Josie's lip trembled and her eyes filled with tears. 'I missed you too. I'll tell you everything later. I'm just so mad with Mum I can't help myself.'

As Ellen prepared some more vegetables and gravy and laid two extra places at the table, she kept glancing out of the window at her parents. They were sitting on two chairs, their backs to the kitchen so she couldn't see their faces, and too far away for her to overhear what they were talking about. But it was clear from the way they were sitting so stiffly, gesticulating with their hands, that it wasn't a happy reunion.

The new school term started the following day, so Ellen thought maybe that was why Violet had brought Josie back now. She had noticed that her stepmother's appearance had improved quite dramatically. She'd had her hair cut and permed, and the navy and white dress she was wearing was new. She also looked as if she'd lost some weight. But however overjoyed Ellen was to have Josie back, she couldn't feel the same about her stepmother. Her gut reaction was that there was more trouble in store for all of them, and she knew she was going to be stuck right in the middle of it.

An awkward silence fell over the dinner table. Violet's mouth was pursed; Josie's eyes remained downcast. Ellen did her best, remarking on how nice Violet looked and passing on bits of village gossip, but there was no response.

'You girls go out for a walk,' Dad said after the dinner had been eaten and the washing-up finished. 'We've got things to talk about.'

Violet shot Josie a malevolent look which could only be a warning she wasn't to speak out of turn, but she didn't countermand her husband's suggestion.

'Mum's stupid and selfish,' Josie blurted out once they got down to the cove. 'She's ruined everything.'

Ellen was well aware from Josie's nervy behaviour that she had been promised a good hiding if she revealed anything. 'I won't let on you've told me anything,' she reassured her. 'Cut my throat and hope to die.'

Josie smiled faintly, they had used that silly vow all the time when they were little. 'Oh Ellen, I don't know where

118

to begin,' she sighed. 'I didn't want to leave here, I thought I'd hate it in Helston, but it didn't turn out like that.'

It transpired that while Violet had stayed looking after her mother in her tiny house, Josie had gone to stay with her Uncle Brian and his wife Susan. They had two boys, Josie told her, John aged seventeen and Mark fifteen, and their house was a very grand place with six bedrooms, a huge garden and a tennis court. It seemed that Brian had made big money in the building trade after the war. Josie liked Mark and John, and right from the start it was her idea of heaven, for her aunt and uncle treated her like the daughter they had never had. They bought her new clothes and made a real fuss of her. Josie started having dancing lessons, and as her aunt was involved with an amateur dramatic society, she had taken Josie along to that too, and Josie had loved it.

'I was really happy there,' she burst out angrily. 'Not just because they made a fuss of me, but because it felt right. I missed you, but that was the only thing from here I did miss. I had a lovely room; I could listen to records, play tennis and go swimming with the boys, watch television and go to the pictures. I felt I belonged.'

Although Ellen felt saddened by what Josie was saying, she could also sympathize. 'So what happened?' she asked.

'Grandma said Mum could have her house when she died.' Josie pulled a face. 'I don't know why she wanted it, it was horrible. But Mum reckoned she could do it up, and she was going to get a job in Helston. She was happy enough for me to stay with Uncle Brian, and go to the secondary school there. I reckon she thought if she left me with them, they'd always look after her too. Then Grandma died, and it turned out her house didn't belong to her at all. Uncle Brian had bought it years before, so Grandma didn't have to pay any rent. He said Mum couldn't possibly have it, he was intending to do it up and let it to holiday-makers.'

Ellen almost laughed, remembering her father's words about Violet's reasons for going to Helston. She might have said 'Serve her right' if Josie hadn't been so upset.

'Mum was like a mad bull,' Josie went on. 'She raged about how she'd looked after the old bat all these weeks when none of the rest of them could be bothered, and she was entitled to something for her trouble. She was hateful to everyone, especially Brian, and she made them all realize she'd only gone to look after her mother because she thought she was going to get something.'

Ellen winced; she knew how nasty Violet could be.

'Uncle Brian laid into her, you should have heard the things he said! He even said she'd only had me to trap Dad into marrying her. Then he said she didn't need any help from any of them anyway, after all she had her own fortune coming to her in this place. He said if she had any sense at all she'd get back here and make Dad see what a goldmine he was sitting on.'

Ellen frowned. She didn't understand how anyone could think the farm was a gold-mine. 'But it isn't,' she exclaimed. 'What did Uncle Brian mean?'

'I couldn't see it either, but my cousin John explained it to me,' Josie said. 'You see, the land and its position are worth a fortune, at least to someone with the imagination and money to put into it. He was talking about a hotel, holiday cottages, that kind of stuff. Uncle Brian had only seen it once, but he's in that business and he knows. He reckoned it might be worth up to a million pounds, and besides that, Dad could still build himself a little cottage to stay in, and work some of the land. So he could have his cake and eat it too.'

This was astounding to Ellen. 'But Dad won't ever sell it,' she said. 'Mum must have flipped if she thinks she can make him.'

Josie shrugged. 'That's what I reckoned too, but Mum thinks she can do it, and I'm supposed to help her. That's why we've come back.'

'Well, I'm glad you have,' Ellen said, even though she couldn't help thinking it might turn out to be a nightmare if Josie didn't want to be here.

They had been sitting on a rock, but Josie got up abruptly, picked up a stone and hurled it into the sea. 'I'm not a bit glad. I've got to get back to Helston; there's a boy there I really like.'

Six weeks before Ellen wouldn't have seen that as a good reason, but she saw things differently now. 'Oh, Josie,' she sighed. 'I know just how you feel.'

She listened while Josie told her about a boy called Dave who was a Mod and drove a Lambretta. She went on and on about how it felt when he kissed her, how she couldn't bear to be parted from him.

Ellen just nodded. Everything Josie said struck a twanging chord inside her.

'I love him,' Josie finally burst out. 'I'll just die if I can't be with him.'

She stopped suddenly, looking curiously at Ellen. 'What did you mean by you knew how I felt? Have you met someone too?'

Ellen felt too wretched to be cautious. She blurted out the whole story about Pierre, including the fact that they'd made love.

'Ellen!' Josie gasped, her eyes widening in astonishment. 'I can't believe you'd do that. You've always been the sensible one.'

'I don't think anyone's sensible when they fall in love,' Ellen said sadly. 'I could have sworn he meant everything he said, but he went away without even saying goodbye.'

'Maybe something happened to stop him. I didn't get a chance to say goodbye to Dave.'

Ellen shook her head. 'I've been through all that in my mind, but I know the truth now. He was just using me. If he'd really cared, he could have left a message at the kiosk.'

Josie took Ellen's hand and squeezed it. 'Don't say that, I can't bear to think of anyone hurting you.'

'I'm getting over it,' Ellen said, but the tears forming in her eyes proved that wasn't true.

Josie looked at her for a moment. 'You couldn't be pregnant, could you?' she said.

'Don't say that,' Ellen exclaimed. 'I feel miserable enough already. You can't get pregnant the first time, can you?'

Josie shrugged. 'I don't know. But Auntie Susan gave me a bit of a talking to when she saw me snogging with Dave. She told me about one of her friends' daughters who got pregnant to a sailor at HMS *Culdrose*, that naval place near Helston. He got shipped off overseas, and she was left to face the music on her own.'

Suddenly Ellen felt very uneasy. She hadn't even considered pregnancy, heartbreak was enough to cope with, but now she came to think about it, the last period she'd had was before she met Pierre. That was at least five weeks ago.

'Are you all right? You've gone all white!' Josie said, and moved to her sister's side to cuddle her. 'You aren't late, are you?'

'I think I am,' Ellen said in a whisper.

'It could be just because you've been upset,' Josie said, tenderly stroking her sister's face. 'I don't always get mine on the right day. Oh shit, I wish I hadn't said anything now.'

'We're a fine pair, aren't we?' Ellen said with a sigh. 'You don't want to be here, I won't either if it turns out I'm pregnant. Dad and Mum are going to be fighting all the time. What the hell are we going to do?'

'Run away together?' Josie said.

For just a second or two that idea sounded wonderful to Ellen. But her common sense came back almost immediately. 'You can't run anywhere; you aren't old enough to

122

leave school. And don't you say a word to Mum or Dad about this, will you?'

'Of course I won't,' Josie promised. 'But before we go back home, I've got to tell you something else.'

'What? You haven't done it too?'

Josie laughed. 'No, but I was tempted to, Dave was so lovely. What I wanted to say is that I'll have to be a real misery at home. It's the only thing that might make Mum send me back to Uncle Brian's. It will mean I'll have to pretend to be nasty to you, and upset Dad too. I'll be just the same as usual when we're on our own. But not when we're indoors.'

Ellen shrugged. She felt so low now that nothing could make her any worse. 'Okay. Well, if I am pregnant, I suppose you being nasty all the time could be a good reason for me leaving.'

'You mustn't do that!' Josie's eyes widened with alarm. 'I couldn't bear it.'

'I'll have to, won't I?' Ellen said, her eyes filling with tears. 'Dad will be furious if I am. And even if he calmed down enough to agree he'd stand by me, could you imagine Mum being nice about it?'

Josie just looked bleak for she was remembering her mother's instructions yesterday as they packed to come home. Her new role was to push Ellen into leaving the farm. If she didn't, she couldn't go back to Helston. Violet's reasoning was that if Albert didn't have Ellen to help him, he'd be much more likely to agree to sell.

When Josie was given this ultimatum, she had been preoccupied with planning her own escape route, and it hardly registered how cruel her mother was being about Ellen. But this latest development was likely to scupper everyone's plans. If Ellen was pregnant, she was far more likely to reveal the truth than just run off. That was the way she was. Dad would fly off the handle too, but in the end he'd stand by Ellen. When the baby was born,

Mum wouldn't have a snowball's chance in hell of getting Dad to sell the farm. And where was it going to leave her?

'I don't think you can really be pregnant,' Josie said hopefully. 'We're just getting carried away. But let's play-act that we've fallen out for good for now, then whatever happens we'll be able to help one another.'

By the middle of October, when no period had arrived, Ellen had to face the fact that she was pregnant. She tried to blot it out, to believe it couldn't be happening to her, but in her heart she knew. Her breasts were tender, she sometimes felt nauseous in the mornings when she smelled bacon cooking, and she discovered by consulting a book in the library that both these things were symptoms.

By day Ellen could blank it out. Being in the sixth form at school gave her many privileges; it was more relaxed than the rest of the school. She liked schoolwork and her teachers. But as soon as she got home, the anxiety came back, for the atmosphere there was stifling.

She couldn't escape by helping her father around the farm, because she had so much homework, and Violet never missed an opportunity to belittle her or blame her for something. As for Josie, she made things even more intolerable because she'd stuck to her plan of never speaking unless they were alone.

Her father had become completely unapproachable. He came indoors to eat his meals, bolted them down and then shot out again. Misery showed in his face, and she guessed that whenever she and Josie were out, Violet harangued him about selling the farm, perhaps even resorting to blackmail by telling him she'd go for good if he made it worth her while.

Ellen so much wanted to search him out and talk to him, to tell him she was firmly on his side, but Violet was very watchful, constantly giving her jobs to do, forcing her to do her homework. And when she was pleasant, it was only to go on about what good opportunities there were for young girls in the big cities, and that only a fool would want to stay in Cornwall.

Dad had even dropped his day of rest on Sundays. October was one of the busiest months, with ploughing to be done and the sheds and barns needing repairs before the winter, but that had never stopped him going to church or snoozing in the afternoon before. Ellen wanted to cry when she saw him outside all day. She knew how important his religion was to him, and she felt he would fall ill if he didn't get some rest.

The holidaymakers all disappeared as the leaves fell from the trees and the autumn storms began. As Ellen battled up the lane to catch the bus to school in high winds, side-stepping the thick mud, she no longer delighted in the squirrels jumping from tree to tree, or the odd sighting of a fox or badger – all she could think of was her hopeless predicament.

She no longer imagined Pierre coming back to claim her. By now she had accepted he had only wanted her for sex and she'd been a mug to have believed it was love.

All her high hopes for the future, college or even university, were dashed. The following May she would have a baby, with no husband and no money. She had no idea what she was going to do.

During half term, right at the end of October, Violet sent Ellen to the village one afternoon to get some shopping. In the past, Ellen had always worked with her father during holidays, but this time Violet had refused to let her. She was so crafty, she made out to Dad that she was so caring, convincing him he mustn't ask for help because Ellen had to study, but all she wanted was to keep them apart.

It was raining hard, and Ellen knew Violet didn't really need the shopping today, all she wanted was to make her even more miserable. Yet however wet and cold it was, it was a relief to get out of the house, for Josie had stepped up her nastiness, and at times Ellen even thought it was for real.

She took the footpath across the fields and as she approached the stile at the far end by the village she caught sight of Mavis Peters walking her dog. Even in the rain she looked elegant, wearing a cream raincoat with a matching hat and shiny brown Wellingtons.

She greeted Ellen with a warm smile. 'Hello, my dear. How nice to see you. I've missed you. But I suppose you get too much homework now to come visiting?'

Ellen nodded, though the truth was that Violet wouldn't let her go anywhere after school. But Mrs Peters seemed to sense something was wrong because she insisted that Ellen come back to her house for a cup of tea and a chat after she'd got her shopping. Just the thought of being in that warm, snug cottage for a while was worth risking Violet's anger, so Ellen agreed readily.

Mr Peters was out somewhere, and once Ellen was settled in a comfortable chair in front of the fire, Mrs Peters asked her gently how it was now that Josie and her stepmother were home. Ellen couldn't help herself, she had to talk to someone about it, and so she told her how dreadful it was.

One of the reasons Ellen had always felt at ease in the company of Mr and Mrs Peters was that they weren't dyed-in-the-wool locals. They weren't gossips, they were interesting, intelligent people who were well read and had travelled widely. During the evenings Ellen had spent sewing with Mrs Peters they had discussed things like politics, religion, art, books and music, and Ellen had always been surprised by the older woman's modern outlook. But it was her ability to understand others that impressed Ellen most. She was never judgmental or critical, she just seemed to have a huge well of understanding about human nature.

On top of that Ellen admired the way Mrs Peters always

looked so neat and attractive; she had retained her interest in fashion, and was never without her face powder and lipstick. But it was her lively blue eyes and her wide smile which made her seem so much younger than her real age of fifty-eight. Her voice was lovely, real BBC English, which made Ellen wish she could speak like that too.

Mrs Peters merely nodded in understanding as Ellen told her how things were at the farm. 'Oh dear,' she sighed eventually. 'I must admit I was worried about you when I heard Violet was back. But when I saw her looking so smart in church, I thought perhaps it was all working out.'

'She only came because someone told her the farm is worth a fortune,' Ellen said with some bitterness. 'Josie is as miserable as me. She liked it in Helston. As for Dad, he just keeps right out of the way.'

They had a cup of tea, and Ellen tried a piece of home-made cherry cake. Then, for no reason she could explain, she suddenly blurted out that she was pregnant. Maybe it was the warm, safe feeling in the cottage that prompted it, or Mrs Peters' previous kindness to her. Perhaps also she knew that it would soon be obvious to everyone, so it was better to tell Mrs Peters herself than let her hear it through village gossip.

As the words tumbled out she was appalled at herself. She half expected Mrs Peters to push her out of the door with abuse ringing in her ears. But she wasn't shocked or horrified, only deeply sympathetic, and the questions she asked were so caring and gentle that she made it easy for Ellen to sob out the entire story.

When she had finished, Mavis Peters got up, perched on the arm of Ellen's chair, put her arms around her and drew her head to her bosom. 'You poor darling,' she said soothingly. 'I sensed something was badly wrong when you didn't call round. You've been looking peaky in church the past few Sundays, but with Violet and Josie there I couldn't really talk to you. But your secret's safe with me,

I promise you I won't say a word to anyone, and I'll help in any way I can.'

Ellen was relieved not to hear disgust in the older woman's voice. 'What should I do?' she asked. 'I can't keep it to myself forever, can I?'

'No, of course you can't, dear,' Mrs Peters replied, her voice calm and soothing. 'The logical thing of course is to tell your father straight away, but I guess you are afraid to do that?'

Ellen nodded. 'It will just make everything at home even worse. I don't want a baby, Mrs Peters. Not unless I can be married and have a home of my own. I can't bear the thought of all the people round here whispering about me. Or when he or she is old enough to go to school being called a little bastard.'

Mrs Peters remembered how Ellen had confided in her about the way she had found out about her real mother and how she had died. It was clear Ellen still felt the shame and hurt about it, and she didn't want the same thing to happen to her child.

Mrs Peters knew from Frank, her husband, what a comfortless place Beacon Farm was. She also knew what a conniving shrew Violet was, and if Ellen had to bring her child up there, it might not be long before she headed for the cliff tops with her baby, just as her mother had done.

'There are people who can help you,' she said gently. 'You don't have to stay at the farm, there are special homes for girls in your predicament, with good people who can give you sound advice and help you decide whether you want to keep the baby or not.'

She explained about how adoption worked, that there were childless couples aching for a baby of their own to love and it might be something Ellen should consider. 'But that's in the future,' she added. 'My concern is for you right now, you're feeling desperate, and I honestly think the answer might be to leave home as quickly as possible, so you can feel at peace for the rest of your pregnancy.'

'I'd leave tomorrow if I had somewhere to go,' Ellen said, sniffing back her tears. 'Anything would be better than having Violet and Josie being nasty and Dad avoiding me.'

'There are mother-and-baby homes for girls like you, but they will only take you for the last six weeks of the pregnancy,' Mrs Peters said. 'You could book a place in one now, though, move closer to it and get work until the time comes.'

'But what about school?' Ellen asked.

'That isn't the be-all and end-all,' Mrs Peters said, patting Ellen's shoulder. 'A bright girl like you could always do your "A" levels later at night school.'

'But I wouldn't be able to if I kept the baby,' Ellen said, fresh tears flooding out again. 'And how can I keep it? You need money for that.'

Mrs Peters had two children herself, and neither of them had been angels, especially her younger daughter Isobel. But they'd come through their family problems by working things out together. Both girls were happily married now, and she had four grandchildren too, but that only served to remind her just how alone Ellen really was.

Albert was an uncommunicative, stubborn and by all accounts difficult man, and his wife little better than a trollop. In Mavis's opinion Ellen's sensitivity and intelligence came from her real mother. She and Frank had grown fond of the girl and believed she would go far, so it was appalling that because of a brief moment of passion her prospects would be ruined. While she didn't usually approve of an outsider standing between a child and its parents, she thought that in Ellen's case someone had to.

'Would you like me to find out about some homes for you?' she asked Ellen. 'I do know of one in Bristol. My daughter Isobel is involved on the committee for it. She might be able to find a nice family who need a mother's help too, so you could stay with them until you are ready to go into the home.'

Hope flooded into Ellen's eyes. 'Oh please, Mrs Peters, that would be wonderful.' But almost as soon as she'd spoken, a cloud passed across her face. 'How will I leave though? I couldn't hurt Dad by just disappearing.'

'No, you couldn't, and you mustn't even think like that,' Mrs Peters said firmly. 'But if the family my daughter finds for you offer you a job, that's a very good reason for going, isn't it?'

'He'll be upset that I want to leave school. So will my teachers.'

'That's true, but your father must know how unhappy you are with Violet. He'll see that as the reason.'

Ellen just sat there for a moment in silence. As she thought about what Mrs Peters had suggested, she felt as if the huge weight on her shoulders was gradually being lightened. She leaned towards Mavis and hugged her. 'You've been so kind to me, I feel so much better now. Thank you so much.'

It wasn't long after Ellen had gone that Frank Peters came in, and Mavis, feeling guilty about coming between father and daughter, told him everything.

'You did right,' he said. 'Telling Albert would have been a calamity all round. By going away Ellen can make up her own mind about what's best for her and her child.'

'He'd be very angry if he ever found out,' Mavis pointed out.

Frank shrugged. 'So what! If he hadn't kept those girls so isolated this probably wouldn't have happened. I can't feel too much sympathy for him; by all accounts he pressured Ellen's mother into marrying him. And some say he drove her to her death with his possessiveness. I wouldn't want little Ellen to be trapped on that farm for the rest of her life, she's worth more than that.'

'I'll have to ring Isobel about it tonight,' Mavis said, heartened to have her husband's backing. 'It would be best if Ellen left here by Christmas or soon after, before anyone notices anything.'

'I wonder if she's confided in Josie?' Frank said.

'She didn't say.'

'I hope she hasn't, adolescent girls can be so treacherous sometimes,' Frank said thoughtfully. 'I can't help thinking Josie isn't made of the same stuff as Ellen, however much alike they are to look at.'

Chapter Eight

Josie refused to go to the station in Truro to see Ellen off on the train to Bristol. She was too cross with her. She didn't even say goodbye when Ellen got into Dad's truck, but stayed up in her bedroom and thumped the pillows on her bed in anger.

Today was 20 December. The Christmas decorations had been up for a week, and a tree cut down and potted up all ready to bring indoors, but just two days before Ellen had received a letter with a train ticket from the people in Bristol she was going to work for, saying they really could do with her help with their children immediately.

Ellen didn't have to go, not now, before Christmas, but she wanted to, Josie felt. She was prepared for Ellen going in January, she wouldn't have been angry then. She was going to Uncle Brian's anyway on Boxing Day and staying for the rest of the holidays. But thanks to Ellen, everything was messed up. Mum had suddenly changed her mind, and now she was refusing to let Josie go.

It wasn't fair. She wanted to be at the big family party on New Year's Eve, to have some fun with her cousins, to go to the pantomime and do all the other things Uncle Brian had organized, and most of all she wanted to see Dave again.

Josie thought he was a dream, with his jet-black hair, chocolate-drop eyes and the longest eye-lashes she'd ever seen on anyone. She loved his college-boy hairstyle, his scooter and that Parka coat with wolf fur round the hood. He had taken her out for a ride on the scooter during the summer and next to being kissed by him it was the most exciting thing she'd ever done.

Josie wasn't fooled one bit by Mum saying she couldn't go now because it wasn't right for their father to be left without either of his daughters at a time that was for families. As if she cared about his feelings! The real reason Mum wouldn't let her go was because she was afraid to be left on her own with Dad.

Over the past months Josie had heard them arguing many times at night. Mum would say that as he didn't love her, why wouldn't he give her some money so she could go and start a new life elsewhere. Dad would say there was no money for that, then Mum would bring up selling the farm again. It always ended the same way. Dad would yell that the farm had been in his family for three generations and he wasn't selling it at any price, ever.

Sometimes there were slaps, china was smashed and pots thrown, and Josie knew that if she and Ellen hadn't been in the house, the fights would have been much more serious. So that's why Mum wanted Josie around, not because she couldn't bear to be separated from her, but so she wouldn't get hurt when she pushed Dad too far.

Josie heard the truck clunking on up the lane and Mum coming back into the kitchen to finish icing the Christmas cake. It was so tempting to go down and tell her that Ellen was only going to Bristol to hide that she was having a baby, but much as she hated her sister at this moment, she couldn't do that to her.

Going away to Helston had given Josie a taste of what life was like in a normal family. They talked to one another, sat around and watched TV together, they had family days out, teased one another, and showed affection openly. When she got back here, all at once she understood why she'd always felt her parents were weird and different from other people. It wasn't as she had supposed just because they farmed and lived in isolation. It was because there was no love between them, not even friendship or

133

shared interests. She felt the hatred flowing between them, and as time had gone by she'd come to despise them for forcing her to live with it.

She lay back on the bed, looking contemptuously around her. Her mother had moved her out of the room she'd shared with Ellen and into this one which hadn't been used for years. She'd painted the walls pink, made new curtains and a frill for a wobbly, scarred old dressing table. She expected Josie to be thrilled and grateful. But she wasn't, she liked sharing the old big room with Ellen, they could chat at night and get into bed with each other when they were cold. But then Josie wasn't stupid, she knew that was exactly why her mother had moved her. The new room felt like a prison cell, and every moment she spent in it she thought only of how lovely it was in Helston.

Nothing had worked out since September. Josie's plan to ignore Ellen in front of their parents had backfired, the only person it made miserable was herself. Ellen didn't even seem to notice, let alone care, so the only person it hurt was herself. As for Dad, he was hardly ever in the house, so it all washed over him. Josie missed the board-games she and Ellen used to play in the evenings, sharing magazines, doing each other's hair, and just chatting. Then, once Mum moved the bedrooms round, they got no chance to be alone together.

The last time they had really talked was when they met in Falmouth after school one day back in November, and Ellen told her about the job she wanted in Bristol as a mother's help. She said she'd got it from a magazine advertisement, and she was going to tell their parents about it that night, saying she wanted to spend a year in a big city before deciding what she was going to do as a career. She made Josie promise she wouldn't tell them about the baby, because she was going to a mother-and-baby home around the end of March and she would almost certainly have it adopted once it was born.

Josie knew then that nothing was ever going to be the same again between them. It was as though Ellen was a different person, so serious and grown-up. But although Josie cried that day about her sister going so far away, and felt as if she was losing her best friend, there was a part of her which was glad, because she thought it would make her mother happier, and that in turn would make things better for her.

But she couldn't see any hope of that now. Christmas was never exciting here, but this year it would be horrible without Ellen. January and February were always long, miserable months, the farmhouse was freezing, she would have to battle through ice, snow and rain to school and this time she'd have to do it alone without Ellen.

She thought too that Dad would blame her for making Ellen go. He had been so sad when Ellen told him she was leaving. He went straight out afterwards, and Josie got the idea he might be crying about it. He wouldn't cry if she left!

'Come down here, Josie!'

Josie sighed at the tone of her mother's voice and reluctantly got off the bed. She couldn't win, Mum had told her to encourage Ellen to leave, but now she'd finally gone Josie doubted Violet would show any gratitude. She expected she'd have to do twice as many chores now too.

'Why didn't you go out and say goodbye to Ellen?' Mum yelled as Josie got to the bottom of the stairs.

Josie didn't reply for a moment, looking at her mother critically. Violet had smartened herself up while they were in Helston, but she'd let herself go again. Her perm was growing out now and her hair was so dry it looked like one of those wire-wool pads for cleaning pans. The apron over her dress was filthy, and her feet were bulging over her slippers, the flesh puffy and grey. Yet it was her face that repelled Josie most.

The bitterness inside Violet showed. Her mouth was pinched and constant frowning had created deep lines around her mouth and on her forehead. It didn't help that her teeth were crooked and stained brown, or that her skin was so sallow. She looked nearer sixty than her real age of forty-one.

'What's it to you whether I said goodbye or not?' Josie replied insolently. Each time she looked at her mother these days she got a stab of fear that she might end up looking the way she did. 'You're glad she's gone, aren't you?'

'That's not the point. I don't want your father thinking we drove her away.'

'I didn't drive her away, you did that.'

Her mother lunged at her and hit her hard across the face. 'Don't you get lippy with me,' she roared. 'I know why you want to go to Helston, and it isn't to see your relatives, it's to see that thug with the scooter you were always necking with, you little slut.'

'I'm not a slut,' Josie held her stinging face and began to cry. 'Just because you are doesn't mean I am too.'

'And what do you mean by that?' Her mother seemed to swell up all over with indignation.

'You got into Dad's bed before his wife was even cold in the ground,' Josie yelled back at her. 'Only a slut would do that.'

That juicy bit of information had been given to Josie by her grandmother just a week before she died. Of course she was an evil old woman, prone to saying all kinds of nasty things, many of them completely untrue, according to Uncle Brian. But Josie didn't care whether it was true or not, she just wanted to hurt her mother as she'd hurt her.

Anticipating another slap, she turned to run back upstairs, but she was halted at the door by a hard wallop on her shoulder. It knocked her right over, down on to the floor, and when she saw her mother was holding a rolling-pin, her face purple with rage, she tried to scramble away.

But she wasn't fast enough. Mum grabbed her by the

hair with one hand and hit her again and again with the rolling-pin. 'You little bitch!' she screamed. 'Everything I've ever done was for you and you repay me like this!'

It seemed to Josie that Mum had gone mad. She showered blows on Josie's head, neck, back and arms, all the time screaming out abuse, so loudly she was drowning Josie's screams of terror.

The front door burst open and Dad came rushing in. 'Stop it, Violet!' he shouted, pulling her away from Josie.

Josie had never been so glad to see anyone, but she was so badly hurt that as her mother let go of her hair, she slumped down on to the floor. As if through a mist she saw Dad restraining Mum, pushing her on to a chair, and slapping her face to stop her hysterical screaming.

The next thing Josie knew, Dad was lifting her up in his arms and holding her protectively to his chest.

'Isn't it enough that one of our girls has gone today, without beating the other one too?' she heard him say.

'She asked for it,' Violet retorted. 'You should have heard the filth she came out with.'

Josie clung tightly to her father's neck, frightened her mother would lay into her again. Perhaps her father sensed this for he ordered Mum out of the kitchen and told her she wasn't to come back until she'd calmed down.

It was the first time in many years that Josie had received such tender care from her father. He lifted her up on to the kitchen table, ran his hands gently over her as if checking for broken bones, then bathed her face and neck with a wet, cold flannel.

'Speak to me, Josie,' he insisted, holding her face in his two hands and looking right into her eyes. 'Do you know who I am?'

It was tempting to say nothing, to make believe she was so badly hurt she'd lost the power of speech, so that she could hang on a little longer to this attention and care. But she found she couldn't do that, she'd never seen such anxiety and fright in his brown eyes.

'Yes, Daddy,' she said. 'Mum was like a mad thing.'

He sighed, and clasped her to his chest in relief. 'I don't think anything's broken,' he said. 'But you'll have some very nasty bruises by tomorrow. What was it all about, my lover?'

The warmth and comfort of his embrace made her cry. 'Because I didn't say goodbye to Ellen,' she sobbed. 'I couldn't say goodbye, I was too upset she was going.'

He held her silently for a few more moments, then got a bowl of cold water, wetted the flannel again and held it against her cheek and then her temple.

'You go and lie down,' he said after a little while. 'I'll bring you up a hot drink.'

Josie felt she had to use this opportunity. 'Send me to Helston to live, Daddy, please! I won't be able to bear it here any more now Ellen's gone. Please, Daddy, I thought Mum was going to kill me.'

'If they was my folk maybe I'd think about it,' he said. 'But they aren't, and you are my daughter, so I have to take care of you. You belong here, Josie, with me.'

'But what if she hits me again?' she asked, fresh tears flooding out.

'She won't do it again, I promise you that,' he said. 'If she lays one finger on you, it's her who'll be slung out of here.'

As Josie made her way upstairs she felt completely bewildered. Although she knew from what Dad had said that she wouldn't even get another holiday in Helston, let alone move there to live, it didn't seem to matter quite so much any more. For he had shown her he cared about her.

January, February and March of 1964 were as miserable as Josie had expected. It was bitterly cold, with endless days of driving sleet which was far worse than snow and she missed Ellen even more than she had thought she would.

It was all the little things, Ellen rinsing the shampoo out of her hair over the bath, the chats on the way to catch the school bus, and bringing wood in for the fire together, that caught her unawares.

Mum was nicer though. She never said anything about that day before Christmas when she attacked Josie, offering no apology or explanation, but she was warmer and kinder. She made little treats for tea, warmed Josie's school coat by the fire in the mornings, and didn't keep making her do chores.

Dad must have laid into her about it, because she even gave Josie the letters Ellen sent, unopened. Not that it would have mattered if she had read them first, Ellen never said anything about the baby. She described Bristol with enthusiasm, spoke of Mr and Mrs Sanderson, her employers, and their two little boys with affection, and it certainly didn't sound as if she was worried about anything.

Josie wrote and said Mum wasn't reading the letters, so she could write whatever she liked, and she wouldn't leave them about to be found. But that didn't make any difference, Ellen still only wrote about everyday matters, not even an oblique word or two about getting fat, or going on to the mother-and-baby home.

By March Josie was convinced she'd been led up the garden path, and Ellen wasn't having a baby at all. Maybe she did think she was pregnant at first, and that's why she'd found this job. But then the pregnancy must have turned out to be a false alarm. Josie couldn't understand why Ellen hadn't told her that, they could have had a secret celebration. Even if Ellen was still set on leaving home, she would have understood, and backed her up.

Once they had shared everything, from their dreams and hopes to their socks and knickers. To Josie, letting her go on believing in a lie was the worst kind of betrayal. It was as though she was nothing, someone who couldn't be trusted.

139

It hurt so much to think Ellen cared so little about her feelings. So when her mother made sarcastic comments like 'A lot of good all those "O" levels did Ellen! Any fool could be a mother's help,' she didn't snap back at her and sometimes she even agreed.

Yet Ellen's absence made it easier to convince her parents there was no point in her staying on at school another year to do exams. She would be fifteen in July, and the local paper was full of jobs for office juniors and sales assistants in both Falmouth and Truro. Not that Josie had any intention of staying in Cornwall for any longer than it took to buy some new clothes. She was set on going to London.

At night in her bedroom, Josie escaped from the loneliness by imagining herself as a world-famous model. She would brush her hair till it stood out like a wild halo around her head, then pose in front of the mirror, draped in a sheet. She had studied lots of pictures of Jean Shrimpton, and it seemed to Josie that she was actually far prettier than 'the shrimp', and had a better figure than the model everyone was talking about. All she needed to do was find a photographer like David Bailey and she'd have the world at her feet.

This dream kept her going when the atmosphere was oppressive at home. It comforted her when she was bottom of the class in tests, and when July and the end of school seemed such a long way away. She barely noticed that Ellen's letters were becoming shorter and further apart during May, for spring had come at last. Josie had never liked any kind of farm work, even feeding the chickens revolted her, but she went out of her way to please her father by offering to help him plant seedlings, hoe down the weeds and clean out the cow shed. She sensed he missed Ellen badly, though he never said as much, and it felt good when he transferred some of the affection he'd once shown his older daughter to her.

There was only one thing that really worried her, and

that was her mother. Although Josie despised Violet for her slatternly appearance and her embittered approach to everything, she was still her mother. What was going to happen to her when Josie left home?

It was blatantly obvious that Dad was never going to sell the farm and give Violet money to set up in a home of her own. The most likely thing to happen was that they would fall out so badly once they were alone that he'd throw her out. Young as she was, Josie knew women fared badly under the legal system, especially when they no longer had any small children. She knew too that her family in Helston didn't want her mother over there. That left only Josie for her to cling on to.

Josie was always reading magazines about life in London, and she desperately wanted to enter that world of swinging discothèques, boutiques, pubs and non-stop parties. But she couldn't be part of all that with her mother hanging on her coat-tails.

It seemed to her that the only answer was for her to disappear without trace, leaving her mother to find her own solution to her problems. She felt a bit guilty about this, yet it wasn't her fault her parents hated each other, they weren't her responsibility. In truth she didn't feel she owed any of her family anything. Dad had always favoured Ellen. Ellen could hardly be bothered to write to her now, and if her mother hadn't been so nasty to all her own family she wouldn't have been cast off by them. Yet disappearing was frightening. What if she didn't become successful in London, what would she do then?

'But you *will* be successful,' she whispered to herself over and over again like a mantra. 'You are not going to be a failure like Mum.'

Josie's fifteenth birthday in early July turned out to be an unexpected turning-point in her life. It fell on a Friday, and for once her mother had agreed that she could spend the whole weekend with her schoolfriend Rosemary Parks at Rosemary's home in Falmouth.

Josie opened her presents and cards in the morning before catching the bus to school and was thrilled to find her parents had bought her the black and white mini-dress she had been drooling over for weeks in a shop in Falmouth.

'It's way too short,' Dad said, shaking his head not exactly in disapproval but rather in bewilderment when she tried it on. 'But I suppose I'm old-fashioned.'

Josie admired herself in the hall mirror. The dress was gorgeous, exactly like the ones she'd seen in fashion magazines. Patterned in a large geometric design, it was cut away on the shoulders and had a slightly flared skirt which ended three inches above her knees. She looked just like all the models in the magazines, and she wished she could wear it to school to show it off, but sadly she had to change back into her school uniform and be satisfied she could wear the dress all weekend.

Ellen had sent her a little white shoulder bag, and Uncle Brian in Helston had enclosed a ten-pound note in his card.

'Don't spend all that money this weekend,' Mum said, as she saw Josie tuck it into the handbag. 'You'll need to buy some clothes to start work in.'

Josie didn't reply to that, it was so like her mother to try to spoil the moment. She was going straight to Rosemary's from school, and she'd packed a small case last night. Rather than disturb the packing by taking something out, she folded the new dress and put it into the case along with the handbag.

'Are you listening to me?' Mum said sharply. 'And behave yourself this weekend. I don't want to hear you've been hanging around on street corners.'

'Okay, Mum,' Josie sighed. 'I've got to go now or I'll miss the school bus. I'll be home on Sunday evening. Rosemary's dad will drop me off.'

Later she thought it was odd that she kissed her parents goodbye, she never usually did. And even stranger too that Dad hugged her, said she looked very pretty and to have a good time in Falmouth.

By four o'clock that afternoon, when school ended, Josie was so excited at the prospect of the weekend ahead, that she couldn't stop giggling. It was a lovely hot day, and the good weather was forecast to remain for several days. She and Rosemary planned to spend the day on the beach tomorrow, and in the evening they were going to a dance in the church hall near where Rosemary lived.

Rosemary got a great deal more freedom than Josie, as she was the youngest of four girls and her sisters took her out with them all over the place and bought her lots of nice clothes. As a result Rosemary was far more worldly than Josie – she'd had her dark hair cut in a short bob like Cilla Black's and she'd been wearing mini-dresses for a few weeks now, while most of the girls in Falmouth were still wearing knee-length ones. She was a really good dancer, and had taught Josie to do the Twist, and the Shake. She smoked and drank cider, and she'd already had a few boyfriends, even admitting she'd lost her virginity back in the Easter holidays in the back seat of a car with a boy who was twenty-one.

The two girls had often discussed going to London together when they were sixteen, and surprisingly Rosemary's parents didn't mind the idea. But then they were a lot less rigid in their ideas than Josie's parents. They weren't Cornish, and they'd moved down here from Surrey some five years ago to open a guest-house. They held the view that Cornwall didn't have a great deal for young girls; their two eldest had already left for London where they were working in a bank.

The girls linked arms as they left school and walked to Rosemary's home down by the harbour. The town was full of tourists, many of them trudging back from the beach to guest-houses, laden with towels, windbreaks and buckets and spades, dragging howling small children who

143

had spent too long in the sun. The girls giggled at the fat women in sun-dresses, their hefty arms and legs glowing with sun-burn they were hardly aware of yet. The men were even more ridiculous, with white flabby paunches bulging out of garish holiday shirts, many with knotted handkerchiefs over their heads. But funny as many of the visitors to the town were, the girls liked to see them, for they made Falmouth a busy, noisy and prosperous place for a few short weeks, and created an exciting atmosphere. The smell of hot dogs was heavy in the air, pop music wafted out of shops, and the girls knew that when they tried to buy a drink later this evening all the publicans would be too harassed to ask how old they were before serving them.

'I hope I get the job in the shipping office,' Josie said. The juvenile employment woman had been to the school earlier in the week and fixed up many of the school-leavers with job interviews.

'You're bound to,' Rosemary said with a grin. 'With your looks you can't fail.'

One of the reasons Josie had made friends with Rosemary in the last year was because she was so admiring. She was pretty too, with her elf-like features, dark hair and eyes, but she always claimed she was ordinary in comparison to Josie. She said she'd die for hair like Josie's, and so would all the other girls who pretended to scoff at it and called her 'Carrots'. She firmly believed Josie was going to be one of England's top models, and her utter confidence helped Josie to believe in herself.

'I can't spell that well, and I'm lousy at arithmetic,' Josie said doubtfully. She wanted the junior's job at the shipping office because lots of men and boys worked there. It also had a starting wage of seven pounds a week, when she'd be lucky to get five pounds anywhere else.

'Juniors don't do much more than make the tea and run messages,' Rosemary said as if she was an expert. 'You aren't going to be there when the time comes for them to expect you to do more. So don't worry about it.'

They were at the gate of Rosemary's house now, and as always when Josie saw it, she felt a tug of pure envy. It might be like the rest of the Victorian terrace from the outside, three steps up to the garden, and a tall, narrow house with a bay window. But the illuminated sign in the garden saying 'Buona Vista Guest-house' made it special. Josie loved the guest-rooms with their pink candlewick bedspreads and flowery wallpaper, the bathroom with the lady in a crinoline dress which hid the spare toilet roll, and the fluffy mats, even one on the toilet seat itself. There were pictures of puppies and kittens on the walls, Spanish dancer dolls in the dining-room, and a lamp in the guest sitting-room which was like a huge pineapple. When it was turned on it glowed a beautiful orangey-pink. To Josie the house symbolized the sophistication of London.

Rosemary and her sister's bedroom was right up in the attic; her other two sisters had to stay in the guest-rooms when they came home from London. Josie liked the way the Parks family lived in the back room of the guest-house, next to the kitchen. It was always warm and cosy, even if a bit cluttered with people and furniture, so very different from the austerity of her own home.

Yet strangely enough Mr and Mrs Parks treated her as if she came from a much grander house than theirs. They said the word 'farm' with reverence, and frequently directed their paying guests to the walk along the cliffs to Mawnan Smith. Rosemary had often told her that they boasted their daughter's best friend lived along there.

Josie never told them how ramshackle the house was, or that they didn't have television or a washing-machine. Sometimes she thought she'd die of embarrassment if Mrs Parks, with her dyed black bouffant hair and elegant clothes, were to meet her mother.

'I'm just going to say we're going along to the coffee

bar tonight,' Rosemary whispered before they went inside. 'I drank too much cider last weekend and I was sick, so Mum's been a bit funny about letting me out since. But she thinks you're really sensible, so she won't say anything in front of you.'

Josie wished she could admit she'd never drunk anything more than a Snowball, and that was in Helston a year ago. Her father liked his beer and cider too, but he drank at the pub, they never had any in the house. Her mother would have a blue fit if she knew her daughter was intending to drink anything but orange juice.

There was beefburgers, chips and beans for tea. It had to be eaten quickly because Mrs Parks had eight guests coming in for an evening meal and she wanted the girls out of the way. Josie saw her filling little glass goblets with lettuce and prawns, adding a cherry and a slice of lemon to each one, and she vowed to herself that one day she'd prepare glamorous things like that for guests in her own house.

It was half past seven when the girls made their way into the town. Josie was wearing her new dress, her curly hair held back from her face with a black velvet Alice band she'd borrowed from Rosemary. Rosemary had a new dress too, very similar to Josie's, but red and white. She had backcombed her hair so much she looked about three inches taller, and she was wearing false eyelashes too. Josie had tried to wear some as well, but they made her eyes sore, so she'd settled for thick black eyeliner and mascara instead. They both looked at least eighteen, and as Rosemary had stolen some vodka from her parents' drink cabinet earlier, they were already a little tiddly. Josie hadn't liked the taste very much, and she'd drowned it with lemonade, but she liked the warm, happy effect it was having on her.

All the pubs near the harbour were packed, and by half past ten Rosemary was very drunk. Josie had only had two more vodkas – once she felt herself getting a bit too silly, she stuck to lemonade only. They hadn't bought a single drink themselves, boys kept buying them for them. They'd stay flirting with them for a while, then pretend to go to the toilet and move on to another pub to check out the boys in there.

When they got back to The Lord Nelson on the quay for the second time, Josie spotted two men standing by the water's edge and pointed them out to her friend.

'They're the ones we have to go for,' she said firmly. 'Just look at them, they're dreamboats.'

The men were in their mid-twenties, both wearing light coloured jackets, smart trousers and open-necked shirts. Even to two such naive girls they were clearly not ordinary holidaymakers or locals, they were too well dressed and classy looking for that. The taller of the two was blond, the other had brown hair and, although long by Cornish standards, well past their ears, it wasn't straggly, or in the Beatles style which most young men seemed to copy.

'They might be in a pop group,' Rosemary said hopefully. She was squinting at them drunkenly, and Josie hoped she wasn't going to blow it by being silly. 'They won't like us, they look like Londoners.'

'So much the better,' Josie said tartly. 'And they will like us, as long as you don't start giggling.'

The alcohol had made Josie feel brave, and knowing time was running out and the pubs would shut soon, she didn't think twice but walked right up to the two men, Rosemary trailing behind.

'Hello,' she said, giving them her most winning smile. 'We haven't seen you here before. Are you on holiday?'

'No, we're down here on business,' the brown-haired one replied, and smiled as if he was really glad she'd spoken to them. 'We were just saying what a nice place Falmouth is. We could be in the South of France, it's so warm tonight.'

He had no accent and his deep voice was like that of a news-reader on the radio.

'I'm Josie, this is my friend Rosemary.' Josie tried not to sound too Cornish for she thought it might put them off. 'Are you going to tell us your names?'

'I'm Will, he's Colin,' the brown-haired man said. 'Is there anywhere round here to go when the pub shuts, a night-club?'

Josie looked round at Rosemary for help, but she was just standing there looking at the men with blank eyes. Josie guessed she was too drunk to be of any help. Stuck for an answer, she decided to go for the truth. 'Sorry, but I don't know. I live a way out of Falmouth, I don't come in here that often in the evenings.'

Will smiled at Josie and she instantly knew that her honest answer had given her an edge over the other girls.

'So you're a country girl?' he said, and moved a step nearer to her. 'What do country girls do on a date?'

She wasn't going to be honest enough to tell him she'd never had a real date, that her only romance had been at fourteen with a Mod from Helston who bought her fish and chips and took her for rides on his scooter.

'On a warm night like this a walk can be nice,' she said, fluttering her eyelashes at him.

There was a kind of moan from Rosemary, and as Josie turned to look she was staggering towards the quayside, hand over her mouth, about to be sick.

'Oh no,' Josie gasped in horror. 'Not that!'

Funnily enough both men laughed, and Will patted Josie's shoulder. 'I don't think she's up to a walk in the moonlight.'

Josie didn't think she'd ever been so embarrassed. Apart from the terrible impression her friend must be making on the two men, there were scores of people outside on the quay. Her shame grew as Rosemary made loud retching noises. If she'd been able to get home she would have made a run for it.

'You look mortified,' Will said, and touched her bare arm. 'I can't count the number of times one of my friends has done that to me, or the number of times I've been the one puking. It doesn't matter, Josie, it's just one of those things.'

Shamefaced, Josie hung her head. 'I suppose I'd better get her home,' she said in little more than a whisper. 'I just wish you hadn't had to see it.'

'Which way do you have to go?' he asked.

'Down along the harbour. Her parents own a guest-house,' she said.

'Well, we'll walk with you, won't we, Colin?' Will said. 'Can't leave a couple of damsels in distress, can we?'

Josie got the distinct impression that Colin would sooner have jumped in the harbour than walk home with a drunken girl, for his smile was forced, but he gallantly went into the pub, got a large glass of water and took it over to Rosemary, making her swill her mouth out, and then drink the rest. As he came back with her he suggested they get her a cup of coffee.

Rosemary seemed quite recovered after a few minutes' walk, and Will bought each of them a takeaway cup of coffee from the fish and chip shop further down the High Street.

'Tell me what you two are doing in Falmouth,' Josie asked. Her embarrassment was fading now, and she hoped she'd be able to pluck up courage and ask them to join her and Rosemary on the beach the following day.

'Colin works for a shipping company in London,' Will said. Colin was in front of them now, holding Rosemary's hand and laughing about something with her. 'He had to check out an insurance claim, I just came with him for the ride.'

'Well, what do you do?' she asked.

'I'm a designer,' he said.

Josie's ears pricked up at that. 'A fashion designer?'

Will laughed. 'No, I design shop and hotel interiors mostly. Why, do you want to be a fashion designer?'

Josie giggled. 'Not me, I can't draw a straight line. But I intend to be a fashion model.'

He stopped her short under a lamp-post, putting his hand on her chin and moving her head this way and that. 'Umm,' he said eventually. 'I think you could be.'

'I will be,' she said with a toss of her head. 'I'm going up to London next year to start.'

'Why wait a year?' he said. 'It's all happening now in London. A pretty girl like you could easily get a job in one of the new boutiques. Get a portfolio together, do the round of the agencies. I'm sure someone would take you on.'

Josie had no idea what a portfolio was, but she wasn't going to show her ignorance. 'You really think so?' She beamed at him.

'I think you stand a better chance than most girls,' he said.

They sat on the harbour wall drinking their coffee, smoking and chatting for some time. The men were staying at the Royal Hotel, and the casual way they spoke of it was evidence they were used to staying in expensive hotels. Will said he lived in a part of London called Bayswater, and he laughed when Josie asked if it was on the river. He said if she ever came to London he'd show her the sights.

A little later they walked on home to Rosemary's house and it was Josie who asked if they wanted to come to the beach with them the following day.

'That would be very nice,' Will said, putting his arm around Josie and squeezing her to him. 'We had planned to stay until the evening and drive home once the roads are clear. A day on the beach with you two would be lovely.'

'They're a bit posh!' Rosemary said in a whisper as they

made their way up the stairs to her room. 'They didn't even try to snog us.'

Josie thought that made it all the better, to her it was a sign they were gentlemen. But she wasn't going to make her friend start giggling by saying that. 'I expect it was because of you throwing up,' she said. 'Would you kiss anyone after that?'

'I'm sorry about that,' Rosemary said once they were up in her room. 'One minute I was all right, the next everything was spinning. I reckon it was those beefburgers Mum gave us for tea.'

Josie said nothing. All she wanted to do was get into bed and dream about Will. If he did turn up at Swanpool beach tomorrow as they'd arranged, she was going to make sure he wanted her enough by the end of the day to invite her up to London.

Chapter Nine

By four the following afternoon Josie had decided that she was going to London that night with Will and Colin. They didn't know yet, and neither did Rosemary, but Josie had it all planned in her head and she had counter-arguments ready for anyone who might oppose her.

Will and Colin were already at Swanpool beach when the girls arrived, a clear sign to Josie that they fancied them. She felt smugly certain that by the end of the day Will would be smitten with her, for the beach was the perfect place to show off all her best features.

Since she was a small child Josie had adored the sea and the feeling of freedom wearing so few clothes. She and Ellen often swam naked down at the little cove by the farm. By the time she was twelve and her breasts began to develop, nearly all of Josie's friends became self-conscious about their bodies. But not her. She felt only delight for it meant she was finally becoming a woman.

There were a few moments of anguish, mainly when she looked at her mother's flabby, shapeless body, and feared hers might become like that. But luckily it seemed that she, like Ellen, had inherited Pengelly traits, for they were both slim and shapely, with long legs.

Another reason Josie felt comfortable on a beach was because she could shed the unfashionable clothes that marked her out as a poor farmer's daughter. In a swim-suit she could compete, and win on all levels. Even her curly hair, which she so often wished could be straight, was an asset on the beach, for girls' hair she so often admired at school looked like seaweed once it was wet.

Hers went into pretty ringlets. And she wasn't burdened with the normal curse of red-heads, skin that became red and freckly in the sun. Both she and Ellen had always turned a golden-brown painlessly.

Academic success meant nothing on a beach either. Josie could swim like a fish, run fast, do leap-frog effortlessly, and she was good at ball-games. The beach was a stage to show off all these talents.

In the early hours of the morning when Josie couldn't sleep for thinking about Will, she had remembered something she'd read in 'Dear Marge' in *Woman's Own*. A girl had written in to ask how to make boys like her. Marge had said there was no magic formula for this, but that she thought showing happiness, both in the boys' company and her own surroundings, was likely to endear her to them rather than trying to pretend she was something she wasn't.

Josie had followed that advice once she'd made up her mind that she wanted to go to London. She didn't attempt to flirt with Will or Colin, or have serious conversations, but treated them in much the same way she did her schoolfriends and boys she knew from the village. She splashed them with water, jumped on their backs in the sea, challenged them to races, laughed a great deal and acted as though she hadn't a care in the world.

Rosemary unwittingly helped her cause. In the past Josie had been embarrassed at the way her friend would speak of her parents' farm in awed tones, as if they were stinking rich. But this time Josie was glad of it, for it gave her the opportunity to make the men laugh still more by talking in a rustic voice and making out she did the milking and mucked out the cow sheds. If they wanted to believe she was talking nonsense, she didn't mind, she'd told the truth after all. It was Rosemary who lied and said she was seventeen and worked in an office in Truro. Josie just said she helped her father, and if they imagined she was seventeen too, that was their fault.

The men bought them fish and chips for lunch, later they paddled in rock pools looking for crabs, and as the afternoon went on Josie sensed Will really liked her. He kept taking her hand as they paddled; he looked right into her eyes, and paid her compliments.

It was a little disappointing that he hadn't turned out to be as handsome as she'd thought on the previous night. Without his smart clothes there wasn't anything special about him. He had a nice enough face, and lovely dark eyes, but he was hardly a real dreamboat. His chest was pale and weedy, and his legs were very thin. He was also more serious than she'd expected, he spoke of books and films that she'd never heard of, and she discovered he'd got a degree in Art and Design, which made her think he was a bit of an egg-head.

Yet when he drew her away from the other two behind a big rock and kissed her, it made her head reel and her legs go all wobbly.

'You must come up to London soon,' he said, holding her face in his hands and showering it with soft little kisses. 'Promise me you'll keep in touch. I must see you again.'

She looked into his brown eyes and knew this was the moment. It didn't matter that he wasn't really handsome, he was clever and had such good manners and a perfect-speaking voice, and he could kiss really well.

'I could come to London with you tonight,' she blurted out.

She half expected him to back away, but instead he laughed. 'Now, what would Rosemary say about that?' he asked. 'Aren't you staying the weekend with her? It would be a bit rude.'

Josie laughed in relief, his good manners hadn't failed him, not even in a tight spot. 'She wouldn't mind if I explained to her,' she said. 'You see, I've been wanting to go to London for so long, she won't come with me for another year. I'm doing nothing here; I could find real work in London. So if you'd give me a lift and let me sleep at your place until I find one of my own, I'd be so grateful.'

He gave her a rather worried look, and it occurred to her that he'd imagined her only coming up to London for a few days, not permanently. 'But what about your parents?' he said. 'You can't shoot off and leave them without a word.'

'I wasn't going to,' she lied. 'I thought I'd tell Rosemary when we get back to her place, then go home and tell Mum and Dad. I could meet you later this evening.'

His forehead wrinkled into a deep frown. 'Isn't it a bit rash, rushing off up there now?'

Josie shrugged. 'It was a bit rash talking to you last night, but it worked out all right, didn't it? Besides you said there's loads of jobs for a girl like me in London. I ought to be there now when it's all beginning to happen. Of course, if you don't want to take me – ' she broke off, leaving it up to him.

He sighed. 'It's not that, Josie, of course I don't mind taking you,' he said. 'But I didn't expect something like this, and I work away a lot, so you'd have to find your way around on your own. My flat's a bit of a tip too.'

'Well, I can clean it up for you.' She grinned and leaned forward to kiss him. 'I don't mind being on my own. I've lived in an isolated farm all my life, remember. I'll surprise you by how clever I can be.'

He still looked doubtful. 'Are you absolutely set on this, Josie?'

'Of course I am. If it doesn't work out I'll just catch the train back.' She grinned again. 'No strings as they say. I'm not asking you to take care of me, Will, only a lift and a place to sleep till I get somewhere of my own.'

She saw the anxious expression fade from his eyes, and knew she'd hit just the right note.

'Okay,' he nodded. 'If you're sure.'

'Don't say anything to Colin in front of Rosemary,' she urged him, grabbing his hand and squeezing it. 'She might

155

get funny and say she wants to come. She can be a bit silly that way, and by tomorrow she'll be regretting it. I'll tell her when we're on our own.'

He nodded, and she thought that pleased him even more as Rosemary hadn't really hit it off with Colin. They didn't seem to have anything to say to each other, and Colin seemed a bit irritated when she kept giggling.

'I'll meet you at nine at the hotel. But if you aren't there on time we'll go without you!' he said warningly.

'I'll be there,' she said, and smiled. She meant she'd be there come hell or high water.

At eight-thirty Josie was lurking in an alley near the hotel, carrying her suitcase. She didn't want to bump into anyone she knew. The enormity of what she was about to do and what she'd already done was overwhelming.

She hadn't told Rosemary the truth, she couldn't because she knew her friend would try to talk her out of it and ask her to wait a year till they could go together. She also didn't want anyone else to know she'd gone off with two men she'd known for less than twenty-four hours.

Josie was a bit ashamed of what she'd done to give Rosemary the slip. She behaved perfectly normally until they got home to her house, chatting about the day, laughing about Will and Colin, and discussing the dance they were planning to go to later. Then Josie began play-acting the minute they got in, she said she had this feeling there was something wrong at home, and she must go back there to see.

Rosemary kept trying to persuade her there couldn't be anything wrong, and Josie pretended she was being convinced as she had a bath and washed her hair. But the minute she was dressed again, she said the feeling was getting stronger and she must go, she promised if there was nothing wrong she'd get the bus straight back. Mrs Parks backed her up and said Rosemary was being selfish, she even said she wished her husband were home so he

156

could drive Josie there. Finally, at half past six, Josie left the house carrying her suitcase, with Rosemary yelling from the doorway she must come straight back, and if there was something wrong she must go to a phone box in the morning and ring her.

Josie felt so silly skulking around the back streets and she was tempted to go straight to the hotel right then, but common sense told her that wasn't a good idea. Will might realize she hadn't had time to go home to tell her parents, and it would give him enough time to change his mind.

At ten to nine Josie walked up to the hotel. It was still very light, and there were so many people around she felt even more nervous, but as she approached the door of the hotel, Will was coming out with a holdall in his hand.

His face lit up. 'I didn't think you'd really come,' he said. 'What did your parents say?'

Josie shrugged. 'They thought I was being a bit daft rushing off on a whim, but they weren't nasty or anything. Everyone leaves here at my age. Tourists only see the good bit in the summer, there's nothing much here the rest of the year.'

'Was Rosemary okay?'

'A bit peeved.' She grinned. 'But she's at the dance now, and she's probably drunk again and forgotten all about it. I told her as soon as I'd got a flat of my own she could come up and join me.'

'Colin chewed my ear off,' Will admitted ruefully. 'He pointed out I'd only known you five minutes and for all I knew you could be pregnant and only asking to come so I'll have to look after you.'

That made Josie smart, but she held her dress tight to her stomach. 'Does it look like I'm pregnant?'

'No,' he said. 'You strike me as being too sensible for that.'

'I am. And I don't need you or anyone else to look after me,' she said indignantly. 'When we get to London you can just drop me off somewhere if you like.'

His face softened and he came forward and kissed her. 'I'm glad you've come,' he said. 'And I certainly won't drop you off anywhere. I want you with me.'

It was a long, long drive to London, but Josie dozed in the back seat and let the men talk to each other. She had felt Colin's annoyance when he came out of the hotel to find her there, so she'd said as little as possible, hoping that way he'd come round.

As they drove through Bristol, Will pointed out a beautiful bridge high up in the sky lit by hundreds of electric lights. He said it was the Clifton Suspension Bridge. That gave her a jolt, for Clifton was where Ellen was. She'd mentioned the bridge and the woods on the other side of the Avon Gorge in one of her letters.

Thinking about Ellen and how she'd left home made Josie realize that what she'd done was not only reckless but stupid. She'd thought she'd worked everything out, but in reality she hadn't even considered the most basic things.

When she didn't arrive home the following night, her father would drive the truck into Falmouth to find her. When he heard from Mr and Mrs Parks that she'd gone home the previous evening, he might jump to the conclusion she'd been snatched or even murdered.

All at once she was frightened. Rosemary was bound to tell him about Will and Colin. If Dad called the police and they went round to the hotel they'd been staying at, they might pass on the men's address in London.

She sat bolt upright in the seat, wondering what to do. Colin was driving now, Will half asleep in the passenger seat. She could tell them the truth of course, but Colin had the hump already about her being with them and he would be really angry if she asked him to turn round and drive back. But then she didn't want to go back; she wanted to go to London.

She slumped down again in the seat, trying to think

logically. If the police traced Will he might get into trouble for taking an under-age girl away. So she would have to get away from him.

Reminding herself that no one would know she was missing until around ten or eleven the following night, she knew she was safe enough for now. She could go to Will's flat, have a sleep, then make some excuse to leave later in the day.

Her natural optimism began to come back as she remembered she still had the ten-pound note she'd got for her birthday. That would be enough to find a room and get by until she got a job, and she'd post a card to her parents saying she was fine and not to worry about her.

Yet all the same she was sad she couldn't stay with Will. He seemed to know everything, and she didn't much like the idea of being all alone in a city she didn't know.

'I warned you it was a tip,' Will said as he opened a door on the second floor and led her into his flat.

It was four in the morning and still dark, and the light he flicked on immediately showed up clothes strewn over chairs, and unwashed plates and cups on a coffee table.

'It's not that bad,' Josie said quite truthfully. It looked interesting to her, for there was a kind of easel set up by the window with all kinds of drawing equipment, and a desk laden with books and magazines. It had exactly the kind of style she imagined a bachelor pad in London would have: simple modern furniture, white walls and lots of fashionable black and grey.

'I've only got one bedroom, but the couch pulls out into a bed,' Will said, yawning as he took off his jacket. 'I'd offer to sleep on it, but the sheets on my bed need changing and I'm too tired for that right now. The bathroom's here.' He pushed at the door to his left. 'The kitchen and the bedroom.' He indicated doors to the right and left of the main room.

Josie put her case down. She saw no point in exploring

for she didn't intend to stay long. 'You must be exhausted with all that driving, do go to bed, Will.'

He gave her a grateful look and rubbed his eyes. 'I'll just pull out the bed for you. Help yourself to tea or coffee. I've got an appointment this afternoon so I'll set my alarm for one. Will you be all right while I'm gone? I should be back by five and we can go out and get something to eat.'

'Don't you worry about me, I'll be fine,' she said, feeling anything but fine. She had a strong feeling he was regretting bringing her here. Perhaps he'd even guessed now that she was far younger than seventeen.

For a second or two she was tempted to tell him the truth. It didn't seem fair that possibly late tonight or early tomorrow morning he'd have police banging on his door. Was it a criminal offence to take an under-age girl away from her home?

But Will pulled out the couch, and brought her a couple of blankets and sheets. Then he said goodnight and went into his bedroom, closing the door behind him, without even trying to kiss her.

Josie took off her jeans and blouse, hung them over the back of a chair and slipped her pyjamas on over her underwear. She didn't think she could sleep, and she wondered why Will had made no attempt to kiss her.

But the couch made a surprisingly comfortable bed, far better than her one at home, and while she was wondering whether Will's chilliness was due to anxiety or tiredness, she must have fallen asleep. She was woken by a dull, droning sound, and it was a minute or two before she realized it was only traffic outside.

It was daylight now, and the clock on a bookcase said it was half past eleven. She got up and went over to the window, pushing back the curtains.

Later that day she was to discover that Will's flat was in Bayswater Road, a main road that ran through Notting Hill to Oxford Street. But that first view of London was a lovely surprise, for though the road was very busy with traffic, on the other side was a huge park.

She had noticed very little as they arrived, only that the flat was up two flights of stairs and the lights kept going out. Will had dropped Colin off in a place he called Hammersmith, but it hadn't been more than fifteen minutes from here.

Across the street there were lots of paintings hung on the park railings. She supposed it must be a kind of exhibition as dozens of people were walking along looking at them. A big red London bus, exactly like the ones she'd seen in pictures and films, came by, and she felt a shiver of excitement. She was here at last, and even if it hadn't worked out quite as she used to plan it, she'd done it now and she was going to make the best of it.

An hour later she was washed and dressed in the clothes she'd worn the previous night. She had washed up all the plates and cups, tidied the kitchen and lounge and folded the bed back into a couch.

A little prying showed that Will was very organized – there was food in his cupboards and refrigerator and he even had some cleaner for the bath and toilet. On a pinboard by his desk were several photographs of girls. One looked a bit like him and Josie thought it was probably his sister. She suspected the others were girlfriends. A notebook by the phone contained hundreds of numbers, and a black diary beside it proved he was speaking the truth when he'd said he had an appointment today. She felt a pang of real sadness that she couldn't hang on to have a meal with him tonight, or even see him again. If she hadn't been so bull-headed, just stayed at home, got that job in the shipping office, kept in touch by letter or phone and come up here later in the year, he could have been hers for keeps.

'You angel, you've tidied up,' Will said as he came out of his bedroom just after one, his hair all tousled and a dark shadow on his chin. 'Couldn't you sleep?'

'I did for a while,' she said, 'but the traffic woke me. I've just put the kettle on, would you like some tea?'

'Coffee please, two sugars. I'll just nip in and shave. I'm a bit pushed for time.'

He emerged from the bathroom some ten minutes later looking exactly how he had when they first met, only his face was a little browner from the day on the beach. He gulped down the coffee and looked anxiously at his watch.

'There's a spare key if you want to go over to the park,' he said, pointing to a set of keys hanging by the door. 'Don't go too far and get lost, jot down the address and phone number before you go out, just in case. Oh, there's a London map on the bookcase if you want to work out where you are. Help yourself to food, won't you?'

'Are you sorry you brought me?' she asked, unable to resist probing.

His face softened. 'No, of course not. But we need to discuss things properly when I get back. I'll be home around five I expect.'

She went over to him and raised her face expectantly for a kiss. His lips brushed against hers, but it couldn't be called a real kiss. 'I've got to go,' he said, snatching up a large slim file which was leaning against the wall. 'I'll see you later.'

At ten that same night Josie was in very different surroundings – a dismal little attic room on the top floor of a house in a place called Ladbroke Grove – and she was crying.

She had left Will's flat full of excitement and gone over to the park where she sat and studied the map of London. Having seen the Tube station called Queensway just a little further down the road, she worked out exactly where she was.

Stopping a couple of girls who looked only a little older than her, she asked them where the best place was to find a flat, and how she should go about it. They said the *Evening Standard* newspaper was the best bet, but that didn't come out on Sundays. She chatted to them for a while and discovered that the Bayswater area they were in was very expensive, even one room could cost as much as twelve to fifteen pounds a week. They suggested she walked along to Notting Hill and looked at adverts in shop windows because she might find somewhere cheaper. They asked if she had a job, and when she said she had only just arrived here and would have to look for one, they recommended she went to one of the employment agencies in Oxford Street on Monday. They were so friendly and nice that Josie thought everyone would be like them, but a few hours later, with blisters on her feet, she had discovered this wasn't so.

She found a shop window with adverts and jotted them all down, and then she began phoning them. Few people even answered the phone and those who did seemed impossibly snooty, asking her all sorts of questions about what sort of job she had and if she had a previous landlord's and bank reference.

Two out of fifteen of the people she phoned said she could call round, and gave her the address, but as soon as she got to the front door, they looked her up and down and said the room had already been let. As they couldn't really have let it so quickly she had to assume that her being so young put them off.

Another thing that surprised her was how quickly the area called Notting Hill changed from smart to seedy. Some roads were lovely, tree-lined with beautiful houses, but then she'd turn the corner and there were overflowing dustbins and paint peeling off front doors. The further she walked away from Notting Hill, the seedier it became, and soon she wasn't seeing neatly typed advertisements in shop windows, but hastily scrawled ones that suggested the owners wouldn't be so fussy.

She had three more invitations to go round and view a room. The first one was so horrible and dirty she backed out with an excuse she had to see somewhere else. In the second, a grubby little man with a bald head touched her bottom as she went up the stairs in front of him and frightened the living daylights out of her. The third house seemed entirely occupied by black people, a group of them sitting on the wall outside. She had only seen two black people in her life before, and that was from a distance, and she was so unnerved she walked straight on past the house, far too nervous even to knock at the door.

Finally she ended up in Ladbroke Grove. It was horrible. Lots of dirty children were playing in the streets, men were lying on patches of bare ground drinking, and there were so many black people that it was as though she was in a foreign country. Even the shops had a sort of pall of dirt hanging over them. She saw an overhead railway ahead of her, but by then she was too tired even to attempt to go somewhere nicer and she sat down on a low wall and began to cry.

Her nervousness of black people abated when a big black lady in a pink floral dress came up to her and asked why she was crying. She had a nice face, soft, sad eyes and a singsong sort of voice. Something about her made Josie pluck up her courage to explain her predicament, and the woman took her into a café, bought her a cup of tea and a sticky bun and tried to persuade her to go home to her mother.

'London ain't no place for little girls on their own,' she said, patting Josie's hand in a motherly way. 'All they do's get themselves into trouble.'

Josie said that she couldn't go home now, and asked if she had any idea where she could get a room, to tide her over until she found a job.

That was how she got this room, right up in an attic in a street called Westbourne Park Road. The lady, who introduced herself as 'Fee', knew the landlord, Mr Sharman, and took Josie round to see him. He agreed to let her have the room for four pounds a week, and because Fee had introduced them he wouldn't ask for any deposit.

Josie didn't really understand what he meant by a deposit, but the fact he didn't want one suggested he was a kind man. So she paid over the four pounds and he gave her the keys.

Yet it was Fee's sweetness that really affected Josie. As they'd walked round here Fee told her a little about herself. She said she and her husband had come from Trinidad ten years ago with high expectations of a better life. But even though her husband now worked as a porter in a hospital, they and their three children had to live in one room. She said people were mean to black people, they made them pay higher rent and gave them all the worst jobs.

Josie was touched that with problems of her own the woman had still taken time out to help her. As Fee left to go home, she patted Josie's cheek and told her to be a good girl. 'I sure hope you run on home to your momma, sugar,' she said. 'But if you can't do that, you get a good job, and then find yourself a nice place to live. You take a good look at what it's like round here. Then get away from it before you get sucked in.'

Chapter Ten

As Josie was crying in Westbourne Park, Ellen was sobbing into her pillow too. She could hold herself together during the day, but as soon as she'd put Nicholas and Simon to bed, grief took over.

When she first arrived in Bristol and Mr and Mrs Sanderson with their two little boys met her at the station, she felt as if all her troubles had vanished. They appeared to be good people, understanding, intelligent and very practical. They had their own wholesale grocery business, but Mrs Sanderson was struggling to cope with working with her husband, plus looking after her home and the two boys. They were as grateful to get help as Ellen was to be offered a job and a home.

From the first evening with them, when they insisted she must call them Roger and Shirley, and Shirley gave her a couple of her old maternity dresses that were really pretty, Ellen felt everything was going to work out just fine. She liked the boys. Nicholas was five, Simon three. They were well-behaved, funny little things, and they welcomed her wholeheartedly because from now on they wouldn't be packed off to their granny's, auntie's or neighbours while their mother went off to work.

The Sandersons' home wasn't a grand one, just a three-bedroomed semi-detached in suburban Westbury Park, but to Ellen it was paradise – warm, cosy, with all the luxuries like television, a refrigerator, washing-machine, fitted carpets, and central heating that she'd never experienced before. Yet the nicest thing of all was that the Sandersons had a very modern outlook. They were young, only in their early thirties, an ambitious couple who wanted to move up in the world. They were fun-loving too; friends called at the house constantly and almost every weekend they either went to a party or threw one themselves. They were very happy to let Ellen have a free rein with their children.

Until well after Christmas Ellen hardly thought about her own family. It was so good to wake up in the mornings knowing there would be no ugly scenes with Violet, no fear of her father discovering her secret. The housework side of the job was very easy, and the boys were thrilled to have someone who would play with them, read to them and take them out for walks.

It was only in January, when Ellen had to go to the maternity hospital for the first time to be examined, that she was reminded of what lay ahead. She didn't relish leaving the Sandersons' in March and going into the mother-and-baby home.

One evening in late February, she and Shirley were in the kitchen. It was snowing outside, and Ellen was doing some ironing while Shirley sat at the table painting her fingernails. Ellen had been impressed from her first day here by how well-groomed and elegant Shirley always was. She was slender, with blonde hair which she put up in a beehive, and she never went out without her full makeup on and her nails painted.

Ellen had been taken by a social worker to see the mother-and-baby home a couple of days previously and she had just admitted to Shirley that she was nervous about going there.

'You don't have to,' Shirley said unexpectedly. 'We've got to think of you as one of our family now, so you could stay here, and we'll take you to the hospital when your time comes.'

'But . . .' Ellen said, thinking that would be wonderful but then she'd have nowhere to go back to afterwards.

'I meant that we'd like you to carry on taking care of

the boys afterwards,' Shirley said, as if she'd read her mind.

A lump came up in Ellen's throat. She hadn't thought for one moment that Shirley and Roger felt so attached to her. 'But I have to go,' she said wistfully. 'They arrange the adoptions and everything at the home.'

'That can be arranged from the hospital, a good deal less painfully,' Shirley said crisply, blowing on her nails to dry them. 'This business of keeping your baby until six weeks after the birth is brutal. I think it would be far better for you to hand the baby over at birth, before you get too fond of him or her.'

'The Matron said it gives us time to really make up our minds,' Ellen said.

'Well, it does for girls who have a boyfriend who might marry them, or a supportive family prepared to step in to help,' Shirley said, putting a second coat of polish on her nails. 'But you haven't got either of those, have you, dear?'

Shirley's suggestion seemed to be the answer to all Ellen's problems, so she was only too happy to let her intervene and make arrangements for her. Within days she had met Dr Fordham, a woman doctor in nearby Clifton, who arranged adoptions privately. From then on Ellen was to have her ante-natal check-ups with her too, and Dr Fordham told her she would arrange for a foster-mother to come and take the baby away from the hospital after the birth.

At that point Ellen hadn't even considered that there might be an alternative to adoption. No one mentioned one, and the implication was that adoption was the easiest, least painful solution. Ellen would be free to go home to Cornwall afterwards if she wanted to, or to choose a college or start a career. No one ever need know her secret.

But Ellen hadn't reckoned on the powerful emotions that came with the birth of her little girl.

She was exhausted after a seventeen-hour labour. She

thought all she wanted to do was sleep, but when the midwife placed her baby girl in her arms, one look at that tiny, scrunched-up, angry face was enough to make the tiredness disappear.

Ellen knew all about the wonder of new life. She'd helped her father with calving and lambing countless times. She'd seen cows and sheep nuzzle and lick their new babies and observed how the adult animal would from that moment on protect their offspring with their own lives, feeding and nurturing it. Yet somehow she hadn't expected that she would respond to her own child in exactly the same way.

As Ellen's fingers caressed her soft skin and felt the firm grip of her tiny fingers around hers, suddenly she was overcome by a fierce desire to put her baby to her breast, to keep her forever, no matter what hardships she had to endure. The feeling was so strong she could hardly bear for her to be taken from her, even to be bathed.

She called her Catherine, and she was allowed just four days with her. Even during that brief time Catherine was always being whipped away to be washed and changed, and for medical examinations. One day Ellen begged the ward sister not to take her away again, and the woman turned and looked at her sharply. 'Why ever not? You're giving her away anyway, aren't you?' she said bluntly.

When Shirley came to visit Ellen, she tried to explain to her how she felt. She cried and asked her if she knew of any way she could keep Catherine. Shirley was sympathetic, but she said adoptive parents had already been selected, and the only alternative was for Ellen to take her baby back to Cornwall.

Maybe if Ellen had been given a little more time to think that idea through, she might have decided on it, for even the thought of Violet's nastiness was far less troubling than the horror of parting with her baby. But she was still too sore to walk anywhere; she had no clothes in the hospital for either herself or Catherine, nor any money.

Without any warning or consultation with her, the foster-mother who would be looking after Catherine for six weeks arrived to collect her and took her away. Ellen had been told that Catherine was only being taken away for a bath in the nursery. When she went to look for her, she found an empty cot with the label saying 'Baby Pengelly. Girl 6lb 5oz' still on it.

That was the cruellest thing of all. She hadn't been allowed to say goodbye, to give her baby one more kiss, or the opportunity to say she wanted time to find a way to keep her. No one had considered she had any rights or feelings.

Shirley and Roger came to take her home to their house a little later and found her in floods of tears.

'You are just overwrought because on the fourth day the milk comes into the breasts and causes "baby blues",' Shirley said. 'Now, buck up, dear, this is what you agreed to. By next week you will have forgotten all about it.'

The ward sister gave Ellen pills to take to make her milk stop, and she wished there was another pill to make her stop picturing her baby, and to take away the terrible feeling of desolation. Yet she couldn't let her true feelings show, even if she did feel she was the victim of a confidence trick. Shirley and Roger had helped her when no one else would, so she had to walk back into their house, kiss and hug the boys and make out everything was fine.

The weather turned warm soon after her return home. Each time she took the boys to the park or up to the Downs nearby she saw women with prams, and she tortured herself by going and looking at their babies. Each day she told herself it would hurt less, but it didn't. Her mind was running on a single track, unable to think of anything but her baby being fed, bathed and changed by a woman she'd never even been allowed to meet.

Only Nicholas and Simon gave her any real comfort. Taking their small hands in hers, holding them on her lap, or washing and dressing them helped. She could lavish the love meant for her own baby on them, and their dependence on her as Shirley stepped up the hours she spent at the office was a kind of balm. Yet alone in her tiny bedroom at night she invariably gave way to tears as she thought of her baby in another woman's arms.

When a letter came from her father in July to say Josie had run away from home, Ellen was suddenly brought up sharply. She had been so immersed in sorrow that although she'd hastily sent her sister a handbag and a card for her birthday, she hadn't written any letters for weeks. Now she had guilt to add to her unhappiness, for it seemed to her that Josie must have thought she didn't care about her.

It was to Dr Fordham that she turned for advice, for even though the woman was rather stern, Ellen had come to trust her. During her ante-natal check-ups, and the two meetings since Catherine's birth, the last one being when she had to sign the first of the adoption papers before the chosen parents took her baby home, she had built up a strong relationship with the doctor. Dr Fordham alone knew just how Ellen felt, and a great deal about her family and home life.

'Why don't you go home to see your parents?' she said, when Ellen had explained about Josie running off. 'It's time you went, you need to see your father, and while you are there you could contact some of Josie's friends. They are far more likely to tell you if they know where she is than your parents are.'

'But I'm so weepy and miserable,' Ellen said. 'What if I let the truth about my baby slip out?'

'People only let slip what they want to,' the doctor said firmly. 'Remember, you have your good friend Mrs Peters there too. You can confide in her, and talking about it can only help, not make it worse.'

'Violet will blame me for Josie going,' Ellen sighed. 'She won't be pleased to see me.'

Dr Fordham took both Ellen's hands in hers. She was a small, rather schoolmarmish woman, but her grey eyes were kind. 'Ellen, my dear,' she said, 'you've come through a terrible ordeal, but it's over now. Catherine is safe and loved by her new parents. I know you won't believe this, but what you've been through will have made you stronger, and you'll be well able to cope with Violet. What you have to do is pick up the pieces of your life again, discard the bits you don't want any more, and decide what you want for yourself. You can't do that until you go back and see what you left behind.'

'I don't know what you mean,' Ellen said.

'You will in time,' the doctor said with a little smile. 'Just go and see what transpires. As for your sister, remember, you aren't responsible for her. Love her, worry about her by all means, but she has her life, you have yours, and you must plan it so it's a good one.'

In early August Ellen caught the train home to Truro. Shirley and Roger were taking the boys away on holiday for two weeks, so she hadn't put them out in any way.

It seemed Josie had sent a postcard home from London, and Ellen had one too, but there was no contact address on either. Ellen had given this a great deal of thought in the last couple of weeks. She had discounted Josie being pregnant, she wouldn't have gone to London if she was, but would have come to her in Bristol to get advice. Not giving an address wasn't necessarily sinister either; she was under age and didn't want anyone dragging her home. But that didn't stop Ellen worrying about her sister. From what she'd heard London was a dangerous place.

'It was you clearing off that made her go,' Violet said spitefully only a few minutes after Ellen arrived at Beacon Farm. 'But I daresay she'll make more of herself than you have – look at you, like something the cat brought in!'

Ellen bit back tears, and later when she looked in the bedroom mirror she saw Violet had a point. She was scrawny and pale, and the cream dress she'd bought for her first date with Pierre, which only a year ago she'd

172

thought so smart, had been washed so many times that it looked like an old rag.

At the end of the two weeks Ellen still didn't know whether it had been a mistake to come home, or a good thing. Violet had never let up in her spite. Her father seemed suddenly old and weary and had little to say to her. None of Josie's old friends had heard from her, all they did was repeat the same story that her father had been told by the police, that she'd got a lift up to London with two men.

But it had been good to talk to Mavis Peters. Ellen found she could tell her all the things she hadn't been able to say even to Dr Fordham. It was good to be entirely alone too, taking long walks along the coastal path and sitting for hours down at the cove looking at the sea. She thought she understood what the doctor had meant now. She *had* to come back here again, if only to see for herself how little the place had to offer her.

While she would always love Cornwall, the farm no longer lured her. She thought she would like to have a career working with children, perhaps in a school or a home. Maybe she'd stay another year with Shirley and Roger, till Simon started school, and then she'd move on.

Dr Fordham was right, she was stronger now. She was sure nothing life could throw at her would ever hurt half as much as losing Catherine. As for Josie, she was certain she would get in touch soon. She had to be doing all right or she would have slunk home again by now.

Chapter Eleven

Two weeks after she arrived in London, Josie was still living in the room at 42 Westbourne Park Road, and hating it like she'd never hated anything before. No air seemed to come in through the tiny window and when she looked out she could see nothing but rooftops. The other tenants, and there seemed to be dozens of them, cooked things which smelled disgusting, and it all wafted up to her room and remained trapped there.

But it was the bathroom that revolted her most. It stank, no one ever cleaned it, the lavatory was disgusting, and there was black mould growing up all over the walls. When she did pluck up the nerve to have a bath, she had to scrub it out first and stay in the bathroom while it ran. She made the mistake of leaving it to run once, and someone else took it, and used the shilling she'd put into the gas meter.

She supposed that the room itself wasn't any worse than her one back home, the same kind of rickety old furniture, worn sheets on the bed, a lack of any comforts. But there she'd had the view, the breeze and the silence. There was never a really quiet time at number 42, people shouted and bawled till the early hours of the morning, televisions and radios blared out. Tow-haired children played on the stairs, and there was always a baby crying. The other tenants seemed to be either black or Irish, and she could see that they were all desperately poor.

Josie felt she was trapped there. She had gone to several employment agencies on the first Monday, but she was hardly through the door when they asked her for her card, without which she couldn't be given a job. This card, she found out, was her National Insurance Card, which everyone had to have, and she could only get one from the National Insurance Office. But she was afraid to go there, thinking it would be the first place the police would check to trace her.

Then someone told her she could get work in the smaller restaurants or cafés without a card. She found a job that very day, in a café in James Street, close to Selfridges in Oxford Street. She saw an advertisement for a waitress stuck in the window, and they were so short-staffed that they took her on immediately. But after just a few days she'd wished she'd turned tail and gone home the minute she found out about the insurance card she needed. It was a horrible job, on her feet all day scraping half-eaten food off people's plates, with everyone, the customers and the owner of the café, complaining all the time that she wasn't quick enough.

But she couldn't go home now, not without losing face completely and getting a good hiding into the bargain. One of the first things she'd done on the Sunday she left Will's flat was to write a postcard home. She had apologized for running off without telling them, but said that London was where she wanted to be and she was safe and happy. She'd stuck a postcard through Will's letterbox too, explaining that she hadn't told him the truth, and if anyone came looking for her he was to show them this card so they'd know he hadn't done anything wrong.

Maybe she could stand the good hiding and her parents keeping her under lock and key in future, but the whole of Mawnan Smith and Falmouth would know about it by now. She couldn't stand the humiliation of having failed, so there really was no choice but to stay here and try to make good before even thinking of going back.

The waitressing job was as bad as her room. The café was busy all day, for apart from shoppers popping in for tea or coffee, the people who worked in offices around there came in for lunch. The owners were Greek and barked at Josie every time a table needed clearing; she got nine pounds a week and some days she got a few shillings extra in tips. But she soon found out that the money she had left after paying the rent didn't go very far.

The loneliness was the worst thing though. No one really spoke to her during the day; it was as though she was so low down the scale they didn't notice her. When she left the café at half past five, her feet were so swollen with the heat and standing all day that she could barely hobble to the underground. But once back in her room there was absolutely nothing to do other than wash her underclothes and lie on the bed listening to the noise from all the different rooms in the house.

She wanted a radio, an iron, a pair of flat shoes to wear to work, some sort of jacket or coat for when it rained, and more clothes. All she had with her was what she'd packed for the weekend with Rosemary. But she had so little money left once she'd paid her rent and fares to work that she couldn't see how she was ever going to be able to buy anything, let alone save something to be able to move somewhere better.

Luckily they allowed her to eat anything she wanted at work, which was just as well as all she had in her room was a single gas ring, a washbasin, one cup, one plate and a knife, a fork and a spoon, not even a saucepan.

Oxford Street was so tantalizing too, so many wonderful shops stuffed with beautiful clothes, and she saw hundreds of girls of her age swinging along in their mini-skirts looking chic and happy. She wondered how it was that they were doing all right and she had gone so wrong.

One rainy Friday afternoon after she had worked at the café for nearly three weeks, two girls came in. Mostly older people used the café, as the food was standard English fare, and the decor dull. So these two girls, one in a shiny white mac and tight knee-length boots, the other in a similar red outfit, stood out. Josie looked at them enviously,

176

for their clothes looked very expensive and they were both extraordinarily pretty.

Archie, the café owner, went over to them and kissed their hands, making a big fuss of them, but as Josie was working at the back and he showed the girls to a table right down by the street door, she couldn't hear what was being said.

They stayed for ages, having one cup of coffee after another, and finally Josie had to go up to their table as the other waitress had left. 'Can I get you anything else?' she asked, changing the overflowing ashtray for a clean one and removing their empty cups.

'You could get us a bit of sunshine,' one of them said. 'It's been pissing down all bloody day.'

Josie giggled. It was the first time anyone had said anything in the café that had amused her. 'I can't even work a miracle for myself,' she replied, 'let alone anyone else.'

'You're from Cornwall!' the dark girl in the white mac said in some surprise. 'What on earth made you leave there for stinking London?'

No one had recognized Josie's accent since she'd been in London and she was delighted.

'Madness,' Josie said with a grin. 'I came on an impulse and have been regretting it ever since.'

'Crummy room and a crummy job?' the girl in red asked sympathetically. She was blonde with large green eyes.

Josie nodded. Just that little bit of sympathy made tears well up in her eyes.

'Come on, love, don't cry,' the dark one said quickly, patting Josie's hand. 'You'll have old Archie there wanting to give you a cuddle, and you don't need that.'

'When do you finish work?' the other girl said.

'At half five.' Josie sniffed back the tears and tried to smile.

'Right, meet us in the pub a couple of doors down when you get off,' the girl said. 'You can tell us all about it then. What's your name?'

'Josie,' she said feebly, feeling a little silly now. 'Thanks, but you don't have to be nice, I'll be fine.'

'We do have to be nice,' the dark one said, and laughed. 'We've been where you are, love. I'm Candy, that's Tina, and we'll be waiting for you in the pub.'

Josie was so down that she really didn't think the girls would be there, but they were. As she walked into the pub they greeted her warmly and insisted on buying her a brandy and Coke to lift her spirits.

It wasn't very busy in the pub, just a few businessmen having a quick drink before going home, and the girls led her over to a table in a corner, sat down and began quizzing her. Candy told her she came from Bude in Cornwall, and once she'd heard the gist of what was troubling Josie, she admitted she'd been through much the same.

'I was so miserable I felt like topping myself,' she said in sympathy. 'I was only fifteen too, and the rent for my room in Earls Court was nearly as much as I earned. But I couldn't go home, I didn't have enough money for the fare, and my folks wouldn't have sent any if I'd asked.'

'Me too,' Tina said with a grin. 'I ran away with a man, and he ditched me after a couple of weeks. I got a job cleaning offices. But we're both evidence you don't have to stay in a rat-hole and work in some crummy café. London's a great place once you know the score.'

'I wanted to be a model,' Josie admitted sheepishly. 'I know it sounds stupid but I really thought that someone would flag me down to photograph me the minute I set foot in London. Some chance of that. No one even looks at me here.'

The two girls smiled and exchanged glances. 'We're models,' Candy said. 'Not fashion models, but we get real good money.'

Josie's heart skipped a beat. 'Really! How did you get into it?' she asked.

'We both answered an ad in the *Evening News*,' Candy

replied. 'It just said, "Pretty girls wanted for glamour pictures, good rates of pay". The ad's in there most weeks, they are always looking for new girls. You could do it too if you want.'

'I could?' Josie downed a huge gulp of the brandy, even though she didn't like the taste. 'Are you serious?' she added, holding on to her throat because it felt as though it was burning.

Candy shrugged. 'It's not *us* that has to be serious, but you, if you want to do it. You have to be prepared to wear very little, like we said, it isn't fashion modelling, it's pin-ups.'

Josie knew what a pin-up was; she'd seen them in magazines like *Tit-Bits*. The girls wore tight, low-cut sweaters, or a swim-suit. She could do that!

'I want to,' she said eagerly, leaning forward. 'Tell me how to go about it.'

For the next hour Josie sat entranced as Candy and Tina told her all about it. They were quick to point out it was a bit more daring than the pictures she'd seen in *Tit-Bits*, and if she was bashful she wouldn't last a day. But they also said they didn't go in for nude modelling or pornography, though they might go nude if they were offered enough money. They said they got paid by the session. That was four hours at a time and the fee was fifteen pounds. Most weeks they did up to six sessions, which they said was more than enough to live well and buy the kind of outfits they needed to be in constant demand.

'We were working this morning,' Tina said. She opened her red mac to show a black dress beneath it. 'The pictures he took were of me in this, with just me undies underneath. That's what they mean by glamour shots. I've got a few skimpy baby-doll nighties, shorts that come half-way up my bum. Lacy stuff, stockings and suspenders, all that sort of thing. You know what I mean?'

Josie nodded. She certainly hadn't known anything about any of this before, but she was cottoning on fast.

When the girls found she didn't have to work on Saturdays, they said she could go with them tomorrow and have a trial session.

'If you can't do it, you've lost nothing,' Candy said reassuringly. 'You can go back to work in the café on Monday and forget about it. But if you're good, and Beetle likes you, then you're made.'

'Beetle' was the boss of 'Glamour Pics Inc.'. The girls laughingly said they didn't know why he was called that, but it suited him. He did the entire organization, arranged the photo shoots, and sold the pictures on to magazines all over the world. They also admitted he gave them a bonus when they introduced a new girl.

'But that isn't why we invited you for a drink,' Tina was quick to add. 'We both could see by your face how down you were. Yeah, we noticed you were pretty and had a good body, but it takes more than that. You've got to be tough and hungry to make a glamour model. I'm not sure you're tough enough, but we'll soon see.'

Josie's feet didn't hurt that night as she went home. Maybe it was just the brandy, but she felt as though she was walking on marshmallows. She was tough enough, and she was hungry for a nice place to live, lovely clothes and fun too. Maybe London wasn't going to be so bad after all.

Josie was washing her hair at seven the following morning, and she was determined she was going to surprise Tina and Candy. They had only seen her with her hair tied back, no makeup, and a nasty nylon overall over a cheap cotton dress. If they thought she looked pretty like that, wait till they saw her in the black and white mini with her hair all loose!

The studio where she had to meet Beetle and the girls was conveniently in Paddington, just a short walk from her room. Tina had said she wasn't to worry about clothes, because Beetle had a selection of outfits for new girls at the studio. Although she wouldn't be paid anything for this first session, if she was any good he'd book her up for five or six next week, and she'd get paid in cash each time. The only thing that really worried Josie was her underwear. She had only one bra and two pairs of knickers, and they were very shabby and grey. She wouldn't want anyone to see her in those, not even another girl. Should she spend some of her week's wages on a new set, before going to the studio?

As she sat by the open window letting her hair dry, she counted her money. She hadn't touched a penny of her week's wages yet, the girls had bought all the drinks yesterday, and she had three pounds too, which she'd managed to hang on to from her birthday money. Once she'd paid her rent for the week that left eight pounds.

A short while ago she would have thought that was a fortune, but she knew better now. Was it wise to blow some of it on new underwear, before she found out whether Beetle would take her on? She decided it was. She would be much more confident today if she knew her underwear was pretty.

At five to eleven, Josie was in Porchester Mews, looking for the studio. The mews was a horribly squalid little place, mostly panel-beating garages, printers and other small businesses, with junk piled outside most of them, and from the street the rooms above what had once been stables looked to be as nasty as the place she lived in.

But she had learned since she came to the city that this part of London, Westbourne Grove, Ladbroke Grove and Paddington, was one of the worst areas of all to live in. While Westbourne and Ladbroke Groves were virtually slum areas, populated by immigrants who were exploited by unscrupulous landlords, Paddington was home to hundreds of prostitutes. Having no real idea what prostitutes looked like, she felt nervous just walking around in case people took her for one.

'Yoo-hoo,' someone called out behind her, and she turned to see Tina and Candy coming into the mews.

It was sunny again today and the girls wore sleeveless mini-dresses. But the skirts were at least two inches shorter than Josie's and she felt a stab of panic that she looked old-fashioned.

'You look gorgeous,' Candy said with a sincere wide smile. 'Beetle is going to be pleased with us. Are you nervous?'

Josie nodded. She hadn't eaten anything because she felt sick with fright, and if she'd had to hang around on her own for much longer, she might just have taken off.

'Remember the first time is the worst,' Tina said, and put her arm around Josie's shoulders. 'A few sessions later and you'll be laughing about how you felt today. Imagine you're an actress, that's all it is really, acting sexy.'

Beetle was aptly named. He was short, squat, with shiny black hair cut in a similar mop-top to the Beatles. He was around forty and his hair looked suspiciously like a wig, yet he had a curious kind of charm that put Josie at her ease. After Tina and Candy had introduced her, they went off to get changed for their session, and Beetle made Josie a cup of coffee and gave her a cigarette.

'You are beautiful, Jojo,' he said, reaching out to touch her hair and twiddling a curl around his finger. 'I find a girl as lovely as you only once in a blue moon. Tina told me about you on the phone last night, and I want to reassure you I won't make you do anything you don't like. I don't try and get my girls to go to bed with me. I pay them for each session, and I look after them. You can trust me.'

The office they were in was tiny, a partitioned-off part of the main studio, but it was very clean and neat, holding little more than a desk, a filing cabinet and a couple of chairs. The walls were covered with photographs of girls in everything from bikinis and negligees to fur coats.

Although many of them had a blouse or a coat undone to reveal they were wearing nothing beneath, there wasn't one picture of anyone completely naked.

The studio beyond, through which Josie had entered, was large. It appeared to run right across the top of two garages beneath. The floor was shiny plain lino, the walls neutral, but it was divided into what Josie imagined film sets looked like. One had a couch covered in a fur rug, there was a beach scene with sand on the floor in another, and a bed piled high with cushions in the third.

As she and Beetle were talking, Josie saw Candy go into the set with the couch, dressed in black shiny boots and a very short black satin petticoat, but the photographer had set up a big white umbrella which prevented her from seeing how he would pose Candy. Tina came out a little later, and she was dressed in a brief bikini for the beach scene. There was a third girl too, dark-haired, and she was lying on the bed in a red negligee.

After about half an hour, Beetle said it was time for Josie to get ready, and he led her across the studio into a small changing-room. He opened a wardrobe, took a white lacy negligee down off a hanger and told her to put it on over her underwear. He then gave her some brief instructions about putting on more mascara and lipstick and defining her cheekbones with rouge. To her relief he didn't stay and watch her.

She was terrified when she was called from the changing-room, even though the negligee wasn't very revealing. But Bob, the man who was to photograph her, barely looked at her, just ordered her to kneel on the floor by an artificial tree. It felt very strange for the first few minutes as the man gave her instructions from behind his camera, and with bright lights shining in her face she could see nothing beyond the little set she was in. She took Candy's advice about pretending she was an actress, and it seemed to work, for she stopped feeling self-conscious and after a little while found she could move into different poses without any prompting.

When Bob suggested loosening the negligee she wasn't frightened, in fact it was much like the way she had posed back at home in her room with a sheet. Soon she was smiling naturally, throwing back her head, running her fingers through her hair, or lying down on her side with one thigh exposed as if she had been born to it.

'No trouble with this one, she's a natural,' Bob said to Beetle when he came over to the set some time later. 'I'll get these developed and drop them round to you this evening.'

'Well, that's it,' Beetle said to Josie, his face very shiny like his hair under the lights, 'looks like you've got yourself a new career now. Phone me tomorrow at midday and I'll tell you what sessions I want you for next week.'

Josie was surprised that that was all there was to it, even a bit disappointed it was over so soon. But Bob was putting a jacket on ready to leave.

Candy was changing into some red underwear when Josie went back to put her own clothes back on. She smiled at Josie and offered her a cigarette. 'How did it go?'

'Fine, I think.' Josie didn't like to repeat what Bob had said, for fear of sounding smug. But she did say how Beetle had said she was to ring him tomorrow.

'Well, you're in then, love.' Candy grinned. 'All your troubles are over, by the end of the week you'll have enough dosh to find yourself a better pad. We'll probably run into you during the week, the sessions usually overlap, and you'll meet some of the other girls too. Good luck.'

Josie was a little disappointed that it was all cut short, she'd kind of expected that she'd hang around and chat with Candy and Tina, maybe even go somewhere with them afterwards. But she tried not to show it, and thanked Candy for introducing her to Beetle.

'You might not be so grateful after a couple of months.' Candy laughed. 'Now, get out in the fresh air today. The summer will be over before we know it, and you need to find your way round London if you're going to stay here.'

Josie did what Candy had suggested and walked miles that afternoon, lost in dreams of fame and fortune. The previous day's rain had washed the pavements and the leaves on the trees clean, and all at once she was seeing the London she'd dreamed off back home in Cornwall, Hyde Park and the Serpentine. Buckingham Palace and Trafalgar Square, all every bit as magnificent as she'd expected. Bubbles of excitement kept leaping up inside her. She was going to be a model, she would earn so much money she could buy all the new clothes she wanted, live in a flat like Will's, have her hair done at the hairdresser's, and never have to scrape other people's left-over food off plates again.

She bought an *Evening Standard* and studied the advertisements for flats. There was a one-bedroom self-contained one in Chelsea which she'd heard was a nice area, for twenty pounds a week. It seemed laughable that only a week before she was looking at ads for bed-sitters and thinking six pounds a week was a fortune.

Her thoughts slipped back to Ellen while she was going home on the Tube later that evening. She had thought of her sister almost daily in the last two weeks, wishing she could contact her, but she hadn't dared to. She wasn't sure she could trust Ellen not to tell their parents where she was in London. What would she think of her modelling? Would she get all high and mighty and say it was a bad thing to do? Or would she just laugh and say good for her?

She really didn't know, and that made her feel rather sad. A year ago she would have been able to predict how Ellen would react to anything, they'd never had secrets from one another. She remembered how Ellen had told her everything about Pierre, trusting her implicitly not to tell Mum or Dad. Why did that trust vanish? What had changed her so much that she could pretend she was pregnant just to justify leaving the sister she said she loved at home alone? Was it simply because she fell in love and that man let her down?

Yet at the back of Josie's mind another thought had taken root. Maybe once Ellen had moved to Bristol she became a bit like Josie had while she was in Helston, thinking her family were all weird, and finding she didn't want to be a part of it any more.

On 1 October Josie was standing inside her new flat, the key in her hand, her heart palpitating with a mixture of pleasure and anxiety.

It hadn't been easy to find a new place. Landlords and agents were a suspicious bunch, she'd discovered. But Beetle had intervened and got her this place in Elm Park Gardens in Chelsea. It was only five minutes' walk away from King's Road.

The block of small flats was new and purpose-built, unlike the rest of the huge Victorian houses in the road. Her flat, on the fourth floor, had two rooms, a kitchen and a bathroom. It was unfurnished, except for a cooker, fridge and fitted carpets, but after the horrors of Westbourne Park Road Josie was quite happy to sleep on the floor. She would have to for a while because she had no money left for furniture.

She never went back to the waitressing job, and she had been doing seven sessions a week for Beetle since she started with him nine weeks ago. Yet even though she'd earned over nine hundred pounds in that time, two hundred of it had gone on key money for this place, plus another hundred for a month's advance rent, and then a huge deposit. The rest had gone on clothes, food and living expenses.

Josie had confided in Tina about this, as she thought that handing over more than half of what she'd earned just for a roof over her head seemed ludicrous. But Tina laughingly said she was earning ludicrous amounts of money too, and to remember she'd get the key money and deposit back if she ever left there.

Josie took off her coat, then carried her suitcase and the pillowcase she'd filled with clothes into the bedroom. There was at least a fitted wardrobe, and as she began to hang up her clothes in it, she put aside her anxiety and thought instead of the future. Beetle kept telling her she was a hot property and that once she was sixteen he'd be able to get her into the prestigious glossy magazines, and she could easily become a celebrity.

Once she'd put her clothes away she went back into the lounge to unpack the box which contained a new iron, a hair-dryer and a radio and kitchen equipment. As she took out each item she reminded herself she had bought them all, and that was concrete evidence that she had achieved a great deal since she arrived in London.

Yet the one thing she really wanted above all was a friend. She hadn't expected to miss Rosemary and her other schoolfriends, but there was hardly a day she didn't think of them and wonder what they were doing now. Did Rosemary get the job in Truro? Who filled the vacancy in the shipping office?

She thought too about her parents, wondering if they'd made any attempt to find her. She thought it was more likely that once they got her postcard they'd just dismissed her, and even if that was what she wanted in one way, it hurt that they could cast her off so easily.

Then there was Ellen. Josie had finally written her a letter, but she put no address on it, making the excuse that this was because she was about to move to a nicer place and she'd let Ellen know the address then. She said she'd got some modelling work (though she didn't specify what kind) and had made lots of new friends. She just wished that last bit was true. London wasn't a very friendly place, she'd found. She couldn't just strike up conversations with people the way she had in Cornwall. If she had a girlfriend maybe they could go to pubs, coffee bars and dance-halls, but she couldn't do any of those things alone, especially not in London.

The girls she met at the studio were mostly much older than her. They were slick and sophisticated and they ignored her. Even Tina and Candy were a bit distant now. They would stop to chat for a few minutes, ask how she was doing, but it was obvious to Josie they didn't want to get involved with her. They hadn't once invited her to go out with them, not even for a cup of coffee. Now she had this flat, and she would give anything to have someone she could invite round.

Beetle had fixed her up with a photographic session this afternoon and again tomorrow even though normally none of the girls worked on Saturday afternoons or Sundays. He seemed to know she was lonely and that her money was all gone, and she supposed he thought work was the answer to both problems.

Once her few things were stashed away in the cupboards, Josie sat on the floor of the lounge, leaned back against the wall and lit up a cigarette. She really didn't know why she kept lighting cigarettes; she didn't like the taste or the smell. Back home she had only ever had the odd one with Rosemary. But everyone seemed to smoke in London, especially the other models, and she didn't want to be different.

As she sat there looking around the empty room, she suddenly began to cry. She couldn't understand why, she'd worked flat out to get this place, had thought of nothing else for the past three weeks, but now she was here she just felt desolate.

After about half an hour she picked herself up off the floor and went into the bathroom to wash her face. It was tiny, but clean and bright, and she gained a little comfort from seeing her face flannel, toothbrush and her own towel, knowing they could stay in there permanently without fear of anyone taking them.

'Put your makeup on,' she said aloud to her reflection in the mirror. 'Stop feeling sorry for yourself.'

When Josie walked into the studio two hours later, Beetle grinned at her. 'I bought you a flat-warming present,' he said, and lifted up a huge carrier bag from Selfridges.

All Josie's sadness vanished at his kindness. 'Oh, Beetle,' she exclaimed. 'That's so nice of you. What on earth is it?'

'Something useful,' he said. 'Go on, open it!'

It was a pink satin eiderdown, the thick, soft kind filled with feathers. All she had was one rough grey blanket she'd taken from the room in Westbourne Park Road, and she'd only thought of helping herself to that this morning when she suddenly realized she didn't have any bedding at all. But for Beetle's thoughtfulness she would have been sleeping with all her clothes on tonight.

She went to hug him, the tears welling up again. 'Come on now,' he said gruffly. 'Don't get all soppy on me and spoil your makeup, Bob's waiting to take the pictures. There's something else I've got to tell you too. Tomorrow you'll be doing the session with Mark Kinsale.'

Josie gasped and looked at Beetle in astonishment. She'd heard the other girls talking about this man, who was a famous photographer. They said he came in here periodically to check on Beetle's girls in the hope of finding someone special.

'Me?' she said stupidly. 'But why?'

Beetle laughed. 'Because you're young and pretty, why else?'

The four hours with Bob flew by, Josie was in such a dream. She didn't mind sitting in rather lewd poses astride a chair, or him getting her to take her bra off and leave her shirt undone, for she was imagining herself in evening gowns, bridal wear and fur coats.

Beetle not only gave her the fifteen pounds for the day's session, but the other fifteen for the following day too, explaining he wouldn't be there, and had given Mark the key to let himself in. 'Now, don't you be late, twelve on the dot, and don't argue with Mark about anything he tells you to do. Your whole future depends on him liking you.'

It was half past three when Josie left the studio, carrying the big bag with the eiderdown, and she took the bus straight to World's End, for there were lots of second-hand furniture shops there, and she intended to try to find a cheap bed.

Her luck was in. The very first place she went into had a double divan that was in really good condition, at only five pounds, and the owner of the shop promised to deliver it to her on his way home at six that evening.

At five-thirty she was staggering up the stairs at Elm Park Gardens laden with her bulky purchases. She'd bought a set of sheets and pillowcases, a pink blanket, two pillows and a table lamp.

As she waited for the bed to arrive she was on cloud nine, hardly able to believe her good fortune. Tonight she would sleep in luxury, and tomorrow, if all went well with Mark, she'd be on her way to stardom.

Later that evening she lay on top of her new bed revelling in its comfort. She had never enjoyed anything so much as making it, smoothing down the sheets, doing hospital corners the way her mother had taught her, and finally placing the eiderdown on top of the blankets.

The new table lamp was sitting on her suitcase, which she'd turned into a bedside table by covering it with a pink dirndl skirt she'd brought from home. Only this morning she'd been tempted to throw it out because it was so old-fashioned, but she was glad she hadn't now.

'A dressing-table next,' she murmured to herself gleefully. 'Some curtains, maybe a pretty chair. Then I'll start on the lounge.'

It was so wonderful to be able to have a bath, to keep her milk and butter cool in a fridge, to press up against the radiators and know that when winter came she'd be cosy and warm. She stood at the window looking down at the quiet tree-lined street below, humming along with the music on the radio and dreaming dreams of when the flat would be all furnished and she'd have dozens of friends to invite round here to share it all with her. She didn't think she'd ever felt so happy in her entire life.

Chapter Twelve

'You must be Jojo?'

Josie could only gulp, as speech was beyond her. The man lounging on the couch in the studio who had greeted her was far beyond even her wildest imaginings of what a famous photographer would be like. This was Mark Kinsale!

He looked about thirty, slender, with straight raven-black hair so long it almost touched his shoulders. His skin was deeply tanned, and he had a long bony face with an aquiline nose. The arrogant way he was lounging made her think of a Roman, even though he had no laurel wreath or toga. But then, he was wearing clothes unlike any she'd ever seen on a man before, even in pictures of pop stars – dark green velvet trousers tucked into long snakeskin boots, and a black leather jacket over a collarless shirt.

'Mr Kinsale?' she managed to get out. 'Yes, I'm Jojo. I'm not late, am I?'

Beetle always called her Jojo, and she'd started using the name herself as it sounded infinitely more chic than Josie. But she didn't feel chic now, not even wearing her favourite black mini-skirt and skinny rib sweater. She felt she looked what she really was, a fifteen-year-old from Falmouth with funny corkscrew ginger hair who had no business to be in the same room as this famous man, let alone imagine he was going to turn her into a top model.

'Take that ribbon out of your hair,' he ordered her, still not moving from the couch. 'I hate those stupid bows, they look like something out of the eighteenth century.'

Her hands fluttered up behind her head to remove the offending ribbon. She had noticed all the smartest girls in London wore their hair tied back at the nape of their necks with a Tom Jones bow, and had copied it. Now she was mortified.

'Now, put your head down to your knees and shake out your hair,' he ordered.

Josie did as she was told. She hoped he knew what he was doing because she knew exactly what she'd look like when he made her stand up, a madwoman or a witch.

'Stand up.'

Josie could feel a blush spreading all over her body, but she obeyed him.

'Great,' he said. 'We'll start.'

'What do you want me to wear?' she asked, appalled that he intended her to leave her hair all wild and bushy.

'What you've got on will do fine,' he said looking her up and down. 'Over there!' He pointed towards a plain wall already lit by one of the big lights.

The other photographers always told her exactly what they wanted, it was usually a sexy pose or as if she'd been taken by surprise. But with no directions and no props she felt silly and awkward. She stood there expectantly, hands clasped in front of her, waiting for Mark to move from the couch and disappear behind a camera, but instead he just stayed where he was, staring at her.

Just as she was about to open her mouth to ask him what he wanted her to do, he moved, uncoiling himself slowly from the couch in an almost feline manner, and she saw he had a small camera in his hands.

It was so strange; he just prowled around her taking pictures from different angles without saying a word.

'Do you want me to smile?' she asked after a bit.

'Do you feel like smiling? Has anything struck you as amusing?' he asked. His deep voice seemed to echo around the studio.

'Well, yes.' She couldn't help but smile then because the whole thing struck her as funny.

'That's nice,' he said, as she put her hand up to her mouth to stifle a giggle. 'You look like a naughty school-girl.'

His words broke the ice and suddenly she realized he wanted to see the real Josie, not the manufactured one the others photographers liked. So she acted just the way she used to back at home when she was playing at being a model, moving around, running her fingers through her hair, looking thoughtful and sometimes sad. His silence seemed to say she was doing the right thing, and as he kept reloading his camera with film, he was clearly satisfied.

Later he did get her to put on a different outfit, a plain long dress that was in the studio wardrobe, and he got her to add a little more makeup. But there was no suggestion of 'glamour' shots, and it wasn't until right at the end that he asked her to put on a bikini.

In over three hours he couldn't have said more than fifty words to her, so she was staggered when after he'd told her to get dressed again, he said he was taking her for something to eat.

Maybe her face registered her shock, for he laughed. 'I've got you on film,' he said. 'Now I want to know a bit about you.'

He took her to a Chinese restaurant close to the studio and ordered for her, as if he knew she'd never eaten Chinese food and wouldn't have had the first idea what she wanted. He had a large Scotch while they were waiting for the meal, but he ordered her a Coke.

'Tell me how you met Beetle,' he said curtly. 'I want to know where you come from, how old you really are, and about your parents. Don't think of telling me a pack of lies. If I'm to use you in the future I need to know the truth.'

She told him exactly that, and it was a relief not to have

194

to make out she was seventeen, or had family in London. She told him about Will, Westbourne Park Road, the café she'd worked in and how Tina and Candy had invited her to meet Beetle.

By the time she'd finished the story, throughout which he hadn't said a word, the food arrived. She stared at all the little dishes of things she didn't recognize and he laughed.

'Put a bit of everything on your plate and try it,' he said. 'You'll find it doesn't taste as strange as it looks. You're too thin. I suppose you hardly eat anything?'

This was true – since she'd left the café she hadn't had one proper meal, only ready-made sandwiches, crisps and the occasional hamburger. So she dug into the food and found she really liked it, even if she didn't know what it was.

'If you are set on being a model you'll have to learn to look after yourself,' Mark said sternly. 'You won't keep that clear complexion on a diet of cigarettes and chocolate. You need a balanced diet with plenty of fruit and vegetables. Exercise too and enough sleep.'

She nodded. Sleep was one thing she did have plenty of, she had nothing much else to do when she wasn't working.

'I'll make sure I eat more,' she agreed. 'Beetle's always telling me that too. He's very kind to me. He even bought me an eiderdown as a flat-warming present.'

Mark gave her a very strange look, one dark eyebrow slightly raised.

'What is it?' she asked, worried she'd said something wrong.

'Beetle's a rogue,' he said abruptly, startling her. 'I don't suppose you've got the first idea that most of the so-called photographers who take pictures in his studio haven't even got film in their cameras?'

Josie frowned. 'But why would they do that?' she asked. She wondered then if Mark was a little crazy.

'Because they get their kicks out of seeing girls with very little on and are prepared to pay for the privilege.'

Josie was winded and for a moment she could say nothing. Then she remembered all those films she'd seen Mark put in his camera, the sounds of winding on, and the finished films which made his jacket pockets bulge. It was very rare to see or hear that in the studio. 'You mean they just look at us?' she whispered, remembering all the times they'd asked her to expose a breast, or lie on the floor with her legs in the air.

Mark nodded. 'If you girls weren't so greedy for money you'd have worked it out for yourselves,' he said tersely. 'In a real assignment the model is told what the pictures are for, there's a makeup artist and hairdresser standing by, the company provides the clothes needed for the job. How you girls can be so thick I can't understand. Who on earth would want photographs of a girl playing with a beach ball on a fake beach?'

'Beetle said they were for holiday brochures,' she said in a small voice, recalling with horror how one of the men had made her keep jumping so that her breasts jiggled around. It had made her feel uneasy, but she'd thought that was part of the job.

'He does handle a small amount of commercial work, for calendars, the tacky end of the girlie mags, stuff like that, but he'd be living in a council flat in Ladbroke Grove and you girls would be earning less than waitresses if it wasn't for the kinky bastards who like to play at being David Bailey.'

The secure feeling Josie had enjoyed for the past few weeks vanished. She had been duped, and now she knew the truth what on earth was she going to do? She couldn't afford to live in Elm Park Gardens on a waitress's wages. Tears sprang to her eyes, and she gave Mark a pleading look, hoping he'd laugh and say he was joking.

'What are you crying for?' he asked brusquely.

'Because I don't know what I'm going to do now,' she

said, dabbing at her eyes. 'I only moved into a new flat yesterday, it's very expensive.'

Mark shook his head; his expression was remarkably like the one her father always had when she'd done something stupid. 'Then you are lucky Beetle spotted that you might have real model potential, and didn't stick you in with any of the real weirdos, and that he called me over to take a look at you.'

It appeared by that statement that all wasn't quite lost. 'Have I got any potential?' she asked timidly.

He looked at her for a moment as if considering the question. Josie held her breath and crossed her fingers.

'Yes, you have,' he said eventually.

Josie beamed.

'Don't look so joyful,' he said dourly. 'You may have a pretty face and gorgeous hair, but it takes more than that.'

'I'll do anything,' she gasped. 'Whatever you tell me to do.'

Mark sighed. 'Look, Josie, it's not as simple as that. There's such a thing as the look of the moment, and no one can forecast what that next look will be. Fashions are changing rapidly at the moment, what's "in" one day is out the next. Besides, there's your age, the estrangement from your family. You are in fact a runaway. That could backfire on me.'

'But I left home almost three months ago now, they haven't come searching for me, so they don't care, do they?' she said defiantly. 'Besides, there's no law against working away from home at fifteen.'

'That would depend on how your parents viewed the work you were doing,' he said. 'If they believed you were in moral or physical danger, they could have you made a ward of court.'

'They wouldn't do that,' she said with a touch of scorn. 'As long as they get letters from me now and then and know I'm doing okay they won't want me back.'

He sighed deeply. 'I'll have to think all this over, Jojo.

I'll get the pictures I took today printed, show them around and see what interest I get. Then I'll get back to you.'

He was already signalling the waiter for the bill. Josie sensed he was dismissing her.

'What do I do now then?' she asked. 'I mean, about working for Beetle.'

Mark turned to look at her and lifted her chin with one finger. His eyes were very dark; she couldn't even distinguish his pupils. 'That's entirely up to you. I'm not about to become your keeper.'

'But is it safe for me to stay working for him?' she asked desperately. 'I need the money.'

'You are safer than the other girls are,' he said. 'If you want the money, do it, but don't go telling any of them about me, or what I've told you.'

That didn't help her at all. 'Shall I give you my address then?' she asked.

He nodded, took a small notepad and pen from his pocket and handed them to her. 'Don't expect to hear anything for a few weeks. And remember to keep quiet about this, for your own good.'

Once outside the restaurant Mark said goodbye to Josie and walked purposefully away to his car. He knew it would have been kinder to have offered her a lift, maybe even gone to her flat to see how she lived, but he didn't want to picture her in any other way than how he'd seen her through his lens.

Mark was older than he looked, thirty-seven, old enough to be Josie's father, but he had no paternal instincts. When she had walked into the studio his only thought was that he could make big money with her. She was lovely, perhaps the most beautiful girl he'd ever photographed, and it was all entirely natural.

'That hair,' he murmured to himself. Her cascade of fiery curls would become her trademark, setting her apart from all other models. Hair product companies would beg for her, and the cosmetic companies would drool. Yet there was more to her than just her hair – her skin, face and figure were all sensational. She wasn't very bright, though, and unbelievably naive. She was likely to be eaten alive once her pictures got around. It was a shame that Beetle had found her. He wasn't going to let her go easily.

Mark knew that great changes were underway in England. He sensed it every day in London, from the little fashion boutiques mushrooming up overnight, the disco clubs, the music in the charts and the mood of the people. He had been aware of something like this before, in 1955 when he was twenty-eight, married with two children and working in a factory in Birmingham. Then it was Teddy Boys and the start of Rock 'n' Roll music with Bill Haley and the Comets that heralded dramatic changes on the way. Photography was only a hobby for Mark at that time, but as he went around taking pictures of the Teddy Boys and the wild jiving at the dance-halls, all at once he realized he wanted to be a professional photographer. If he stayed in Birmingham the most he could hope for was a few weddings and school photographs. He saw his pictures as art, and he knew the only place he was likely to be taken seriously was London.

He had been seventeen at the end of the war, and the two years of National Service which came a year later had done nothing to broaden his outlook. Like so many of his friends he had married young, and children quickly followed, giving him no choice but to stay in a secure but dead-end job. He reasoned that maybe it was callous of him to walk away from them and go to London to try his luck, but he knew that if he stayed he would only end up resenting them for trapping him.

The revolution he expected didn't happen after all. Married women remained at home with their children. Their men worked long hours to keep them and found solace in buying a television or a car. Yet apart from improving their quality of life with material things, for most people life went on in much the same way as before the war. But Mark stayed in London, recording with his camera the subtle changes that were taking place, and he never considered going back home.

He managed to scrape a living from selling his pictures of Teddy Boys, tramps and prostitutes in Soho, and beatniks in jazz clubs, and gradually developed a reputation for pictures that were a social comment. In 1957 he won a prize for capturing the anxiety and hope on the faces of West Indian immigrants as they got off the boat in Southampton. In the following year his pictures of the Manchester United fans grieving after their idols in the football team had been killed in a plane crash in Munich, and the ones he'd taken of the race riots in Notting Hill, got him further acclaim. Soon he became known as the photographer with a social conscience, and newspapers called on him when they wanted particularly poignant pictures of a story they were covering.

But now, a decade since he left Birmingham, Mark knew that what he sensed in the air wasn't going to be a damp firework like the changes in the mid-Fifties. People were tired of being grateful for regular work, and the new innovations of the post-war period like the Health Service and improved housing were all old hat. A 'we-want-everything-now' attitude was emerging, people no longer saved for things they wanted but got them on the never-never. There was also admiration for conspicuous wealth and decadence, and it was this that he intended to capture on film. He would still take pictures that were a social comment on the times, but to hell with down-and-outs, slum dwellers, racial tension and men on picket lines; he wanted to move up to a more ritzy level, personally and professionally.

However, Mark knew that if he was seen to be selling out, he would be vilified by those very newspapers who had given him his fame. Until today he had been troubled by how he could move on up without revealing that he'd never cared tuppence about the plight of the people he photographed. All he'd ever been interested in was getting an outstanding picture.

Jojo could be the first rung on the ladder. Nothing succeeded better than Cinderella stories, and with her he had the makings of one. The poor farmer's daughter who fled to London and was rescued from the dangers of the sex industry would appeal to even the most cynical. He could see it all in his mind's eye – a few shots of a frightened, doe-eyed girl with a battered suitcase at Paddington station, which he would pretend he took quite by chance. He could say the pictures haunted him after he'd had them developed, then he'd spent several weeks looking for her. With the help of a good journalist, they could do a piece about the places runaway kids often end up in, designed purely to shock. Then lo and behold, he finds the unknown girl again, rescues her from the edge of a precipice, and takes her under his wing.

Mark smiled to himself as he drove out of Paddington, on towards Belsize Park where he lived. It had always grated on him that David Bailey got so much acclaim when he only photographed beautiful women who could be done equal justice by an amateur with a box Brownie. Let him eat his heart out when he saw Jojo. Mark intended to get her sewn up so tight in a contract that she couldn't be photographed by anyone but himself. Jojo was going to be the face of the Sixties.

While Mark was shut in his dark-room developing his pictures of Josie later that evening, gloating over them as he hung the prints up to dry, she was lying on her bed crying. She was frightened, confused and she didn't know what she should do about anything. She hadn't shown Mark how horrified and dismayed she was to be told that Beetle's studio was a front for something very nasty, but then it wasn't until he walked away from her at the restaurant that the full implications of it hit her. Had she been told in advance that the job consisted of displaying herself to dirty old men, she would never have taken it, not if she'd been offered a hundred pounds a day.

But now she knew, how could she go back to it? Just the thought of it made her flesh crawl. She wasn't a tart, even if the other girls were; she was still a virgin, and she'd never let a boy do anything more than touch her top half.

But if she didn't go back to Beetle tomorrow, how would she live? All she had to her name was around three pounds, and in another month she had to pay another hundred pounds' rent. She couldn't earn that kind of money anywhere else.

All she had was a ray of hope that Mark was going to come back to her with a real modelling job. But what if he didn't?

She wished she'd never got this flat, but now she came to think of it, it was Candy and Tina who had egged her on to find somewhere grand. Had they always known exactly what was going on at Beetle's? Were they laughing at her behind her back? And Beetle too, she'd trusted him, but wasn't it more likely that he wanted her to get in over her head with this place so she'd never walk out on him?

She clutched at the satin eiderdown he'd given her. She'd thought it was so generous and thoughtful of him to buy it for her, but now it seemed more like a bribe to do as she was told and not ask too many questions. She didn't know who she was most angry with, Candy and Tina, Beetle, or herself. What a prize fool she'd been!

For the first time since she left home Josie wanted her mother, just to feel her arms around her and to know she was safe. Cornwall might have been dull, but at least she could trust people there.

A high wind was getting up outside and rattling the window-frames, and that was another reminder of home. The track up through the woods to the road would be deep in fallen leaves now, a carpet of brown, gold and orange. If she opened her window there tonight she would hear the sea pounding on the rocks down in the cove, and the sheep would be huddling up against the hedges to keep warm.

She got off her bed and walked over to the window. Down below, the streetlights showed up the puddles on the pavements and the sludge of fallen leaves. There were lighted windows everywhere she looked; yet she didn't know anyone. Back home they might not be able to see a single light from their house, but they knew everyone in a ten-mile radius around them and could call on any of their neighbours in an emergency.

But it was no good thinking longingly of home; she had to go back to Beetle tomorrow. She could go home next weekend, though; she would have enough money then not to go empty-handed. Or maybe Mark would come round before then, and everything would be all right.

All that week Josie felt as if she'd suddenly been given a pair of glasses and could see her new world as it really was – a very shabby, nasty one. She remembered now how Fee had told her there were landlords in London who preyed on the weak and the poor, packing them into their houses, charging them exorbitant rents so that they would have to sub-let just to eat. She hadn't really believed it then, but now, when she passed by slum properties in Paddington, she felt for the tenants. She knew now too why cafés and restaurants would take on staff without insurance cards. It was so they could get cut-price labour out of people who wouldn't dare to complain.

She looked at the men who came into the studio and wondered how on earth she could ever have believed they were real photographers. The seediness of their natures showed in their lined faces and flabby bodies. They couldn't meet her eye, they couldn't hold a conversation, and it sickened her to think that once they were behind those big fake cameras it gave them power.

She saw too that the other girls did know. Maybe like

her they'd been duped in the first place, but they knew now and it didn't bother them. Overheard conversations took on new meanings now she knew the truth. Kate, one of the oldest of the girls, came back into the dressing-room grinning from ear to ear on Monday afternoon. 'I cut his session short,' she said. 'I opened my legs and let him have a good look. He came straight away.'

Just two days before Josie would have imagined she was only talking about making the photographer move closer or something like that. Yet now she saw the situation in all its awfulness – these men didn't just look, they relieved themselves while they were at it.

She worked out for herself that the only times she'd really been photographed was when Beetle kept her back after the other girls had gone, or got her in early. Those were the only times when he was fussy about what she wore, or checked her makeup and hair. This was probably why the other girls didn't speak to her too, they were jealous that she was getting some real modelling work.

Yet that didn't make up for all the times she'd been one of four girls in the studio, bathed in bright light and unable to see what was going on beyond them. It was almost laughable that she'd tried so hard to look gorgeous and alluring, she might just as well have slipped her top off or exposed her private parts and got it over with twice as fast.

But she said nothing to anyone, not even Beetle. When he asked her in private how it had gone with Mark, she made herself look as innocent as possible and said she really didn't know, he hadn't said much. Yet she was burning with anger inside, for the money she'd wasted on the sort of underwear she would never want to wear anywhere else, or the pair of long black boots which pinched her toes and were so high she couldn't walk in them, but most of all for being made a fool of by Beetle and his treacherous girls.

By Friday evening she knew she couldn't stomach any

more, and she was just weighing up whether she should hang on in the flat till the end of the month, living on what she'd earned this week, or go home now before the loneliness drove her mad, when the door-bell rang.

She jumped. Apart from the man who delivered her bed, the bell had never been rung since she got here. As she ran down the stairs she hoped it might be Mark, but she was so down now that she didn't really think that was likely. Yet it was him and he asked if he could come up.

Josie was embarrassed when he glanced around the flat and looked surprised at how bare it was, with not even a chair for him to sit on. But he made no remark, just sat down on the floor as if that was quite normal and offered her a cigarette.

'The pictures were good,' he said, without showing any expression. 'I think I can work with you, but I have to tell you now it will be on my terms. Whatever I ask you to do, you do it.'

Josie thought this was another trap, that maybe he wanted to take pornographic pictures of her. She didn't trust anyone now.

'I'm not taking my clothes off,' she said nervously. 'So if that's what you want me for, you'd better forget it.'

'I'm a serious photographer,' he said sternly. 'If I wanted to take pictures of naked girls I would find one older and better endowed than you. Now, listen to me.'

Much of what he said went over her head. Then he went on to describe the kind of photography he was noted for, and showed her a small notebook of prints. All of them were of people, strange-looking in the main – black people, old people, tramps, tired-looking women pushing prams. One was of a group of both black and white people with angry faces as if they were about to start fighting. Josie became even more puzzled.

'My plan for you is that we kind of chart your progress since you came to London. Arriving at the station with no money, working as a waitress and living in a slum. It's a human interest story, Jojo, people love them, especially when little Cinderella gets to go to the ball in the end and marries the Prince.'

Josie couldn't bring herself to admit she didn't understand what he was talking about. He'd already commented the previous time she'd seen him that girls would have to be stupid not to know what was going on at Beetle's. Well, she knew now that they did all know, all except her, so she was the only fool.

'Story?' she said, thinking that was one point which wouldn't make her look too dense. 'Do you mean someone will write it?'

He nodded. 'A journalist, and I'll do the pictures. Bit by bit the readers will see you becoming transformed, as you buy more fashionable clothes and get to know people here in London. At that point we're going to be approached by model agencies, they'll all be competing to get you. But I shall insist that I take all the photographs.'

He said he already had a journalist lined up, and that tomorrow they would start working on her arrival in London. He asked her to go and get dressed in whatever she'd worn the day she first came to the city.

'This is it,' she said as she came out of the bedroom wearing jeans and a white sleeveless blouse. 'I haven't really got to wear this though, have I? The jeans are horrible ones.'

Mark had to stifle a laugh; she really did look as though she'd come up from the sticks. The jeans were the cheap kind from Millet's, and fitted where they touched; the blouse was rayon and shapeless.

'You look just how I want you to look,' he said. 'Except I want you to part your hair in the middle and put it in bunches.'

Her expression of horror proved she hadn't worn it that way for a very long time and didn't ever want to be seen like that again.

'I know best,' he said gently. 'It's kind of acting, Jojo. I'll be taking these pictures on a crowded station, I want you to look lost and forlorn – I'm sure you did look that way when you first arrived.'

She couldn't argue with that, she could remember how desperate she'd felt when she was sitting on the wall in Ladbroke Grove before Fee spoke to her. At least he wasn't suggesting taking her off to some studio where anything might happen.

'How will I get paid?' she asked, more out of bravado and to prove she wasn't a complete fool than really wanting to know at this point.

'I shall pay your rent when it comes due next. I can't give you money like Beetle does. But if you want to carry on doing a few more sessions with him each week, that's all right with me.'

'I can't go back there,' she said in alarm, just the thought of it made her tearful. 'I'd already planned that I wasn't going to.'

Mark smiled. That's what he'd hoped she'd say. He didn't want Beetle getting wind of any of this just yet. By the time he did, he'd be under police surveillance, if not arrested. That was all to be part of the story.

'Well, that's fine, there's always waitresses needed in the King's Road, you could do a few days' work a week for pocket money.'

'You'll really pay my rent?' she asked. 'It's a hundred pounds a month!'

'Yes, I'll pay it, but it will be a loan until you start earning big money again. I don't think it will be very long, just as long as you do as I say and keep all this to yourself.'

'I haven't got anyone to tell,' she said, and the thought of that made her want to cry again.

Mark saw her lips tremble and he realized that was entirely true. 'You will make new friends soon,' he said, momentarily feeling a little sorry for her. 'There will come a time when you'll be very glad to escape up here on your own, I promise you. But I've got to go now. Tomorrow afternoon at half past four I want you to go to Paddington station, dressed just like I said, except you can put a cardigan on as it's likely to be chilly. No makeup other than a bit of mascara, and put some things in your case to make it heavy. I'll meet you there.'

It was quarter past five when Mark arrived at the station; he'd delayed his arrival purposely, knowing she'd get into a panic when she couldn't see him. The station was very busy as the first rush of commuters made their way home, and as always at this time of day it was a dirty and unpleasant place to be.

He spotted her immediately; her hair was like a beacon. She was standing with her case by the newspaper stand looking completely bewildered. He had worn a raincoat, with his long hair tucked up beneath a trilby hat, as he didn't want her to notice him until he was good and ready. He took up a position by a coffee stall to take the first pictures with a zoom lens. He was stunned by how young and vulnerable she looked with her hair in bunches, yet he clicked away, delighted at how well his plan was working out.

Then a man approached Jojo. At first it seemed to Mark that he was merely asking her for directions or something harmless, for he was middle-aged and well dressed in a camel coat. But as he viewed the scene through his lens, he saw Jojo's eyes widen in shock, and she backed away in panic.

Mark knew it was time to reveal himself, but he found he was rooted to the spot, almost enjoying Jojo's distress as he photographed it. She was wringing her hands, alternating between looking up at the clock and around her in fear.

From Mark's vantage point he could almost sense the predators around her, a man in his mid-twenties eyeing up a handbag left on top of a suitcase, a scruffily dressed older man wandering apparently aimlessly, but his eyes shifting from side to side. He wondered how many men were lurking around the station looking out for young girls and boys on their own, ready to offer them an ostensibly helping hand which could very well turn out to be the ruin of those young people.

Jojo moved, carrying her case over to a corner and then sitting on the top of it. At that point Mark was just about to walk over to her, when he saw through his lens that she was crying.

He felt only delight to get the pitiful picture he'd been hoping for, not a shred of sympathy that she'd be feeling let down again, or that it might be running through her mind that he was going to renege on paying her rent too. He kept clicking the camera as he walked over to her, his heart pounding because he knew he'd caught images that were potential prize-winners. Then all at once she looked up, saw him walking towards her, and, perhaps not recognizing him as Mark, but thinking he was another pervert about to try to force his attentions on her, she flew at him, her fists raised in anger.

'Fuck off, you dirty bastard,' she screamed at him, almost knocking the camera from his hands.

'It's only me, Jojo,' he said, sidestepping her. 'I'm sorry I kept you waiting. I got held up.'

She seemed to shrink before his eyes, all fight gone. Tears had washed tracks of mascara down her cheeks; she looked nearer ten than fifteen. 'I thought . . .' she said, but cut off what she was going to say. 'I was scared,' she added lamely.

'Let's go and have a cup of tea,' Mark said, only too aware of people watching them. 'I've got all the pictures I need, your job is over for today.'

He thought she'd be pleased, but instead she looked cheated and indignant, her eyes flashing with fire he hadn't seen before. 'You took pictures when I didn't know?' she asked, and her voice shook. 'I wouldn't have been looking my best!'

'You looked just perfect to me,' he said, and put his hand on her shoulder in an attempt at showing some affection. 'Now, let's have some tea and cake.'

Chapter Thirteen

Ellen saw her father's old truck parked outside Truro station and ran towards it through the rain. Her small suitcase was heavy with Christmas presents, banging against her legs as she ran. But as she got closer to the truck she knew there was something badly wrong, her father's face was taut with anger.

A cold chill ran down her spine. Had he found out about the baby somehow?

'Hello, Dad,' she said nervously as she opened the truck door. She supposed if he got too nasty with her she could go and stay with the Peters. They wouldn't turn her away at Christmas. 'Is something wrong? You look awfully fierce.'

'It's bloody Josie,' he snapped. 'She's shamed us all.'

Ellen's last visit home had been back in August. Since then she'd received two letters from Josie. Her first reaction was one of hurt, as Josie hadn't asked anything about her baby. Not what sex it was, its weight or how Ellen had coped with giving it up. All she wrote about was herself.

But reminding herself Josie was only fifteen, still a child really, Ellen put the hurt aside and was pleased for her sister that she'd managed to get into modelling. She sounded happy in London, and the lack of address on the letters was understandable, given Josie's fear that Violet might turn up on her doorstep. It was sad for Ellen to think she couldn't write back, but she had taken Dr Fordham's advice to get on with her own life, and if Josie didn't feel she could trust her, well that was her problem.

Thoughts of the baby still tormented her, and she often cried at night over her, wishing there had been a way she could have kept her. But once Catherine was six months old, she'd had to sign the final papers and the adoption was then legal and binding.

Shortly after that she had a letter from the adoptive couple, sent via Dr Fordham. That letter gave her far more than she'd ever hoped for, every little detail: what she ate, that she had three teeth and more coming, and that she was a happy, placid baby who smiled and gurgled all the time.

Aside from all the detail, Ellen was deeply touched by the way they thanked her for what they called 'her gift to them'. They said Catherine had given them more happiness than they could measure and they understood at what cost to her. They said that they sincerely hoped she too would find happiness and success in her life, and that when Catherine was old enough to understand they intended to tell her she had been adopted.

There were also three photographs, one taken in a studio, the other two in their home. Catherine was as fat as butter now, with a few tufts of hair sticking up and a wide, gleeful smile. Those photographs meant everything to Ellen, for they bore out all that Catherine's new parents had said, and more. She could look at them whenever she wanted, and although it would always be painful to know she'd allowed her child to be taken from her, she knew she had secured Catherine a far better life than she could have given her.

Now she was able to look ahead, for it was done and there was no going back. In the spring she intended to start to look around for another job, perhaps with children in a residential home. While she knew the Sandersons weren't going to be very pleased, as they'd come to rely on her completely, she wasn't going to let that stop her. She felt she was entitled to a job that had set hours so she could go out or away for a weekend without having to beg for it. She also thought she deserved more than the three pounds a week pocket money she got now.

As the truck roared away, Ellen turned to her father. 'Shamed us? Whatever has she done?' she asked, not only relieved that it wasn't her that was in trouble, but a little amused at his old-fashioned turn of phrase. 'Shamed us all' smacked of Victorian melodrama.

A year influenced by the Sandersons' modern outlook, plus reading extensively on childcare and development, had made Ellen look closely at the way she had been brought up. While she didn't feel hard done by, she thought most child psychologists would consider her and Josie lucky to have turned out so well adjusted.

'What's she done?' her father roared over the noise of the truck engine. 'Haven't you seen the paper?'

It was too noisy in the truck to get the full story, but as soon as they got to Beacon Farm her father thrust the previous Sunday's paper at her. It wasn't the paper the Sandersons read, but one of the more down-market tabloids. Ellen was shocked to see a large picture of Josie looking very forlorn on a London railway station. She was sitting on her suitcase crying. The headline above it said *Do you know this girl?* Then there was an article which stated that the award-winning photographer Mark Kinsale had taken the picture and was now haunted by what might have become of her.

As Ellen read on about the many youngsters who flocked to the big cities, her heart began to pound with fear for her sister. According to the article they were targets for unscrupulous employers, usually in catering or in the dress-manufacturing sweatshops and, more frightening still, in the Soho sex industry. It said the only places they could afford to live were shared rooms in some of London's worst slum areas, where they could easily be induced into crime to supplement their low wages.

'I rang that bloody paper and they wouldn't help me,' her father raged, while Violet stared stony-faced at Ellen as if it was somehow her fault. 'They said she must have been unhappy at home to run away. How does that make me look?'

'I can't see why you think she's shamed you though,' Ellen said. 'They haven't said she's done anything wrong, have they? She sounded well and happy in the two letters I've had. She's been gone nearly six months now, so this picture is an old one.'

'So you know where she is then?' Violet pushed past Albert and stuck her face right up to Ellen's. 'She didn't put an address on our letters.'

'Nor mine,' Ellen said, wishing she hadn't come home now. 'I haven't any idea where she is. She said she had lots of new friends now and she was doing some modelling.'

Ellen's previously good spirits plummeted as Violet raged about her daughter and once again said she held Ellen responsible. All at once Ellen knew she had to fight back or get this kind of treatment every time she came home. Her father was silent now but he still had a thunderous expression and she thought he should at least have asked how she was getting on in her job.

'Don't take it out on me or I'll be off too,' she finally said when she could stand it no longer. 'It isn't my fault at all, and well you know it. Look to yourself if you want someone to blame.'

Violet moved to clout her, but Ellen was too quick and moved out of reach. 'Don't you dare,' she exploded. 'Lay one hand on me and I'll be out that door for good.'

After she had gone up to her room, Ellen giggled to herself about Violet's shocked expression. She wished she'd had the guts to stand up to her a long time ago. She couldn't make Violet love her, but she might have won her respect.

Later that evening, once all the preparations for Christmas dinner had been made, Ellen studied the newspaper article again. She thought it strange that Josie had her hair in bunches, she hadn't worn it like that since she

214

was eight or nine. It was also odd that she was at a station, when it was common knowledge she'd gone up to London in a car. Then there was the question of the time gap. If this picture had worried the photographer so much, how come it took him six months to show it to the paper?

As her parents seemed to have calmed down a little, and were now sitting in the parlour in front of the fire with a large whisky each, Ellen thought she would tell them her opinion.

'I don't believe any of it,' she said. 'It's some kind of a set-up. That picture looks staged to me.'

Ellen wasn't exactly surprised that they didn't agree with her. They were simple people who knew nothing of life outside Cornwall. She didn't know much more herself; she certainly didn't know anything about the workings of newspapers and journalists. All she had was a hunch.

Christmas passed quietly and uneventfully, aside from Ellen noticing her parents seemed to be drinking quite a lot. They had never to her knowledge had drink in the house in the past, and although it was quite normal for any household to get some in for Christmas, she had the feeling this was more than that.

Maybe it was a way of dealing with their disappointment in their children, or some kind of mutual comfort and support. It certainly seemed to have stopped them being as nasty to one another as they used to be. As it did seem to be mellowing them, or at least creating some sort of buffer between them, Ellen was all for it.

She had to return to Bristol on Sunday, the day after Boxing Day. That morning there was another article in the paper related to the one the previous week. This time there were pictures of young girls who worked as striptease artists in Soho. It seemed as if they were going to do a series of stories about the exploitation of youngsters who arrived in London. Right at the bottom of the article there was the picture of Josie again, with the same plea that if anyone knew where she was, to contact the paper.

'If they really cared,' Ellen pointed out to her father, 'they wouldn't have been so off-hand with you. They've got something up their sleeve, I'm sure of it.'

Ellen was very glad to go back to Bristol that afternoon. Apart from Violet's constant barbed comments and her father's sullenness, it was so cold and comfortless at the farm. Clearly she'd been softened up by central heating, but she couldn't understand why her parents were so miserly with wood for the fire, and didn't do something about the windows and doors to stop the terrible draughts everywhere. She wondered what would happen when they got really old. She wished she could find it in her not to care.

Over the next two weeks there were more articles about runaway youngsters in the same Sunday paper. Then at the end of January there was a large picture of Josie wearing a man's shirt and very little else.

'Found!' was the headline. Mark Kinsale had tracked her down to a studio in West London where she and many other girls were posing for men who only pretended to be photographers.

Ellen's first thought wasn't one of dismay. Josie looked so adorable and pretty she couldn't help but feel a surge of pride. Yet as she read on her pride did turn to anxiety. It all sounded so terribly seedy.

Later that day her father rang her from the village phone box. He wasn't used to phones and he shouted down it, nearly perforating Ellen's eardrums. 'Did you see it?' he kept asking, even though she kept telling him she had. 'It'll be the talk of the village by tonight.'

There was nothing much Ellen could say to calm him down.

When she showed the paper to Mr and Mrs Sanderson, they didn't seem shocked at all. 'Don't get all worked up

216

about it,' Roger said. 'Newspapers do features like this to sell papers, they exaggerate and they exploit. You can bet your life this is all hatched up between the photographer and the paper. If that Mark Kinsale was on the level, when he found Josie he'd have packed her off on the first train home, not photographed her again.'

'But why would they do all this?' Ellen asked. She felt confused by their attitude being so far removed from her father's.

'I'd say Kinsale thinks he can make money out of her,' Shirley said thoughtfully. 'He's hooking the public with this picture, and you can bet your boots it won't be the last one. A pound to a penny he thinks he's got another Twiggy or Jean Shrimpton on his hands. I'd say he has too, she's prettier than either of them.'

Over the next few months Ellen saw that Roger and Shirley were right, for pictures of Josie kept appearing in newspapers and magazines. They played it up as a sort of Cinderella story, the poor little farm girl who'd come to the big city to seek her fortune. While Ellen enjoyed seeing pictures of Josie, or Jojo as they called her, in London's Carnaby Street, kitted out in outrageous clothes, she was repelled and horrified by what they were saying about her home life.

According to the press, Josie had run away from cruelty and severe hardship. Someone had taken pictures of the farm, and they'd gone out of their way to make it look sinister. Violet appeared in one, and she looked even more of a dirty harridan than she did in real life, clearly unaware she was being photographed as she fed the chickens.

Ellen wanted to be glad for Josie as it really looked as if she was going to attain her childhood dream and become a famous model. But she felt ashamed of her sister too for being so disloyal as to allow her parents to be shown in such a bad light.

Her father didn't telephone Ellen again, and only wrote

very brief notes which never mentioned Josie. But Ellen heard from Mrs Peters that Violet was distraught, and Albert had become even more of a recluse, not even going to the pub at the weekends. Mavis Peters also said that Violet had come to her, pleading for help. Mavis had helped her write a letter to Josie care of the Sunday paper that had started it all. In this letter she'd begged Josie to let her know where she lived, saying she was frantically worried about her.

Ellen was afraid that Josie had cut her out of her new life too, as there were no more letters or cards. Yet she collected all the press clippings about her sister, and the first few magazine advertisements for shampoo she modelled for, and pasted them in a scrapbook. That way she felt she was still close to her.

Two letters arrived for Ellen on the same morning in July. One was from a school for handicapped children in South Bristol, offering her a position as general assistant in September. The other was from Josie. Both thrilled her.

She hadn't thought she'd get the job at the school, because she had no relevant experience. Yet the headmistress had recommended her over twelve other applicants.

But Josie's letter, this time with an address in Chelsea, and even a telephone number, almost eclipsed the job offer.

Dear Ellen, she read. *I bet you're really angry with me for not writing, or letting you know where I was. But I was scared to in case you told Mum. You know what she's like and if she came up here it would spoil everything. Promise me faithfully you won't tell her yet? I still can't face her and I expect both her and Dad are hopping mad about the stuff in the papers about them. I didn't say all that to anyone, most of it came about because Dad was such a pest ringing up the* Mirror *and making himself sound like an ogre.*

Anyway, I'm doing just fine, I've got a fab flat in a posh

218

*part of London and so many lovely new clothes. Mark says
I'm going to be The Face of the Sixties, he's my photographer
and manager. He takes me to lots of smart places, and he says
everyone thinks I'm gorgeous.*

*But I miss you. If you aren't too angry with me will you
come up to London for the weekend? I could show you King's
Road and Carnaby Street, you'll love it, it's really exciting.*
My love
Josie

Ellen read and reread both letters several times. Wonderful as they both were, she knew Shirley wasn't going to be very pleased about either. Ellen hadn't asked for any time off since Christmas because she had no desire to go home and face her parents. So Shirley and Roger had got used to her being there every single weekend to look after the boys. While they couldn't really refuse her one weekend to see her sister in London, as soon as she told them she had another job for September they were likely to be difficult.

In the eighteen months she'd been working for the Sandersons Ellen had gradually come to see they weren't such kind, big-hearted people as she'd first thought. While it had been good of them to give her a job and a home when few others would have done so, with hindsight she could see they were really only thinking of themselves.

Once they'd got her there, and saw she cared for their boys as tenderly as if they were her own, they hadn't wanted to lose her. That was the real reason they'd suggested she stayed with them instead of going to the mother-and-baby home. Shirley's advice that it was less cruel to hand over Catherine in the hospital was based on self-interest, not the truth, or concern for Ellen's feelings or the future for her and her baby. She had been manipulated, robbed of all choice to ensure the Sandersons had continuing help around the house.

Ellen had observed that Shirley was not at all maternal.

Although she did love her boys, business was far more important to her. She was already expanding the wholesale company and had future plans that relied on everything running smoothly at home. She would find it impossible to get anyone else prepared to live in a box-room and be nanny, cook, housekeeper, cleaner and gardener for three pounds a week.

Ellen had often had to bite her tongue when Shirley went off to work even when one of the boys was ill, or when she expected her to cook a meal for guests on top of all her other duties. Lately she'd been coming home later and later, sometimes long after the children were in bed. Ellen knew that from the moment she gave her notice, Shirley was going to sulk and imply she was letting her down.

On top of that, Ellen would have to find somewhere of her own to live in South Bristol for when she began her new job, but while she was working such long hours, based on the other side of the city, she didn't see how it would be possible.

After mulling all the problems over for a couple of days, Ellen could see that the best way to solve them all was to find a temporary cheap room somewhere in nearby Clifton. She could easily get a clerical or waitressing job for the remainder of the summer, and find somewhere permanent to live for September. That way she could go and see Josie for a weekend, and she could earn more money.

Just after clearing away the evening meal, Ellen took the plunge and told Shirley she wanted to leave. It was a Monday night, the boys were in bed, Roger had gone into the sitting-room to watch the news and Shirley was in a good mood because she'd won a contract earlier in the day for supplying food to a chain of hotels in the west.

Ellen was careful how she broke the news. She mentioned first how good Shirley and Roger had been to her, but that she felt the time had come when she had to move on.

Shirley looked much younger than she usually did that evening as she'd changed into pale blue slacks and a gingham shirt and combed out her beehive when she'd come home from work. But as Ellen began talking, her previously cheerful expression changed.

'You want to leave? Just like that, after all we've done for you?' she snapped at Ellen. 'You ungrateful little baggage!'

'I'm not ungrateful at all,' Ellen retorted. 'I've worked hard for you for eighteen months, but I want something more than being a mother's help. I've been offered a job that's a real career.'

'If you wanted a career you shouldn't have got yourself pregnant by the first man who came along.'

Ellen's heart hardened at that spiteful remark. 'Don't you think I paid enough for that mistake?' she said coldly. 'But I'm damned if I'll spend the rest of my life paying for it again and again. I'll be leaving next week.'

'Oh, will you now?' Shirley's eyes narrowed with malice. 'Suppose I choose not to give you a reference?'

'It won't matter to me if you don't,' Ellen said, not caring now if she had to be rude. 'They've given me the job on the strength of my ability and on the word of Dr Fordham. She vouched for me and said how well I looked after your children.'

'Fat lot you care about them.' Shirley's voice rose higher in anger. 'Who's supposed to look after them now?'

'You could look after them yourself,' Ellen said tartly.

With that Shirley seemed to swell up, her face turning purple with anger. 'That's it,' she shouted. 'You can go right now. I don't want you in the house another minute.'

Ellen's heart plummeted. It was eight in the evening and she hadn't got anywhere to go yet. She'd planned to find a place on her Saturday afternoon off. Yet as she looked at Shirley she saw an expression so like the one she'd often seen on Violet's face. Pure malice.

'Right, I'll just go and pack then,' she said. She wasn't going to back down, even if she had to walk the streets tonight. Her days of being subservient were over.

Less than fifteen minutes later she was walking up the hill towards the Downs and Clifton which lay beyond them. She had little more with her than when she'd left Cornwall – just new clothes that had replaced her old ones, and a few personal items she'd bought to make her bedroom more homely. But the case was heavy and it was starting to rain. She thought Roger might have come and said something to her before she left. He had always been more considerate and appreciative than his wife, but he'd stayed in the sitting-room throughout the row, and she thought he was cowardly.

But she was most saddened by not being allowed to say goodbye to the boys. She had grown to love them, and she was going to miss them terribly. Yet she bit back her tears and walked on determinedly.

She thought of telephoning Dr Fordham, but dismissed the idea immediately. She wasn't going to beg for a bed for the night, she still had some pride.

It was another two weeks before Ellen was able to go and visit Josie. On the evening she'd been thrown out of the Sandersons' home, she had got the local paper and seen that several hotels were advertising for live-in chambermaids. She rang several of them, although by then it was very late. All but one said she could come for an interview the following morning, but the St Vincent's Rocks Hotel in Clifton sounded so desperate that she felt able to suggest she could call on them immediately.

They took her on there and then, at six pounds a week all found, and gave her a tiny room up in the attics. That night, as she looked out of her window and saw the Suspension Bridge across the Avon Gorge all lit up in the rain, she felt happier than she had for a long time. She was free for the very first time in her life.

As the coach drove into the bus station at Victoria, Ellen's stomach was full of butterflies, afraid Josie might not be there to meet her as she'd promised. She had never been to London before, and she hadn't expected it to be quite so vast, or so busy with traffic and people. But as she stepped down from the coach, Josie came whirling through the crowds and enveloped her in a tight hug.

'I was afraid you might miss the bus or not be able to come after all,' she blurted out. 'I've thought of nothing else all week but you coming.'

For a moment or two Ellen could only stare at her sister in wonder. She looked so grown-up and beautiful in an emerald-green mini-dress with matching shoes. It was one thing to see her pictures, she knew that someone did her hair and makeup and chose her clothes for her, but she hadn't expected her to look like a fashion plate in the flesh.

'You look so gorgeous,' she said reverently, then blushed, realizing how frumpy she looked in comparison. 'I should have bought something new to wear,' she added.

Josie giggled and looked Ellen up and down, as if agreeing that her cotton skirt was far too long and her blouse only suitable for the dustbin. 'You can wear some of my things,' she said. 'You won't believe how many clothes I've got now, they often give me stuff I model.'

On the bus back to Chelsea and her flat, Josie never drew breath once, pointing out sights, talking about restaurants and pubs she'd been to, and she mentioned Mark in almost every sentence.

It was only as they got off the bus that she asked how Ellen's job was.

'Dead easy,' Ellen grinned. 'Especially after how hard I was working at the Sandersons'. I only work from seven in the morning till twelve, doing the rooms and stuff. Then I get the afternoons off, go back to turn the beds down around seven, and that's it for the day.'

'So what do you do with all that time off?' Josie asked.

Ellen shrugged. 'Go round to flat-letting places to see what they've got, read, sunbathe on the Downs. Look in the shops. There's another girl there called Anne, we often go out together in the evenings.'

'What, to pubs or night-clubs?' Josie asked.

'No,' Ellen giggled. 'Just for a walk, or to the pictures. We aren't old enough for that sort of stuff yet.'

'Neither am I,' Josie said airily. 'But I go to them all the time with Mark.'

Ellen was really impressed by Josie's sunny, spacious flat, although there wasn't much furniture. 'Where do you hang your washing?' she asked, and Josie got a fit of giggles.

'Don't be daft, Ell,' she said. 'People in Chelsea don't hang washing out. They take it to the laundrette.'

Ellen wanted to know what that was, and how much it cost, but Josie wasn't interested in talking about such mundane things.

'Get something out to wear,' she insisted, pointing to the wardrobe. 'And put some makeup on, then we'll go down the King's Road.'

Ellen wasn't sure she had the courage to wear the dress Josie eventually selected for her. It was pale lemon with cut-away shoulders, and so short it barely covered her bottom, but she was pretty certain her sister wouldn't be seen dead with anyone looking dowdy, so she said nothing. She made no comment either when Josie insisted she did her makeup for her. She never normally wore anything more than lipstick and mascara, and she thought the dark eyeliner was too much. But she was in London now after all.

It turned out to be the most wonderful day Ellen had ever spent. All down the King's Road there were boutiques that sold amazing clothes, all too expensive for Ellen to buy anything, but it was fun just to look at them and try a few things on.

They went into coffee bars and watched other people walking by, and they all amazed Ellen too. All the girls wore minis, as short as the one Josie had insisted she wore, and there were no beehive hairstyles here like in Bristol. Everyone had sleek, bouncy, loose styles, short like Cilla Black's, or long and flowing. The men were very different too. Few went in for the Mod style Ellen was used to – very short hair, heavy boots and jeans, or sharply tailored suits and winkle-pickers. Here the men wore their hair longer, influenced strongly by the Beatles, and their clothes were more individual – coloured shirts, and jeans so tight Ellen wondered how they could sit down. She and Josie attracted a great deal of attention, and several times Josie was recognized as Jojo the model.

'I expect I could have the pick of any man walking along here,' Josie said at one point in the afternoon as they stopped for another coffee at a place with tables outside in the sun.

'I'm sure you could.' Ellen smiled, a little embarrassed at her sister's high opinion of herself. She had plenty of admiring glances herself, and she was enjoying it, in fact for the first time since Catherine was born she felt she would actually like to have a boyfriend. 'So why don't you pick someone then? Go on, I dare you!'

'I can't, because I'm in love with Mark,' Josie replied, and for the first time during the day she looked uncertain.

'So he's your boyfriend then?' Ellen wanted to meet and get to like this man she'd heard so much about, but so far she had only formed the opinion there was something fishy about him.

'Not exactly,' Josie said, and her eyes dropped. 'Well, not in the way you mean, kissing and stuff. He does everything for me, manages me, gets me work and takes the pictures. But that's all.'

This came as a bit of a relief to Ellen. She had made it her business to find out about Mark back in Bristol, and she knew he was in his mid-thirties and divorced. There was a great deal to admire about his work; she'd managed to find a book at the library with some of his award-winning photographs in it. But she was still waiting for an explanation as to how he really got involved with her sister, and why.

'Tell me everything that happened after you left the farm,' she suggested.

Josie told her a great deal, about the awful room she'd had, waitressing, and then how she got into working at the fake photographic studio. Then she explained how Mark came to her rescue.

'He said he was going to make me a big star,' she said with a toss of her head, making her corkscrew curls tumble about her face. 'We're getting there too, I'm in great demand already.'

'So how much money are you making?' Ellen asked. She wanted to let Josie know how much she had hurt their parents and berate her for not letting her know where she was earlier, but she didn't want to start playing big sister just yet.

Josie shrugged. 'I only get pocket money now, Mark sees to the rent and everything for me.'

Ellen knew nothing whatsoever about what models earned, but she reckoned it had to be quite a bit. She didn't like the sound of this at all, and said so.

'Don't try and make out you know everything,' Josie snapped at her. 'Mark isn't pocketing the money if that's what you are thinking. It takes a long time for it to come in. Besides, he gave me twenty-five pounds yesterday so I could treat you to meals and stuff.'

Ellen didn't want to upset Josie so she said nothing. But later, when they went to a hamburger place, it occurred to her while Josie was crowing about how plain most other models were when you saw them without makeup, that her sister still hadn't asked her anything about when she had her baby.

She waited until late that evening when they'd gone back to the flat. They had been in a pub where they'd both had three half pints of cider. That was quite enough for Ellen, but Josie had insisted on buying a flagon to take home too.

They each had a glass sitting on the bed, and suddenly Ellen had to speak out. 'You haven't asked about my baby,' she said in a small voice. 'Have you forgotten that's why I went to work for the Sandersons?'

Josie gave her a blank look. 'You really had one then?' she said. 'I thought when you didn't say anything in your letters to me when I was still at home that it was a false alarm.'

'I was over four months pregnant when I left, how could that be a false alarm?'

Josie had the grace to look crestfallen then. 'Well, I told you that it was all right to say anything in your letters because Mum wasn't reading them.'

'I didn't dare take the risk,' Ellen said. 'I put the telephone number on the letters, I expected you to ring me from a call box around the time Catherine was due.'

'Catherine!' Josie looked surprised and almost ashamed. 'It was a girl then?'

Ellen nodded, waiting for Josie to ask some more questions, but instead she changed the subject and started talking about what kind of furniture she was going to buy once she got some big money.

'I'd like a couple of those really modern big round chairs like eggs, that swivel around,' she said. 'They've got one at the model agency.'

'I'd like to stick you in a swivelling chair and spin you round and round until you are sick,' Ellen snapped. 'Don't you bloody well care what happened to my baby and me? Have you got any idea what it was like?'

Josie's eyes opened wide. 'Well, you had it adopted, didn't you? It's over now.'

'It will *never* be over,' Ellen said fiercely. 'She's on my mind all the time, she probably will be forever. You could show some sympathy. She was your niece after all.'

Josie got up from the bed and wandered off into the kitchen to fill up her glass. 'You'll get married before long and have another one,' she called back through the door.

On the coach the following evening as Ellen travelled back to Bristol, she thought about how callous Josie had been, and decided it was because she was too young to comprehend the heartbreak of giving away her own flesh and blood. She'd been so callous about her own mother too; she just didn't care about Violet's feelings.

Ellen couldn't find it in her to wish heartbreak on her sister so she'd discover what it was like. Josie thought she had the world at her feet, and Ellen fervently hoped she would find real fame and fortune.

Chapter Fourteen

1966

'Come on, Jojo,' Mark pulled back the bed covers and forced her to sit up, 'get yourself together. We've got the *Vogue* shoot today.'

'I'm too tired,' Josie said, and tried to get back under the covers.

It was mid-November, and dark still, but Josie knew it had to be seven in the morning if Mark had come to collect her.

He yanked her up again, more roughly this time, and forced her to take the cup of coffee he'd made. 'Drink that now and take those,' he said, indicating a couple of bright red pills on the bedside table. 'By the time you've had a bath you'll be on top of the world.'

Josie forced her eyelids apart; they were gummed up with a combination of glue from false eyelashes and mascara. She had meant to take her makeup off before going to bed, but she'd been too drunk to bother. She reached eagerly for the pills Mark had put down, popped them into her mouth and washed them down with coffee.

Mark stood in the doorway looking scornfully at her. 'You look disgusting,' he said. 'If you don't pull yourself together I'll drop you and find someone else.'

Josie was still too sleepy to make any retort, and besides, she didn't believe he would ever drop her. She was too famous. Absolutely everyone wanted her, the fashion magazines and the big companies who wanted her to advertise their shampoos, makeup and perfume.

But she was worried about how horrible he was being to her these days. He didn't even seem to want to sleep with her any more. Last night he'd brought her home drunk from a press party, carried her up the stairs, then flung her down on the bed and left without even a good-night kiss.

He went off to run her bath, and she got gingerly out of bed and pulled on a dressing-gown. Looking in the mirror, she could see he was right. She did look disgusting. Her skin was muddy and she had dark circles under her eyes.

By the time she'd had her bath and washed her hair, she felt better, for the speed was beginning to work. She put on clean underwear, jeans and a sweater. There was no need to put on makeup or arrange her hair, they'd do that at the shoot.

'If you'd just give me a few days' rest, I wouldn't need pills to wake me up and more to send me to sleep,' she said wistfully, as she gave her hair a rough rub with the towel. 'Let me go down to Ellen's for a few days?'

Mark was lounging in her one and only chair, watching her contemptuously. He did that all the time now; Josie felt sometimes that he hated her. Yet she couldn't quite see why; the maroon leather jacket and snakeskin boots he was wearing were evidence of how much money he was making from her.

'Are you stupid? You work when it comes in. Right now it's still coming in thick and fast, but it won't for ever. You can rest then.'

Josie's eyes prickled with tears. There were times when she wished she'd never met him. Sometimes she even wished she'd never left Cornwall. It was exciting to see her face on big hoardings, in every magazine and newspaper, and to be recognized on the street, but it wasn't any fun being bullied and forced to dance like a puppet on a string, day after day.

It had been like this for over two years, and what had she got to show for it? She was a seventeen-year-old star, but she was still in the same old flat with no furniture and a wardrobe stuffed with clothes that she rarely got the chance to show off. And her parents had disowned her.

If it weren't for Ellen she'd have no one at all. Mark only said he loved her when he wanted her to do something for him.

'Leave your hair, it will dry in the car,' he said impatiently. 'Put on some shoes, for God's sake! Do I have to tell you everything?'

The shoot that day was in a mansion out in Hertfordshire. There was a time when Josie had been interested enough to ask who lived in these places, when she wanted to look around and marvel at her surroundings. But she no longer cared about any of that. It was just a job, the place a backdrop, she might as well be back at Beetle's studio – at least she wasn't harangued all day there: 'Move this way. Put your head back. Arms up. Arms down. To the side. Shake your hair.'

As they drove out of London Josie stared listlessly out of the window at the steel-grey sky. She was trapped, and she didn't know how to escape. She had read in a magazine that she was reputed to be one of the highest-paid models in the world, but precious little money came her way. Mark said she shouldn't believe all she read, and that after deducting her rent and expenses there wasn't much left. She didn't believe him, but there wasn't anyone else she could ask about it, Mark saw to that. He never left her side when there were press about, all interviews were directed by him. She didn't go anywhere without his say-so, and even though he left her alone most nights in her flat, she couldn't go out without him finding out. She was too well known.

He owned her, body and soul, and there was nothing she could do about it.

Her mother's face came into her mind, and tears welled in her eyes as she remembered their last parting. Mark had been right in saying that a mother like Violet would only bring her down, but why did he force her to get rid of her in such a cruel way?

Last February Josie had had flu. She was so ill she could barely get out of bed to use the toilet. When Ellen unexpectedly telephoned from a call box and said it was half-term and she was down in Cornwall, Josie felt pangs of homesickness, and said she'd give anything to see her mother.

Josie hadn't for one moment thought Violet would react to that message. She had after all been instructed by Albert that she was to have nothing more to do with her daughter. Josie certainly didn't expect her to get on the next train to come and see her. Violet had only ever been to London once in her life, and that was with Dad, when they tried to get the *Mirror* to tell them where Josie was. They'd been brutally turned away from the newspaper offices then and both vowed they'd never return under any circumstances.

Yet Violet did come, despite everything, and found her way to the flat all on her own. Josie nearly died of shock when she opened the door, and she was mortified that her mother should find her in such a terrible mess. The whole flat was filthy; Josie hadn't had time or energy to clean it for weeks. There was no clean bed linen, there were heaps of dirty clothes everywhere, and not a thing in the entire flat to eat.

Violet just took over. She rushed out to the laundrette with all the washing, bought food, and then tucked Josie into a clean bed while she cooked a meal. Josie was happy to be her little girl again, to be cared for.

Violet stayed for four days and in that time they talked to each other as they never had before. Josie apologized properly for running away and not contacting her mother. Violet said she was sorry for being so nasty sometimes, and explained that it had never really been directed at Josie, it was because things were so bad with Albert.

Mark hadn't been round since the day Josie went down

with flu, when he'd given her a box of aspirin and shot off hurriedly. He didn't even phone. Then when he turned up five days later and found Violet there, he was livid. He sent her out on an errand, and while she was gone he told Josie to get rid of her. She had to tell her mother to clear off and never come back, or he would find a new model. He promised too that she would never find work with anyone else, he'd see to it. He wouldn't even give her time to do it gently, it had to be done that day, on Violet's return, and he was going to stay to check she did it.

'You can't have that old bag hanging around you,' he said forcefully. 'Just look at her, Jojo, she's like a disease. And I know her sort, unless you are heavy with her she'll always be turning up, spoiling everything.'

Josie knew he was right. He was only voicing things she'd thought so many times in the past. She knew too that if she hadn't been so ill, she wouldn't have welcomed her mother's unexpected arrival anyway.

But knowing all that didn't make it any easier, for the only way to get rid of Violet was to be cruel. When she returned to the flat, Josie shouted at her, called her names and told her to fuck off out of her life forever because she was an embarrassment.

It was awful. She saw her mother sag visibly with hurt and disappointment. 'How can you be like this to me?' she whimpered. 'I'm your mother, I only wanted to look after you.'

Josie couldn't look at her, if she had she might have weakened. Instead she turned her face away and flung Violet's coat at her, saying that a mother who looked like her was far worse than no mother at all.

She was so ashamed once Violet had slunk out like a whipped dog. She knew only too well that she was her mother's whole reason for living. She was afraid for her having to make the long journey home alone in such a distraught state. She also knew when her father got to hear of what she'd done, he would never let her back in Beacon Farm.

Even Ellen, who had never liked Violet, was deeply shocked. She heard about it from Mrs Peters and was on the phone immediately asking Josie how she could be so ungrateful and wicked. Of course Josie made out she didn't care, she said Violet had it coming to her, but she did care really, she cried over it for days on end.

To make matters worse, Ellen felt so sorry for Violet that she began going home more often, and now it seemed they were becoming much closer. It was as though Violet had switched all the love she had once had for her real daughter to her stepdaughter.

'Damn Ellen,' Josie muttered.

'What's she done to you?' Mark asked. He had never met Ellen on the few visits she made to London; Josie always made sure he wasn't around. Mark made her feel so insecure that part of it was fear that he would like Ellen more than her, part was because she knew Ellen would tackle him about the money.

'Oh, she's just so bloody perfect,' Josie sighed. 'Flogging her guts out for those cripples. Keeping Mum and Dad happy, visiting the neighbours. Never puts a foot wrong.'

'I thought you said she was a bit of a goer?' Mark said. He was being nice again, as he always was when they had work in front of them. 'Always in the sack with someone?'

Josie *had* said that, but only because she didn't have a better way to describe how Ellen was with men. It was bizarre that her whiter-than-white sister loved sex. Anyone would expect that someone who'd given themselves to one man and been let down would be put off it. But not Ellen – soon after she found her little flat in South Bristol she began going out with men, and went to bed with them when she wanted to.

She talked about it quite candidly, though the subject only came up because she wanted to advise Josie to go on the pill, as she had. She said she liked men and sex, and she no longer believed in waiting for a fairy-tale romance. Josie had stayed with Ellen twice in the last year for a weekend. On both occasions she'd met the latest man in her sister's life. While she couldn't fancy either of them herself, she sensed something animal and earthy between them and Ellen. She even felt envious of the relaxed way Ellen was with them – she didn't dress herself up, didn't put on any show other than feeding them a nice dinner. There was a kind of happy glow around her, and it was obvious that both men adored her.

When Josie didn't reply to Mark's question, he looked sideways at her. 'You're jealous of her,' he said, and laughed. 'Why, because she's Miss Perfect with her worthy job, or because she's sexy and you aren't?'

That stung Josie, for there was a time when Mark used to tell her she was the sexiest girl he'd ever known. It was of course before he conned her into love-making by telling her it would help her to relax when he was photographing her. But then he'd said he loved her too, and he didn't act as if he did now. She wished so much that she had refused him, perhaps he'd have a bit of respect for her then. But when he crooked his finger, she obeyed him.

It happened for the first time on her sixteenth birthday. He took her for a Chinese meal, then back to her flat with a bottle of champagne. He sweet-talked her, telling her how beautiful she was, and describing the wonderful life they were going to have together.

Josie knew from other girls that the first time wasn't usually very good, so she didn't expect much. But suddenly he went from kissing her and telling her he loved her to brutality. He didn't even stop to undress her, or let her get into bed properly. He just got on top of her like a wild thing. He was so rough, pushing her legs apart, thrusting his fingers inside her so hard it hurt. And all the time he was saying crude, dirty things.

She truly became his property then; he took her whenever he felt like it. There was never a warm cuddle first, or any tender kisses, just animal behaviour, as though he was the stallion and she was the mare.

Pretending to like it seemed the only option. On a few occasions when she had tried to refuse him, he just got nasty and hit her, and then it took longer because he seemed to enjoy it more. So mostly she put on Oscar-winning performances of total bliss. But perhaps he wasn't fooled after all?

'Who says I'm not sexy?' she snapped. 'That's not what men in the street think. Don't you remember that news-paper article that said men all over England have pictures of me stuck up in their garages and sheds?'

'Just because you look sexy doesn't mean you are,' he said, and laughed. 'I think it's time I put you through a little test.'

'What kind of test?' Josie asked.

'Wait and see,' he said.

The test came when Josie had long forgotten that Mark had ever said he was going to set her one. In May the following year they went to the South of France for a photo shoot with six other models. Things had been very bad between her and Mark for months. She felt insecure because he was always saying he was going to drop her, and the more she tried to please him, the nastier he was.

He had gone from demanding sex practically every day to going weeks without as much as kissing her. And although this should have pleased her, she was afraid it meant he had someone else. He was always criticizing her too, saying she was stupid, lazy, that her Cornish accent irritated him, and that she did too many drugs.

It was true that they dominated her life. Sleeping pills at night, speed to wake her up in the mornings and cope with the pressure of work. She smoked pot or drank to mellow herself out, then took another sleeping pill at night to calm herself down. Yet Josie couldn't see how he could blame her for this, he'd introduced her to drugs in the first place, and he smoked joints all day, and snorted coke too.

When Mark did seem to be really concerned about the weight she was losing, and said he'd arranged this job as it would be something of a holiday, she thought he'd begun to realize how badly he'd been treating her. They would be staying at a luxury hotel, dining out with millionaires and film stars on their yachts, and she would also have time to lie in the sun and recuperate. In a rare moment of real tenderness he said she was very precious to him, he even agreed he was overworking her. He promised the hectic pace would slow down soon, that he'd arrange for her to have driving lessons and get her a car when they returned from France.

Josie was overjoyed at that. Ellen had already learned to drive and bought a car, and from what she said about her visits back to their parents, they were more impressed by the car than anything.

Josie often wondered how she'd get by if she didn't have Ellen. She was so utterly dependable, the only person in her life she knew she could rely on, whatever happened. She wrote every week, she would catch the train up to London whenever Josie asked her to, and Josie knew she could turn up at her flat at any time and always get a welcome. Not that she went very often, she wasn't organized enough to catch trains. But she did phone her at least once a fortnight, wherever she was working.

Ellen could be counted on to listen to her grievances, to be impressed when Josie had met someone famous, to collect up her press cuttings and stick them in an album. She was even trying to lay the ground for their parents to accept an apology from Josie and forgive her. But that was her all over, she liked her life nice and tidy, and it couldn't be, not when her sister wasn't welcome at home.

As Josie set off for France with Mark she was feeling confident and optimistic. Mark seemed to value her again, and once she could drive she could go down to Cornwall and put everything right there. Her parents might not be impressed with her pictures in the papers, but tangible evidence of success, like a car, and perhaps buying them some luxuries, was bound to change their opinion of her.

Yet as soon as the photo shoot started in St-Tropez, Josie felt inadequate. The other models were older and far more sophisticated than she was, stunningly beautiful girls who'd made their names on the catwalks of Paris and Milan. They were chilly with her, perhaps resentful that she hadn't paid her dues in gown showrooms and couture houses.

The hotel where they were staying and being photographed in evening dresses and ball-gowns was the grandest Josie had ever seen, with its white marble terraces, fantastic gardens, huge lounges and vast chandeliers. Maybe she wouldn't have felt so intimidated if the French press hadn't kept swarming round her, or if the hotel guests had been banned from the photo shoots. She felt so awkward, and for the first time in her life plain, as she watched the other models glide regally around as if they were born to such surroundings.

Normally she had no opportunity to drink while working, but here in a luxury hotel, she had only to wave her hand and a waiter brought her a cocktail. That and the heat made her drowsy and less receptive to instructions. She knew Mark was growing angry with her, but somehow she couldn't seem to do anything right.

On the third afternoon when the shoot was over, Josie ran off down to the beach and leapt gleefully into the sea for a swim. She had only been in for a few minutes when Mark appeared and ordered her out and back to the hotel.

'But why?' she kept asking. He'd said the trip was to be a holiday too.

'You can't risk getting sunburn until the whole shoot's over,' he said curtly. 'Now, go on up to your room, and put something fetching on, I'm bringing someone up to meet you.'

Mark never shared her room when they were working on location, he said it was because he had to treat all the models the same. This time Josie hadn't minded at all, for the room was beautiful, with a six-foot bed, a white marble floor and its own balcony overlooking the sea. It was nice to have it all to herself and not have to put up with Mark urging her into sex games.

She had just showered and changed into a white mini-dress, when a waiter called with a bottle of champagne for her. He opened it and poured her a glass, then left. Assuming it was Mark's way of making up to her for not letting her go swimming, Josie drank it down and poured herself another glass.

She had finished the whole bottle by the time Mark arrived, bringing with him a man he introduced as the Duke. He was a big Frenchman, with a large Roman nose and soft brown eyes, wearing a white linen suit.

Josie was too drunk and giggly to care whether he was a real duke or not. He was charming, kissing her hands and her cheeks and telling her how lovely she was in perfect English, and it didn't even cross her mind that it was odd for Mark to get them to meet in her room.

Another bottle of champagne arrived and they drank most of it, Josie having the lion's share, and then suddenly the Duke was urging her back on the bed and kissing her.

At first it seemed like a bit of fun, for Mark was sitting on the bed watching them and laughing. But as the Duke began unzipping her dress Josie grew alarmed and struggled.

'Don't be silly, Jojo,' Mark said reprovingly. 'I said I was going to set you a test to see how sexy you are. The Duke's got a reputation of being the best lover in France, so just lie back and enjoy it.'

In her fuddled state Josie couldn't tell whether the test was really to see if she enjoyed sex with another man better than with Mark, or if it was to see how loyal she was to him. But Mark seemed cross when she struggled, so she gave up and let the Duke make love to her.

It was lovely at first, he was far more gentle and sensuous than Mark, and a good kisser, so she closed her eyes to shut out Mark watching and just gave herself up to the pleasure of his probing fingers.

But suddenly she felt something cold and hard being pushed into her, and her eyes flew open. The Duke was naked now, and she could see he was hairy-chested with a pot-belly which almost hid his penis. He was kneeling up in front of her open legs and he was pushing what appeared to be her plastic shampoo bottle into her.

She looked at Mark in alarm, but he had his trousers open and he was masturbating as he watched. It was clear from his rapt expression that he wasn't going to take kindly to her calling a halt to the proceedings.

In that moment she saw how little she meant to him, yet at the same time she also knew that if she broke up this scene, he would abandon her altogether. Better, she thought, to play along with it. Mark might even get jealous and value her more. She forced herself to let out a deep moan of simulated pleasure as the Duke pushed the bottle into her. She arched her back and thumped her arms down on the bed as if in the grip of passion.

It hurt, but as she glanced towards Mark she saw he was flushed with excitement, his eyes screwed up and his mouth open. Her reward was getting the bottle shoved into her even harder, and it was all she could do not to scream out in pain.

'You like it, leetle one,' the Duke said, leering down at her as he pushed the bottle in harder still. He had an erection now too, but his penis was a lot smaller than Mark's.

'Fuck me with your cock,' she yelled out, thinking that was the only way out of it.

'Not yet, my pretty one,' he said, sweat running down his face. 'I like to see you take all this first.'

She didn't think there was room inside her for it to go any further, but still he forced it in, ramming it so hard that the pain went right through to her back.

'Enough!' she screamed out. 'I want your cock, now.'

All at once he was into her, but even though his penis was half the size of the bottle, she was so sore it still hurt terribly.

His rasping, laboured breath seemed to fill the room, and she bucked under him trying to speed him along. But he was in no hurry, grinning down at her, his sweat dripping on to her face. Mark was watching them, gradually moving closer and closer to her until the tip of his penis was by her cheek. Josie knew he wanted her to take it in her mouth, but she wouldn't, couldn't do that.

With a guttural roar from deep inside him, the Duke came, and at the same time Mark did too, and his semen spurted all over her mouth.

It was shameful enough during the act, but even worse to be left there on the bed naked, as the two men hurriedly got up.

'Thank you, madam,' the Duke said, giving a little bow before reaching for his clothes.

Josie couldn't bear even to look at Mark. She just hoped he would leave immediately and never come back.

'There's one more glass of champagne in the bottle,' he said as he opened the door to go. 'Enjoy!'

The door was hardly closed behind them when Josie began retching. She only just reached the lavatory in time. Again and again she vomited until there was nothing left but green bile, and the marble floor beneath her knees hurt her as badly as the bottle had.

She lay in a hot bath for hours, constantly sinking right under the water and staying there for as long as she could hold her breath. She had locked the room door from the inside so even a pass-key wouldn't let anyone in. She hoped she would lose consciousness and drown so her misery would end.

When she finally came out of the bathroom, she saw it was dark outside, and she could hear the sound of music, laughter and clinking glasses wafting in through the open balcony doors from the terrace three floors down. The lights festooned on trees and along the seashore looked so pretty against the blackness of the sky and sea, it made her break down and sob like a small child.

It had been said so often in the press that she had the world at her feet. Yet it seemed to her that her life was more like being in one of those ghost trains at a funfair, lurching from one frightening and sickening scene to another, unable to get out of the car.

What had she done to deserve such humiliation? How could Mark say he loved her, then force her to do that with another man?

She was tempted to pick up the telephone and ring Ellen, to tell her what had happened. But she couldn't. Ellen would tell her to pack her case and insist that she be given her ticket home immediately.

While the thought of walking away from Mark, the cameras and the other haughty models and the press was very appealing, she knew she'd pay dearly for it. The shoot had another two days to go and Mark would take his revenge by cutting her off from any further work. He'd stop paying her rent, and she'd be finished.

Mark came knocking on her door at midnight. By then Josie was all cried out, and she pulled on a long tee-shirt and opened the door readily, hoping for an apology.

Mark looked very distinguished in a black dinner jacket and a frilly dress-shirt, with the black tie hanging loose at his collar. His dark hair was slicked back into a pony-tail. 'Why have you been skulking up here all evening?' he asked coldly.

'You know why,' she said, turning away from him. 'How could you do something like that to me?'

'I didn't do anything to you,' he said with a shrug, walking into her room. 'You let it happen.'

'I didn't, I didn't want to.' She began to cry again. 'How can you share me with someone when you're supposed to love me?'

He shut the door and turned to face her. His eyes were narrow with scorn. 'Love you?' He laughed mirthlessly. 'I don't even like you most of the time. Look, get this straight, Jojo. I gave you what you wanted. I made your name for you. We have a business relationship, nothing more.'

'But why do you sleep with me then?' she bleated, her lips quivering.

'You are such a child,' he said contemptuously. 'I have to get you up in the mornings, tell you what to wear, what to eat, what to do. So I fuck you now and again too. It doesn't mean anything to me, but you expect it.'

Josie felt as though she had been punctured, as if all the beliefs she'd held on to were now whistling out of her. She hadn't got the words to be able to tell him what he'd done to her. She felt completely powerless.

'Let me go home,' was all she could think of to say. 'If you don't love me, let me go.'

He caught hold of her arm and twisted it up and around her back. 'Listen here, you silly bitch,' he almost spat in her face. 'I've invested a lot of time and energy in you. You will stay with me as long as I want you to. There's no let-out clause.'

'I won't stay with you,' she screamed at him. 'You can't make me.'

He let go of her arm and caught hold of her by the neck, digging his fingers hard into her skin. 'You will stay,' he said, his dark eyes boring into her. 'I have enough material about you, your drinking and pill-popping to make the biggest stink you've ever smelt. Walk away from me and you'll never work again as a model. All you'll be good for is blue movies and tits-and-arse magazines. That won't last long either, a few years down the line and you'll be washed up, no one will want to look at you. So wake up. See how good you've got it. Or else!'

Josie was frightened now, she knew he meant it. But she had to say one more thing while she still had the courage.

'You've got to pay me what I earn then!' she said, wriggling out of his grip. 'I want real money, not pocket money. I'll pay my rent myself, get my own car and all that. And I want to be able to go out without you around.'

He just stood there for a moment, a slight smirk twisting the corner of his mouth. 'Okay,' he said eventually, 'if that's what you want. You haven't got a brain in your head, Jojo, and I know you'll end up spending it all on drink and drugs. But as long as I get another year or so out of you, that's all right with me.'

He turned and left then, banging the hotel door shut behind him. Josie reached for her bag and took out a sleeping pill.

Chapter Fifteen

1970

Ellen sat at the table in the window of her flat, a pile of photographs and press cuttings of Josie in front of her. It was the end of September and raining too hard to go out for a walk as she usually did on Sunday mornings, but she was happy to stay in and paste all this in her scrapbook. She'd been meaning to do it for weeks.

She loved her little flat above a shop next to the post office. It was on the busy Wells Road going out of Bristol, and a bit noisy from the traffic, but the open countryside was only a mile up the road, and the school where she worked only a ten-minute walk away. The rent was very low because when she first saw the flat, it was in a bad state, and the landlord was too old to cope with getting it done up. Ellen took one look at it and decided she could never find anything better in her price range. She liked the idea of scrubbing it out and doing it all herself anyway.

It wasn't a daunting task to decorate two rooms plus a kitchen and bathroom. The whole row of shops and the flats above them had only been built in the Thirties so structurally it was quite sound. Once she started her job at the school, she soon met people who offered her help. The caretaker knew about electrics, and she found a plumber too, to put in a new gas fire.

She adored rooting round junk shops, and it was fun buying old things and doing them up. She loved the feeling of total independence, and making a real home of her own.

Fortune had certainly smiled on her. She loved the school from the first day there. Physically handicapped children were a challenge, and they took some time to get used to, but she found the job far more rewarding than caring for the Sandersons' boys.

She soon found a social life too. The assistants and teachers at the school were friendly and warm-hearted, and right from the start she fitted in. The married ones often invited her to their homes for dinner or a party, and the single ones often came down to The Happy Landings, the pub right by her flat, for a drink after work.

Six years on, she could look back at Catherine's birth and the subsequent adoption without crying. She didn't berate herself about it any more, for she knew decent flats like this, and a good job, didn't go to single mothers.

Instead she imagined Catherine going off to school in a little uniform, with a satchel on her back. She wondered if she had dancing lessons, or would learn to play a musical instrument. She could never have done all that for her.

When a wave of sorrow came over her, she would think of the children at her school, and how much more help they needed than normal children. She could channel all her maternal instincts into improving life for them. That was enough for her for now.

She picked up her scissors to cut round the edge of a magazine page. Josie was modelling a sweater on it, looking like a real country girl, holding a big Afghan hound on a lead.

Her sister's beauty and fame never ceased to astound Ellen. It seemed funny that they'd gone in such different directions, become such opposites, when once they had been so incredibly alike.

Ellen smiled to herself. Each time they met, Josie was always urging her to be more fashion-conscious, to wear makeup or do something with her hair. But it wasn't Ellen's thing; she didn't yearn for glamour or attention. She was happiest in jeans; she really couldn't be bothered thinking about which shoes went with which clothes. When she did make the effort to dress up for a special occasion, do her nails and put makeup on, it was nice, but she didn't want to do it every day.

Men seemed to like her just the way she was anyway. Jack, a man she'd recently had a bit of a fling with, called her 'Mother Earth'. She liked that image. Meanwhile she could always look at pictures of Josie and see what real glamour was!

She leafed through her scrapbook of Josie and found the pictures taken in the South of France, back in '67. Josie looked like a princess in a cream silk ball-gown, the low bodice dripping with seed pearls, a pearl tiara in her hair. It was one of Ellen's favourite pictures, a glimpse into a different world from the one she knew.

People at work had often asked her if she felt jealous of her sister. She would laugh and say 'Only for the money she earns', but in fact even that wasn't true. Her real feelings, and she would never divulge those to anyone, were just of sadness that Josie hadn't found happiness along with her fame.

The picture in the South of France was a fine example. Josie looked stunning, she'd stayed in a fabulous hotel, mingled with the super-rich. Yet something unpleasant had happened to her during that time. Ellen had never got to the bottom of what it was, Josie had emphatically denied it, but her drug-taking had accelerated shortly afterwards.

Ellen grimaced. Josie was so hard to understand. She could be such good fun, generous and loving too, but there was a very dark side to her as well – she could be devious, nasty, totally selfish and destructive. Try as she might, Ellen couldn't put her finger on exactly why. They'd had the same upbringing, were so close in many ways, yet why were they poles apart mentally?

It seemed such a waste to Ellen that Josie had achieved her childhood dream, yet that still wasn't enough to make her happy. What was it that was missing in her life that made her plunge into drink and drugs the way she did?

Although Ellen's personal experience of drug-taking was limited to smoking a few joints with friends at parties, she was quite clued up about the subject. Lots of her friends were into speed and acid. It was all part of the Flower Power culture, and as rife here in Bristol as it was in London. As far as she was concerned, taking something for an extra high now and again didn't do much harm, as long as it didn't start to control a person's life.

But it was controlling Josie's.

Ellen knew Mark had been responsible for starting her on that road. She suspected it was his way of binding Josie to him so he could siphon off all the money she earned. But their relationship had changed soon after they came back from France. He still took all the photographs of Josie, but he wasn't her lover any more, and she was paid directly by her agency. It wasn't as if that rift was the cause of Josie's troubles, she claimed to be glad, as now she could do what she liked, see whom she liked. And she seemed sincere. So that left no one to blame for Josie's unhappiness but Josie herself.

Ellen picked up a photograph of herself and Josie taken down in Falmouth. Josie had bought the camera that day, and asked people to take pictures of them together. This one was taken down by The Chain Locker in the harbour. They were both laughing their heads off because the man who was taking the photograph kept saying Josie reminded him of someone, but he couldn't think who. They wondered if later he would suddenly realize who Josie was, and kick himself for not knowing in the first place.

Ellen sighed deeply. They may have spent all that day laughing, but the rest of the visit home had been awful. Perhaps Josie hadn't really been ready for a reunion with their parents.

Right from the time Ellen found out where Josie was in London, she had worked on their parents to forgive her sister. Albert was unable to forget the humiliation of Violet and himself being thrown out of the *Mirror* offices, or the lies Josie had told about her family. He had said then that he would never speak to her again. Yet he did relent and let Violet go up to London to look after her when she was ill. Ellen had thought that was a real breakthrough, but Josie blew it by throwing Violet out of her flat.

Eventually, by constantly chipping away at them both, Ellen had managed to convince her parents that Mark Kinsale was responsible for everything. As he was off the scene by then, they finally agreed to try a reconciliation.

Had Ellen got her way, that first meeting would have been on neutral ground, perhaps at her flat. But Josie had bought a flashy blue sports car, and suddenly she wanted to drive down to Cornwall. She didn't seem to take on board that she would need to win her parents over, as they were still feeling hurt by her. So Ellen only went along with her as a mediator.

If Josie had restrained herself, worn something ordinary like jeans and been prepared to help with a few chores, everything could have worked out. But she insisted on dressing up to the nines, kept complaining how cold draughty and miserable the house was, and went on and on about the smart hotels she stayed in as if her own home wasn't good enough for her any more.

Then there was the incident of the fridge. She just went out and bought one and got it delivered. Ellen couldn't help but grin as she remembered Violet's shocked expression when the deliveryman carted it in and plonked it down in the kitchen.

Josie was right, they did need one, food and milk went off quickly during the summer. But she should have known their parents were old-fashioned country folk. They were happy enough with their larder and meat safe, and they didn't like being forced to accept charity, which was how Josie made it seem.

Of course Josie got nasty when they didn't fall and kiss the hem of her dress in gratitude. In pure spite she flung insults about the state of Violet's clothes, her mottled legs, and Albert's long hair.

Ellen wished she could forget that awful visit. She had wanted to slap Josie for being so insulting, and for spoiling all the hard work she'd put in on her behalf.

Sometimes Ellen thought her sister was a bit deranged. She just never knew when to stop or back off, or to hold her tongue. She showed off continually and had no respect for others. Was it the drugs she took that made her like that? Or was she born with this defect?

Ellen hadn't had any contact with her for months now. Josie hadn't phoned or written since the last time she came down to Bristol when she'd just broken off an affair with a rock guitarist. Yet Ellen knew she'd been down to Cornwall, showing off in Falmouth, because Mrs Peters had told her.

That was another strange thing about her sister. She claimed to hate the farm and always ended up rowing with their parents, yet she persisted in going down there. Rumour had it she'd been asked to leave a restaurant because she'd taken a bunch of people into it who were all drunk and abusive. It was also said she wasn't too welcome in several of the pubs because of bad behaviour and the company she kept.

Ellen could only suppose the attraction was purely because she was such a celebrity among her old school-friends. Maybe she needed that unconditional admiration to bolster up her private fears that when her looks faded she would be a nobody again.

A familiar car engine made Ellen look out of the window, and there to her huge surprise was Josie in her blue sports car, driving on to the forecourt of the shops beneath her flat.

As always, Ellen forgot her concerns in her delight at seeing her sister again. She leapt to her feet and rushed downstairs to the front door.

'What a lovely surprise!' she exclaimed as she opened the door. 'Good job it's raining or I'd have been out walking.'

Josie was wearing sunglasses, but Ellen put that down to affectation. All she really noticed was that Josie didn't start rabbiting on the way she usually did.

'How was the drive down? How long can you stay for?' Ellen asked as they went back up the stairs.

'How long can you put up with me for?' Josie said wearily.

That sounded a bit ominous, and Ellen hedged round it by saying she'd make some tea. When she came back into the living-room with the mugs, Josie had taken off her long coat, beneath which she was wearing a red crushed-velvet hot-pants suit and knee-length black boots. She had also removed the sunglasses, and one eye was red and puffed up, the start of a black eye.

'Don't start preaching,' Josie warned Ellen. 'Okay, I had a bit of a fight with Mark. I need somewhere to crash for a few days to give him a fright.'

'You know you can stay here, though I'll be working tomorrow,' Ellen said. 'But what was the fight about?'

'He's got another woman,' Josie said. 'Another model told me yesterday. He called round early this morning to tell me about a job tomorrow, and when I asked him about her, he said it was none of my business.'

'Well, it isn't, Josie, you've been apart for over two years,' Ellen said gently.

'It *is* my business,' Josie snapped. 'He should have told me before everyone else found out. He's going to marry her! They've been carrying on for years while she was still married to someone else. When I think what I've done for that bastard! How can he treat me so badly?'

'Is he still getting you work and paying you?'

251

Josie nodded.

'Well, I can't see that he's treating you badly,' Ellen said tartly. 'He was always much too old and manipulative for you anyway. You'd have been much happier with someone who really cares about you.'

'I suppose you want me to have one of those peace and love types that you like so much?'

'You could do worse,' Ellen said with a grin. 'Most of them are great in bed because they've tuned into what women want.'

'I don't want sex,' Josie snarled. 'I want someone to look after me. No one's ever done that.'

Ellen believed in looking after herself, men were for entertainment only in her book. But she knew better than to say that now. Besides, Josie always did seem to draw the short straw with men. Mostly she picked the ones who just wanted her as a beautiful accessory. In the last two years she'd been out with several rock stars, two actors and a Harley Street surgeon. All of them appeared to have been cold-hearted, egotistical bastards.

'Drink your tea, Josie, then maybe you could do with a little nap while I make us some lunch.'

'Got any booze?' Josie asked.

Ellen had a feeling this visit was going to be heavy. If Josie had already had some speed this morning, she would talk and talk all day and half-way through the night. She'd stay in bed most of the following day while Ellen was at work, and that pattern would be repeated every day till she finally cleared off, leaving Ellen wrung out and exhausted.

'Only the home-made wine you sneered at last time you were here,' she said.

'Why do you make that crap?' Josie said nastily. 'No one wants to drink it.'

'Well, my friends like it.' Ellen tried not to get annoyed. 'I make it because I enjoy doing it. It's also a lot cheaper than buying wine.'

'You're so . . .' Josie fluttered her hand as she searched

for a word, 'together,' she said eventually. 'It's really boring. Look at this place, patchwork cushions, handmade pottery, all crafty and rustic. I bet you listen to folk music too.'

Ellen snapped. 'Oh, stop being nasty or you can clear off right now.'

By Thursday evening, Ellen had had enough. Her worst fears had been realized. Josie was still in bed when she left for work each day. When she got home each evening the place was like a tip, clothes and makeup strewn everywhere. All the towels in the bathroom were wet and left in a heap on the floor, records out of their sleeves. Josie never thought to prepare a meal, much less get any shopping, and she was like a stuck record, repeating all the same old stuff about Mark.

This time she was stretched out on the couch smoking a joint. Ellen could see burn holes where some of the cannabis had fallen out.

'I think you should go home in the morning,' she said, trying not to sound harsh. 'It's too much having you here when I'm working. I can't stand to come home and find things like this.'

'Come and have a drag of this, then you won't mind,' Josie said, offering her the joint.

'I'd prefer it if you got off your arse and cleared up,' Ellen said, gritting her teeth.

'You're not so cool as you make out, are you?' Josie said, still not moving. 'You're really uptight. Get down the doctor's and get some tranks.'

Ellen ignored that and asked her sister what would happen if she missed some assignments.

'Mark will get really pissed off,' Josie giggled. 'I told you, that's why I came down here.'

Had she said she needed Ellen it might have been different. 'Well, if you want to continue to piss him off, do it somewhere else,' Ellen retorted angrily. 'Go on down to

253

the farm, you can piss your mother off at the same time.'

Josie sat bolt upright. Today she was wearing royal blue hot-pants and a skinny rib sweater, her hair up in a pony-tail. She looked about fifteen, not twenty-one.

'Look here, you bitch,' she hissed, 'don't make cracks about Mum. If it wasn't for you there wouldn't have been any trouble between us.'

'If it wasn't for me you'd still be an outcast,' Ellen reminded her. 'I had to work very hard on them to make them forgive you.'

'I know you work hard on them. But not for me.' Josie's eyes narrowed with spite. 'It's to make sure you get the farm when they snuff it. You don't fool me one little bit, you know how much the land is worth and you can't wait to get your hands on it.'

Ellen wanted to hit her, but she resisted the temptation and turned away towards the door. 'I'm going out now. Be gone by the time I get back or I'll throw you out,' she said. 'You've gone too far with your nastiness this time. Don't come back again until you've changed your ways.'

Ellen drove her car out towards the village of Pensford, just outside Bristol, and pulled up in a lay-by. She was livid with her sister, and at that moment she never wanted to see her again. Why did she say such evil things? What was wrong with her?

She watched the sun till it sank right down behind a hill, and as it disappeared so did her anger. She had studied enough child psychology books to see that many of Josie's problems came from her mother. Violet was such a bitter woman, and since Josie was born she had dripped poison into her daughter's ears at every opportunity. It was she who had fed Josie the idea that Dad didn't love her. She had probably also convinced her that her older sister would snatch her share of any inheritance too. Even Josie's belief that a man's role was to take care of a woman came directly from Violet.

Ellen could agree that in most marriages that was the norm, but not in the way that Violet saw it. She didn't think of love, Ellen doubted she even understood that concept. To her it was trading sex for the security of a home and food. She'd put that into practice with Albert.

Now Josie was the same. Ellen couldn't remember Josie ever raving about a man she liked. All she ever gloated over was what kind of car he drove, how rich or successful he was. She doubted too that she'd ever leapt into bed with anyone just because she fancied him like mad, only for what she hoped it would bring her.

'Poor Josie,' she murmured to herself. 'When will you learn?'

As she drove back on to the forecourt and saw Josie's sports car had gone, Ellen didn't know whether to be pleased or sad. She went upstairs wearily, wondering what she could cook for supper that would be quick, and how soon she could get to bed.

It was no surprise to see that Josie hadn't tidied up before she left, but at least all her clothes and cosmetics were gone. By the time Ellen had straightened everything out, she was too tired to cook anything more than a bacon sandwich.

She woke refreshed the following morning and stripped her bed with the intention of leaving her washing at the laundrette to be done while she was at work. It was a lovely morning, and she considered driving down to Cornwall that night and staying for the weekend, as it might be the last good weather before autumn really set in.

She was ready to leave for work at half past eight when she remembered it was the end of the month and the rent was due. She thought she'd leave it with Bert in the post office next door just in case she wasn't here tomorrow.

But when she went to the drawer in her dressing table to get it, it wasn't there. The rent book was there, so obviously she hadn't moved it and forgotten. The four ten-pound notes tucked inside it were missing.

'You couldn't have taken it, could you, Josie?' she said aloud, unable to believe anyone would sink that low. Yet it was clear she had. She must have seen it while she was gathering up her things.

'You fucking bitch!' she yelled in rage. Apart from the fact that her sister had actually stolen from her, there was the question of how she was going to pay the rent now. She wasn't due to be paid for another week, and if she used that money, she'd be short next month too. 'I'll never forgive you for this,' she muttered to herself. 'Turn into a bloody junkie if you like. I won't care. We're finished.'

Chapter Sixteen

1991

'Why am I so dizzy, Fred?' Daisy nuzzled the terrier's white fur with her nose as she lay on her bed with her Whitney Houston album playing in the background. 'It's not just the question of a job, or where it's going with Joel. I've got to do something about my real mum too.'

Fred yawned noisily and snuggled closer to her. The gesture said he didn't mind how dizzy she was, in fact he liked it.

It was March, nine months since her mother's death, yet Daisy felt she hadn't moved on at all. She couldn't claim it was purely grief for though that came in waves, often unexpectedly knocking her for six, time could pass without her thinking about Lorna too much.

But without being able to sound ideas off her mother as she was used to, Daisy found it hard to be positive, to make plans and stick to them. She often had a lonely, desolate feeling that even her friends and Joel couldn't eradicate.

The only positive step she'd taken was to enrol in an intensive chef's course. She had used some of the money her mother had left her to pay for it, and begun it last September, having spent the summer doing agency office work. While she felt she had found the only thing she really had a talent for, and the praise from her tutors had boosted her self-esteem, now the course was close to ending, and she was nervous. Cooking fabulous dishes in a calm and friendly environment was one thing, to do it professionally in a busy restaurant was quite another.

Daisy sighed. She couldn't afford any further failures, so whatever job she plumped for had to be the right one, or at least the first rung on the right ladder. But how was she supposed to know if it was the right ladder?

Her tutor had suggested two alternative plans. One was to get an assistant chef's position in a first-rate London hotel or restaurant, the other to go out of London to a smaller restaurant or hotel, where Daisy's diploma would get her a position as head or sole chef.

The first plan appeared to be the best. She would gain experience of working with staff under her, and could continue to live at home and still be able to see Joel. But she knew how busy central London kitchens could be and it wasn't that appealing.

Going out of London would mean either living in or finding a flat of her own, and it would be difficult to see Joel. But on the plus side it would be a more prestigious position, probably with more money too, and her tutor had said he thought she would be far happier in charge of a kitchen.

Daisy knew she didn't take kindly to being ordered about. She also liked the idea of going somewhere new and reinventing herself, but she wasn't so sure she could cope without seeing Joel for weeks on end. Her downfall in the past had been that she tied herself to men, and she was trying not to include him in the equation. But she found old habits died hard. She really couldn't imagine life without seeing Joel two or three times a week.

Yet going away might solve the problem with Lucy. They were still frequently at loggerheads, mainly because her sister wouldn't do a hand's turn around the house. But that problem might just go away anyway, as the twins were planning a round-the-world trip after taking their final exams.

Daisy reached out and turned the stereo up louder,

singing along to 'Miracle'. She smiled to herself, knowing that was exactly what she was hoping for, some blinding flash in which everything would be solved for her, and the road ahead clearly marked out.

'Miracle' ended and Whitney Houston began singing 'All the Man that I Need'. Daisy reached out again and switched it off. She didn't want to hear it, for she wasn't so sure Joel was 'all she needed' any more. It was a warm and comfortable relationship, but then so were thermal vests, and she wasn't ready to slip into those just yet. She hankered for a few fireworks, some real evidence that this was the real thing. Moving away might bring on those fireworks again, but then it could just as easily put the flame out for good.

She wished so much she could be like some of her girlfriends, who were so sure of what they wanted, what they were capable of, that they zapped through life without any anxiety. She knew she was pathetic, she couldn't even make up her mind about whether or not she wanted to find her real mother!

She'd had plenty of excuses up till now to put that off. Between the chef's course, looking after the house and seeing Joel she hadn't had time. But recently it had started to niggle at her, not so much because she had promised her mother she would do it, but out of her own innate curiosity.

The desire to know the whole story about Ellen was consuming her, yet at the same time she wasn't so sure she wanted to come face to face with her. Was it fear of opening up Pandora's Box? Or was it that she also had quite enough people leaning on her right now, without adding someone else?

She had mentioned this to Joel recently, and his sarcastic retort had cut her to the quick. 'You want the sandwich, but not the crust. But then you're like that about everything, including me!'

He was right of course. She wanted a job she loved,

without too much hard work, her family minus the problems, a love affair with only passion, all the boring bits cut out, even a new mother with no stress involved.

'You're the only person I like absolutely and completely,' she said to Fred, tickling his ears. 'I wouldn't change one bit of you.'

He licked her face as if to say he felt the same about her and it made her laugh.

'Daisy!' She was startled to hear her father's voice, as she hadn't heard him come home.

'Come in, Dad,' she called out.

'I thought you had someone in here with you, I heard you laughing,' John said from the doorway.

'It's just me and good old Fred.' Daisy giggled. 'I was just telling him he was my favourite person.'

'He's taking more and more liberties these days,' John said, sitting down on the bed and stroking Fred.

One good thing was that her father was recovering. He was going out with friends for supper and to the theatre, he was laughing again, even looking forward to going sailing in the summer. Daisy hoped that in time he'd find a new lady, he was much too nice and young in outlook to remain on his own.

'Why are you up here lolling around?' he asked her. 'I expected you to be out.'

'I got off early today,' she said with a yawn. 'I've been lying here pondering what I should do next.'

She briefly outlined her predicament. 'Why am I so dizzy?' she asked. 'No one else seems to waver as much as I do.'

'If I knew the answer to that I might have cured you years ago,' he said, smiling at her affectionately. 'But I've done a bit of wavering in my time too, and I found a way out of it.'

'Tell me how?'

'You stop thinking about those serious things, and do something else instead. You could take a holiday, for instance, once you've finished the course. Once you get some distance from the problems, the solution to them often becomes clear.'

'But Joel can't take a holiday with me then,' she said. 'He'll have to wait until June or July.'

'Who said anything about going on holiday with him?'

'I couldn't go on my own,' she retorted.

'You could very easily. Maybe not a holiday abroad, but there's places in England you've never seen. Take the West Country for instance. You could start by going to Bristol to look up the doctor who arranged the adoption. I bet she could tell you enough to satisfy your curiosity.'

'Mmm,' Daisy murmured. 'Perhaps. I suppose afterwards I could meander down through Somerset and Devon to Cornwall.'

'You could even check out a few restaurants and hotels as you go,' John said with a grin. 'You never know, you might find a summer job that would suit you, and that way you'd get some experience without committing yourself to a permanent job.'

'But surely lack of commitment is one of my most serious flaws?' she said, only half joking.

'It's an awful lot smarter to test the water with your toe than plunging in blindly.' He put his hand on her shoulder and squeezed it affectionately. 'Besides, if you got a job in a good hotel, I'd have the perfect excuse to come and stay there to see you. I love Devon and Cornwall.'

'Do you?' She was surprised, he'd never mentioned it before.

'Your mother and I used to go camping in Looe before you came along, we loved it,' he said, looking a little wistful. 'But once we had three of you, it was too long a drive with small children, so we never went again. I've often thought if I sell this house I might buy somewhere down there. I could work just as easily from Barnstaple or Exeter, say, as from London. Most of the properties we work on are in the west.'

His enthusiasm stirred Daisy and suddenly she really wanted to go. 'I could take Fred with me, that would give me an excuse for long walks.'

At the word 'walks' Fred's ears pricked up.

'Not now,' Daisy giggled. 'I've got to get my diploma first.'

At nine in the morning of 9 April Daisy set off for Bristol in her Beetle with Fred sitting in the back. She had passed her chef's exam with distinction, gained her diploma, and she had a curious sense of satisfaction that for once she'd stuck at something long enough to achieve a goal.

Her thoughts turned to Joel, whom she'd seen the previous day. He had been so chilly, but whether that was because she'd been talking about getting a summer job away from London, or just because she wanted to go somewhere without him, she didn't know. He had checked her tyre pressure, oil and water, but he'd had a sullen expression on his face, and he kept saying the Beetle was too old for such long journeys.

But then he'd been a wet blanket about her appointment with Dr Julia Fordham in Bristol too. Daisy had written to the doctor a couple of weeks ago, and even then Joel had been scoffing, saying she'd be well over seventy and even if she was still alive she was probably senile. Maybe he was peeved because he was proved wrong. Dr Fordham still lived at the same address and she didn't sound senile when she agreed to see Daisy on 9 April at one. Her father had claimed Joel was just being protective, because he was worried about Daisy going there alone. To Daisy it just looked like a schoolboy sulk.

She wasn't going to think about him any more. Tonight she was booked into a guest-house in Bristol that didn't mind dogs, but from then until the end of the week when she had arranged to stay at a cottage in St Mawes in Cornwall, she hadn't made any advance plans. Perhaps that worried Joel too.

Yet armed with maps, visitors' guides and a booklet of guest-houses in Devon and Cornwall, Daisy felt in control and very excited. To her it was a magical mystery tour that might very well result in a whole new direction.

Bristol was a very confusing city to drive in, with seemingly no directions signs except to the airport. She pulled into the bus station and asked five different people the way to Clifton, and was baffled when they told her there was a village, somewhere called the Triangle, and another part called Whiteladies Road. It didn't help that they spoke so strangely too, it reminded her of television adverts for cream with one of the Wurzels saying 'Give 'em a gurt big dollop'. So she took the road that had been pointed out and kept on it. When she asked for directions again, she was almost at Pembroke Road.

Number 7 was right at the end of a long, lovely road of huge old houses. There were cherry and magnolia trees in full bloom in almost every garden, and though many of the houses had clearly been converted into flats for students, judging by the copious amount of dustbins, they didn't have that seedy, run-down look student houses in London had. There were many roads off to the right and left that begged to be explored, little communities with a few shops, restaurants and pubs, and she felt like a child on a Sunday school outing.

She was very early for the appointment, so she parked her car and took Fred for a walk on the Downs, which was at the top of Pembroke Road. She was staggered to see such an enormous green space in the middle of a city. Bristol certainly was a city of surprises.

'We'll come up here again later,' she told Fred as she put him back on his lead. He had gone mad for a while after being cooped up in the car for so long, rushing about and rolling on his back on the grass with evident delight.

She put Fred back in the car, and taking her notebook and the adoption documents her mother had given her, she walked up the path of number 7. It was strange to imagine that Ellen must have walked on this path, both before and after Daisy's birth, and that her parents had collected her from here too.

She looked up at the old house and wondered if Ellen had been intimidated by it when she first came here. It was very grand with its stone steps up to the front door and its huge bay windows. But like the other houses in the road it appeared to be divided up into flats as there were six bells. She rang Dr Fordham's and for the first time felt a little nervous.

'Dr Fordham?' Daisy asked when the door was opened by a white-haired lady in a lavender knitted two-piece. She didn't fit the image of a hard-bitten professional woman that her mother's note had created. She just looked like a sweet old granny.

'You must be Daisy,' she said with a warm smile. 'I am Dr Fordham, do come in. Did you manage to find your way here without too much difficulty?'

'Yes, I found it easily. What a lovely place Bristol is. I just took my dog up for a walk on the Downs, I can't believe that a city has so much open space.'

'Clifton's not what it was, my dear,' the doctor said as she led Daisy through a door into her flat which was on the ground floor. 'It used to be very smart, the shops comparable with Bond Street, now it's all restaurants and take-aways.'

'But the houses are so lovely,' Daisy replied.

Once she was inside the flat she wondered how Dr Fordham could afford to heat such vast rooms on her pension. It had clearly been very elegant once, but the velvet drapes were dusty, and everything was very worn. She wondered why she didn't move somewhere smaller and easier to manage.

'Do sit down, Daisy,' the doctor said. She looked delighted to have a visitor. 'I was so pleased when I got your letter, for I remember you well as a baby, and your parents of course. I am so sorry to hear of your mother's death, I remember her as being such a vivacious woman.'

Daisy had explained in her letter that she only wanted to know a little more about Ellen at this stage, and that she wasn't sure she was ready to meet her, even if that were possible. She hoped the old lady had taken that in and wouldn't suddenly produce Ellen from behind a door.

'The first thing I want to know is, why was it a private adoption?' Daisy asked. 'I didn't think that was allowed.'

Dad had told her that he and Lorna had got so fed up with the red tape and all the endless visits and questions from the National Adoption Society that when a friend of theirs offered to put them in touch with someone who dealt in private adoptions, they had jumped at the chance. Daisy was just testing Dr Fordham to see if she answered the question truthfully.

'It was frowned on by the main societies,' the old lady said carefully. 'Of course that was because there are so many unscrupulous people around. But doctors often get to know girls in trouble, and in turn know ideal couples who want to adopt. You mustn't get the idea I was running some kind of baby farm here, dear me no.'

'I didn't mean that at all,' Daisy said quickly. 'I just wanted to understand how it came about that I was matched with John and Lorna.'

'Ellen was brought to me for an examination by the people she worked for in Bristol. She was intending to go to a mother-and-baby home later. As it happened, I had friends in London who knew John and Lorna well. I had already been told how badly let down they felt by the National Adoption Society, for they were just kept hanging on, their hopes built up only to be dashed again and again. I knew they were good people with everything to offer a child, and like natural parents they weren't the least concerned about its sex, they just wanted a baby.

'When I saw what a sweet girl Ellen was, they

immediately sprang to mind. I had a feeling it would be a perfect match.'

That was almost exactly what Daisy had been told by her father, and the fact that the doctor could recall it so clearly made her think she must be entirely trustworthy.

'Of course there were other circumstances too, which prompted the private adoption.' Dr Fordham frowned as she spoke, as if this was the one area she wasn't quite happy about. 'The family Ellen was working for didn't want to lose her, she was so good with their children, and they were afraid if she went through the normal channels of a mother-and-baby home, she would be tempted into keeping you. So it was in their interests too, to encourage a private adoption where the baby is taken away at birth, rather than the mother looking after it for six weeks.'

'So Ellen was pushed into it then?' Daisy said bluntly.

Dr Fordham sighed. 'Yes, she was rather. Not by me of course, I was merely a mediator, and in those days we all really believed we were doing both the mother and child a favour. But I'm older and wiser now, and with hindsight I would have given Ellen more time, and counselling too.'

'Do you think she might have kept me then?'

Dr Fordham looked at her sharply.

'Who can say, dear? Things were very different then, so very difficult for a single mother. She wanted the best for her baby, and John and Lorna were the perfect couple. I never had the slightest qualms about them, I was delighted I could help to make their dream come true. But looking back, from this more enlightened era, I'm not so sure that we were fair to Ellen.'

'Do you know where she is now?' Daisy asked.

The old lady shook her head. 'The last contact I had with her was when I sent her on the letter and photograph from your mother, about six years after the adoption. I didn't send the original letter of course, but copied it, omitting the address. At that time she was still working at the handicapped children's school in South Bristol where she'd been since leaving the family she worked for. After I got your letter I contacted the Education Department, and asked if she was still there, or working at any other school in the county, but it seems she left their employ in 1978. She was still single then.'

Daisy did a quick mental reckoning and found Ellen would have been thirty-one at that time.

'Maybe she left to get married?' she said, feeling a bit disappointed as this would complicate tracking Ellen down.

The doctor nodded. 'Well, I'd always assumed she'd married years before and that was why she suddenly stopped sending me a card. But I suppose once she had that letter from your mother she felt more at peace, and didn't feel the need to keep in touch with me any more. She was very involved with the children she worked with too, I daresay that helped her.'

'What about the family she worked for when she was expecting me, might she have kept in touch with them?' Daisy asked.

'I doubt that very much, my dear.' Dr Fordham made a sort of flurry with her hands. 'You see, they were angry when she wanted to leave them. She was the perfect nanny for their children, a real-life Mary Poppins. They couldn't understand why she wanted to go and work with handicapped children when she could be looking after their two dear little boys. I believe the woman was quite unpleasant to her about it.'

'So how long was she with them then?' Daisy asked.

'I can't remember exactly, but for at least a year after you were born, she adored the little boys. But she was right to move on. She had a fine brain and she was worth a great deal more than just being a mother's help. She came to me for a reference for the school in South Bristol, and I applauded what she intended to do.'

Daisy noticed then that the doctor had a slightly distant

expression. 'Do you think now that was wrong for her too?' she asked.

'Oh no, it was very laudable. But it was at that time that I began to regret my part in hurrying along the adoption. I could see she hadn't got over it. I had a feeling she never would.'

Daisy felt her eyes prickle with unexpected tears, and all at once she knew she wasn't going to be satisfied with just the information Dr Fordham had to give her. 'Have you got any idea where I could go from here?' she asked.

The doctor thought for a little while. 'It might turn out to be a dead end, but Ellen was very close to a lady called Mrs Peters. She was the wife of a school teacher and lived in the same Cornish village Ellen came from. It was through her that Ellen came to Bristol to have you, and I remember her telling me at the time she took the position at the school here that she still visited Mrs Peters regularly when she went home to Cornwall. The village has a funny name, Mister Smith or something.'

'Mawnan Smith,' Daisy smiled. 'I was intending to go on down to Cornwall so I'll try and find her there,' she said. 'If you think of anything else, will you contact me?'

'You are very like Ellen,' the old lady said suddenly, her eyes looked suspiciously damp. 'Your hair is just like hers. Not just the colour and the curls, but the way the light from the window catches it. It takes me right back to sitting here talking with her.'

She paused for a moment, looking at Daisy reflectively. 'You have a much bolder attitude than her, she tended to hang her head and rarely asked questions, but you are lovely, just as she was. Of course I'll let you know if I think of anything more.'

Daisy felt that was the end of the interview and got up, holding out her hand. 'Thank you so much for your help,' she said. 'But I ought to go as I've left my dog in the car.'

Dr Fordham got up too, and shook Daisy's hand firmly.

'It was a pleasure to meet you,' she said, smiling with her eyes. 'Do let me know if you find her, won't you?'

All at once, for no particular reason, Daisy had a *déjà vu* feeling. 'Was I handed over to Mum in this room?' she asked.

The old lady half smiled. 'Indeed you were, dear. This was still my sitting-room then, the surgery was in the basement. The foster-mother who took care of you for the first six weeks brought you here at midday to meet your parents. They were so happy and excited. But that's adoption for you, one woman's joy comes from another woman's anguish.'

As Daisy left the house the doctor's last words rang in her ears. Until now, somehow it hadn't quite clicked in her mind how terrible it must be for a mother to give up her baby.

That night Daisy sat up in her bed in the guest-house with Fred close beside her and thought about everything Dr Fordham had said.

She had walked miles with Fred after leaving the old lady, right over the Downs, all the way to Clifton village. She'd seen the Suspension Bridge and Avon Gorge, explored all the little shops in the village and felt she was falling in love with Bristol. Although she had always thought of herself as a Londoner, in fact she was born in Bristol, so maybe that was why it enchanted her. She felt at home here, in touch with something she couldn't quite explain.

Later, after checking into the guest-house, she'd gone out again, found a pub that didn't mind dogs, and bought fish and chips to eat on the way back. Yet now, in bed, she felt suddenly saddened as she thought over all that Dr Fordham had told her. Reading between the lines, Ellen was probably just an innocent little country girl, no match for the predatory woman she worked for who wanted the baby whisked away so that her life wouldn't be disturbed.

If she had really cared for Ellen wouldn't she have let her keep her baby and her job?

'But people aren't like that, are they, Fred?' she said stroking him. 'Shall we stay another night here and go exploring again, or move on to Devon?'

He half closed his eyes, as if saying he didn't care what happened tomorrow, all he wanted was a sleep now.

Daisy stayed another night in Bristol, spending the second day exploring the city further. Then early on Wednesday morning she set off for Cornwall, planning to go straight to Mawnan Smith and find somewhere to stay for the night before going on to the cottage at St Mawes on Thursday.

It began raining as she got to Bodmin, but even the grey sky couldn't detract from the rugged beauty of the Cornish landscape. As she got closer to Truro, Daisy began to feel excited at the prospect of seeing all those places immortalized by Daphne du Maurier. She had read most of her books as a young teenager and felt she knew Cornwall from them, never realizing at the time she was reading *Frenchman's Creek* and loving it that her real mother had lived nearby.

It was a little after two when she finally drove into the village of Mawnan Smith. She stopped her car by a small row of shops in the centre of the village and sat there looking at them for a few minutes. They must have been built since her birth, for despite being constructed mainly of Cornish stone, they had a distinctly late Sixties and Seventies style. Where was her grandfather's farm? Would Mrs Peters still be living here?

The post office seemed to be the best place to inquire. That at least looked as if it had been there for a good fifty years.

'Mrs Peters?' The dumpy middle-aged woman in a floral-print overall beamed at Daisy. 'Oh yes, she's still here, though her husband passed away a few years since.

You'll find her cottage just up the road, past the pub, it's called "Swallow's".'

Fred was desperate to get out of the car, so Daisy put him on the lead and walked him up the road towards the cottage. It had stopped raining about half an hour earlier and the sun had come out again. She thought she'd just make a reconnoitre, then take him for a short walk before returning him to the car.

She sensed which cottage was 'Swallow's' even before she got close enough to see the plaque on the gate. It was the kind of place Londoners dream of, painted white, with small lattice windows, roses growing round the door and as ancient garden wall smothered with purple aubrietia. A young man was working in the garden.

As she got right up to the cottage she hesitated for a moment, not knowing whether to walk on past or speak. But the man took matters into his own hands – he stood up, grinned at her and said hello.

Daisy grinned back. He was nice-looking, probably in his early thirties, with floppy fair hair and bright blue eyes.

'Nice dog,' he said, leaning over the wall to take a better look at Fred. 'I like West Highland terriers, they are a big dog in a small suit, aren't they?'

Fred put his paws up on the wall and woofed a greeting.

'I think he liked that description,' Daisy said with a smile.

'You here on holiday?' he asked, looking very interested. 'Only I haven't seen you before.'

'Well, actually I'm here on a mission,' she said. 'I was looking for Mrs Peters. They told me in the post office she lived here.'

He nodded. 'She's my grandmother. Come on in, she's always glad of visitors.'

'I can't bring Fred in,' Daisy said, a little alarmed that now she had no chance to compose herself. 'I was just taking him for a walk before putting him back in my car.'

'Oh, don't do that.' The young man came along to the gate and opened it for her. 'We're both dog lovers. Fred doesn't want to be stuck in a car.'

'Well, if you're sure,' she said. 'I'm Daisy Buchan.'

'I'm Tim Peters,' he said, and shook her hand. 'Why do you want to see Gran?'

Daisy liked this friendly, rather inquisitive man. 'That's a tough one to answer easily. I believe your grandmother knew my mother.'

He raised his fair eyebrows and his eyes twinkled. 'Well, this is a first. Mostly when anyone wants to talk to Gran about village history, they are about a hundred and ten. Gran!' he yelled as he led Daisy into the cottage. 'Someone to see you!'

As he was kicking off his shoes in the tiny hallway, Daisy stood in the doorway of the sitting-room. Like the outside of the cottage it was very pretty, with a low-beamed ceiling, a stone fireplace and cottage furniture. Through the French windows at the far end of the room she saw an old lady holding a bunch of flowers in her hand.

'A visitor, Tim?' Mrs Peters called out, then stopped short as she saw Daisy. 'Oh, my goodness,' she gasped. 'I thought for a moment it was Ellen.'

A thrill ran through Daisy. Countless times she had heard people remark on Lucy and Tom's similarity to their mother, and it had often hurt that she was excluded. It felt good to have someone recognize a family likeness, even if she knew very little about that family.

Daisy took a few tentative steps towards the woman. 'I'm her daughter, Daisy,' she said.

Mrs Peters' eyes widened with shock. 'My dear! How absolutely wonderful,' she gasped incredulously. 'Oh, I'll have to sit down, you've knocked me for six. Tim, don't stand there with your mouth hanging open, make us all some tea.'

Ellen wondered how old Mrs Peters was. She had to be

at least eighty, perhaps even older, yet she didn't look frail, her skin was lovely and she looked well.

'Am I allowed to know who Ellen is?' Tim asked, going over to his grandmother and taking the bunch of flowers she'd picked from her hands. 'You know me, Gran, nosy to the last!'

'Ellen Pengelly,' she replied. 'Beacon Farm.'

Daisy saw a look of shock and bewilderment on Tim's face, and the sharp look the old woman gave him as if warning him to say nothing more. Afraid that she might really be an unwelcome visitor, however tactful Mrs Peters was being, she hastily apologized for coming in unexpectedly with Fred, and asked if it would be better if she called at another time.

'Of course not, dear,' Mrs Peters said. 'I'm delighted you called, just a little taken aback, that's all. I like dogs, I've kept them all my life, and do call me Mavis. Sit down and tell me how you came to find me.'

Daisy explained about her mother's death, and the trip to Bristol to see Dr Fordham. 'Well,' she finished up, 'the doctor hadn't any idea of what had become of Ellen, but she knew about you, and said she thought you might be able to tell me more about her.'

'I can tell you quite a lot about the past,' she said. 'But I haven't heard from her since . . .' She faltered. 'Well, since the fire.'

'Fire?' Daisy asked. 'What fire?'

Mavis looked at her grandson as if for support.

Tim came right over to Daisy, leaning towards her. 'I'm sorry, Daisy. This isn't going to be the best introduction to your family history. You see, the fire at the farm wiped them all out.'

Chapter Seventeen

Daisy looked from Tim to Mavis in horror. 'No!' she gasped.

'Not Ellen,' Mavis said quickly, giving her grandson another sharp look. 'But your grandfather, step-grandmother and your Aunt Josie. Ellen was in Bristol when it happened.'

'But how? When?' Daisy stammered out.

'It was at night, in October of '78,' Tim said. 'No one really knows for certain how it started. I was staying here with Gran at the time, just about to go up to Newcastle to university. Nobody knew about it until the next morning, and by then the farmhouse was just a smouldering pile of stones. You see, it was on a very quiet road, the one up from Maenporth beach, I expect you came that way today. Beacon Farm was in a dip, hidden from the road by woods.'

'How terrible,' Daisy gasped. 'How come they all died in it though? Couldn't they escape?' She might not have known her relatives but it was awful to think of anyone burning to death.

Tim shrugged. 'They could very well have been overcome by the fumes from foam filling in a couch. It was a windy night too, so that would have made the blaze even fiercer. By the time the fire brigade got out there, there wasn't much left to pick through.'

'We'd better have that tea now, Tim,' Mavis said sternly. She looked back at Daisy. 'I'm so very sorry, dear. We shouldn't have launched into something so ghastly the minute you got here.'

After Tim had brought in the tea tray and poured them all a cup, Daisy asked about Ellen.

'This must have been terrible for her.'

'Yes, it was. It changed her,' Mavis said, and her voice quavered a little. 'We had kept in touch ever since she left the village, she wrote or phoned at least once a month, always came round when she was visiting her parents. But she was so distraught when the police called on her in Bristol to tell her the news that she couldn't even come down for the funeral.'

'Good God,' Daisy exclaimed.

Tim leaned forward in his chair. 'Would you like to see where the farm was?' he asked. 'I don't want to drag you away from Gran, but it will be getting dark soon, and you ought to see it. We could walk across the fields to it with Fred.'

Mavis looked at him gratefully. 'That's a very good idea, Tim,' she said. 'But make sure you bring Daisy back for tea with us. By that time I'll have gathered my thoughts about all the things I really must tell her about Ellen and her family.'

Daisy realized then that Mavis was very shaken, and clearly Tim wanted to give her time to compose herself again. She wasn't sure she wanted to see where the farm was, but under the circumstances she thought it best to go with him.

'That's very kind of you,' she said. 'I must find somewhere to stay for tonight too. Do you know of any guest-houses near here that won't mind Fred?'

'You can stay with us,' Mavis said immediately. 'Now, don't argue,' she said as she saw Daisy's mouth open to protest. 'I have a spare bedroom and we'd love to have you, wouldn't we, Tim?'

'Of course, Daisy,' he said with a smile. 'Besides, you two have got a lot of catching up to do.'

'Your grandmother is a lovely lady,' Daisy said as she and

Tim started off on a footpath that skirted round the back of the village.

'Yes, she is, and very sentimental,' he said. 'I'm sorry if you didn't really want to go to the farm right now, but I could see Gran was getting a bit wobbly. That's mainly the shock of you turning up, but also because of Ellen. I realized I needed to warn you about certain things which might upset her further, out of her hearing.'

Daisy looked up at him in puzzlement.

'You see, Gran adored Ellen,' he went on. 'As a kid I had no idea what the connection was between them, I suppose I thought she was a relation. But for some time after the fire Gran was in a very low state and my grandfather explained she was grieving over Ellen and he told me how close they had been. I was a bit mystified about the word "grieving" – after all Ellen didn't die in the fire – but grandfather said it was because Ellen had dropped her, and she couldn't understand why.'

'Dropped her? She didn't write or visit ever again?' Daisy asked.

Tim nodded. 'That's about the size of it. Immediately and completely. Gran's letters to Ellen came back marked "Gone away". It wasn't until a couple of years later that my Aunt Isobel told me about you being born and Gran's part in it. Even my own mother didn't know about that.'

'How strange all this is,' Daisy said thoughtfully. 'But there must have been some very good reason why Ellen cut her off.'

'Oh, Gran will tell you a dozen of those tonight.' He smiled wryly. 'She used to make up a new excuse for Ellen every time I saw her. That she needed to make a new life for herself, with no reminders. Her bleak childhood, even her commitment to her work. But none of them really hold water, Daisy. Between you and me, and I'm sorry if this will hurt you, I think Ellen was a bit of a selfish bitch.'

Daisy was shocked by such vitriol. 'Well, you've put that plain enough.'

He blushed furiously. 'Oh dear, I've said too much,' he said, hanging his head. 'But my gran is one of the kindest, most generous-hearted women on this planet. She doesn't lean on people, she just cares. Ellen must have known that, so I'm sorry I can't make excuses for her too.'

Daisy thought that was a reasonable enough explanation for his sharpness. 'Do you stay with your grandmother a lot?' she asked.

'Whenever I get a chance,' he said. 'I teach at a boarding school near Exeter so I usually spend the holidays with her. But as a kid I was always here. My mother was very much a career woman, and she used to dump me on Gran almost every holiday.'

'Did you actually know Ellen?' she asked.

'Yes, in as much as she visited several times while I was there. I remember her as being nice, asking me about school and stuff, but I can't say she made much of an impression. You know how it is as a kid, you don't take much notice of grown-ups unless they give you money or act strange. But I did take notice of your Aunt Josie, even though I only met her once.'

'Did she give you money or act strange?' Daisy said with a grin. There was something rather engaging about Tim's openness.

'No,' he laughed, 'but she did kind of flirt with me, I was really knocked out by it, after all I was a spotty eighteen-year-old and she was gorgeous and famous.'

'Famous!' Daisy exclaimed, stopping in her tracks. 'What for?'

Tim looked at her in consternation. 'You don't know who she was?'

Daisy shook her head. 'All I knew until today was that there was a younger sister called Josie. Now it seems she died in the fire. What else was she famous for?'

'She was Jojo, the model!'

Daisy frowned. That name did ring a very faint bell, as

if she might have heard it on the radio or seen it in a magazine, but that was all.

'Even if I had heard of her, how could I possibly know she was my aunt? If she died in '78 I was only fourteen.'

He looked embarrassed. 'Of course you wouldn't. Silly of me. I suppose I thought the doctor in Bristol would have told you about her.'

'No, not a word,' she said.

'She was as well known as Twiggy and Jean Shrimpton in the late Sixties and early Seventies,' he said. 'You know, one of those faces of the Sixties.'

'Really?' Daisy exclaimed. This was all becoming very bizarre.

'I was too young to take any interest at the height of her fame,' he said, and grinned. 'I didn't prick up my ears till I was about fourteen, by which time she was on the downward slide, hanging around with rock stars, taking drugs and generally behaving pretty wildly. That of course was fascinating to a boy cloistered in boarding school, especially as she came from my gran's village.

'I used to lap up every new bit of gossip about her in the papers. There were pictures of her everywhere when she was at the height of her fame. You know the kind of thing, tiny mini-skirt, all eyes and cleavage. I almost became a celebrity myself because I had a vague connection with her. But I didn't actually meet her in the flesh until the day before the fire. She was in the post office and she spoke to me.'

Daisy half smiled, imagined a bunch of adolescent boys drooling over such pictures. 'I feel a bit out of my depth,' she admitted. 'First the shock of the fire, then this. No wonder your gran said we had a lot of talking to do.'

Tim didn't reply to that for a minute, just picked up a stick and threw it for Fred. 'Talking about Ellen to her is like walking on thin ice, one word of criticism and she gets snotty. But she can be really funny about Josie too. She's a very liberated old girl in many ways, but some of the things Josie was reported to have done were too shocking for her.'

'That's a shame.' Daisy grinned. 'She sounds fascinating.'

'I agree.' He laughed. 'I've dined out on my vague connection and one meeting with her. I suspect Gran knows far more about what went on in the entire Pengelly family than she's ever told me. She can be very cagey, especially if she was told things in confidence. But I do know that Violet, that's Ellen's stepmother, was very mean to Ellen when she was a small girl, while she doted on Josie. I also know Albert and Violet were at each other's throats most of the time. So I've drawn some conclusions of my own.'

'And they are?' Daisy asked.

'That Gran might have been blind to faults in Ellen, because she loved her. Maybe she only latched on to Gran because she wanted a mother figure, then once she got the money she found she didn't need her any more.'

Daisy frowned. 'You've lost me,' she said. 'What money?'

'Her inheritance after the fire. She was left the land the farm was on. She sold it to a hotel group and made herself a fortune.'

'This story is getting more and more outlandish,' Daisy thought to herself. 'On the way down here from Bristol I was imagining Ellen as a sweet, gentle girl, maybe even a long-suffering martyr. Now she seems to be turning into a selfish, cold-hearted gold-digger!'

'I'm sorry, I've jumped ahead, forgetting you don't know the family history,' Tim admitted. 'My interest began after the fire, so I had to back-track to find out the rest. What Gran and I should do is sit you down and go right through the family history, from beginning to end, then you can draw your own conclusions. You see, I don't think you can get a true picture of Ellen without seeing the family in its entirety first, or without knowing about the hostility between Albert and Violet and their wrangling

279

over the value of the farm. I'd say Ellen's character was forged by that, along with what happened to her, and Josie's fame too.'

'I see,' Daisy said, even though she didn't.

Perhaps Tim saw her puzzlement for he chuckled. 'Gran once said she wondered how she would explain it all to you if you ever turned up. Of course, she never really supposed you would. Then out of the blue you breeze along the road with your dog, and suddenly it's real, and possibly very hurtful.'

Then he went on to astound her even further with the story of how Clare, a society girl, had married Albert and come to live at the farm, and of her death on the cliffs with her baby in her arms.

'My grandmother did that!' Daisy exclaimed. 'Come on, you're making it up!'

'I'm not,' he said firmly. 'That's exactly what I mean about the history of the family being so important.'

He went on to explain that no one ever knew for certain whether it was an accident or suicide, and told her how Violet came into the picture, married Albert and then produced Josie. 'The girls were two and a half years apart and almost like twins, with the same hair as yours. Ellen didn't know they weren't real sisters or that Violet wasn't her real mother until someone in the village let the cat out of the bag.'

'I see what you mean,' Daisy said, thinking back to when Lucy told her she was the cuckoo in the nest. She was an adult and knew perfectly well she was adopted, yet it had still stung her. 'What was Violet like? Was she the kind to explain gently?'

Tim gave a mirthless laugh. 'Hardly. I used to see her when I went down to the cove. I always thought she was a witch. Ellen told Gran that Violet laid into her for being upset about it. I don't think you'll find anyone with a good word to say about her. Gran did try to find something to like about her, but I think even she failed.'

When they came to a stile which brought them back on to the road Daisy had driven along earlier in the day, Tim pointed out that although there were houses along it now, most had only been built in the last twenty years.

'Ellen and Josie must have felt very isolated,' he said thoughtfully. 'No television, no phone, I don't think they even had electricity until they were in their teens. Stuck in the middle of nowhere between parents who never stopped fighting.'

A short walk along the road from the stile brought them to a tree-lined drive with a very elegant sign in gold lettering for the Rosemullion Hotel. A low wall separated the grounds from the grassy bank at the side of the road, and through the thick bushes Daisy caught a glimpse of smooth lawns. 'That's not it, is it?' she asked, stopping in her tracks.

'Yes, it is, but a far cry from what it looked like when it was Beacon Farm.' Tim laughed. 'As I remember there was a broken-down fence along there under the bushes, and the drive to the farm was just a muddy rutted track.'

Daisy was staring at it in wonder.

'Try not to see the sign, the lawns or the tarmac drive.' He grinned. 'I'll try and give you a glimpse of what the old farm was like for Ellen and Josie by taking you through the woods.'

Whistling to Fred, he took Daisy's arm and led her back a little way to a footpath which was signposted to the beach. It was almost hidden by thick bushes on either side. 'This is the way I used to come down to swim in the cove with Grandpa,' he said. 'It's not that different now, except someone has put some gravel down in the muddiest places.'

Daisy was charmed by the way trees formed an archway above their heads. To either side of the sloping footpath was a blanket of yellow celandines, wind-flowers, and bluebells about to flower. It seemed to go on and on, but finally the woods thinned out and she could see down across the fields to the sea.

'All the land on both sides of us and right down to the sea belonged to Albert, his father and his grandfather before that,' Tim explained. 'But it was hard to farm by all accounts, and he refused to make part of it a camp site or caravan park which would have brought in some extra money.' He stopped suddenly as the front of the hotel came into view to their left.

If Daisy hadn't been told it had only been built in the last twelve years she might have believed it had been there forever, for it was in the style of an old country house, with sash windows, wide steps leading up to the huge front doors and a stone porch covered in wisteria.

'Try and wipe that picture out,' Tim said, making a sweeping gesture with his arm. 'Replace it with a low, ramshackle stone cottage which had bits added in a haphazard fashion over the years. It didn't even face the same way. The back of it was right up in the woods, the front door faced the sea. In fact the hotel isn't even in the same spot as the old cottage, that's under the drive now. When the guests sit in the dining- and drawing-rooms admiring the view of the cove, they'd be where the old front garden was. That had a scrubby lawn, a few fruit trees and a dilapidated wooden fence. Then of course there were several old wooden outbuildings too and a barn to the right of it.'

Daisy nodded. The photograph she had of Ellen and Josie as little girls had part of the farmhouse, and one of the fruit trees in the background, so she had a picture in her mind. But this smart place with its manicured lawns and carefully planted flower-beds was overriding that image of rural poverty.

'Well, I suppose if nothing else I can get some kudos from boasting that this was once all my grandfather's,' she said with a smile.

'Let's go on down to the cove,' he said, whistling again

to Fred who was rooting around in the woods. 'There at least nothing has changed, other than the National Trust putting in a proper footpath along the cliffs.'

As they put the manicured gardens of the hotel behind them, Daisy could easily imagine why her grandfather hadn't wanted to sell the property. It was simply awe inspiringly beautiful. The tumbling stream, the mix of heather and wild flowers, lush grass and craggy boulders were far beyond any landscape gardener's capabilities.

There were a few sturdy little ponies and some goats in the steeply rising fields to either side, where presumably Albert once kept his cows and sheep, but Daisy doubted anything much else had changed. Down at the little cove, she could almost visualize two small tousled red-heads in woolly bathing suits, catching crabs in the rock pools, and it all seemed so familiar to her, as if she had carried the memory of this place with her in her mother's womb.

'I used to wish Grandpa owned the farm when I was little,' Tim admitted as he threw pebbles into the sea. 'This was my idea of the most perfect place in the world to live.'

Daisy stood looking all around her in wonder. It was too early in the year for tourists to have found their way here, and the utter peace and tranquillity, with nothing but the soothing sound of waves and cries of seagulls, brought a lump into her throat.

'Yet Ellen got pregnant and ran away to Bristol, and Josie became a model and moved away too,' she said with a sigh. 'I don't think I would have wanted to leave it.'

'Josie ran away too, when she was only fifteen,' Tim said. 'But then we're looking at this enchanted place from a different perspective to the one they had. We know what big cities are like, we aren't children deprived of company or luxuries. Ellen was supposed to be the one who loved it, yet when it became hers, she couldn't get rid of it fast enough.'

Back in 'Swallow's' much later that afternoon, with a fire

lit because it had grown chilly once the sun faded, Mavis told Daisy how she came to know Ellen, and about the girl's home life. Daisy listened spellbound to the tales of the primitive conditions at the farm, of the difficult and uncommunicative Albert, and Violet, the harsh, slatternly stepmother.

Having painted the background picture, she then went on to tell Daisy of the part she had played in Ellen going to Bristol to have her baby.

'I've never been able to make my mind up about whether I gave her the right advice or not,' she sighed. 'Maybe I should have encouraged her to tell her father about you.'

'It doesn't sound to me as if that would have been a better solution,' Daisy said thoughtfully. 'And I certainly had a better childhood than Ellen could have given me.'

'But she never got over giving you up,' Mavis said with real feeling. 'She made a good life for herself, she worked hard, had good friends, she claimed she had put it behind her, but I could sense the sadness within her. I used to hope she'd meet some nice young man, get married and have more children, but she said she believed her path in life was to help other children, ones that really needed her. She meant it too, she was entirely dedicated to her work, she didn't even care about her appearance.'

Mavis shook her head as if she still didn't understand it. 'Sometimes when she came down here to see me, I used to plead with her to let her lovely hair loose, to put on a bit of makeup and buy herself some pretty clothes. But she would just laugh and say she'd leave all that to Josie who was enough of a sensation for both of them.'

'Was this sadness just the result of giving me up, or was she badly hurt by my father too?' Daisy asked. 'Do you know about him?'

'Yes dear, I do know.' Mavis stopped short, glancing nervously at Tim. Daisy guessed this was something she hadn't shared even with him, and wasn't sure if she should now.

'Tell me,' Daisy begged her. 'It's all water under the bridge now, and I'm sure she wouldn't mind either Tim or me knowing. Was he a married man? Is that why she couldn't tell anyone else about him?'

'No, he wasn't married, at least as far as Ellen knew. It was just what he did for a living, and the fact he went off without a word to her. He worked in a circus.'

Daisy's eyes opened wide in shock, then she giggled. 'Really! Don't tell me he was a clown, I'll never live that one down.'

Tim laughed and his grandmother reprimanded him. 'No, he wasn't a clown. He was a trapeze artist.'

'But that's fabulous,' Daisy said with delight. 'You aren't teasing me, are you?'

'Of course not. But though it may sound fabulous to you, to Albert it would have been as bad as consorting with Old Nick himself. All that is irrelevant now, because the circus moved on without him saying goodbye, even before Ellen knew she was pregnant.'

'Oh God, yes, I can see what you mean,' Daisy said reflectively, suddenly aware of how terrible that would be for a young girl.

'He was actually one of the top stars of that circus,' Mavis said. 'Nowadays he would probably be something of a celebrity, but people didn't view circus folk like that in those days.'

'It explains something about me though,' Daisy said. 'I'm good at gymnastics, I was even once a bit of a child star, winning prizes and stuff. It's nice to know where it came from.'

'You seem rather bucked about it,' Tim chuckled.

'I am,' she admitted, grinning broadly. 'It was my one talent, and it always seemed so extraordinary in a family where no one else could even do a hand-stand.'

'Well, Gran, you don't have to worry now,' Tim said laughingly, looking pointedly at his grandmother. 'Your dark, dark secret never to be spoken has made Daisy happy.'

'Don't talk such rot, Tim,' Mavis said heatedly. 'I only kept it to myself because Ellen asked me to. I didn't think there was anything shameful in it.'

'It could have been a lot worse, he could have been a rat catcher.' Daisy smiled. 'I wish he'd come back for Ellen though, that would have been very romantic.'

'I never felt she was ashamed of having loved him. Only hurt that she'd been fooled into thinking he loved her back,' Mavis said.

'I've loved some pretty unsuitable men myself,' Daisy admitted, 'so I can sympathize with that.'

Over a meal of steak and kidney pie, followed by a lovely chocolate mousse, Mavis told Daisy everything she knew about the Pengellys, in much greater detail than Tim had. She was good at telling stories, giving so much detail, and having seen where Beacon Farm once stood, Daisy could now visualize all the characters and the settings.

'What do you think happened to Clare?' she asked. She supposed if this grandmother of hers had lived she would have been older still than Mavis. 'In your opinion was it suicide or an accident?'

'It had to be suicide,' Mavis said. 'If she'd gone up there for a walk with the baby in her arms she would have been doubly careful to keep away from the edge of the cliff. I think it must have been post-natal depression. Of course in those days they didn't know about that sort of thing, they passed it off as "trouble with her nerves"! Clare was by all accounts an artistic, highly strung young woman.'

Mavis paused, looking reflective.

'I suppose she married Albert in the heat of passion, he must have seemed wildly romantic to such a gently brought-up girl. He was a good-looking chap when he was young too, by all accounts. But two babies in such a short time, in primitive conditions which she wasn't used to, must have become too much for her.'

Daisy pondered on this for a moment. 'No wonder I've never been exactly normal,' she said, and half smiled.

'Sullen, difficult men, mad women, trapeze artists, what a family history!'

'Your mother was one of the best people I've ever met,' Mavis said sharply. 'She was highly intelligent, sweet-natured and hard-working. Her only fault was that she always tried to make things right for other people. Never herself.'

'But she changed when she got that money, didn't she?' Daisy retorted, forgetting she wasn't supposed to say anything unkind. 'She didn't want the farm, or her old friends.'

Mavis looked accusingly at Tim. 'You shouldn't have put it like that,' she said indignantly. 'You know I don't believe it was the money that stopped her keeping in touch. I honestly think she must had some kind of mental breakdown, most sensitive people would after something so terrible happening to them.'

'I'm sure you're right, you knew her better than anyone after all,' Daisy said hastily, ashamed of herself for hurting such a kind and loyal woman. 'Maybe she will come back to you too one day. I hope so. But tell me about Josie now.'

She took the photograph of the two girls together out of her bag and showed it to Mavis. 'Ellen sent this to my mother when I was about six or seven,' she said. 'I only want to understand the significance of it. Why didn't she send a recent picture? I know it must have meant something special to her, I feel it really strongly. That's why I want to know about Josie too.'

'Ellen loved Josie, they were best friends as well as sisters,' Mavis said eventually. 'That picture was taken not long before Ellen found out that Violet wasn't her real mother.'

Daisy listened carefully as Mavis repeated Ellen's story about the revelations in the school playground, how nasty Violet was to her about it, and her feelings afterwards that nothing would ever be the same again.

'In my opinion that picture signified real happiness to Ellen, everything that came after was tainted with sorrow. Most of us have dozens of pictures of happy times, but that was her only one. So she wanted you to have it.'

'I see,' Daisy said, feeling tears prickling in her eyes. 'But please tell me about Josie. I'm sure she must have been very important to Ellen, and if I ever get to meet her it will help if I know about her already.'

'I suppose the first important detail about Josie is that she ran away and caused so much misery for all her family,' Mavis said. 'She went just after her fifteenth birthday in July, two months after your birth, when Ellen was in a very low state. All of us here in the village got to hear about it immediately because Albert called the police from the pub when Josie didn't come home after a weekend in Falmouth. He rang Ellen in Bristol too, checking to see if she'd gone there.'

'How long was it before they knew where she was?'

'Apparently she sent a postcard just a few days later saying she was in London. She sent others too later on, saying she had a room and a job, but she didn't send an address. I'm sure you can imagine what that did to the rest of the family.'

'My parents would have been distraught.' Daisy shook her head sadly.

'Albert and Violet were too. Most of us in the village half expected more tragedy to follow – Josie was, after all, Violet's whole life. Yet Ellen told me when she came down that it seemed to be pulling Violet and Albert closer together. She took some comfort in that.'

'So Ellen came back down here then, did she?' Daisy asked.

'Only for a week, and that was one of the bravest things she ever did. After all she'd been through already, the last thing she needed was Violet blaming her for Josie running off, but she felt she had to try to comfort her parents. But that was how she was, Daisy, always thinking of others before herself.'

Mavis paused and dabbed at damp eyes.

'I really don't know how she managed to get through that visit without them guessing something awful had happened to her too. She used to come up here and sob her heart out to me. About both you and Josie. She said she could understand perfectly why Josie wasn't letting their parents know where she was, but she was desperately hurt that Josie hadn't even telephoned her in Bristol before she left to tell her what she was going to do, and to ask if she'd had her baby and what it was.'

Daisy thought of her own relationship with Lucy. 'Sisters can be cruel and thoughtless,' she said.

'I know, but they had been everything to one another all their childhood,' Mavis said. 'Ellen had confided in Josie when she first found out she was pregnant, Josie was the only person other than me that knew why Ellen really went to Bristol. So you can imagine how hurt she was that Josie couldn't trust her with her own secret, and didn't seem to have remembered that Ellen would need some support too.'

'So when did they all find out where Josie was living?' Daisy asked.

'They didn't for absolutely ages, well over a year as I remember. But around Christmas of the year you were born, they ran a story in one of the tabloids about a young runaway girl photographed on Paddington station. It was Josie.'

Mavis got up and went over to a bureau, and took a cardboard folder out of a drawer. 'You'd better read it all yourself,' she said. 'I'm sure you'll understand how we all felt.'

Daisy opened the file and gasped as she saw the headline 'Runaway' and the heart-breaking picture beneath of a girl who looked little more than twelve, her hair tied up in bunches, tears rolling down her cheeks, and clutching her suitcase fearfully.

'It was just a scam,' Tim said, as she was reading about Mark Kinsale, the photographer who took the picture. 'According to what Ellen told Gran much later on, that guy Kinsale had plans right then to do a sort of Cinderella feature with her.'

'But Albert and Violet just saw this, and thought it was all for real?' Daisy asked incredulously. 'God almighty, that must have been terrible for them.'

Mavis nodded. 'It was, absolutely shattering. The whole village saw it, everyone was so frightened for Josie. You'll see the article is all about young girls disappearing into vice rings and such things. Violet was nearly out of her mind. To make matters worse they ran a whole series of grisly stuff about runaways, and every week that picture of Josie was repeated. It was four weeks before they announced they'd found her. Go on turning the pages, you'll come to it.'

Daisy winced when she came to the page headlined 'Found'.

In this picture Josie was looking a great deal more adult and knowing, wearing a man's shirt over skimpy underwear. The journalist said she had been given a tip-off that Josie was working in a so-called 'photographers' club' where men paid by the hour to take pictures of young models. She stated that invariably the men had no film in the cameras and the girls were being conned into 'glamour poses' which often verged on the pornographic.

Then Mark Kinsale was alerted and he visited the 'club' and took this picture of Josie. The article ended with a gushing piece about her innocence and beauty and how Kinsale felt she had the ability to be a real fashion model if she was given the opportunity.

'I can see how contrived it is,' Daisy said, looking up at Tim and Mavis. 'But I don't suppose Albert and Violet could. Was it true that she was really about to be sucked into vice, or was that just hype?'

'I think the newspaper knew she was working in that place all along, even before they put the first picture in the paper. And a fat lot they cared if she was in danger,' Mavis said angrily. 'Albert and Violet went up to London to see them, they begged the editor of the paper to tell them where Josie was living, but they were sent away and told to keep out of it. That was criminal. If they'd done that to one of my children I think I would have killed them.'

'If you can distance yourself from the misery that newspaper caused for the Pengellys,' Tim said, 'it was rather a clever scam to launch Josie. In the four weeks they ran it, they caught the attention of every parent in England by showing all the dangers runaways can fall into and making every single one of them desperately want her to be found safe and well.

'Then, when they showed where she was, they squeezed people's hearts a bit more. They twisted quotes from Albert so he sounded like a vicious bully, her mother a monster, and the farm a hell-hole. It was all preparing the way for when Josie would be launched as Jojo, the model, the little-girl-lost with the tragic childhood.'

Daisy began to turn over the cuttings. She could see exactly what Tim meant. The farmhouse photographed in mid-winter did look stark and primitive. Violet was caught looking fat and frowzy in wellington boots and a dirty apron as she fed chickens. As for Albert, he looked like an ageing gypsy with long, straggly hair, brandishing a stick at the photographer. She thought if such a story were to be run today, she'd be crying over it too.

'It's hard to believe such a beautiful girl had such awful-looking parents,' she said, looking at Mavis and Tim. 'To be truthful, I wouldn't want to show that one of my grandfather to anyone.'

Mavis gave a little snort of disapproval, but Tim grinned.

'Shame we haven't got one of your father up on his trapeze,' he said.

Yet as Daisy looked at more pictures of Josie, she couldn't help but feel a little grudging admiration for Kinsale. Setting aside his somewhat sinister motives, he had clearly worked hard on Josie, gradually building her up from the waif on the station to a real glamour-puss. Maybe it wasn't ethical, but then the film industry and the pop music world were both full of talentless people who had been hyped into stardom. She wouldn't mind someone doing it to her.

One article amused her particularly. Josie had been taken to Carnaby Street to buy new clothes, and she was photographed in several different outfits, including a mini-fox-fur coat and long tight boots.

It was all very Sixties, with quotes from Josie like, 'Wow, this is out-a-sight,' 'I feel fab,' and 'It just blows my mind to think a few months ago I was milking cows.'

'I stopped collecting cuttings then,' Mavis said as Daisy came to the end of them. 'I couldn't bear to look at her, knowing what she'd done to her parents. Of course, her home life wasn't idyllic, but neither was it hell. We all saw how it affected Albert, he became even more of a recluse, drinking at home which he never did before. As for Violet, time and again she sat here in this very room, sobbing her heart out. I couldn't take to the woman, but I know how much she loved her daughter.'

'Was Josie in on it?' Daisy asked. 'I mean, if she was only fifteen, was she mature enough to know what the newspaper was doing to her parents?'

'Ellen always said she didn't, but she could be very gullible where Josie was concerned. Whether she did or she didn't, that still doesn't excuse her hiding away in London and not telling her parents where she was. Or for the way she treated them later on.'

'Did she come back here eventually?' Daisy asked.

'Not for a very long while. We saw her face in every magazine and newspaper. Adverts for shampoo, bridal gowns, swimwear, everything. She looked lovely. But none of us down here could really feel proud that she was a local girl, we all felt so bad about Albert and Violet.'

'But obviously she must have made it up with them, or she wouldn't have died in the fire. When was that?' Daisy asked.

'I don't know if you could say they ever really made it up,' Mavis said thoughtfully. 'She'd come down here and swan around showing off from time to time. But she usually managed to upset them again because she was so scornful of the farm and country life.'

'And she got into drugs too?' Daisy said. 'When did that start?'

'Almost as soon as she started modelling,' Tim said. 'Well, it was that era when everyone was at it, wasn't it? Judging by the amount of pictures of her, that guy Kinsale must have worked her very hard too. But she didn't really come unstuck until after she'd split with Kinsale. That was when she seemed to fall apart.'

'Was he her lover?' Daisy had seen a picture of him in one of the cuttings and she thought he looked a mean sort, one of those ageing Sixties rock star look-a-likes with a pony-tail and a frilly shirt.

'I think he was right from the beginning,' Mavis said. 'He was old enough to be her father too! But that's not for me to judge. Violet met him once, she went up to see Josie when she had flu. She stayed for a few days in her flat in Chelsea, then he came round and threw her out.'

Daisy raised her eyebrows.

'Well, Violet said it was him who threw her out. I always suspected it was really Josie,' Mavis said seriously. 'That was around the time she got really famous. She was off to New York one minute, the South of France the next. Always on Kinsale's arm. After they split up he was still her photographer, which I suppose meant he was making huge amounts of money from her, but they weren't as they say these days, an "Item" any more. Soon afterwards she

293

was going out with rock stars and actors, mentioned in the gossip columns nearly every day.'

'How much did Ellen have to do with her during that time?' Daisy asked. She found it hard to imagine a famous model wanting to spend much time with a quiet girl like Ellen who worked with handicapped kids, not even if she was her sister.

'Ellen's flat in Bristol was her bolt-hole,' Mavis said. 'She would turn up there when she needed her. But it wasn't until she really began to slide down the slippery slope that it became a regular thing. I think Ellen gave her money, she tried very hard to straighten her out. But nothing worked. Ellen told me Josie would cry to her, say she was going to change, and she'd leave to go back to London resolute, but in a few weeks she was back on drugs, worse than she was before.'

'So what happened to her in the years after her career was over and before she died?' Daisy asked.

Mavis suddenly got up and went into the kitchen. It was clear to Daisy this was something she didn't want to discuss.

'Porn,' Tim whispered. 'Gran can't cope with that. So don't ask her anything about it. After Josie died, that's when I started digging into everything about her. I got hold of a video with her in, it was pretty seedy. But don't tell Gran that either!'

Daisy grinned. 'Well, how come she ended up back down here then?' she asked.

'The end of the road, I guess.' Tim shrugged. 'According to what Gran's told me, she would turn up about once every six months, always with a tale for her mother that she was about to go into films, television or something.'

'Poor Violet used to confide in me,' Mavis said as she came back into the room with three cups of hot chocolate on a tray. 'Heaven knows I didn't want to hear it, but I had to anyway. Josie would weave all these stories, than shoot off again, usually borrowing money which she never repaid. But it was different the last time she came. Even I could see she really seemed to have quietened down. She was here for over a month and Violet said she had left her flat in London, and she was going to buy a place down here. It seemed definite, she'd made a formal offer for a small cottage in Truro, got herself a job, we both thought she'd turned over a new leaf.'

'But then she died in the fire,' Daisy mused. 'Strange how things work out for some people, isn't it? Did she have any money left to pay for this cottage she was going to buy?'

Tim looked at Mavis sharply. 'Well, did she, Gran?' he asked.

'No, I don't think she did,' Mavis admitted. 'My husband spoke to someone in the know who said she hadn't left a will, but that hardly mattered as her bank account was overdrawn.'

'Hmm,' Daisy murmured, and the other two looked at her. 'Makes you wonder if she started the fire and intended to get out just in time.'

There was an uneasy silence while both Tim and Mavis stared at her.

'I've often thought that,' Tim finally admitted, fingering his collar nervously as if he was afraid Mavis would snap at him.

'I did too,' said Mavis in a small voice. 'I've often wondered if that was the real reason Ellen wouldn't come back here. Maybe she thought so too.'

Chapter Eighteen

'You will come back and see me again?' Mavis asked as Daisy put Fred's lead on in readiness to leave the following morning.

The note of sadness in the old lady's voice surprised Daisy, and she suddenly realized Mavis half expected her to disappear just as Ellen had.

'I can't promise to come down here for a while. I've got to get myself a job,' Daisy said. 'But I'll keep in touch and tell you any news. Of course, if the solicitor in Falmouth comes up with anything positive, I'll be on the phone immediately.'

Tim had said his goodbyes and gone out an hour earlier, out of diplomacy, Daisy suspected – he must have thought the two women had things to say to each other in private. There was indeed a great deal Daisy wanted to say to Mavis, she very much wanted to express the depth of her gratitude. But as yet she couldn't find the words.

As she had lain in the pretty little guest-room upstairs the night before, she had thought back to the way the old lady had welcomed her into her home. She didn't think many people would be so generous and open-hearted.

How could Ellen have cast such a wonderful friend and mother figure out of her life? Daisy had known Mavis less than twenty-four hours, yet already she felt attached to her. In some strange way that made her want to find Ellen even more now, if only to put the old lady's mind at rest. She must have suffered agonies wondering if Ellen had lost her mind after the tragedy. Now Daisy knew so much about the Pengellys, that really did seem to be the only plausible explanation.

Daisy was pinning all her hopes on Albert's solicitor being able to help her in the next stage of the search. Mavis had given her his name and the address of his practice in Falmouth, and she planned to go to see him the following day.

'It's been almost like having Ellen back here again,' Mavis said, a tell-tale break in her voice. 'I've felt so comfortable with you, just the way I did with her. You don't get that feeling with just anyone.' She paused for a moment looking reflectively at Daisy. 'You aren't that alike physically, although the shock of seeing that hair again made me think you were at first. Your eyes are blue, hers were brown, and you are much more direct and outgoing. But then you've had a different kind of upbringing, and advantages Ellen didn't have. And you are a very modern girl – Ellen was the old-fashioned kind, even when she was your age.'

It suddenly occurred to Daisy then that she didn't have a mental picture of Ellen in her mind. She had one of Josie, as firmly engraved as if she'd known her personally, but Ellen was still very cloudy.

'I didn't think to ask before,' she said, 'but do you have a photograph of her?'

'Only one,' Mavis said, glancing towards the sideboard. 'I used to keep it over there, but I put it away a few years ago, it only made me sad. I don't know why I didn't think to show it to you yesterday.'

Mavis rummaged through the sideboard. 'Here it is,' she said, pulling out a colour picture in a silver frame. 'Tom, my husband, took it in the garden. We had it enlarged because it was such a nice one.'

Daisy studied it carefully. Ellen was sitting on a bench with an arch of white roses behind her. She wore a demure print dress with a scoop neck and a frill round the hem. It looked like one of the Laura Ashley dresses Daisy could remember her mother wearing during the Seventies.

Ellen's similarity to Josie was remarkable. But for Ellen's prim style of dress and the unflattering way her hair was scraped back off her face, it could easily have been the model a few years on, for the delicate bone structure and huge, expressive eyes were the same. The difference was only in the smile; in all the press cuttings of Josie, her exuberant smile was a traffic-stopper, revealing an outgoing nature. Ellen's smile was shy, as if smiling didn't come easily to her. She looked somehow as if she'd seen the whole world, and it had disappointed her.

Yet Daisy could see herself in that face. Not the way she looked when she was excited and happy, but those glimpses she'd had of herself sometimes when everything seemed against her. Was that how Ellen felt?

'When was this taken?' she asked.

'It was the summer before the fire,' Mavis replied. 'Ellen was thirty-one, and it must have been June because the roses are in full bloom. I remember her saying that day you'd just turned fourteen. She hoped you did ballet, or were into horses, because fourteen can be such a difficult age, and girls with a hobby didn't seem to get themselves into as much trouble as those without.'

'That's when I was doing gymnastics all the time,' Daisy said thoughtfully. 'I wonder what she'd make of that!'

'I think she'd be pleased,' Mavis said and came forward to embrace Daisy. 'Anyone would be proud to have you as a daughter. I hope you can track Ellen down, it's going to turn her life around completely.'

Daisy hugged Mavis back, and she felt a sting of tears in her eyes and a lump in her throat because the hug and Mavis's words made her think suddenly of her adoptive mother. Lorna would have liked Mavis; they were very similar in their manner.

'You've been so wonderful,' she said, her voice sounding oddly strangled as she leaned into the older woman's shoulder, 'so kind, so understanding. Even if I never find Ellen, you've given me such insight into her and her family.'

Mavis took Daisy's face in both hands and smiled at her. 'You've made me feel better too by coming here. At least I know you really did go to a good home. You are a credit to your adoptive mother. Now, you keep that picture of Ellen. I've got all the ones I need still in my head.'

After saying goodbye to Mavis and promising to keep in touch, Daisy went straight to St Mawes. Tim had given her clear directions, and the cottage was right by The Rising Sun pub on the harbour. It belonged to an associate of her father's, and they'd agreed Daisy could stay for a week for nothing, on the understanding she would give it a good cleaning and airing before the owners arrived for the Easter holiday.

The cottage had been described to her as 'basic', so she wasn't expecting much, but it was in fact delightful, a turn-of-the-century fisherman's cottage, two up and two down. The owners had stripped and varnished the floorboards, painted all the walls white and the old wooden furniture bright blue.

It wasn't even cold and damp as Daisy had expected it would be, though that was probably because it had been mild and sunny for a few days. As she stood up in the bedroom, looking out at the serene view of the fishing harbour, she felt happier than she had in a long while. It was as if in coming away from London she'd finally managed to take a real step forward, and now she could begin to look ahead again.

Later in the afternoon she took Fred for a walk along to the castle which stood at the mouth of the estuary facing Falmouth on the other side. Now it seemed more than just coincidence that she'd been offered the cottage, for Mavis had told her this morning that Ellen had only had one real date with Pierre, the trapeze artist, and this is where he'd brought her.

As she walked past the castle, down to a footpath that went along the river, she wondered whether she was conceived here, in the long grass of a meadow perhaps. The thought made her smile; if Joel had come down here with her she would have been only too keen to do a little romping in long grass herself!

Yet thinking of him made her suddenly sad. She felt their love affair was all but over. Maybe she'd never really known him as she once thought she did. He'd been so dismissive of her coming here, as though he couldn't see the importance of it for her. 'Clutching at straws' was how he put it.

Daisy sighed. It was going to be even more difficult when she got home. In her wildest dreams she hadn't expected to discover so much fascinating information, and she knew now that she was probably going to become like a dog with a bone about it all, chewing on it, burying it for a while, then digging it up again. Joel wasn't going to like it one bit. She supposed she ought to phone him really, but she couldn't bear the thought of him pouring cold water on her enthusiasm.

Fred was rooting around among the bushes, so Daisy sat down on a bench to look at the view. It struck her that this was the first time in her life she'd really been on her own. She'd always been one for needing company in whatever she did, and often she panicked at the thought of being alone for longer than a few hours. That seemed quite pathetic in the light of hearing about both Ellen and Josie leaving home so young and the ordeals they'd both been through.

But she wasn't the least bit lonely or panicky now; it felt good to be independent and to have this time alone to sort out her feelings. Maybe she was finally turning into an adult, as she didn't feel the slightest desire to rush off to a phone box to share all her news with anyone. She knew she needed space to be able to collate all the information she'd received, and to plan her next move.

The view before her was further inspiration. A yacht was out in the middle of the estuary, going towards Falmouth. It looked so tiny in the wide stretch of water, its sail ballooning out, the owner leaning right back over the side to hold it on its course. She knew from her father's experience at sailing that it took a great deal more than just wind to get to the desired destination. You had to know how to harness the boat, often patiently tacking back and forth to move forward.

She was likely to have setbacks in her search for Ellen. But she was going to continue doggedly, whatever it took. Maybe Joel would come aboard too, maybe he wouldn't. But she wasn't going to give up now.

At nine the following morning, Daisy drove into Falmouth. It had turned colder again, and rain was expected later, but even if the solicitors wouldn't see her without an appointment, she wanted to explore the town.

'May I see Mr Briggs?' she asked the receptionist in the offices of Briggs, Mayhew and Pointer. 'I'm afraid I haven't been able to make an appointment as I'm only in Cornwall for a few days. It is a matter of some urgency.'

She doubted the wisdom now of having brought Fred with her, and being dressed like a hiker in a padded jacket and jeans. It didn't create a very good image. But she smiled brightly at the snotty-looking woman in her pink-tinted glasses, and prepared to stand her ground.

'May I know the nature of the business you wish to discuss with Mr Briggs?' the woman asked starchily. 'He doesn't usually see anyone without an appointment.'

'It's a delicate matter, regarding the estate of Albert Pengelly of Mawnan Smith,' Daisy replied.

'I see.' The woman nodded, and Daisy got the distinct impression that she was noting her red hair and connecting it with the Pengellys. 'I'll just pop in and see Mr Briggs,' she said, getting up off her chair. As she disappeared down a corridor behind a frosted-glass door, Daisy smiled to herself. Clearly the woman wanted to warn him what she looked like, or she would have spoken to him on the intercom.

She came back very quickly. 'Mr Briggs can see you for a few minutes before his next client,' she said. 'It's the third door on the right.'

Feeling more confident now that she knew the name Pengelly had some clout to it, Daisy shortened Fred's lead and marched down the corridor.

Mr Briggs opened the door for her as she got there. 'Daisy Buchan,' she said, holding out her hand to the small elderly man. 'I am Ellen Pengelly's daughter.'

He was visibly taken aback by that announcement, but shook her hand and pulled out a chair for her in front of his desk.

'I don't suppose you knew of my existence,' Daisy said, making Fred sit down beside her chair. 'That is the delicate part of the matter.'

As quickly and concisely as she could, she explained when and where she was born, and the background to the reasons she'd come to Cornwall. 'It was only yesterday I learned about the tragic fire,' she said. 'And I understand Ellen moved away and has not contacted anyone down here since.' She produced her adoption certificate and the note her mother had made regarding the letter from Ellen to verify she had expressed a desire to meet her one day. 'I was hoping you might be able to help me find her.'

'Well, Miss Buchan,' said Mr Briggs, pale eyes flickering nervously behind thick glasses, 'Ellen isn't one of our clients, we only acted for her father. I haven't had any contact with her since the estate was wound up, that was over ten years ago now.'

'Where was she then?' Daisy asked.

'At her flat in Bristol,' he said. 'But I know she was intending to leave it shortly afterwards.'

302

'But you must have had some contact address,' Daisy said with her brightest and warmest smile. 'Even if it was only her solicitor's. After all, her entire family died in that fire, I can't imagine the police or the coroner would have allowed the only living relative to just disappear.'

Mr Briggs looked at her hard for a few moments. 'It was a very difficult time for Ellen,' he said at length. 'She was traumatized by what happened, so much so she couldn't even come to our offices to sign the papers. I did all I could to hasten the winding up of the estate, as she was too sick to work and needed it settled.'

'Sick?' Daisy repeated. 'What kind of sick?'

'I really couldn't say,' Mr Briggs said in a manner that suggested she shouldn't be asking him questions like that.

'She would have been paid if she was off sick, and she'd lived in Bristol a very long time, so why was she in such a hurry?'

'People are often in a hurry to have an estate wound up, sometimes because they believe they will stop grieving once it's all finalized.'

Aware she was putting his back up by asking so many questions, Daisy tried another tack.

'I'm sorry if I sound pushy, I don't mean to be.' Daisy gave him a wide smile. 'I'm just worried about Ellen. You see, Mrs Peters in Mawnan Smith who was a very close friend of Ellen's told me she has estranged herself from all her old friends, and most people in the village think it's because she came into so much money. But Mrs Peters and I can't believe that. We think it's far more likely she had some kind of mental breakdown after the tragedy.'

Mr Briggs nodded. 'I would agree with you,' he said. 'She never struck me as being materialistic.'

'If that was the case,' Daisy went on, heartened by his agreeing with her, 'it might help her deal with the past if I turn up. What do you think?'

The man's face softened. 'I think you are right. Now I

know about you, Miss Buchan, it does cast some light on why Ellen left Cornwall so young, and went in for work which must have been very punishing. I had always got the impression from her father that it was more to do with the difficult relationship she had with his wife. I take it he never knew of your existence?'

'No, the only people who knew down here were Mr and Mrs Peters.'

'Ellen often spoke of them before the tragedy.' Mr Briggs nodded. 'You see, she sometimes popped in here with messages from her father when she was down visiting him. I always used to ask when she was going to come back for good.'

'What did she say about that?'

'That she and Violet couldn't live under the same roof, however much she'd like to run the farm with Albert.' Mr Briggs smiled. 'That's what she was like, kind-hearted, realistic and straight-talking. Knowing how much she loved the place, it was something of a shock that she wanted to get shot of it almost the minute the disaster happened.'

'Well, no one would be able to be objective about the future at a time like that,' Daisy said.

'True, that's why I tried to persuade her to wait a while,' Mr Briggs replied. 'Maybe if I'd been able to speak to her face to face, I might have been able to offer a different solution. But she wouldn't or couldn't come down here, wouldn't wait, and of course in the end I had to accept my place as merely her father's solicitor and executor, and go along with her wishes.'

'What would your different solution have been then?' Daisy asked, relieved that Mr Briggs had warmed up.

'To sell most of the farmland, keeping a small part for herself, and apply for planning permission to build herself a small cottage on it. There would have been no problem with that. She would have had enough capital left to live on, and there are dozens of schools in the surrounding area who would have been only too delighted to employ her. Apart from being good for her, it would also have made Albert very happy. He would have hated the farm to go entirely out of Pengelly hands.'

'Now I've seen where the farm was, and been told so much about her, I really think she must have cracked up,' Daisy said. 'I just hope she wasn't another casualty of that terrible fire.'

'Me too,' he nodded. 'Let me look in the file. I don't remember there being any contact number or address, but of course I couldn't possibly remember everything in there.'

The receptionist interrupted them at that moment, announcing the arrival of his next appointment. Briggs frowned. 'Could you possibly come back in a couple of hours, Miss Buchan? That will give me time to go through it. Let's say at twelve?'

'That's fine with me,' Daisy said, getting up to leave. 'Thank you so much for your help, Mr Briggs. I'll go and explore the town now.'

Daisy was a bit disappointed with Falmouth. Despite its great age and its having been one of England's great ports, she found it surprisingly drab. It had too many tacky souvenir shops for her taste, and it didn't help that it was such a miserable day. Even down at the harbour, the sea and sky were both dark grey, and the many oil tankers and container ships lying at anchor out in deeper water waiting to be unloaded had a desolate look about them. But she was glad to have had the chance to spend some time there.

At twelve she presented herself back at the solicitors' and this time the receptionist welcomed her with a warm smile and sent her straight in to see Mr Briggs.

'I've found one lead,' he said, 'a firm of London solicitors, who requested a reference for Ellen in relation to renting some accommodation. She may well have used the same solicitors later if she bought a property.'

Daisy was disappointed, she had hoped so much that he was going to come up with an address. Perhaps he saw that in her face for he looked sympathetic. 'I've photocopied the letter and written her old address in Bristol on the back. You could try calling there and ask if she left a forwarding address. Let me know how you get on,' he said with real warmth. 'I liked Ellen very much, and I'd like to hear you became reunited.'

Daisy was just about to leave when she turned at the door. 'Did Albert leave anything to Josie or Violet in his will? I know it hardly matters seeing as they died with him, I'm just curious.'

'No, he made no provisions for either of them, everything was to go to Ellen.'

'That was a bit hard on Violet,' Daisy said.

'I think he trusted Ellen to make sure she was taken care of,' Mr Briggs said. 'He altered his will at the time there were allegations in the papers that he'd been cruel to Josie. He vowed then she would never set foot on his property again. I think the reason he left Violet nothing was all tied up with that, he said Josie could wind her mother round her finger and that Violet hadn't got the sense to see it.'

'Were Josie and Violet aware of this?' she asked.

'I doubt it. Albert wasn't the sort to divulge his business to anyone.'

'And the police didn't find it suspicious that Ellen was the sole beneficiary?'

'Why should they be? Firstly, that will was made many years before the fire. And everyone knew how Albert felt about his farm; it was common knowledge that Violet and Josie had no interest in it other than the money it would raise. He had always hoped that in the event of his death Ellen would want to farm it.'

'But she let him down!' Daisy said.

'Yes, I suppose she did. But don't judge her for that, Daisy. Think how hard it would be for anyone to settle in a scene of so much tragedy.'

The weather improved again over the weekend, and Daisy spent it taking long walks with Fred and thinking over everything she had learned about her mother.

She telephoned Joel on Sunday afternoon when she knew he'd be at home. He seemed delighted to hear from her at first, but as soon as she started trying to tell him what she'd found out about her mother so far, he seemed to clam up. She hadn't really expected him to share her excitement, but she was dismayed when he began throwing up objections to her continuing the search.

'If she's had a mental breakdown, she could be very needy. I don't think you could cope with someone leaning on you.'

'Why do you have to be such a downer?' she asked, intensely irritated that he didn't want to know every little detail.

'I'm not being a downer; I'm just trying to make you think things through before you rush off half cocked. Even if she isn't in need, she might have married; she could even have other children now. She might not welcome you turning up out of the blue and exposing a past she'd never spoken of to anyone.'

'I haven't even found her yet,' Daisy said, exasperated. 'Can't you just offer to help? Couldn't you contact the police down here and see if they kept any tabs on her?'

'No, I can't,' he said curtly. 'Just because I'm a policeman doesn't mean I can get access to files for my personal use.'

'Well, stuff you,' Daisy snapped, and flung the phone down.

She was far too angry with Joel to phone back later, even though she could see he had a point about Ellen maybe not wanting her past churned up. The more she thought over their conversation, the more she read into it. He didn't want her having anyone else in her life, in fact he didn't want her to have a life of her own, he wanted to be the centre of her world.

As she lay in bed that night listening to the sound of the

307

waves on the harbour wall, she forced herself to remember other times when he'd objected to things she wanted to do. There were the parties for one thing, raves in old empty houses. She had loved them, it was fun having a party somewhere you shouldn't really be. But he said he didn't think it was much fun paying inflated prices for cans of beer and drinking them in a dirty old house with a mob of head-bangers.

He objected to driving to Newquay in her Beetle for the annual Run to the Sun too. He said obsessive Beetle owners with surf-boards strapped to the roofs of their cars weren't his kind of people.

She had come round to his way of thinking because he was good at surprise outings like a booze cruise on the river, or a night away in a pretty country village. But that wasn't the point – however good his ideas were, he stopped her making decisions. It was always him who decided what they were going to do on a night out: films, concerts, it was always his choice, and she'd gone along with it because she was easy-going.

He'd even changed the way she dressed. When she first met him she used to wear outrageous clothes, tight skirts split to the thigh, low-cut tops, but although he never actually said he disapproved, she felt he did. So she changed, just to make him happy.

Well, she vowed she wasn't going to bow to his wishes any more. She wouldn't phone him or go round to his place when she got back to London. He could get stuffed permanently.

Chapter Nineteen

Daisy left Cornwall on Thursday, a week after she'd been to Mawnan Smith, and arrived home in Chiswick in the evening for the Easter weekend.

'Daisy!' John Buchan shouted out joyfully as she walked through the door, and without even stopping to pat Fred he scooped her into a bear hug. 'It seems like you've been gone for months. We've all missed you so much.'

Over his shoulder Daisy could see into the sitting-room which was very untidy. She dreaded to think what the rest of the house was like.

'It's good to be home,' she said, hugging him back, and despite her anxieties, it *was* good.

Lucy and Tom came running down the stairs and their welcome was just as warm. They all fired questions at her at once. What was the cottage like? The weather? The scenery? But it was Lucy who asked if she'd found Ellen.

'I've got a photograph and a solicitor's address here in London, but that's all,' Daisy said, her voice shaking with emotion because she hadn't expected such warmth from them all. 'But you aren't going to believe some of the stuff I learned about her and her family. It's all too amazing.'

The kitchen was a mess, with a fetid smell coming from the sink drain-hole. The dining-room table had got white rings on it and someone had yanked the curtains too hard in the sitting-room and partially pulled them off the rail. Yet none of that mattered to Daisy, for as Lucy and Tom hastily prepared a chicken salad for them all, Dad sat her down, made her a cup of tea and insisted she started right at the beginning of the story without missing anything out.

Daisy was no stranger to being the centre of attention, but she couldn't remember a time before when she had the whole family hanging on her every word. Their rapt faces spurred her on, and she put a lot of drama into parts of the story, embellishing the tale of her mad grandmother jumping off the cliff, her grandfather being a surly Worzel Gummidge, Violet the vicious stepmother, and her real father a smooth operator in a spangled suit. She could sense their excitement growing even greater as she told them that Josie became a famous model and later slid into drug-taking.

But when she finally got to the part about the fire, and how they all died in it except Ellen, they looked completely stunned.

'I don't believe it, you've made it all up,' Tom said, looking at her doubtfully. 'Come on, Daisy! This is a wind-up, isn't it?'

Daisy shook her head. 'I promise you it's all absolutely true. That's why I didn't phone you while I was down there. I would have told you it all garbled, left bits out. So I thought I'd wait till I got back when I'd had time to put it all together properly.'

'Good God, Daisy,' her father sighed. 'When you didn't phone I thought you must have drawn a complete blank, then made some new friends and forgotten what you'd gone down there for. That would have been completely in character. We even laughed about it!'

'I said you'd come back with a taste for rough cider, or maybe a mania for sailing,' Tom admitted with a chuckle. 'We really thought that you'd got into something else.'

'I even thought you'd found a new man,' Lucy said, and had the grace to look sheepish. 'Sorry about that, but we *were* all glad you seemed to be having a good time.'

'I did have a good time,' Daisy grinned, 'but nothing

like you imagined. My head's been whirling with all this information. It still is, and I've still got to find Ellen.'

They fell into silence for a while, Lucy staring at the photograph of Ellen and Tom gazing into space.

John got up from the table and went out into the hall. He came back with the telephone book. 'I wonder how many Pengellys there are in London?' he said. 'Anyone want to make a guess?'

'More than fifty, I expect,' Tom said. 'Too many to try ringing them all. Besides, she might have changed her name.'

Lucy looked up from the photograph. 'You are like her,' she said. 'But she looks a bit serious and po-faced.'

'She does, doesn't she?' Daisy agreed. 'I've been told so much about her, but I still haven't got a real fix on her. Everyone else, even Violet the wicked stepmother, seemed so vibrant, so real. But not Ellen. She sort of wafted in and out of the stories. A pleasant, do-righting kind of person, but a bit shadowy somehow.'

'Maybe that's just because she was the only survivor,' Tom said, and patted Daisy's hand. 'People enjoy saying what they really thought about a person once they're dead, good and bad. But it's different when the person is still alive.'

'She sounds a fine woman to me,' John said. 'I think that it was quite understandable that she severed all connections in Cornwall after the fire, too. I know I find it hard to talk to Lorna's old friends and relations now. Of course I wouldn't cut myself off from them, but then it's different when you've got children.'

'So you don't think she went barmy then?' Daisy asked. 'I mean, if she did have suspicions her sister started the fire, that would prey on her mind, wouldn't it?'

John shook his head. 'She might have floundered for a while, after such a terrible thing anyone would. But she must have been strong and in control of herself otherwise she couldn't have made dramatic changes in her life like

311

moving away. Maybe she suddenly couldn't face the school any more, didn't want her old friends to try and keep her there. You said she came up here quite often to see Josie, and for all we know she might have always had a yearning to live in London.'

'I wonder if she was ever jealous of Josie,' Lucy said.

'I wonder that too,' Daisy replied. She had been touched by Lucy's enthusiasm and interest – for once she'd dropped her guard, there wasn't a trace of ridicule in her voice and her eyes were thoughtful, not hard. 'I think I would have been. But then I'm not the kind to make a career with handicapped children.'

'And I'm too plump and plain to be a model,' Lucy added with a giggle.

'You've got too good a brain for that,' Daisy said quickly. 'Josie was quite thick by all accounts. But it made me think about how it is between me and you Lucy, too. We might not be blood sisters, but we're all we've got, so let's try to be nicer to each other, eh?'

'I really missed you while you were away,' Lucy admitted, blushing a little. 'I even got to feeling sorry for the horrible things I've said in the past.'

Daisy grinned. 'Me too, so let's just forget them and start again, shall we? I won't bear a grudge if you won't.'

They moved on to talk about things that had happened while she'd been away, including the new cleaner who came once and never returned.

'I've tried all the agencies,' Dad said dolefully. 'It seems good cleaners are like gold dust. I thought I'd put an ad in the local paper. Is there anyone around here that doesn't think they are above a bit of charring?'

'There's me.' Daisy laughed. 'I'll get stuck into it tomorrow.'

Daisy was delighted that the evening had gone so well, and very relieved no one had mentioned Joel. But after the twins had gone up to their rooms, Dad suggested they went into the sitting-room and had a drink together. As he was pouring her a gin and tonic he asked what Joel had made of everything.

'I didn't really tell him much,' she said, 'we only spoke on the phone once.' She paused.

'What's gone wrong?' her father asked. 'I know something has, there was a time when you brought his name up in every sentence but you haven't mentioned it once tonight.'

Daisy had no choice but to tell the truth. 'He was so full of himself,' she ended up. 'Didn't really want to know, didn't want to help. Anyway, I think it has burned itself out. I don't think we have a future together any more.'

'Only you know whether that's true or not,' her father said. 'But don't make the assumption he didn't want to know just because he threw up a few objections. I'd say that he was just worried about you getting in over your head.'

'Why should he think that?'

'Well, you are rather well known for rushing into things,' he said with a grin. 'I suppose Joel was afraid that the quest to find Ellen might take over your life, excluding him and all of us too. He has a very logical mind. I daresay he thinks if you met up with Ellen and she wasn't exactly what you wanted her to be, you might be badly hurt.'

'I don't *want* her to be anything,' Daisy said indignantly. 'I'm quite happy to accept her as she is.'

'I think Joel might be thinking you want another Lorna,' John said gently. 'I know when I think of another woman I want one in the same mould. It's natural when you've lost someone to hope for a replacement.'

'I don't want that,' Daisy retorted, and began to cry.

John put his arm around her and drew her close to his chest. 'I might not be your biological father, Dizzie, but I loved you from the moment I first held you in my arms. I know you pretty well. You are big on ideas, but less good at carrying them out. You are afraid of commitment. I think that's why you want to sweep Joel out of your life.'

'That's stupid,' she said heatedly. 'It would be really harebrained to drift on with Joel under the pretence of *commitment*. He isn't right for me, he's too bossy, too opinionated.'

'Is that so?' John gave her a quizzical look. 'Funny you never brought up those two objections until you wanted to do something he was trying to deter you from!'

'I've felt for some time that things weren't right. Going away gave me time to mull it over in my mind,' she said. 'He's a control freak.'

'I never saw him in that way.' John stood up and moved away to the door. He paused for a second, looking back at her. 'His objections sound rather more like caring to me. Think about it carefully before you do something irrevocable, that's all I want to say. Finding Ellen will be like winning a prize in a tombola. You might be lucky and get the star prize. On the other hand, you might be left with the booby prize.'

Chapter Twenty

Straight after the Easter weekend, Daisy went to Shawcross and Hendle in Marylebone Road, the solicitors from whom Mr Briggs had received a request for a reference for Ellen.

On the Tube ride there Daisy thought over the advice her father had given her, and decided he was right. If she said she was trying to find her mother, they were likely to be wary of giving her any information. So she planned to pretend she was Mr Briggs's secretary, and that he needed to contact Ellen with regard to the family estate. Fortunately she had one of Mr Briggs's office cards, and she hoped that and the letter would be enough to convince them.

The offices were on the first floor of one of the more imposing old houses in Marylebone Road, close to Baker Street. Before going up the stairs she checked in the mirror in the hall and decided she did look like a secretary in her black suit, with her hair tied back, carrying Lucy's leather briefcase.

The reception area for the solicitors was very plush, with deep blue couches and oil paintings on the cream walls. It was manned by a plump, grey-haired lady in a navy blue suit, who smiled brightly as Daisy walked in. 'How can I help you?' she said.

Daisy had always prided herself on being able to act out a part. She had used it to advantage in the past to get work, and to interest men. As she launched into her rehearsed story she felt she sounded perfectly plausible, and taking the letter to Mr Briggs out of her briefcase, she showed it to the woman.

'After the estate was wound up, Miss Pengelly moved to London and we had no further contact with her. But now something has cropped up again, and we need to find her. Could you look in your files and see if you have her current address? It is a matter of some urgency.'

Fortunately the woman didn't seem the least bit suspicious, and asked Daisy to take a seat while she took a look. She went into an adjoining room which appeared to be a typing pool, and Daisy could hear her talking to someone else.

Several minutes passed before she came back with a slim brown file in her hand.

'I'm afraid we don't have a home address for Miss Pengelly,' she said. 'We only represented her once in preparing a commercial lease, and all I have is that address.'

Daisy stared blankly at the woman. She didn't understand what she meant. 'Commercial?' she repeated.

'Yes, a shop,' the woman said. 'Miss Pengelly took out a fifteen-year lease on it.'

'Where is it?' Daisy tried to sound casual, but having steeled herself for coming away with nothing she felt like grinning like a Cheshire Cat.

'14 Heath Street, Hampstead,' the woman said. 'I'm sorry, but I don't have a telephone number.'

'That's fine,' Daisy said, forcing herself to keep calm, and jotted down the address. 'Mr Briggs will write to her there. Thank you so much for your help.'

Once back outside in Marylebone Road, Daisy was forced to light up a cigarette to calm herself down. She couldn't believe it had been so easy. She had always been under the impression solicitors never gave out any verbal information about their clients.

Her father had asked her to ring him if she had any news, but knowing if she told him this he'd tell her to go home and write a letter to Ellen, she decided against phoning him. She would go to Hampstead now, and just look in to see if Ellen was still there and what the shop was like. Then she'd speak to him.

Daisy knew Hampstead fairly well. In her late teens she'd often gone to pubs there with her friends. There was a time when she'd day-dreamed of getting a flat there, she loved the quaint, arty feeling about the place, but sadly it was far too expensive for her.

She turned right out of the Tube station and began walking up Heath Street, her heart thumping like a sledge-hammer as she checked the numbers. She passed an art gallery, a baby clothes shop and two antique dealers. Then she saw a green swinging sign ahead marked Number 14 and 'Chic Boutique'.

Somehow she'd expected it to be a toy or craft shop, not a boutique. Perhaps it had changed hands and was no longer *her* shop?

She stopped dead just before the bow windows, afraid to look in. But she could already see part of the display because of the curved windows, and the sheer femininity of it urged her to move closer.

A pale yellow suit was displayed artfully and beneath it the floor of the window was strewn with yellow and white artificial daisies. There was a cream leather bag, the very expensive kind, with a green and white silk scarf draped over it.

She stood there for some time, unable to move. If she went right up to the window and looked in, would she come face to face with her mother?

Eventually she made herself saunter past. The part of the window she couldn't see before held a green dress – although the style was too old for her, it was her favourite colour.

There was a step down into the shop, but she could see little beyond the first rail of clothes. Yet just the closed door and the ivory and pale pink decor were enough to let her know it was an extremely expensive designer shop.

There didn't appear to be anyone in there, neither assistant nor customers.

She turned and walked back past it again. Mavis had said Ellen had no interest in clothes, so how could it be hers? Yet she felt sure it was. Even though Daisy could only afford clothes from chain-stores or charity shops, and *never* went into designer boutiques, she knew she would have been drawn into this one whatever the circumstances. That had to mean something.

She went down past the Tube again, and found a coffee shop. Common sense told her to go home and write a letter to Ellen. Yet when she'd finished her coffee she went up to the shop again.

This time there was someone inside. A slender woman in a black dress was tidying clothes on a rail, her back to the window. Her hair was red and curly, just touching her shoulders.

Daisy was rooted to the spot, her eyes glued to the woman, wanting her to turn and face her, yet terrified that she would see her looking in. She drank in everything about her, the gold chain-belt around her small waist, her narrow hips, slim but shapely legs, and black court shoes with just a strip of gold above the three-inch heels.

She hadn't for one moment anticipated such glamour and elegance. She had pictured Ellen in flowing ethnic-type clothes, but it couldn't be anyone but her, not with hair that colour. Daisy knew that if she was dressed the same and made to stand next to this woman, the only difference would be that her hair was longer, wilder and badly needing a trim.

She suddenly felt faint. Her heart seemed to be beating too fast, the palms of her hands were sticky with perspiration. She knew she ought to walk away and prepare herself properly before making any contact, but her need to look at Ellen's face, to hear her voice, was too strong for caution.

A bell tinkled as she opened the door, and the woman

looked round and smiled, not a smile of recognition, just an ordinary smile of welcome to a potential customer.

'May I just look?' Daisy managed to say, for she was overwhelmed by how lovely the woman was with her soft brown eyes, with only a few tiny lines around them, peachy skin and still plump, girlish lips. While there was no doubt that this was the woman who had been photographed in Mavis's garden thirteen years earlier, the shyness of the smile had gone, she had the poise of a woman who knew her worth.

'By all means,' she said, a trace of laughter in her voice. 'Don't mind me, I'm just tidying up after the weekend. I had so many people in here on Saturday that everything is in a muddle.'

There was just a faint hint of a Cornish accent, but if Daisy hadn't been in Cornwall so recently she wouldn't have been aware of it. She put her briefcase down on the floor and moved over to a display of sweaters, feeling even fainter now she was in an enclosed space.

The shop was one of the prettiest she'd ever seen, cream and palest pink with touches of gold on the counter and around the frames of the many mirrors. It smelled of expensive perfume, the cream carpet was thick and luxurious. Even the curtains around the changing cubicles at the back of the shop were perfection, pale pink brocade, each one held back with a heavy gold tasselled cord.

She picked up a pale green lacy sweater. It was an exquisite, dainty Italian one, something she would give her right arm for.

'You'd look fabulous in that,' the woman said from behind her.

Daisy knew then she couldn't contain herself any longer, for the woman was looking at her hair, as if appraising it as being so similar in colour to her own.

'Are you Ellen?' she said.

'Why, yes,' she replied and smiled, showing perfect even teeth. 'Have you been recommended to come here?'

Daisy took a deep breath. 'No. Not exactly. I'm your daughter.'

There was utter silence for a moment or two. Ellen stared at her, large brown eyes wide with shock, her lips slightly apart.

'You called me Catherine, but my adopted parents named me Daisy,' Daisy managed to blurt out. 'Mum died last year but she said I ought to find you.'

'Oh, my God!' Ellen exclaimed, and she clutched at her heart almost as if she was having a seizure.

All at once Daisy was horrified at herself. In her eagerness she hadn't considered what a shock announcing herself would be. She was mortified that she'd acted so recklessly without any thought of the possible consequences.

'I'm *so* sorry,' she said in panic. 'I shouldn't have just come like this, but when I saw you through the window I just couldn't wait any longer. I should have known better, it's inexcusable.'

Ellen reeled towards a padded bench by the counter and slumped down on it, her carefully made-up face suddenly drained of colour. 'I don't know what to say. I never expected this,' she said breathlessly.

'Can I get you a drink of water?' Daisy said, moving over to Ellen and laying her hand on her arm. 'Or maybe I should go now and come back another time?'

'Yes. No. Oh, I don't know what to say,' Ellen gasped out, and her carefully manicured hands fluttered with anxiety.

'Yes, you'd like some water? Or yes, you'd like me to go?' Daisy ventured. 'Oh God, this is awful, I didn't mean to shock or embarrass you.'

Ellen got up and steadied herself by holding on to the back of the bench. 'Just give me a minute to get a drink and pull myself together,' she said, her voice shaking. 'I'll just go out the back.'

As Ellen went out, leaving her alone in the shop, Daisy

thought of how her father had often teased her about charging into things like a rhino. It had always been something of a family joke. But this wasn't funny, the poor woman could have had a heart attack.

The time seemed to pass very slowly. Daisy could hear water running from behind the door. Then it opened again. 'I'm making some coffee,' Ellen called out. 'How do you like yours?'

Daisy breathed a sigh of relief. The crisis seemed to have passed, and it didn't look as if Ellen was going to send her packing. 'White with sugar,' she said.

Ellen came back a few minutes later carrying two pretty bone-china mugs. 'That's a bit better now,' she said with a wobbly smile. 'Goodness me! What a turn you gave me. Are you always so impetuous?'

'I'm afraid so,' Daisy admitted. 'I try not to be, but I always seem to jump in with both feet without thinking things through. I only found out about your shop this morning from a solicitor and I planned just to look and then go away and write to you, but once I saw you, something entirely different took over. It was your hair, I think, it's so much like mine.'

'Pengelly hair,' Ellen said, and lifted a lock of it up and half smiled. 'I've never been able to work out if it's a curse or a blessing. Looks like you've inherited my impulsive nature too. God, I could do with a cigarette.'

'Me too,' Daisy grinned.

'Well, let me close the shop for a while and we'll nip out the back,' Ellen said.

She put a note on the door, locked it, then led Daisy out through a small kitchen and storeroom to a little yard beyond. There was a wooden bench and a couple of tubs of spring flowers. Because it was sheltered from the wind it was quite warm in the sunshine.

'I won't take up your time now,' Daisy said as she offered her cigarettes to Ellen. 'But maybe we could meet again soon for a real talk.'

321

'Yes, that would be good,' Ellen replied, drawing deeply on her cigarette. 'Do you live in London, and how did you find me?'

Daisy told her she lived in Chiswick, and explained how Lorna had given her the details of her birth and adoption. She didn't want to talk about Mavis right now, so she just said she had called on Mr Briggs in Falmouth and he'd given her the London solicitors' address. 'I'm afraid I told them a few "porkies",' she said with a grin. 'I made out I was Mr Briggs's secretary and that there were a few things to sort out about your father's estate. Then I came straight here.'

'I'm very glad you did,' Ellen said. 'You see, I always hoped you'd come looking for me, though I long since gave up expecting you.' She paused, looking at Daisy thoughtfully. 'This is a bit like a dream. I can't quite believe it's happened, or that you are so like me. It's so strange.'

'Strange' was exactly how Daisy saw it too. It was so strange to be confronted by someone so like herself, to know that she had grown in this woman's belly, been held in her arms and grieved over after she had given her up. Yet there was a sense of anti-climax too, for Ellen didn't seem excited, in a rush to ask her questions. Suddenly Daisy was sobbing.

'I'm so sorry,' she said through her tears. 'I'm behaving like a needy lunatic, and I'm not either of those. But you are so like me, I didn't expect that. How on earth can we fill in twenty-five years?'

Ellen turned on the bench to face her. She put one finger under Daisy's chin and tilted it up to look at her. 'We've met, that's the first step. But we're both in shock. We meet again in a couple of days when we are calmer, and we talk our way through it. Does that sound like a good idea?'

'Yes,' Daisy whispered, dabbing at her eyes. 'But just tell me, are you pleased?'

'Pleased!' Ellen gave a little chuckle. 'Of course I am. But just give me a little time to get my head round it.'

Daisy sensed that she should leave. She stood up, saying she had to meet a friend for lunch.

'I'll give you my card with my home address,' Ellen said, getting up too and smoothing down her dress. 'It's Tuesday now, isn't it? What about if you came over to me on Friday evening?'

'Great,' Daisy said. She thought she needed a few days to get all her questions sorted out in her head. 'I'm sorry I gave you such a shock.'

As they went back into the shop, Ellen took a card out of the counter drawer and handed it to her. 'My flat is easy to find,' she said. 'It's a rather plain Sixties block, overlooking Primrose Hill. About eight, if that's all right with you.'

Daisy said it was and put the card in her jacket pocket. She moved forward to kiss Ellen on the cheek and Ellen caught hold of her shoulders.

'Don't talk to anyone about this, will you?' she said, a note of urgency in her voice. 'Not just yet anyway. You see, no one knows I've had a child. I have to think about how I disclose it. As I'm sure you discovered, I've been through an awful lot. I learned the best way to cope with it was to avoid confidences.'

'You mean you don't want me to tell my family?' Daisy said in some surprise, knowing that would be extremely difficult for her.

'I think it would be better if you waited,' Ellen said gently. 'Until we've had time to get to know one another. I'm sure you understand what I mean.'

Daisy went home on the Tube in a daze. While on one level she very much wanted to tell someone about Ellen, on another she was glad she'd promised to say nothing about their meeting.

As soon as she got in she phoned her father at work and told him that the solicitors had been unable to give her any information about one of their clients, but if she'd like

323

to write a letter to Miss Pengelly, they were willing to pass it on. Fortunately her father was busy, so he couldn't discuss it any further. All he said was 'That's for the best really. Be careful what you write though. As Joel said, she might have got married or have other children, and you don't want to embarrass her.'

Daisy spent the rest of the day cleaning. She had always found that doing mundane jobs was an excellent way to think through problems. Yet this time it didn't seem to work. It *was* thrilling to find Ellen was so smart and together, she'd take great pleasure in rubbing Joel's nose in that. But on deep reflection about everything Ellen had said and done, she supposed she was a little disappointed her mother hadn't shown any emotion.

Still, that could be the shock. It must have been quite traumatic having someone walk in and announce herself as her daughter. Daisy guessed she would have to wait until Friday evening to see how she reacted when she'd had time to collect herself.

Then Joel phoned at six. He was nice, considering she hadn't contacted him again since telling him to get stuffed. He asked if she'd had a good time in Cornwall, what the cottage was like and if the car had played up at all. But she was so on edge, dying to tell someone about seeing Ellen, yet afraid to because she'd promised she wouldn't, that his questions just irritated her.

'What's this, an interrogation?' she asked.

'Don't be silly,' he said. 'It's just normal stuff you ask people when they've had a holiday.'

'So I'm silly now,' she snapped. 'If that's what you think of me then I haven't got anything further to say to you,' she said, and slammed the phone down for a second time.

Her father appeared at the top of the stairs. 'Dear me, Daisy,' he said, shaking his head in bewilderment. 'Is that any way to treat a man who was so supportive and caring when your mother was dying?'

'It's the only way to treat any man who's an arse-hole,' she retorted angrily, and ran upstairs to her room and stayed there for the rest of the evening.

She was ashamed of herself. Joel didn't deserve that kind of treatment, but somehow Ellen seemed more important than anything right now. She wanted to be alone to think about her. She didn't want anyone questioning her about anything.

Wednesday, Thursday and Friday seemed endless. She cleaned, polished and tidied until there was nothing left to do. She cooked meals to put in the freezer, cut the grass, repainted the garden seats and weeded the borders. On Friday afternoon she went to the hairdresser's for a trim, and bought a new cream sweater because by now she had come up with the idea that Ellen had probably thought she looked plain and uninteresting in the businesslike black suit.

Finally it was Friday evening and she set off for Primrose Hill just after seven, having told the family she was going to see a girlfriend. Despite butterflies in her stomach, she felt more confident now; the new sweater toned well with her favourite brown velvet trousers and she had put on a chunky amber necklace that had been Lorna's. The trim had done wonders for her hair, and she'd let it dry naturally so it was a mass of corkscrew curls. No one could accuse her of looking plain or uninteresting.

Askwith Court was easy to find. Most of the houses in the road were big Georgian or Victorian ones, and clearly the three-storey block of flats had been built at a time when planners weren't so stringent about keeping a uniform period feel to the area. It was as Ellen had said typical of bland Sixties architecture, with large picture windows and iron balconies, but set in landscaped gardens so the flats could be said to be 'luxury apartments'.

Daisy left her car in the car park at the back of the block, then went round the front to find Flat 9. It was listed first on the entrance door, so she guessed the flat was on the top floor. She rang the bell and within seconds she head Ellen's voice coming from the entryphone.

'It's me, Daisy,' she said, and a buzzer sounded as the front door opened.

The staircase was carpeted, but there was no lift, and Daisy was breathless by the time she got to the last flight of stairs and saw Ellen smiling down at her.

'Puffed?' she asked. 'Sometimes I can't imagine why I picked a flat on the top floor. But I suppose it keeps me fit.'

She looked more than fit to Daisy. She was radiant, in a cream trouser suit, no one would ever guess she was forty-three. As Daisy reached the top stair she came forward to embrace her, and she was enveloped in a heavenly perfume.

'I haven't been able to think of anything else but you all week,' Ellen said as she hugged her. 'It seemed like tonight would never come.'

This was the kind of welcome Daisy had hoped for but not expected, and it made her eyes prickle with tears. 'It's been the same for me,' she admitted. 'But I was scared I'd frightened you off.'

'I don't frighten easily.' Ellen laughed. 'Now, come on in, I've got some champagne on ice so we can celebrate. By the way, you look gorgeous. Your hair's just the same as mine was at your age.'

Daisy wasn't exactly surprised at the decor of Ellen's flat, it was so similar to the shop with its cream settees and carpet, pale pink walls and curtains. But there seemed to be far too much gold – ornate mirrors, picture frames, cushions, coffee tables and even gold cherubs holding up lights. It was how she expected the owner of Chic Boutique to live, but it wasn't in keeping with a girl who loved farming and had worked with handicapped children.

Maybe Ellen guessed what she was thinking for she giggled. 'It's a bit glitzy, isn't it?' she said. 'I think it's a back-lash against my childhood. I wanted sumptuous comfort and luxury. But I bought the flat for the view.'

She went over to the window and pulled the heavy curtains back. It was too dark to see the grass and trees of Primrose Hill clearly, but beyond that was a panoramic view of the twinkling lights from the city. 'I sit out there on the balcony for hours in the summer,' she said. 'I have my plants around me to remind me of home, and the world at my feet.'

Put like that, Daisy could understand Ellen's feelings perfectly. She also thought Ellen must be very astute to have bought a flat in such a good part of London. From the way property prices had risen since she bought it, and would continue to rise, she'd certainly have kept her inheritance intact.

Ellen closed the curtains and told Daisy to make herself comfortable, then she opened the bottle of champagne which she had sitting in an ice bucket, and poured two glasses.

'To us, and our future,' Ellen said, clinking her glass against Daisy's. 'I'm sorry I was so shell-shocked when we first met. After you'd gone I had a cry because I realized I hadn't really welcomed you.'

'It was my fault for dropping the bomb.' Daisy giggled. 'My dad is always going on about me charging in like a rhino and he's right, it does put people off.'

'Well, you can see how pleased I am that you've come back into my life now,' Ellen said, patting Daisy's knee. 'And I've done a few rhino charges in my life too. Now, tell me from the beginning about why and how you came to find me.'

'Mum always told me I was adopted, but it didn't really mean anything very much to me, not until after she died and I saw this.' Daisy opened her handbag and brought out the picture of Ellen and Josie as little girls. 'You sent it to Mum when I was about six, I think.'

Ellen took the picture and suddenly tears were welling up in her eyes. 'I'd forgotten I sent it,' she said in a croaky voice. 'We thought we were real stars the day that was taken. We were so excited because it was very rare for anyone to come to the farm, least of all a photographer.'

As they continued to drink the champagne, Daisy told her how she found Dr Fordham in Bristol, and then went on down to see Mavis Peters.

'It was she who told me all about you, your family, why you had me adopted, and about the fire,' she said. 'I was so shocked by that, Ellen, it must have been terrible for you.'

'It was,' she agreed. 'I didn't want to live myself for a while either. I expect you were also told by Mavis that I've never been back?'

Daisy nodded.

'I just couldn't,' Ellen said, her voice shaking. 'The thought of seeing the farm gone, of imagining their panic as the flames engulfed them, was too much to bear. I couldn't even speak to Mavis on the telephone. I know I should have, but I couldn't do it, just the sound of her voice would have been too much for me.'

'She's been so worried about you,' Daisy said gently. 'She loves you.'

'I know, but that kind of made it worse.' Ellen turned on the settee to face Daisy. 'When there's only one person in the world who really knows how it is for you, sometimes that is the hardest person to face.'

Daisy knew just what she meant. Often when she had been in trouble she couldn't face her mother, even though she knew she would always stand by her and understand.

'I know,' she said softly, and took Ellen's hand and squeezed it.

'Starting out all over again, putting everything, my job and friends behind me seemed the only way I could cope,' Ellen went on. 'I didn't care that people would be hurt, not then, I was hurting too much myself to think about them. I changed everything, the way I dressed, the way I used to think. People use that expression now, "reinvented myself", well that's exactly what I did. Then much later, when I'd come to terms with everything, I was so different to the old Ellen, I just didn't think I'd be able to fit back into those old friendships any more.'

'I can understand that,' Daisy agreed. The story was slipping into place now, making perfect sense. She had nothing but admiration for this woman who had clearly suffered so much.

'I started drinking just after the fire,' Ellen said. 'Oh God, it was awful when I think back. I felt so low I used to slip out and buy a bottle as soon as I woke up, it was the only thing that seemed to help. Of course I didn't want anyone to see me like that, so I didn't answer the door. That flat became like a prison, hour after hour of lying in bed hurting. I didn't even buy newspapers any more, because I knew there'd be so much stuff about Josie in them. I didn't answer the phone because I guessed journalists would try and get me to talk about her.'

'But you pulled yourself together,' Daisy said. 'That shows how strong you really were.'

'I wasn't strong when I left there,' Ellen said, then gave a mirthless chuckle. 'I packed up the few things I really cared about, and left at night so no one would see me go. I left everything else inside, sent a note to the landlord, and left no forwarding address.'

'Why did you choose to come to London?' Daisy asked.

Ellen shrugged. 'Because it was big enough to swallow me up. Besides, it was the only other place I knew. I'd had some good times here with Josie.'

'Weren't you terribly lonely at first?'

'Not really. I wanted anonymity, and I got that. For the first time ever in my life, I found I could be myself, not that person other people thought I was.'

Daisy must have looked puzzled for Ellen smiled. 'Well, I'm sure you've been told by Mavis about what a good girl I was? Just because I was reliable, honest, hardworking and good with kids, I ended up with a bloody halo. You can get very tired of that, just as I got tired of wearing hippie clothes and never putting on makeup. There was always a bit of me who wanted to be a rebel, that's why I dressed like that in the first place I suppose. That and feeling the need to be as opposite to Josie as possible.'

'You obviously did know something about clothes all along for your shop to be so successful,' Daisy said.

Ellen smiled. 'You can learn anything if you try hard enough, and I must have picked up a few pointers from Josie over the years. But I've been fortunate.'

Daisy thought that the cream suit she was wearing tonight, timelessly elegant and beautifully cut, was evidence of her good taste. She looked comfortable yet glamorous at the same time. Daisy hoped that she could look like that at her age.

'Did you envy Josie?' Daisy asked a little later when the conversation was gradually moving away from the Pengelly family on to Ellen's shop and London in general.

'Only occasionally,' Ellen said. 'For all the seemingly good things about her fame, she had it so tough most of the time. I expect you were shown press cuttings about how she got started?'

Daisy nodded.

'Well, what the press said was all rubbish, she was set up between the newspaper and the photographer Mark Kinsale. He was an evil bastard, but she didn't realize that until long after he had her completely in his clutches. He took her virginity and her heart, and her money too.'

Ellen got up and opened a drawer in a bureau. She pulled out a large, thick leather-bound book and sat beside Daisy to show her it. It was all of Josie, pictures and press cuttings, many that Daisy hadn't seen before.

As Daisy turned the pages the single thing which struck her most was the care and love with which they had been collected. A large picture of Josie in evening dress would be surrounded by other smaller complementary ones, then on another page there would be ones of her in swimwear or casual clothes. Appropriate quotes from her had been cut out and used as a way of bringing her character into the album. One that made Daisy smile was above one of her topless: 'I was blessed with a good figure, so I see no sense in hiding it.'

'It still makes me sad how she was portrayed,' Ellen said with a little break in her voice. 'She was "The Face of the Sixties", so very beautiful, so much part of the era. Everyone who was anyone then dabbled in drugs, lots of the models posed in the nude too, but they didn't hound them for it the way they did Josie. Look at this cutting, for example!'

She turned the pages quickly towards the end of the album and stopped at a picture of her sister wearing a witch's pointed hat and a diaphanous black net dress – she appeared to be naked beneath it. The heading on the cutting was 'I'm a witch, I can put a spell on you.' Daisy read on to find the journalist reporting that Jojo professed to be a witch and was studying the work of the famous satanist Aleister Crowley, including satanic rites and orgies.

'It was just a joke.' Ellen grimaced. 'She was photographed at a fancy-dress party, for goodness' sake. Lots of people talked about Crowley at that time, it made a welcome change from those who were banging on about becoming Buddhists and stuff. Any fool would have known she was just teasing, but they put that in the paper as if she was serious. She was wearing a body-stocking under that dress too. But they implied she was wafting about in the semi-nude.'

'Why didn't she set the record straight then?' Daisy asked.

Ellen frowned. 'She was told the old adage "All publicity is good publicity", and she got to believe it! But she wanted her real story known and she got a well-known journalist interested in writing her biography. I have her notes for it here, in which she told the whole truth about our family. And about how she had been seduced, conned and used by Kinsale, and how he fleeced her of the money she earned and forced her into drug-taking. The journalist never did anything with it, instead he betrayed her by writing an article about her being treated for drug abuse in a Harley Street clinic. Talk about twisting the truth! She'd only been in there for a gynaecological complaint.'

'But surely the real story about her would have made better copy?' Daisy said, a little puzzled. She didn't know if Ellen's version was the true picture; Mavis had said she was sometimes blind to her sister's faults.

'The newspapers weren't going to expose exploitation, not when some of their own were involved.' Ellen shrugged. 'Besides, they'd hit on a winning formula, the more outrageous they made Josie seem, the more papers they sold. She couldn't fight it, she didn't know how.'

Ellen paused for a moment looking at one astoundingly lovely picture of Josie in a ball-gown. 'They said she was the most beautiful girl in England,' she said with a break in her voice. 'But Josie didn't think so. They made her feel ugly inside with what they made her do.'

Again Daisy was a little confused. 'Are you saying it was them who introduced her to drink and drugs?'

'Mark Kinsale was the one who did that,' Ellen spat out. 'That evil swine used every trick in the book, drugs, drink, sex and blackmail, to get what he wanted out of her. She thought he loved her, she was too young and naive to see what was going on. He made her have sex with a guy he said was a film producer once, he said if the guy liked her he'd include her in his next film. But the "producer" turned out to be just an actor in blue movies, and Mark got it all on film. Every time Josie tried to get work with another photographer, he'd threaten to send the film to her parents and the newspapers. She was trapped.'

Ellen shut the album sharply and got up and put it back

in the bureau. The dispirited way she moved touched Daisy deeply. 'You must have felt equally powerless knowing this was going on, but being unable to stop it either?'

Ellen sighed. 'Yes, it tore me apart. But I'm working on her biography, and if I ever get it finished and published, perhaps then I'll have put the record straight. I wish there was something that could be done to punish Mark Kinsale too. But only last year I read in the paper that he died in the States. Too many drugs, I expect. But enough of him and Josie. Tell me about yourself now.'

'There's not a great deal to tell.' Daisy blushed a little. She went over her recent history quickly, explaining how her mother's death had given her more focus, and how she got her diploma as a chef. She spoke too of her relationship with Joel, and her sadness that it had fallen apart. Then she went on to say she'd fallen in love with Cornwall and fancied finding work down there if only for the summer.

'You don't want to do that.' Ellen looked horrified. 'It might be pretty and quaint, but you can't bury yourself down there at your age cooking for holidaymakers. You want to get yourself work in some up-and-coming place here in London, somewhere with a future.'

'But you loved Cornwall. I heard you wanted to farm your father's land,' Daisy retorted, though she couldn't imagine that being really true, not now she'd met Ellen.

'A silly girlish dream,' Ellen said firmly. 'Three generations of Pengellys broke their backs on that land. All it was good for was what it is now, a hotel for people who want to look at the view and romanticize about the past. There's nothing in Cornwall except the views and the tourists that go there to gape at them. No industry, no decent shops, no work and no decent housing for half the poor devils who were born there.'

Daisy didn't know what to say. If she mentioned a quality of life which was missing in London and other cities, or that she'd met more real people in a week down in Cornwall than she'd met in years up here, she had a feeling Ellen would shoot her down in flames.

'Well, I love it,' she retorted. 'I think London is dirty, overcrowded and full of get-rich-quick fakers. The whole Thatcher ethos gives me the willies.'

Ellen laughed. 'I used to say that when Ted Heath was Prime Minister, but I was in my twenties then too and idealistic.'

Daisy glanced at her watch and saw it was after ten, and she still hadn't asked the burning question.

'Were you pushed into giving me up?' she asked. 'Both my mother and Dr Fordham seemed to think you might have been.'

Ellen gave her a blank look, as if she didn't understand the question. 'Pushed?' she repeated.

Daisy nodded. There was a long silence.

'There wasn't any choice then,' Ellen said eventually. 'Unmarried mothers weren't accepted like they are now. Now, I'll just go and make us some coffee.'

Daisy was a little disappointed Ellen didn't seem to want to give her version of the events at that time, but as she waited for her to come back with the coffee, she saw why. Ellen was a strong woman, that was clear from the way she had rebuilt her life after the fire. It obviously wasn't in her character to put blame on to others for her own actions, or to agonize over things past.

'You must have thought me very odd asking you not to say anything to your family about finding me,' Ellen said as she came back into the room with a tray of coffee and sandwiches. For the first time that evening, she looked a little anxious and unsure of herself.

'Not really, I was too overwhelmed by just finding you to think of anything else,' Daisy replied.

'That was how it was for me too,' Ellen said as she put the tray down on the coffee table. 'My first reaction was how on earth can I suddenly spring a daughter I've never mentioned before on my friends? Then I got to thinking about it later and I realized I was still suffering from the bigotry of the past, and that's ridiculous because it's over and gone now. So I'll be proud to say you are my daughter. I want to show you off.'

Daisy felt a warm glow run through her. 'I very much want to tell my family about you,' she said.

'You go ahead, but you won't want me to meet them, will you?'

Daisy looked at her in surprise.

'Oh, I don't mean I don't want to meet them at all. Maybe a meal in a restaurant or something like that, something formal on neutral ground,' Ellen said quickly. 'You see, I don't know that I could cope with all the many reminders of what I lost by giving you up, not if I came to your house. I'd really rather we had a relationship that was separate, and special, where we can make a future together without all the trappings of the past.'

In the last two days Daisy had pondered on how it would work if Ellen came to Bedford Park. While she was dying to see Dad's and the twins' reaction to such a beautiful woman, she could see it might be awkward and strange for them, and it could possibly set her apart from them again.

'I think that's the perfect solution,' Daisy said eagerly. 'I am so glad I did find you. You are better than my wildest dreams.'

Ellen smiled. 'Bless you, darling. That's the loveliest thing anyone has ever said to me.'

Chapter Twenty-one

Joel sat in an armchair, staring at but not seeing the ironing board littered with the remains of the previous night's takeaway. The whole flat was in much the same state. Since he'd fallen out with Daisy he had no interest in cleaning up, or doing anything else for that matter.

It was four weeks ago that Daisy had put the phone down on him while she was in Cornwall. He could kick himself now for not calling round to Bedford Park over Easter when she got home to talk it out with her.

He understood perfectly why she wanted to find her mother, and he wasn't against it at all. But he had maintained right from the beginning that she should go through one of the agencies who specialized in finding birth mothers. That way there would be a mediator on hand to smooth out any potential problems.

It was when Daisy had said she thought Ellen might have had a nervous breakdown following the fire at the farm that he became worried. In his opinion, the last thing Daisy needed in her life so soon after Lorna's death was involvement with someone unstable. She had been so strong for Lorna and John, but she could easily start to bend if someone else began to lean on her. Maybe he should have been more diplomatic, he also supposed he didn't need to refuse to use his work connections to help in the search. But her wild exuberance caught him short.

The next time he phoned Daisy, he tried really hard to be diplomatic. But she seemed so irritable, everything he asked her appeared to annoy her further. He still couldn't see what was wrong with saying 'Don't be silly.' It wasn't meant to be offensive. But he supposed she'd have flown off the handle whatever he'd said. So he'd left her alone, thinking that time would bring her round.

Another mistake! She didn't phone him or call round. He was left in limbo, not knowing whether she considered him persona non grata or if she was waiting for a gesture from him.

He loved Daisy. From the first night he met her in the wine bar, he knew she was the only girl for him. He could remember how, as he helped her pick up the contents of her handbag from the floor, she tossed back that glorious hair, and beneath it were those forget-me-not-blue eyes. If she hadn't agreed to go out with him that night, he thought he would have prowled around that area forever, just looking for her.

He'd never felt that way about any woman before.

She was dizzy, but in the best possible way. She fizzed like lemonade, she made every occasion a special one. He wanted her to be his wife, the mother of his children. The only reason he didn't ask her within just a few months of knowing her was because her mother was so ill. He wished he'd told her now how great he thought she was while she was nursing Lorna. For it was then that he saw her true strengths, capable, kind, unflustered, keeping the whole family together with her humour and warmth.

He'd finally phoned John at his office a couple of weeks before. They had always got on well, and he wanted John's advice as to whether Daisy would welcome a reconciliation. Before he could even broach the subject, John told him Daisy had already found and met Ellen and she was, in his words, 'walking on air'.

It seemed John wasn't entirely happy though. Daisy had made no attempt to find a job, she seemed to be living from one meeting with Ellen to the next, with no thought to her own future. John was quick to say he had no doubts that Ellen was an admirable woman, for Daisy had raved about her shop, her home, her elegance and beauty. Yet at the same time he did seem concerned that Ellen might be turning Daisy's head by giving her expensive clothes and drawing her away from her family.

'You know what she can be like,' John said at one point. 'She's an all-or-nothing type. Right now it's all Ellen this and Ellen that. We don't get a look in.'

'So I haven't got a cat in hell's chance of getting a look in either then?' Joel said, keeping his tone light.

John sighed. 'I have to just wait till it's run its course. But there's no reason why you should, Joel. I can't advise you, I really don't know what's going on in her head any more.'

Joel sent Daisy some flowers the day after, with a little note saying he missed her. But it drew no response, not even a phone call to thank him, so he could only conclude that she'd lost interest in him entirely.

It was as though all the light had gone out of his life. He woke each morning feeling as if he had lead weights lying inside him. Without her there didn't seem to be any point to anything.

He loved Daisy, he wanted to spend the rest of his life with her. And he had believed that she'd felt the same way too. He wondered what she could be thinking of, to let something so good just slip away.

Daisy was thinking about Ellen. She had thought of little else since she found her. But on this occasion she wasn't just hugging herself with glee that she'd turned out to have such an interesting and beautiful mother, but considering what she could do to bring them closer.

They had met eight times now, several times at Ellen's flat. They'd had a couple of meals out, and drinks in the wine bar near her shop. Yet even though Ellen had bought her several presents, including that lovely green sweater from her shop, Daisy felt she was still holding back.

It didn't matter that she said she still wasn't ready to

meet Daisy's family, Daisy didn't think that was really important. But it did bother her a bit that Ellen still didn't want to talk about her past. Daisy's conception, birth and the subsequent adoption was something she dismissed as being too sad to talk about. Daisy was burning to hear about it, and she thought they were crucial issues that needed airing. But then Ellen didn't talk about her life in Bristol either, what her friends were like, or her work. Mostly when she spoke of the past it was only about her childhood.

It seemed to Daisy as she listened to amusing tales about the awful clothes she and Josie had to wear, how hard her father was, and how slatternly and vicious Violet could be, that Ellen was trying to trivialize her loss. She remembered that she and the rest of her family had been like that when Toby, the dog they had before Fred, died. Had they talked about all their best memories of him, they would have got terribly upset. So they only ever spoke of the things he had destroyed, the holes he dug in the lawn, and his constant barking at nothing.

It seemed to her that Ellen still carried a burden of guilt about Josie, though why she didn't know. Perhaps Ellen felt she hadn't tried hard enough to stop her downward spiral, or that she should have tried to get her sister out of London to start a new career.

The more Daisy mulled over things about Ellen, the more she thought that if she were to go back to Cornwall, or to have some contact with her past there, she could really put it all behind her. She didn't dare suggest this, knowing Ellen would snap at her. But she couldn't stop thinking about it.

She also hadn't dared tell Ellen that she had telephoned Mavis almost immediately after their second meeting and told her everything there was to tell. Mavis had wanted to come up to London right then and see Ellen, but Daisy had explained things and said it might spoil the relationship if she went against Ellen's wishes.

But now, a few weeks later, Daisy felt sure that it would be better in the long run to bring everything out in the open. Ellen did appear to have some friends in London, she did mention the odd supper or drinks parties. Yet she had no man in her life, and it looked as if she was alone for much of her spare time. She might say she liked her life the way it was, but Daisy suspected that was just bravado and she was in fact lonely.

Mavis wanted to see Ellen so badly that she was prepared to risk possible rejection. Daisy didn't believe for one moment that Ellen would reject her, why should she? The rift between them had only been caused by grief. Once Ellen had got over that first hurdle, maybe she'd open up fully. She might start to contact her old friends in Bristol and begin living again, rather than just putting all her energies into her shop.

Daisy knew too that she should be putting her own house in order, whether that was moving away to work or finding a job in London. Tom and Lucy were revising for their final exams and planning a trip around the world afterwards. In one unusually generous moment Lucy had suggested Daisy came with them too. But since she found Ellen she had been preoccupied by her to the exclusion of everything else.

Then there was Joel. She was ashamed she hadn't thanked him for the flowers or had the grace to tell him whether it really was over, even though he still came into her mind with monotonous regularity.

She missed a great many things about him, sometimes so much that it hurt. Love-making was one. Finding a mother was wonderful, but not quite in the same league as hot sex! Sometimes she would take out his front-door key and imagine going round to his flat when he was on night duty, to wait in his bed till he got home. Just the thought of it made her quiver.

Then there was his sense of humour. She missed that, it seemed ages since she'd had a good laugh. She also missed that feeling of being looked after. It had always been Joel who organized taxis, booked tables in restaurants, thought up new things to do on his weekends off. She felt ashamed now that she'd told her father Joel was a control freak. He wasn't, he was just far better at arranging things than she was.

Yet if she did phone him and things started up again between them, wasn't he likely to be funny about her seeing Ellen so much? And how could she fit a chef's job in around him and Ellen? So she was doing what she always did when she couldn't see a way forward – nothing.

It was that knowledge that finally made her phone Mavis and hatch up a plot for her to meet Ellen. She was taking action, even if Joel, and possibly her father too, would see it as meddling in other people's lives. Tim's sister Harriet, Mavis's granddaughter, lived in Finchley; Mavis could come up and stay with her for a long weekend, and on the Saturday afternoon Daisy would take her to see Ellen in the shop.

'Are you sure this is a good idea?' Mavis said doubtfully when Daisy put it to her. 'Of course I want to take the bull by the horns, so to speak. But it is a bit of an intrusion.'

'It was even more of one when I walked in and announced myself,' Daisy said with utter confidence. 'Look how well that turned out! Let's be reckless.'

The weather was glorious on the Friday evening in the middle of May when Mavis rang to say she'd arrived safely in Finchley. She was very excited about spending a few days in London with Harriet and seeing Daisy again, but most of all about looking up Ellen.

'I'll pick you up at twelve tomorrow,' Daisy said. 'We'll have some lunch, then go to Hampstead in the after-noon.'

'What are you up to?' John said curiously at eleven on Saturday morning. He had heard Daisy go out early with Fred, then she had come home to shower and wash her hair. Just the way she was bustling around, all spruced up with a wide grin on her face, made him suspicious. 'Have you made it up with Joel?' he added hopefully.

'No, but I might try to if things go well today.' Her grin grew ever wider. 'I do miss him.'

'So what is it, a job interview?' He looked her up and down and thought that the new pale blue dress and little jacket she was wearing were very attractive, but hardly suitable for an interview.

She giggled and put one finger to her nose. 'Keep that out,' she said. 'Until I'm ready to tell you.'

John was looking out of the bedroom window later, admiring the cherry trees which were in full bloom and almost forming an arch over the road, when Daisy left the house. He watched her walk down to her car; she had a bounce in her step and she looked so pretty with the sun shimmering on her curls. She had looked that way when she first met Joel and he really hoped they could make it up.

Pleased as he was that she'd found Ellen, he was finding her preoccupation with the woman a little tedious. From the day Daisy visited the solicitors, she hadn't been herself at all. There seemed to be something a bit furtive about it all too. Daisy hadn't shown him the letter she got back from Ellen, just announced she'd got one a couple of weeks later, and rushed off to meet her.

She kept saying she wanted to arrange a meal in a restaurant so he and the twins could meet her, but that hadn't happened yet either. Was he suffering from jealousy?

'This was a bit of luck,' Daisy exclaimed when she found a parking space in Haverstock Hill, right around the corner from Heath Street. She had been worried about Mavis walking – she might be fit enough to walk some distance on the flat, but hills were different.

'I love Hampstead,' Mavis said, looking all around her.

Frank and I always came here when we were in London. We'd have afternoon tea somewhere, then he'd insist on buying me a present. I bet I've been in Ellen's shop before, there was a lovely handbag shop in Heath Street. Frank once bought me the most beautiful beaded evening bag in there. I hardly ever had an occasion to use it, but I loved it.'

Daisy smiled. Mavis had been reminiscing a lot since they left Finchley, about lunch with Frank in The Spaniards, walks on the Heath, and even swimming in one of the ponds. It was clear the pair of them had remained in love until his death.

'Let's hope she hasn't got a shopful of customers,' Daisy said as she locked up the car, then, taking Mavis's arm walked across the street with her. 'If it is crowded, maybe we'd better go and have a cup of coffee or something until there's a lull.'

Daisy was very nervous now, suddenly aware that it was a breach of Ellen's trust to foist Mavis on to her like this. But there was no going back, Mavis was determined to see her, and besides, Daisy was sure Ellen would be glad once the deed was done.

'That *is* the place where we bought my bag,' Mavis said excitedly when Daisy pointed out the swinging sign up ahead. 'It wasn't called "Chic Boutique" then, but I remember the bow windows.'

'Just wait here while I look and see who's inside,' Daisy said as they approached.

The sunshine had brought out crowds of people, but hopefully most were only window-shopping on the way to the Heath. Daisy darted forward and glanced through the window. She could see Ellen bent over the counter writing something. The shop was empty, unless of course there was someone in the changing-room.

'It's okay, no one there,' Daisy reported back to Mavis who was leaning heavily on her walking stick, looking a little anxious now.

As the door-bell tinkled, Ellen looked up, saw it was Daisy and smiled. 'Hello, sweetheart,' she said.

Daisy stepped down into the shop, Mavis following right behind.

'Look who I've brought to see you,' she said.

There was utter silence for a second or two. Ellen looked at Mavis as if she didn't know her, and when Daisy turned to see the older lady's reaction, she saw she had turned very pale and had her hands up to her mouth.

'What is it?' Daisy asked, thinking the surprise meeting was too much for the old lady.

'That's not Ellen,' Mavis gasped out. 'It's Josie!'

Chapter Twenty-two

Mavis's statement seemed to hang in the scented air of the shop. Daisy looked from her to Ellen in astonishment. Ellen looked equally astounded and shaken, her brown eyes wide and staring.

The total silence seemed to last minutes. Daisy was unable to think of anything to say. But Ellen broke it. 'Oh, Mavis,' she said reprovingly, 'of course it's Ellen, I've just smartened myself up, that's all.'

Mavis took a step forward, tottered and her stick fell from her hand. All at once she appeared to be about to faint.

It was Ellen who rushed forward and caught her while Daisy stood by, too stunned to move. 'Help me take her out the back,' Ellen ordered her. 'It's quite a climb up that hill and very warm in here. Quickly now.'

Taking one arm each, they half carried Mavis through the shop and storeroom out to the little yard and sat her down on the bench. Ellen nipped back in doors and returned seconds later with a damp cloth and a glass of water.

'Fancy you thinking I was Josie,' she said tenderly as she put the cool damp cloth on Mavis's forehead, but she smiled as if it was amusing to her. 'Surely I don't look that much like her? Now, what are you doing up here anyway, gallivanting around Hampstead? You've given me quite a turn too.'

'I'm sorry, Ellen, it was all my idea,' Daisy blurted out. 'I thought I had to bring you together again.'

'You are too impulsive for your own good,' Ellen said

tartly. 'As it happens, I'd been thinking that I should contact Mavis again. I *am* very pleased to see her. But shocks like this aren't good for anyone, let alone someone of her age. Go and make us all a cup of tea and lock the door.'

Daisy went off feeling very ashamed of herself.

After locking the shop door she returned to the yard while she waited for the kettle to boil. Mavis's colour was coming back and she was looking up at Ellen as she continued to hold the damp cloth to her forehead.

'Why did you shut me out of your life?' Mavis asked in a small shaky voice.

Daisy felt a surge of relief. Clearly Mavis was only confused earlier.

'It was never anything personal,' Ellen said in a soft, sweet voice, stroking the older woman's head. 'I was in such a state after the fire. I could hardly wash and dress myself, much less talk to anyone, especially you who would have brought back so many more memories.'

'But just a little note would have done.' Mavis's lips were quivering. 'Anything so I knew your mind was still intact.'

Ellen looked shamefaced. 'I never meant to hurt you,' she said. 'I was so caught up in my own hurt I didn't think of anyone else.' She put her hand on Mavis's shoulder. 'Then there came a time when I knew I had to step out on a new road, and that meant putting aside everything that went before, even you.'

'Frank died five years ago,' Mavis said reproachfully, her voice still a little quavery.

'Oh Mavis, I'm so sorry.' Ellen pressed Mavis's two hands between her own. 'He was such a good man, and had I known I would have sent flowers at least, but I haven't kept contact with anyone from Cornwall.'

'It doesn't matter,' Mavis replied, looking up at Ellen, her blue eyes watery. 'He was eighty-eight, a good age as

346

they say, and I'm lucky to still have my children and grandchildren around me.'

They had a cup of tea together, but Daisy could see that Mavis still wasn't right. She wasn't trying to talk to Ellen, in fact her expression was vacant, and when Daisy suggested she took her home to Finchley she nodded gratefully.

Ellen was very solicitous, she took Mavis's telephone number in Finchley and said she'd ring her later, and perhaps the following day they could meet for lunch. Mavis did appear to rally a little then, she said that coming up to London had been more tiring than she expected, and perhaps it was time she acted her age.

Ellen took Daisy aside before she went to get the car. 'That was a really stupid and dangerous thing to do,' she said curtly, and her brown eyes were dark with anger. 'Now, just make sure you get her home safely and make her have a lie-down. And don't you dare try to interfere in my life again. I won't stand for it.'

Mavis was very quiet on the way home, she appeared to be in a world of her own, and coupled with Ellen's angry words, Daisy's anxiety deepened by the minute. At the door of her granddaughter's house the old lady fumbled in her handbag for the key Harriet had given her, and failed to find it, so Daisy had to dig it out for her.

As Harriet had said earlier that she was going out, and wouldn't be home before five, Daisy led Mavis into the house with the intention of making them both tea. As they got into the hall Mavis stumbled, almost falling right over, and Daisy saw she was still very pale and that her hands were shaking.

'I think you'd better have a little nap,' she said gently, and helped her into the lounge and down on to the couch. 'I'm sorry, Mavis, I shouldn't have talked you into it. Have a little sleep and I'll stay until Harriet gets back.'

'Daisy, sit down,' Mavis said, and though her voice was

tremulous it still had a note of command. 'That wasn't Ellen. It *was* Josie. I know it was.'

Daisy groaned inwardly, she had thought that silliness was over. But given how shaky Mavis was, she thought she'd better humour her, so she sat down beside her on the couch.

'You always said they were very alike,' she said, keeping her tone light. 'Thirteen years is a long time not to see someone. You're just confused because she doesn't look frumpy any more.'

'Thirteen years is nothing when you're eighty-six,' Mavis said, fixing her eyes on Daisy as if daring her to argue with her. 'That woman's voice isn't Ellen's, it's too London. She never had a waist as small as that either, and she couldn't have walked in those high-heeled shoes, not if she practised for fifty years. She certainly wouldn't have a dress shop like that one. That was Josie.'

'Oh, Mavis,' Daisy said in exasperation. 'How can it be Josie? She died in the fire.'

'Someone died in the fire. A young woman with red hair and good teeth. Everyone thought it was Josie because she was staying there at the time, and because the police found someone who called herself Ellen in her flat in Bristol the next day.'

Daisy said she was going to make the tea. She hoped that after a rest the old lady would come to her senses.

'I don't want more tea,' Mavis said petulantly. 'I'm not senile yet. If that had been Ellen you wouldn't have got me out of that shop so quickly. But I had to get away, to think it through.'

'And what did you come up with?' Daisy said sarcastically.

Mavis had a faraway look in her eyes. 'The day of the fire was Albert's birthday. Ellen always tried to get down for that, I only remember her missing it once or twice. I bet she was there too, but arrived so late in the evening no one saw her.'

'Wouldn't she have told you if she was coming down?' Daisy asked.

'Not necessarily, she liked to surprise people, you take after her in that respect! Josie knew this as well as anyone, maybe she even set it up by getting Ellen to leave her car up on the road so Albert wouldn't hear it! I can just imagine her bursting through the door with a cake and a bottle of whisky for him. That was her style.'

'Oh, Mavis.' Daisy wanted to laugh. It was such a far-fetched idea.

'I bet you anything that's what happened,' Mavis insisted. 'They all had a lot to drink and then went off to bed. Except for Josie. She set the fire, then drove Ellen's car back to Bristol, let herself into her flat and became Ellen from that moment on.'

'Mavis! No one could get away with that,' Daisy said impatiently.

'Couldn't they?' Mavis raised one eyebrow. 'As little girls everyone mixed them up. It was only once they were older and began to have distinct styles of their own and different kinds of clothes and hair-styles that it became obvious which was which. No one knew Ellen as well as Josie – once she was in her flat she could put on her clothes, do her hair like hers, and who would know the difference?'

Daisy shrugged. She wasn't going to buy that one.

'Only someone like me,' Mavis said tartly. 'Someone who knew Ellen inside out. That's why Josie wouldn't come down for the inquest or the funeral. It was rubbish about her being out of her mind with grief. She knew she wouldn't fool me for a minute. Even with her being as sweet as honey just now, I knew. I didn't say any more, because if she can kill her parents and her sister to get what she wants she wouldn't think twice about you or me.'

Daisy gulped. Mavis's idea did have a peculiar ring of truth to it. But then some of the more outrageous things she'd told her about Josie did too, and Ellen had given a quite different slant on many of those.

'But her signatures on legal documents, cheques and things?' Daisy pointed out. 'How would she get round that?'

'People can learn to copy others' handwriting,' Mavis said with a shrug. 'Look at all the credit card frauds there are! If Josie was clever enough to fake her own death, she's quite clever enough to do a bit of forgery.'

Daisy just sat there for a minute mulling everything over in her mind. She couldn't believe Mavis's idea, it was just too melodramatic. Besides, such an audacious and cunning plan could only have been executed by someone utterly ruthless or half mad. If Ellen really was Josie she'd need to have nerves of steel, acting ability and incredible determination to continue to hold it together for such a long time afterwards. From what she'd heard about Josie she was weak and even a little stupid.

Harriet got home at five. She was very like her brother Tim, tall and with a slim build. She wore wire-rimmed spectacles and her fair hair was tied back in a single bunch. When she saw her grandmother looking so nervy and pale and heard what had happened, she was quite sharp with Daisy.

'She's an old lady, Daisy, and she's entitled to calm and peace of mind at her age,' she said. 'I didn't think it was a good idea to see Ellen again, not after what she put her through before, and now it's sent her gaga.'

'I am not gaga,' Mavis insisted indignantly. 'You should call the police and get them to arrest that woman. She's a murderer.'

Daisy didn't know what to say or do. She certainly didn't think Mavis had gone gaga, as Harriet put it, but on the other hand she didn't believe Ellen was really Josie either. If they called the police they would all look ridiculous.

Daisy went out into the kitchen with Harriet, apologized

for being responsible for upsetting Mavis, then ran through her theory again. 'Do you think she might be right?' she asked. 'I don't, I can't believe anyone could do such a thing, let alone someone like Josie, who was nothing more than an air-head model on drugs. But you know your grandmother a great deal better than I do, and you must have known the Pengellys.'

'Yes, I do know my grandmother very well,' Harriet said. 'She's got a keen mind, but she reads too many murder mysteries. I didn't know any of the Pengellys, I didn't go down to Cornwall as often as Tim, but I well remember how hurt she was by Ellen after the fire. Shock has brought on this lapse of common sense, nothing more. She has had years of thinking and worrying about that woman, during that time she lost her husband too. Then you swan into the picture, bring back all that hurt, and finally take her to see Ellen. Her mind can't take it. It's like a fuse has blown.'

'Well, what should we do?' Daisy was on the point of bursting into tears now, she felt so ashamed of herself for causing all this. 'Should we call the police?'

'Don't be ridiculous,' Harriet snapped at her. 'Go home, Daisy. You've done enough damage for one day. I'll put Gran to bed and call my doctor to take a look at her.'

Daisy left feeling like a whipped dog. As she approached the North Circular Road, which would be the quickest route back to Chiswick, she suddenly changed her mind and thought she had to go to see Ellen. She didn't want to, she was afraid she would still be angry with her, but she felt she must.

As Daisy drove on down the Finchley Road towards Swiss Cottage, she felt queasy with anxiety. It suddenly occurred to her that she had been wrong in thinking that finding Ellen was the answer to everything. She had lost Joel along the road, she still had no job, and in the last few weeks she'd sensed that dad and the twins were growing cooler towards her because of her preoccupation with Ellen.

Maybe that was why Lucy suggested she went travelling with her and Tom. They wanted to remind her she was still important to them. She blushed as she remembered she'd said back-packing wasn't her style, and that she thought she might have a holiday in Italy with Ellen.

Ellen's car was parked at the back of Askwith Court, and as the back door, which was only used by the residents and normally locked, was propped open, Daisy nipped in that way and up the stairs.

Ellen's door was also propped open, so Daisy stepped into the tiny hall and called out.

Ellen came out of her bedroom and frowned when she saw it was Daisy. 'What is it now?' she snapped. 'I've seen quite enough of you for one day.'

'I had to come round. Mavis was still odd when I got her home,' Daisy blurted out. 'I thought I ought to warn you before you phone her that her granddaughter is quite angry with me and she might be nasty to you too.'

'I don't blame her for being angry with you,' Ellen said crisply. 'Now, clear off home. I'm going away for the weekend, and I'm in no mood for post-mortems.'

Daisy turned to leave, she was too demoralized for any further discussion. But as she turned, the propped-open door jangled something in her mind. People only did that when they were carrying a lot of things out. The door downstairs was also left open, so Ellen must have already put one load in her car and had returned for another.

No one took that much stuff for just a weekend. She was going somewhere for longer than that.

'Go on then,' Ellen said, her tone impatient now.

Daisy knew Ellen hadn't been planning to go anywhere this weekend, otherwise she wouldn't have said she would phone Mavis and make arrangements for taking her out to lunch the following day. So it had to be a spur-of-the-moment thing. But why? Because she was rattled by Mavis thinking she was Josie?

'Let me stay and help you down with your things,' Daisy said, and without being asked brushed past Ellen and into her bedroom.

'Get out now!' Ellen shrieked at her.

The fright in that shriek, along with the mayhem in the bedroom, told Daisy everything. She was flitting, there were clothes and shoes strewn everywhere. Two half-packed cases lay on the bed, and drawers were gaping open.

'You *are* Josie!' she exclaimed. 'You're running because you've been rumbled.'

'You're as daft as that old bat,' Ellen retorted. 'I'm going away for a weekend, that's all.'

Daisy pushed her way past Ellen and into the lounge. Calling Mavis an old bat was further evidence to her – the real Ellen, from what she knew of her, would never call her that.

Ellen grabbed her arm as she reached the lounge and tried to pull her back. But it was too late, Daisy had already seen what was there. On the table was a large open cash-box, several bundles of banknotes beside it, and her passport.

'I'm getting the police,' Daisy said as she tried to shrug the woman off her.

'Oh no you aren't,' Ellen yelled back. She kicked the door shut behind her and almost in the same movement, lunged at an object on the sideboard.

Daisy tried to get away as she saw what it was, a kind of gold wooden obelisk with figures carved on it. She had admired it on a previous visit to the flat and had been surprised by the heaviness of it when she picked it up. Ellen had said she'd bought it in a flea market – it was weighted with lead and she'd sprayed it with gold paint herself.

Now Ellen held it by the thin end and advanced on her.

Daisy backed away but was hampered by a coffee table, then the settee. She had no doubt the woman fully intended to hit her with it, her eyes looked mad now, almost popping out of her head, and her lips were curled into a savage snarl.

Daisy went to leap up on to the settee and over the back, but she had forgotten how tight her dress was, and she toppled forward. She heard the blow coming as she tried to cover her head. There was a rush of air, a dull sound of wood against bone, then a sudden searing pain above her ear before she slipped into unconsciousness.

Chapter Twenty-three

'Do we have to wait any longer for Daisy?' Lucy asked plaintively. 'It's nearly eight o'clock and I'm starving.'

'I can't imagine where she's got to,' John said, looking worried. He looked up at the kitchen clock and then at the electric slow-cooker, still gently simmering. 'She said she was coming home for supper. It's not like her not to ring if she's changed her plans.'

Tom came into the kitchen and lifted the lid of the slow-cooker, inhaling the smell of beef, garlic and herbs. 'Let's start without her,' he suggested. 'She won't expect us to wait for her.'

'It's a shame she isn't as good at time-keeping and getting her head together as she is at cooking and house-keeping,' Lucy said with a grin. 'I bet she's even made us pudding too.'

'Turn those spuds on then,' John said, and frowned. Daisy might not be a good time-keeper when it came to getting to work, but she always let him know when she was going to be late. Besides, family meals were important to her. Just the careful way she had made this casserole and peeled the potatoes too, was evidence she wanted to be home with him and the twins tonight. She had been a bit mysterious this morning about where she was going though. Could something have happened to her?

Leaving the twins to set the table and look after the potatoes, John went up to Daisy's bedroom to see if he could find her diary. She tended to scrawl telephone numbers in there and with luck there might be one for today.

His luck was in – the diary was by her bed, and for Saturday, 19 May there was a number marked Harriet. Taking the diary with him into his bedroom, he rang the number from there.

Five minutes later, after having his ears bashed by an irate woman who had called Daisy feckless, stupid and totally irresponsible, he had got the gist of what Daisy had been doing today. It also explained her excitement this morning.

John sat there for a few moments mulling over the strange story of Mavis Peters mistaking Ellen for her dead sister Josie. But where was Daisy now? She'd left Harriet's house soon after five with a flea in her ear, so surely she'd have come straight back here?

It seemed very odd to him that Mavis Peters was still insisting Ellen was in fact Josie. Everything Daisy had told him about the woman led him to believe she was completely in command of all her faculties. And what if Daisy had gone to see Ellen again after leaving Mavis?

A cold chill ran down his spine. While common sense told him he was daft even momentarily to consider Mavis might have been right, he had a gut feeling all was not well with Daisy. He felt he had to ring someone else and get their opinion, and who better than Joel, who was the most rational man he knew?

Luckily Joel was home, he said he'd just walked in as the phone rang. John told him the story and fully expected that Joel would make some disparaging remark about Daisy and tell him to do nothing and wait for her to turn up.

But he didn't. 'Going to Ellen would have been the most logical thing for her to do,' he said. 'But I would have expected her to phone from there if she was going to be late.'

John said that she'd made supper for the whole family.

'I'm going to drive over there,' Joel said without a second's hesitation. 'Have you got the address?'

Ellen's card was stuck in the front of the diary, so John read it out. 'Do you think this old girl could be right then?' he asked.

'Well, let's just say I care too much about Daisy not to take her seriously,' Joel said.

As Joel was setting off from Acton, Josie was already half-way to Bristol, driving her silver Golf flat out and muttering the same thing over and over again to herself. 'It's all her fault. She should've kept her nose out.'

She didn't know where she was going, this road was just the one she always used to take when things went wrong for her and she rushed to Ellen who always straightened her out. She frowned as she remembered there was no Ellen now, no one to take her in and care for her. But in thirteen years of posing as Ellen, thinking like her, acting like her, mostly she even believed she was her. Josie was dead and buried, with all the bad memories that went with her.

Yet each time a car's headlights came into her rear-view mirror she felt frightened. Was she being chased? Was Daisy coming after her? Everything was so confusing.

When Daisy turned up at the shop with Mavis she thought she had handled it just as Ellen would have. There was one brief moment of blind panic, but she controlled it and she knew she had convinced Daisy that Mavis was mistaken.

Yet on the way home after closing the shop, she suddenly had a panic attack. What if Mavis stuck by her story and Daisy's family called the police to investigate? All at once she was trembling all over with fear and apprehension, and making a run for it while she still could seemed the only thing to do.

She had packed one suitcase and put it in her car, then all at once Daisy was there at her door. Up till then Josie had been frightened, but she had a plan and felt she was in control. She was off to the airport to catch the first plane out to Spain or Italy. She had enough cash to live for several months, she would change her name, and start all over again.

Then suddenly Daisy was calling her Josie, saying she was going to call the police. She just had to stop her, and hitting her with that obelisk was the only way.

From then on it was all hazy. She could remember fragments, the girl's blood on the settee, getting the tow-rope to tie her hands and feet. But it didn't seem real, more like memories of a nightmare. Yet she could remember very clearly packing her money, passport and jewellery into her vanity case, and going into the bathroom and looking at it for one last time.

She had loved that bathroom. Every time she slid down into a scented bubble-bath she would think of how it had been when she was a girl and had to use the tin bath in the kitchen. The rough patches rubbed against her skin and a draught came under the kitchen door and nearly cut her in half. That image had never left her.

She had many luxurious baths in beautiful hotels later, but almost all of them were spoiled by a man wanting to have sex with her. When she moved into Askwith Court and had her own pretty pink bath, she vowed no man would ever use it. The big mirrors reflected only her, and the soap and the fluffy towels only ever touched her skin. She began to feel clean at last.

She had sobbed as she looked at it, hating Daisy for forcing her to leave it. The whole flat had been a sanctuary, every piece of furniture, every ornament, picture, utensil and cushion chosen by her alone. She'd been happy there for the first time in her life, with no memories of the past, no voices telling her she was no good. She was reborn as the person she'd always wanted to be. Then Daisy came along, like a living ghost of Ellen, and ruined every-thing.

She could remember locking the front door as she left, and carrying the last two cases down the stairs. It was dusk then, and she hoped none of her neighbours would see her drive out.

If she could recall some things so well, why hadn't she turned off the M4 into the airport? Where was she going now?

The blue signs on the motorway were very familiar with place-names like Reading and Swindon that had once meant she was getting closer to Ellen with every mile. Yet Ellen had let her down in the end too.

All at once an old memory of the last time she made this same journey began coming back to her. She tried to suppress it, and the events which led up to it, but she couldn't.

It was a hot sultry evening in the summer of '78 and she was at a party somewhere in West London, close to the river. She had just finished filming, six weeks of tacky soft porn for the German market. She was on a natural high that night, for she'd made enough money to get a better place to live, take a holiday and have some fun. She had already had a lot to drink when a man offered her a line of coke. It was good, and she danced, chatted and laughed, having the time of her life.

Much later, the man came back to her and said he was off with his friend to score, and if she wanted some too, she could go with them. She *had* wanted more coke, but she had no money on her. The man said that was no problem, they could stop off at her place to get some, and once they'd scored she could get a taxi back to the party as they were going on somewhere else.

They gave her another couple of lines as they drove to her place in Shepherd's Bush. She remembered them teasing her as they got out of the car, saying she must have fallen on hard times to live in such a dump. She told them it was only temporary, and that she'd just had a big pay-out. It was true too, she had nearly a thousand pounds up in that hideous room.

Then suddenly everything turned nasty. As soon as the

men were in her room, one of them punched her and demanded to know where her money was. She tried telling them she had been lying and that all she had was about thirty pounds, but it did no good. While one of them held her down with a knife at her throat, the other ransacked the room until he found the money.

They packed up everything she had of value, her jewellery, leather and fur coats, even her stereo. Then they raped her in turn, laughing as they did it. They punched her to the floor and the bigger one pissed all over her as she lay there crying, then they left.

Ellen was the only person she could run to.

The sun was coming up as she drove out of London, crying with the pains of her injuries, stinking of those evil men. They had taken every penny she had, even her cheque-book and bank card. Everything she had left in the world was thrown in the back of the car, but she even had to leave her last valuable, her wristwatch, in a garage in exchange for petrol.

Josie could see Ellen now in her mind's eye, as she opened her front door. She looked innocent and clean in one of those white cotton nightdresses with ruffles, her bare arms and legs a deep golden-brown.

Yet that time there was no welcoming hug, no concerned words that Josie had a black eye. Ellen just took one look at her sister and turned away, her lips pursed in disgust.

'You can come in and have a bath, I'll even let you stay for the rest of the weekend while you tell me your latest sordid story. Then you can go,' she threw over her shoulder.

Ellen didn't relent even after hearing every last thing the men did to Josie. 'I've had it with your hard-luck stories, you bring it all on yourself,' she said, her eyes as cold as a February morning. 'I've helped you hundreds of times, but all you do is shit on me. This time you're on your own.'

Josie had no choice but to go down to Cornwall. There

was nowhere else to go. But it was much worse than on any previous occasion, for this time she knew with utter certainty there weren't going to be any more breaks for her. She was twenty-nine, her body wasn't so firm anymore, tiny lines were appearing round her eyes. She really was washed up.

Getting a job in an office in Truro appeased her parents a little. But hardly a day passed without Violet whispering that she should find an older man with money, seduce him and get him to marry her, just as she'd done with Albert. Josie wanted to scream at her that she was a filthy old cow, that sex disgusted her, and so did she, her mother. But she had to pretend to agree with her, just for some peace.

Setting fire to the farmhouse was an idea Josie had toyed with and even joked with Violet about in the past. It had seemed a good way to force her father's hand to sell his land, but nothing more. Land prices had leapt up during the early Seventies, and her parents could retire comfortably to a house in Falmouth with the proceeds.

If she hadn't found a copy of Albert's will, she would never have seriously considered it. The will was tucked into a box-file beneath his work-bench at the back of the shed where he kept his tractor. Josie had only gone there looking for a screwdriver to try to mend her hair-dryer. She dropped the tool accidentally, and as she was picking it up, she saw a box of old magazines tucked beneath the bench. Thinking they were ones with her in them, she had pulled it out, but as she lifted the magazines, she saw the file hidden beneath them.

Most of the papers were very, very old, relating to Albert's father and even his grandfather. But there among them was the will, and when she discovered Ellen was to inherit everything, that she and her mother would get nothing, she felt suddenly murderous towards her father. Coming so soon after his refusal to lend her two hundred pounds as a deposit on a cottage she'd found in Truro, and countless other slights and humiliations, it was the last straw. The cottage was a real bargain at only two thousand pounds. She knew by the way house prices were rising that even without improving it, it would be worth double that in a couple of years. She had even got an offer of a mortgage for it.

Albert refused point-blank, even though she knew he had the money. 'You want a cottage, then work for it,' he said, looking her up and down scornfully. 'Or sell yourself, that's what you've done before, in't it?'

As she stood there in the shed, the will in her hands, all at once she began to erupt with anger and hatred. She had always known he preferred Ellen to her, she'd accepted that along with his sarcasm and lack of interest and praise. Yet she'd somehow always imagined that the farm would go to both of them.

From that day on in late August, every sharp word, black look or angry retort added fuel to the fire burning inside her. When Ellen came down for a holiday in early September she noted how Albert always smiled whenever she came into the room. He would be enthralled by her boring stories about her crippled kids. She saw him hug her spontaneously, and remembered he hadn't kissed or hugged her since she was fourteen.

Yet Violet was every bit as bad. Ellen could buy her a cardigan in a charity shop, and she went around beaming all day. Josie had bought her a lovely Shetland wool one the previous winter, but she never wore it, saying it itched.

Ellen got thanks for helping around the house, yet when Josie washed up, she was taken to task for leaving a smear on a plate or a stain in a cup. Ellen's opinion counted with Violet, it was 'Ellen said this, Ellen said that', as if she was some kind of oracle who could never be wrong about anything. But then, she'd only changed her tune so she'd get more out of Ellen.

As a young girl Josie had been able to balance Albert's indifference to her with the affection she got from Violet.

But there was no affection any more, Ellen got it all. Albert, Violet and Ellen were family, bound together by shared interest in the farm. Josie was an embarrassment, a disgrace. They would be happy if she disappeared, never to return.

The planning of the fire was intensely satisfying. In her lunch-break at work Josie would make lists of potential problems and ideas, and work on a timetable. On the drive to and from work she would happily think of the fortune that would come to her afterwards, and tell herself that if Albert had just given her that deposit, it wouldn't be necessary.

She planned it for Albert's sixtieth birthday because she knew Ellen would jump at the chance of a surprise party. The weather was often bad in October with storms and high winds. Yet the leaves on the trees wouldn't have begun to drop, so the fire would remain hidden until it was too late to put it out.

Josie came out of her reverie as she approached the turn-off for Bristol, all at once aware that the city now held nothing for her but memories of that time after the fire when she'd come back here.

The memories were disagreeable ones of living in fear of the police coming to arrest her. They called again and again at first, questioning her about every detail of her parents' and her sister's lives. But her portrayal of a woman torn apart by grief must have convinced them she had no hand in the fire.

She practised Ellen's handwriting and signature constantly, burning the evidence afterwards. She tried on every last thing in her wardrobe, tied her hair back, and even let her eyebrows grow naturally until she felt she was a replica of her sister.

Even after all this time she could still hear that door-bell ringing, the shouted pleas from Ellen's friends through the letter-box to open the door. Sometimes she would just stand by the window long enough to convince the caller she was alive and well. She took the phone off the hook for long periods, and never answered it when it rang.

The callers gradually faded away, but still she stayed indoors watching television, sleeping and drinking. She typed a letter of resignation to the school, then lived on sickness benefit once no further wages were paid into Ellen's bank account.

She spoke to no one on the telephone except Mr Briggs the solicitor. She would drive to the other side of town to buy food, she didn't dare go to the local supermarket for fear of running into anyone Ellen knew. She hated every moment of the long, long months in that flat. It was frightening, boring and lonely. But every day that passed without the police calling, or Ellen's bank refusing to cash a cheque because her signature didn't match the one on their records was another day nearer to her goal.

Rain splattered down on the windscreen just as she saw the sign to Bristol, and for a moment she wavered, tempted by a place she knew, yet knowing it held nothing for her. She drove on.

The intersection for the M5 north to Birmingham, south to Exeter, and the M4 on to Wales came up too quickly for her to decide which direction she wanted to head in. She was in the inside lane which would take her to Exeter, and it was too late to signal and pull out as the traffic was suddenly heavier.

She didn't care. All she hoped for was a service station so she could get a cup of coffee and some more cigarettes.

A sign to Clifton brought back a long-forgotten memory of Ellen. Josie had come down to Bristol to spend the weekend with her. It must have been '69, because Josie remembered it was at the height of her fame when people stopped her in the streets to get her autograph.

Ellen had insisted on showing her the sights of Bristol. It was a hot, sunny day and she was wearing a long white cheesecloth dress, with a beaded band round her forehead. She looked very cool and pretty – hippie clothes suited her. Josie on the other hand, was sweltering in a black leather maxi-skirt and waistcoat, and she'd been grumpy with Ellen all day.

They went to see the Suspension Bridge, then sat on the Downs to eat an ice-cream. There were families having picnics all around them and a long-haired, bare-chested boy in brightly patterned loons was playing a guitar.

'Isn't Clifton lovely?' Ellen said, looking around her joyfully. 'I'd love to live here.'

'Well, get a decent job and you'd be able to afford to,' Josie snapped at her.

'I wouldn't leave the children for all the money in the world,' Ellen replied.

'You left your own kid,' Josie threw back at her.

For a moment Ellen said nothing, but her eyes filled with tears. 'Why do you say such nasty things?' she said eventually. 'You know perfectly well that I had to give Catherine up. Have you got any idea how painful it was?'

Josie felt her face blushing, even though it happened so long ago. Why did she have to be so hurtful? Ellen's gentle way was so much nicer. She never picked on people's weaknesses, and she always looked for the best in them too. That was one of the things Josie found hardest to imitate once she became Ellen. Yet once she had managed to master it she found it made her happier, and before long she could sometimes see the world as Ellen did.

'But she had to die too,' Josie said aloud. 'It wouldn't have worked otherwise. You had no choice.'

The rain was growing heavier and heavier, and she was forced to slow down. It had rained like this the night she drove back from Cornwall to Bristol in Ellen's car. It didn't start until she was nearly at Exeter, but she recalled pan-icking that if it was just as heavy back home, it might have put the fire out.

*

Yet there was no rain in Cornwall that night. She couldn't have picked better weather for her plan, for it was not only dry but very windy. Josie had given her father a bottle of whisky for his birthday, but even though he'd had several glasses by eight in the evening, he was as silent and brooding as usual.

The three of them were in the kitchen, Josie washing up the supper things at the sink, her parents on either side of the fire with their full glasses in their hands. Everything was just how it always was, Violet in the same wool dress she put on at the start of each October, a tweedy shapeless thing, almost hidden by her stained apron. Her slippers were new though. They'd been bought by Ellen during her summer holiday and were red tartan with a fleecy lining, Josie remembered.

Albert looked like a wizened old gypsy in his dirt-encrusted moleskin trousers, flannel shirt and old brown cardigan. The shirt collar was frayed, and his grey hair hung to his shoulders, looking like something that approached dreadlocks.

Josie recalled thinking how dismal and dirty the kitchen was. She couldn't remember when it was last given a coat of white paint, it seemed to have been that same yellowish colour since she was a child. The table was cleared, but the clutter of old newspapers, bills and farming magazines had only been moved to the dresser, where it shared space with various hand-tools, china and several bottles of pills.

Josie heard Ellen approaching the front door, but then she'd had her ears pinned back waiting for her arrival. The door burst open, and there she was.

'Happy Birthday, Dad,' she yelled.

She was wearing her old long brown coat and an emerald-green scarf around her neck, and was loaded down with bags. She smelled of outdoors, cold and clean.

Albert was on his feet in a second, his wide smile making him look almost youthful again.

'You remembered then?' he said, and hugged her so tightly Josie felt almost sick to watch them.

'Would I forget?' She laughed. 'But it was Josie's idea. She thought your sixtieth needed a real surprise.'

Josie supposed she ought to have been touched that Ellen gave her credit for it. But as she watched her get the birthday cake box out of one bag, another bottle of whisky and two of her own home-made wine out of another, all she could feel was resentment that she'd never once had a welcoming homecoming like this one.

'I didn't think you'd appreciate sixty candles,' Ellen said excitedly as she opened the box to show Albert a cake decorated with a toy tractor and a few plastic animals, along with 'Happy 60th'. 'But I put just one on, so you can make a birthday wish.'

She turned to Violet then, gave her a hug and a kiss, and put a present in her hands too.

'It's not brand new,' she said, making a little grimace. 'But I saw it in the charity shop near me and thought it was just the job for working outside in the cold weather.'

When Violet opened it Josie saw it was like all the presents Ellen bought, perfect for the recipient. It was a brown waterproof jacket with a thick quilted lining and a hood, sturdy enough for farm life, the right size, and not so smart Violet would feel she had to keep it for best.

Violet cooed with pure delight. 'Just what I needed,' she said, smiling and showing her horrible brown teeth. 'You are a kind, thoughtful girl, Ellen.'

'I didn't hear your car,' Albert said. 'Where is it?'

'Further up the track,' Ellen said. 'I didn't want you to hear me coming. Now, let's have a party.'

'You go and get the fire going in the parlour,' Violet ordered Josie. 'Put on the electric one for a while too to warm it up.'

Josie was in the parlour for some time getting the fire going with a really good blaze. She wasn't anxious to go back in the kitchen until Albert had grown tired of telling

Ellen how pleased he was, and how lovely she looked.

When she did go back in there, Ellen was helping Albert out of his chair and rubbing his back for him. 'Oh, poor Daddy, you're so stiff,' she said in her sweet, caring way.

Josie stuck a smile on her face and kept it there all evening, yet inside she was hating them for not loving her, for forcing her to live in this dirty, draughty old house, for being so peculiar.

Every time she glanced down at her mother's feet and saw the purple mottled flesh oozing over the new slippers, got a whiff of her body odour, or noticed the cast in her eye again, she knew she wouldn't fail to carry out her plan later.

Ellen looked incongruous with her hair loose, dressed for a party in a flouncy Laura Ashley dress in dark green needle-cord with a lacy collar and cuffs. It was mid-calf length, like something from Edwardian times, and she wore lace-up boots.

She opened her home-made elderberry wine once they were in the parlour, and within minutes they were all chatting away, laughing and guzzling down the wine as if it was lemonade. Josie didn't have more than the first glass, it was too strong, but just watched the others and pretended she was enjoying it all as much as they were. She remembered thinking that she couldn't get her parents to laugh like they did with Ellen, not even if she had dressed one of the pigs up in Violet's Sunday best!

The candle on the cake was lit, they all sang 'Happy Birthday', and Albert said his best present was Ellen coming home.

Josie pulled into Taunton Deane services, not so much for coffee, but because she was crying now. She turned off the engine and leaned her head on the steering-wheel, trying to control herself, but she couldn't.

Watching her parents with Ellen that night had been torture. They hung on every word she said, laughing fit to bust at her stories about her kids at school. Josie remembered how often she'd tried to make them laugh with some of her old stories about modelling, but they always turned away and said they didn't want to know about 'that'.

The talk turned to farming later, Albert going on about what yield of corn so-and-so had, how many tons of potatoes someone else had dug up. He said he'd planted daffodil bulbs in the top field just recently as he'd been advised flowers for the London markets were becoming a lucrative crop. Ellen sat there listening, entranced the way she always was.

Finally Josie got up and made them a night-cap, hot toddies with whisky, fresh lemon juice and a spoonful of honey. That was about the only thing she could do right for Albert. He always liked the way she made them.

But this time she dropped a few drops of an antihistamine into them. She had been given this mixture years ago by a chemist in London when she had an allergy, and had always kept some by her in case of another flare-up. One of its side-effects was that it acted like a sleeping draught. She looked around at her family as she took the glasses in and realized they were so drunk now that she could have given them arsenic and they wouldn't have known.

The hot toddies were drunk, but still they kept talking, and Josie began to get nervous they'd fall asleep down there in the parlour and she wouldn't be able to move them.

Just after eleven, Albert finally said he was going to bed, and then they all went staggering off up the stairs. The last thing Josie heard Albert shout out was 'Don't forget the fire-guard, Dumbo.'

That favourite insulting nickname of his wiped out the last of her qualms. He thought it was funny, but every time he used it Josie felt he'd slapped her. That was how he saw her. Dumb.

She waited until she heard their bedsprings creak, then waited and waited until she could hear both Albert and Violet snoring. Then she went up to check on them.

Her parents were both out cold, the room stinking of whisky. She stood there for some time just looking at them. They lay there back to back, Violet so fat, Albert so thin and scrawny, and thought how repulsive they were with their mouths open, snoring lustily. They had brought her into the world without love, their meanness and coldness to her had ruined her life. They deserved to die.

Ellen was fast asleep too, her curls like golden foam on the pillow. She was wearing a pair of Josie's pyjamas. Josie took off her jeans and sweater, and put on Ellen's dress and tights which were on the chair beside the bed. Finally her slippers were replaced by Ellen's lace-up boots.

It was only then that she felt bad about what she intended to do. She and Ellen had had some good times up in that cold, miserable room. She looked at it one last time, the old torn posters of Elvis Presley and the Beatles, pictures of animals they'd stuck up there when they were kids. But she hardened her heart and reminded herself that Ellen had failed her too when she really needed her. She bent to kiss her cheek, then went downstairs and set to work.

First she turned on one electric ring on the cooker and left the tea-cosy on top of it, with another tea towel right by it, the end trailing down to a paraffin can on the floor.

The parlour was next. She scattered some newspapers about and opened one of the paraffin cans she'd put in there earlier in the day, then prised a burning log out into the hearth and waited till it caught on the hearth rug before moving the settee nearer.

Putting on Ellen's coat and scarf, and picking up her handbag, she was ready to leave. She took the top off the paraffin can by the stove, then turned off the lights. The tea-cosy on the hot plate was already smoking.

Once outside she waited a few minutes, shivering in the

cold wind. She looked at her car, remembering with some nostalgia how proud she'd been of it when it was new. But it was rusted and unreliable now, and she would be glad to drive Ellen's carefully maintained Ford.

She could see a bright glow in the parlour windows. The fire had clearly reached the settee now. It was time to go.

Half-way up the track to the road in the pitch darkness, she heard a sort of whoosh from behind her. She guessed that was the first paraffin can going up. But suddenly there was so much light she thought they'd see it for miles around, so she ran the rest of the way to Ellen's car.

Josie sensed someone peering at her in the darkness, and looking up she saw a man staring in at her from the services car park.

'Are you all right?' he shouted. It was still pouring with rain and the man was wearing a waterproof jacket with a hood pulled over his head.

She wound the window down just enough so he could hear her. 'Just having a rest,' she said.

'I thought you were crying,' he said, coming a little closer. 'Want a cup of tea and a chat?'

She shook her head and put the window back up. Ellen would have said he was just a kindly trucker. Josie knew he was a dirty bastard hoping for a shag.

Something strange hit her as she went into the services. The lights were suddenly too bright, the noise from the games machines and the piped music were too loud. Everyone seemed to be staring at her.

She ran to the toilets in panic, yet on checking her face in the mirror there didn't seem to be anything that unusual about her, other than that she was pale and her eyes red-rimmed. But the feeling of oppression wouldn't leave her, so she bought a cup of coffee to take away, and some cigarettes, then rushed back to the safety of her car.

Back on the road again she became aware she'd have to

make some sort of plan. Where was she going, where was she going to stay? Yet she couldn't seem to get to grips with making a decision. And having felt so strange in the services, she knew she couldn't face going to a hotel or guest-house.

Weird, disjointed things kept coming into her head as she drove on and on through the rain. She saw Daisy lying on the settee, her red hair tumbling down, vivid against the pale blue material of her dress. One moment she knew it was Daisy, the next she was thinking it was Ellen. She saw her mother's face too, her lips curled back like a snarling animal's. Then faces of men from her past came at her as well – Mark, Beetle and a whole procession of others whose names she'd long forgotten.

At one point well past Exeter she was so agitated she pulled up and thought she'd turn round and go home, unable to remember why she'd come this way in the first place. But there was a barrier in the middle of the road, and that seemed to mean she could only go one way.

A red light came on by the speedometer. She looked at it again and again before realizing it was warning her she was low on petrol.

There were no more cars now, just her headlights sweeping out through the rain ahead of her. She began to get the idea she would overtake the lights if she drove too fast, and she slowed right down. But the slower she drove, the more aware she became of the darkness beyond the side windows and behind her. Not a light anywhere, just deep blackness which seemed to be pressing in on her.

When she saw a petrol station up ahead, golden light spilling out across the road, she began to cry again. She didn't know if it was relief, or fright at having to get out and fill up the tank.

Terror engulfed her as she got out of the car. A man was watching her from behind a glass screen in the kiosk, and her hands were shaking so badly she could barely manage to unlock the petrol cap. The whirring noise of the pump frightened her still more, and the pitch darkness just beyond the oasis of light on the forecourt made her shudder. She glanced around fearfully as the tank filled, and she thought she saw eyes glinting in the darkness. Stuffing the nozzle back into its holder, she leapt back into the car and drove off without paying, the accelerator pressed right down to the floor.

On and on she went, panic making it hard for her to breathe. A sign to Bodmin seemed to have some significance but she couldn't work out what, and when the odd car came towards her, she swerved, thinking it was going to hit her.

Then suddenly she came out of country lanes into a town with street lighting. With a sharp jolt she recognized it as Truro. The cathedral to her right and the houses on her left were unmistakable, comforting in their familiarity.

'Going home,' she muttered. 'Going home. I'll be all right when I get there. Just a few more miles.'

But as she turned on to the road to Falmouth and the street lighting ended, her fear came back worse than ever. The road was winding, trees came right overhead like an arch. Her headlights picked out hideous faces on tree trunks, and the rain was falling so fast the wipers weren't sweeping it away.

Nothing looked familiar now. She came to a huge roundabout she'd never seen before, then another, and thinking she'd taken the wrong turning she went round it again and turned off into what she thought was the road to Maenporth.

It had similar houses for a little way, but they suddenly ended and she was going down a winding hill with high hedges on either side. Yet it didn't seem right, she thought she ought to be coming to the beach by now. Thirteen years was a long time to be away, but surely she'd know it still even after such a long time?

The road bore round sharply to the right, confirming in her mind that she'd taken the wrong road, but she went on anyway, hoping to come to some lights or a signpost.

Suddenly a village green with white painted cottages all around it was before her. A telephone box stood on the grass, its light glowing yellow in the darkness. Ahead of her across the roof of a low cottage was the sea – although it was not clearly visible, nothing else glistened quite like water.

It wasn't a place she recognized, and she slowed right down, looking longingly at the telephone box. But whom could she phone for help?

In a flash of lucidity everything suddenly came back to her. Her vanity case on the passenger seat, stuffed with wads of notes and her jewellery. Cases of clothes and shoes in the back seat and the boot. She'd almost certainly killed Daisy, and when they discovered her body, which they would very soon, as her car was still in the car park of Askwith Court, they'd come after her.

Josie was trembling all over, and icy cold even though the heater was on. She stopped the car and leaned on the steering-wheel, trying to think.

Once again she'd been drawn back to Cornwall against her will. It was probably too late to try to get out of the country, besides, she knew she was in no fit state to try an airport or one of the car ferries. Even now the police might be looking for her, by morning they definitely would be. Hotels and guest-houses were out of the question. She was too noticeable with her red hair to remain hidden.

She drove on very slowly round the green and down towards the sea, glancing back at the cottages as she went. Sturdy, well-built old places, with roses round the doors. The kind people dreamed of spending a holiday or their retirement in.

The road bent round sharply to the right, and then again to the left, and all at once she was by an old quay, grassed over now with age and lack of use.

She stopped the car engine and just looked. The tide was high, and when she opened the window she could hear the loud slapping of waves and smell that wonderful salty smell on the wind that she'd missed so much when she first went to London.

There was too much cloud for moon or stars, yet her headlights beamed out on to the black choppy water and it seemed, in some strange way, to be beckoning her. She thought for a moment of all those hundreds of little boats that had put out to sea from there over the last two centuries.

Her mind turned back to Daisy, and how she'd suggested that they made a trip to Cornwall together. She'd refused point-blank, making out she hated everything about the place, but that wasn't so. It was in her blood and she had always loved it, however hard she tried to fight it.

Thinking of Daisy made her start to cry again. She had really liked her. She was like Ellen without her righteousness, Josie without her weaknesses. A sunny-natured girl who made life richer for everyone whose lives she touched. Josie hadn't wanted to hurt her.

The game was up now, there was nowhere and no one to run to, she was already growing wet from the rain coming in the window. She looked at the fence around the quay, it was a feeble wire one, broken down completely in parts, and as fate had brought her to this place, it seemed a fitting spot to end it all.

Putting the car into second gear, she revved it up and then let the brake off. The car shot forward over the broken fence and bounced as it hit some ruts. She put her foot right down on the accelerator and felt it sail through the air momentarily as it left the quay wall. A loud splash, then a wall of water engulfed it, cutting the engine and the lights.

The water which had rushed through the window was icy, but she could feel the car still floating and bobbing in the waves. It struck her then that this was not going to be a quick or painless death. But then, after what she'd done, she couldn't expect that.

Chapter Twenty-four

Joel saw Daisy's Beetle in the car park of Askwith Court and parked next to it, then ran straight round to the front entrance and rang the bell. When he got no reply from Flat 9, he rang the bell of Flat 8.

'It's the police,' he said when a woman spoke on the entryphone. 'May I come up and speak to you?'

The door opened with a hiss, and Joel raced up the stairs. When he reached the top, a middle-aged man and a woman were standing outside their front door looking a little puzzled.

He explained he was looking for the owner of the blue Volkswagen parked outside and that she must have been visiting their neighbour, Miss Pengelly.

The couple exchanged glances. 'Someone did call on Miss Pengelly around quarter to six,' the man said. 'We heard voices. But she went out later on. I heard a noise and looked out to see what it was. Miss Pengelly was just going down the stairs with a suitcase.'

Joel ascertained they hadn't actually seen Daisy and that they didn't know Miss Pengelly well. They said she kept herself to herself.

Joel knew it was feasible Daisy had gone with Ellen, but he thought it unlikely. He also knew if he broke into Ellen's flat and Daisy wasn't there, he'd be in serious trouble. But he was prepared to take that risk.

'I've got to check Miss Pengelly's flat, so I'm going to force the door,' he explained to the startled man, 'I'd be grateful if you'd come in with me in case I need a witness.'

The door was a strong one and didn't yield to his

376

shoulder. But a hard kick opened it. Joel went in with the neighbour close behind him.

It was immediately obvious Ellen had made a hasty departure. The bedroom door was open and clothes, shoes and other belongings were strewn about, wardrobe doors and drawers left open. The door into the lounge was closed, but as Joel opened it and switched on the light, he saw Daisy lying bound on the settee, blood splattered everywhere.

'Oh my God!' the neighbour exclaimed in horror. 'Is she dead? Did Miss Pengelly do this?'

Joel was every bit as horrified, but he was in no mood now to answer questions. 'Call the emergency service,' he ordered, already bending over Daisy and feeling for a pulse. 'She's alive, but only just, so make them hurry. Tell them she's been viciously assaulted and has a bad head wound. Hurry!'

As the man disappeared, Joel knelt down beside Daisy and gently removed the scarf used as a gag. She was lying on her side, the wound on the side of her head already congealing. Her hands and feet were tied clumsily with a single piece of tow-rope.

'Can you hear me, Daisy?' he asked, even though she was unconscious. He felt sick with fright for her, for the wound looked very serious. 'It's Joel. I love you, baby, and I'm going to get you to hospital.'

Nurse Franklin approached Daisy's bed. Daisy's head was swathed in bandages, her face was almost as white as the sheets, and she had a drip in one arm.

'You've got a visitor, Daisy,' she said gently, for her patient hadn't been conscious for very long. 'It's your sister, I said she could have just a minute with you.'

It was now Monday morning. Daisy had been rushed to University College Hospital on Saturday evening and had been operated on immediately to remove small fragments of bone embedded in the head wound. Joel, John and the twins had kept a vigil in the waiting-room all that night and most of Sunday. They had only gone home in the evening once the nursing staff had convinced them she was out of danger.

'Lucy?' Daisy said weakly. She was still very confused about what had happened to her.

'Yes, Lucy,' said the nurse. 'The poor girl looks frantic. But then all your family and that lovely man of yours have been here all weekend. We had to chase them all out last night so they could get some rest.'

A few seconds after the nurse had gone, Daisy saw Lucy hovering at the foot of her bed. Even though her vision was slightly out of focus and her mind confused, she could sense her sister was distraught.

'It's okay,' she managed to whisper. 'I'm all in one piece.'

Lucy came round to the side of the bed and bent over her, gingerly trying to hug her. 'It's been the worst weekend of my life,' she gasped out. 'I couldn't believe what that woman did to you.'

Daisy only knew what Ellen did to her because the nurse had told her when she first came round. She certainly wasn't up to discussing it yet.

She lifted the hand without the drip in it, and tentatively touched the bandages around her head. 'Have they cut off my hair?' she asked in a whisper.

'Some of it, round the wound,' Lucy said. 'But don't worry about that, it will soon grow again. You'll be as good as new in no time.'

Even through the fog in her mind Daisy was aware Lucy was terribly afraid she wouldn't be. 'I'm so glad you came,' she managed to get out. 'I'm sorry if I'm not really with it.'

'Just to see you awake and hear you speaking is enough,' Lucy blurted out, and bent closer to her. 'That's why I came alone. You see, when I thought I was going to lose you, it made me see how much I love you. I knew I must tell you.'

Confused and groggy as Daisy was, Lucy's words struck right through to her heart. She was deeply touched that her little sister who was always in control, so unemotional, could be moved enough to express her feelings.

'Bless you, Lucy,' Daisy whispered, and her eyes filled with tears.

The nurse came back and said they'd had long enough. Daisy felt Lucy kiss her cheek and squeeze her hand and she was gone.

By the time Tom and John came in much later in the day, Daisy was a little more alert. Some of the events of Saturday afternoon and early evening were coming back to her, though a little jumbled, and she wanted them to fill in the gaps. After reassuring them she was feeling better, she asked a few questions.

Her father ran through what he'd found out from Mavis's granddaughter, and told her how he rang Joel for his advice.

'It was Joel who went over to Ellen's and kicked the door in,' John explained. 'Thank heavens I phoned him, Daisy. If I'd just rung the police they would have told me to wait at least twenty-four hours.'

He didn't have to add that would have been too late. Daisy could see it in the concern on his face.

'So he found me?' she said. 'One of the nurses said something about my boyfriend, but I was too dopey to take that in. After the way I treated him I didn't deserve rescuing.'

'He still loves you,' Tom chimed in. 'If you'd heard his voice when he rang to tell us you were in hospital! He sounded like he was crying.'

Daisy mulled that over for a moment or two. 'Do you know what happened to Ellen?'

'Joel wants to tell you that when he comes in tonight,' Tom said. 'But you'd better start calling her Josie. That's who she really was, not your mother.'

John took Daisy's hand in both his and stroked it. 'It's going to be hard for you to come to terms with all this,' he said soothingly. 'I know you got very attached to her, but remember we are your real family, and we'll be there for you through it all.'

After they'd gone Daisy lay there trying to piece everything together. She could remember driving to Askwith Court and the events with Mavis which preceded it. She also remembered suddenly realizing that Mavis had been right, the woman she thought was her mother had to be Josie or she wouldn't be packing to run off somewhere. Yet she didn't remember being attacked.

The doctor had said earlier that head wounds like hers often resulted in complete amnesia and the fact she could remember most of what happened was an excellent sign. Yet Daisy almost wished she had lost her memory, it was embarrassing to think how she'd raved to her family about the woman, and now she'd turned out to be a murderess. So much for her judgement of character!

Yet after cringing with shame for some time, Daisy came to see that embarrassing was all it was. Not painful really, for now she could look back objectively on the time spent with Ellen/Josie, she could see with some relief that she hadn't exactly bonded with her. She had liked her, admired her business acumen, her taste and her aura of glamour, but there wasn't anything about her that had made Daisy feel 'Now I know where that came from' or the sense of completeness she'd expected. In fact the woman had been something of an enigma right from the start.

By the time Joel came into the ward at seven-thirty that evening, Daisy was feeling very much better. Her head ached, she didn't like lying down flat, but her vision was perfect again and she was far less confused.

Yet as she saw him coming in hesitantly, almost dwarfed by a huge bouquet of flowers, she suddenly felt choked up. He looked more handsome and fit than she remembered, a

380

tight black tee-shirt and jeans showing off his muscular body. A drastic hair-cut emphasized his rugged face. He had rushed to her aid without a second thought. She had made some very bad judgements about him too.

'Hello, Action Man,' she said as he approached her bed. 'I should be sending you flowers for rescuing me, not you bringing them to me.'

'I'm not the flower kind.' He smiled a little shyly and she noticed that his brown eyes were still as lovely as she'd thought when they first met. 'I'm just happy that you look pleased to see me. Or is that just a polite façade?'

'No, it's not,' she said, and blushed furiously. 'I'm sorry I was so . . .' She paused, unable to think of the right word.

'Stroppy?' he suggested, and grinned. Daisy thought he looked gorgeous.

'That'll do,' she smiled. 'Now, put those lovely flowers over there and sit down. Dad told me you were going to tell me about what happened to Josie.'

He put the bouquet down on the bed table, and pulled up a chair. 'How are you feeling, first?' he said.

'Sore head, getting bored already,' she replied flippantly. 'Tell me.'

A shadow crossed his face. 'I thought I knew how I was going to tell you when I came in,' he sighed. 'But now I'm here, it's tougher.'

'She's been nicked and she's in prison?'

'No,' he said. 'She's dead, Daisy.'

He told her about it all in a rush. Early on Sunday morning, Josie's car with her still strapped into the seat-belt was found stuck in the mud at a place called Point about four miles from Truro. She had drowned.

'Point is on the Restronquet creek. Apparently there's a little old quay there from the times of the tin mines. She must have driven over the edge of it at high tide.'

Daisy knew roughly where that was, she'd been to a pub called the Pandora Inn on that creek while she was staying at St Mawes.

'Are you saying it was accidental?' she asked.

Joel shrugged. 'I spoke to one of the team down in Truro that fished the car out and they don't think so. It was tipping down on Saturday night, and there's no street lighting at Point, but the sea is always visible and the quay at least partially fenced off. They said that even if she'd got on to it by mistake, or used it to turn the car, it's too wide for an accident to happen. Besides, if it were an accident she'd surely have made an effort to get out of the car.'

'But why kill herself that way? It must have been so slow waiting for the car to sink,' Daisy said.

'I think she must have been out of her mind,' Joel said thoughtfully. 'I've been thinking about it ever since I got the news. She must have intended to run for it when she left London, or she wouldn't have taken so much stuff. But it was crazy going to Cornwall, the one place where people were likely to recognize her. So I reckon she flipped on the way. Maybe she'd kind of blanked out that she set that fire, but attacking you brought it all back with a vengeance. She must have known the game was up, and perhaps that freaked her out completely.'

Tears trickled down Daisy's face.

'I don't know why I'm crying for her,' she said, trying to stop. 'She killed my mother, and did her best to kill me.'

Joel took out his handkerchief and tenderly wiped her eyes. 'I'd have been disappointed in you if didn't see a few tears, after the mammoth effort you made to find her and all it meant to you.'

Daisy looked at his face. She saw no animosity, nothing but concern for her, and she felt soothed.

'If I hadn't searched her out, no one would have ever known she was responsible for the fire. So why didn't she tell me to get lost when I turned up?' she asked him. 'That would have been the smartest thing to have done.'

'Maybe she was like me and didn't see you were potential trouble straight off.' Joel grinned. 'Maybe because she'd acted out the role of Ellen for thirteen years, she actually believed she was her. Or maybe she was lonely and liked the idea of a daughter. She could also have been afraid you'd make waves if she sent you packing. But whatever her reasons, I think she must have been mad. What sane person would burn three people alive?'

Daisy remembered when she first called on Mavis and she'd said something to her about mad relatives. That reminded her what a turn the old lady had had when she recognized Josie.

'Do you know how Mavis is?' she asked.

He nodded. 'I went to interview her this morning with another officer. She was of course very upset that you'd been hurt, but I think glad in a way to be proved right about Josie. She said both she and her husband had always thought there was something very fishy about the fire. She said in her opinion the police should have been more thorough in their investigations. But she's a strong, bright old girl, she's going to be fine. She said she was going home tomorrow and sent you her love.'

'No one has told me when I can go home,' Daisy said plaintively.

'It won't be for a while,' Joel said. 'You've had a very serious head wound. They have to check for brain damage.'

'What brain?' she said, and began to cry again. 'I don't see any evidence I've got one, losing you, chasing murder-esses, alienating myself from my family.'

'You haven't alienated yourself from your family at all,' he said stoutly. 'And nor have you lost me. I'm here, aren't I?'

'But I've spoilt it.'

'We'll see when you are better.' He bent down and kissed her on the lips. 'Maybe we'll have to start at the beginning again.'

Daisy's recovery didn't come as quickly as she'd expected.

Shock set in soon after Joel's visit, bringing with it nightmares, a high temperature and a very bad sore throat. After a fortnight in hospital she was sent on to a convalescent home in Sussex for a further three weeks. She tired easily, there were vicious headaches to contend with, and now and again she found herself falling into fits of deep depression when she didn't want to speak to anyone and spent hours just staring into space.

'It's just nature's way of giving you time to come to terms with what's happened to you,' one doctor explained. 'Don't try to fight it, Daisy. Just go with the flow of it.'

Gradually she began to understand what he meant as she found herself sifting through her mind, picking up previous incidents, experiences and even conversations and examining them. She thought it was a bit like sorting out her bedroom, chucking out the rubbish, polishing up the things which were of value to her, rearranging it all in a tidy fashion. She found she wasn't sorry she began looking for Ellen any more, she knew the truth now, and however bad it was, the cobwebs had been cleared.

She knew the value of her adopted family too. She loved them, and they loved her. Nothing else mattered.

When Josie's death was announced, the press were desperate to discover what the connection was between Daisy and her, and made a real nuisance of themselves, waylaying, Lucy, Tom and John at the house and the hospital for information. But John, with Joel's help, eventually managed to convince them it was just a friendship which had turned sour, and insisted they left Daisy alone. Fortunately the once famous model's resurrection after being thought to be dead for so long, and the fact that she had murdered her family, was more than enough for them to feed on, and they soon lost interest in Daisy.

John kept all the press clippings for her to read once she was able to cope with them. Along with all the old stuff about Josie's past, there was a great deal about Ellen too. Old friends from Bristol had been interviewed, and there were photographs of Ellen and children she worked with at the school. It was heartening to read how distressed they were to hear what had really happened to her. Many of them told touching stories about what she had meant to them.

Through this, Daisy was able to put a few further pieces back into the jigsaw to complete the picture of her mother.

The police in turn had sifted through the records and reports on the fire at Beacon Farm, and it seemed that Mavis's theory of how Josie engineered it was probably a fairly accurate one. In the Fire Officer's report there was a mention of an unusually large amount of paraffin stored in the farmhouse, but at the time this had been put down to Albert's eccentricity, as he was known for keeping fuel for his lamps indoors.

The reason why the coroner had found no reason to consider that the body of the younger woman found at the farm was anyone other than Josie was because of a lack of any dental records. It seemed neither girl had ever visited a dentist.

Yet throughout all this, it was the love and concern Daisy received from her family and friends that helped her on the road to full recovery. And above all it was Joel to whom she felt most indebted. He had not only rescued her in the nick of time, and supported and protected her family under the barrage of press interest, but he'd been a constant visitor, making her laugh again and encouraging her to talk through her feelings about Ellen and Josie.

Daisy told him about the book Josie had claimed to be writing, and expressed her fears that if it existed it might fall into the wrong hands when her belongings were disposed of. Joel used his connections to discover which solicitor had been appointed to wind up her estate, and got an assurance that if it was found, it would in due course come to Daisy.

With his work commitments, Joel couldn't visit Daisy so often in Sussex, but he telephoned her daily. When she returned home, hardly a day passed without him popping in.

In late July, when Lucy and Tom finally saw that their sister really was on the mend, they decided to go off on their planned round-the-world trip. Seeing them off with her father at the airport, Daisy knew the time had come to start on some plans of her own.

Her first priority was to seduce Joel.

It had become more and more obvious to her that she did truly love him. The misgivings she'd had in the past seemed absurd now, for since waking up in hospital, all the fine qualities – his strength, kindness and sense of humour – which had attracted her in the first place seemed to have been expanded. She knew without any doubt that he was the only man for her, but although she was sure she could always count on his friendship, she wasn't convinced he still fancied her the way he had. She guessed it was hard to feel desire for someone with their head bandaged, but she was afraid she might have hurt him too badly for him to take the risk again with her.

So it was up to her to make the first move, and as her father was going away for a week's sailing, and Joel had a few days off starting around the same time, she invited him to come round for a meal that Saturday night.

Saturday arrived with the promise of another long hot day, and Daisy spent most of it lying in the sun in the garden, contemplating the night ahead. She was only making a simple meal, pasta with a creamy prawn sauce, salad and garlic bread, strawberries and cream to follow. But food wasn't on her mind, that was secondary to how she had to look for Joel.

She wanted him to see the girl he'd fallen for nearly two years earlier. In those days she'd been pretty sensational – slinky dresses, four-inch heels, a *femme fatale* by anyone's definition. But as time had gone by she'd modified her appearance. She had always claimed this was because he didn't approve, but in her heart she knew the truth was that she'd grown lazy.

It wasn't going to be that easy. After the operation her hair had been a mess, for she had a large shaved area on the left side of her head. A visiting hairdresser in the convalescent home had cut the other side short to even it up, and cropped her curly hair on top so it partially covered the bald section. For a while, she felt ill every time she looked at herself and despaired of ever looking nice again. But the hair had begun to grow at last and now the scars were hidden.

She had washed her hair that morning and let it dry naturally in the sun and for the first time since she left the convalescent home, she could see the old Daisy was coming back. She stayed out in the garden until four o'clock, then went in to prepare the food, tidy up and lay the dining-room table. She opened the French windows wide, moved the table closer to the doors, and cut a bunch of heavily perfumed pink roses as a centrepiece for it.

Later, as she lay back in a scented bath, she felt happy and secure in herself, the way she used to when her mother was alive.

Daisy smiled to herself as she remembered how in her late teens she had rejected all her mother's standards and thought her parents were so terribly starchy and old-fashioned. She could remember watching her mother preparing for a dinner party, wondering why when it was only neighbours and old friends coming in she found it necessary to polish the silver, arrange flowers and have candles on the table – not to mention scrub out the bathroom, polish the furniture and put new pot-pourri in dishes everywhere. Daisy had once stated that no one would ever catch her doing such unnecessary things. But now, a few years on, she seemed to have acquired those same values, wanting the whole house to look beautiful, the dinner to look and taste perfect.

She supposed she had finally grown up. The last year

might have been fraught with sadness and hurt, but she had probably learned more about herself, her family and the world in general than she'd learned in the previous twenty-five.

'Wow! You look gorgeous!' Joel exclaimed as Daisy opened the door to him at seven-thirty.

Daisy blushed. Her emerald-green lacy dress was an old one, and she had been a bit shocked by how tight and revealing it was, but by the gleam in Joel's eye, it was going to have the desired effect.

'You look pretty gorgeous yourself,' she retorted. He was wearing a white polo shirt and chinos, his face and arms golden from the sun. She kissed him on the cheek, and he smelled as delicious as he looked.

They sat outside in the garden for a couple of drinks before eating, and Daisy asked him about his work. He had just been moved on to the Vice Squad, and he was enjoying it immensely.

She went back into the kitchen and put the pasta on to cook, and reheated the sauce in the microwave. Everything else was ready. Within fifteen minutes they were sitting down to eat.

'Mmm, this is the business,' Joel said as he tasted the prawn sauce. 'I've been living on those oven-ready meals for so long I'd forgotten what real food looked like, let alone tasted like.' He speared a piece of avocado in the salad. 'Ah, what's this? Something alien.'

Daisy laughed. When they first met and she began cooking for him, he claimed everything was alien. He'd been brought up in a home where even pasta was considered exotic and weird. In the navy, like in the police force, he'd had ordinary canteen-type food, and when the ship had docked in foreign countries he'd always been too suspicious to try anything he didn't recognize. He'd overcome this prejudice very quickly after meeting Daisy, but then she had bludgeoned him into trying everything.

It was so lovely being alone again with him. It was such a warm evening, only the lightest of breezes making the candles flutter. As the daylight gradually slipped away into darkness, the scent of the roses on the table, the good food and the wine made it easy to talk.

He said that when Daisy shut him out of her life his world had fallen apart. 'Everything seemed so pointless, getting up in the mornings, cleaning the flat, washing my clothes. I didn't know until then how attached I'd got to your family or how you'd coloured every aspect of my life. My mates soon got tired of me being miserable, at work they said I was a grouch. I'd always prided myself on being so self-contained too. I suppose I imagined that I was too tough to go to pieces over a woman.'

Daisy reached out and stroked his cheek tenderly. 'I'm sorry I put you through that,' she whispered. 'Yet it's nice to find you can be so emotional. That was one of my misgivings about you. I got the idea sometimes that you didn't *feel*. You did seem very self-contained.'

'I suppose I got the idea that I had to be masterful and bossy with you, because you seemed to be so dizzy and frothy,' he admitted.

'Frothy!' she giggled.

He smiled and took her hand in his, kissing the tips of her fingers. 'Yes, frothy. And you still are sometimes, like that day I got to the convalescent home and found you in tears. I thought you'd had some terrible news, that you needed another operation or something. You were only upset because you couldn't bend to paint your toenails without your head throbbing.'

'A girl's toenails are important,' she laughed.

'Am I important to you too?' he asked, his dark eyes looking right into hers.

'Extraordinarily so,' she whispered.

'Then let's go to bed,' he said, getting up and pulling her up too. 'Right now, before we have pudding or coffee.'

'I planned to put on some soul music and dance with you,' she said.

'We can do that later. We've got all night.'

She looked at his face and his brown eyes were pools of mischief, so sexy they made her shiver. His lips were soft and full, pink and moist from the red wine. Then she looked at his hand in hers, so big, so capable, and she remembered how sensitive those fingers could be.

'Kiss me,' she whispered. 'I've forgotten what a real one is like.'

His arms came round her and his lips down on to hers. The kiss began gently, his tongue teasing hers, but his arms tightened around her and all at once it was fierce and passionate, with more fire than she ever remembered before. Scooping her up in his arms, he carried her upstairs and laid her on the bed. He stood for just a moment looking down at her.

'What is it?' she asked.

'Just thinking how much I want you.' His voice was husky with emotion.

It was even better than when they first met, all the raw excitement yet the security of familiarity too. Joel undressed her, kissing her shoulders and arms, unhurried, wanting to make it last.

As he made gentle love to her, she could feel the last of the tension inside her ebbing away. There was no room in her mind for anything else but him – time, place or tomorrow didn't exist as he brought her to a fierce climax.

'I love you,' she heard him murmur at the height of it, and his body and hers seemed to flow into each other in a way she'd never felt before, then suddenly she was crying at the sheer beauty of it.

'No tears,' he whispered, licking them away. 'Fred will think I'm hurting you and savage my backside.'

Daisy glanced to the side of her bed to see Fred sitting there, his head on one side, ears cocked, as if questioning what they were doing. All at once she was laughing.

'The new model Daisy goes from tears to laughter in one point five seconds,' Joel said, imitating the voice of a man who did car adverts on a local radio station. 'A smooth ride, with plenty of excitement, that's what you can expect with the new Daisy.'

They were still laughing later when they went downstairs again to eat the strawberries and cream and drink more wine. Taking a bottle with them, they went out into the now dark garden and swung on the swing seat, Joel in his boxer shorts and Daisy wearing just her knickers and his polo shirt.

'We could make love again here,' he said, swinging fast. 'With the added thrill of not knowing whether the neighbours are watching.'

Daisy lay back looking up at the stars. 'We've had this swing as long as I can remember,' she said. 'Mum would never part with it even though it's a bit rusty and the cover's shabby. I wonder if that's because she and Dad used to frolic around out here when we were little?'

'I expect so.' Joel smiled, lying down beside her. 'One of the first things I sensed in this house was the feeling of love. It kind of wraps itself round you. Shame we could never afford to buy it from your dad if he sells up and moves on.'

Daisy looked at him questioningly.

Joel smiled again. 'I suppose I ought to ask you to marry me before discussing buying houses. Would you marry a poor copper who can't keep you in the manner you are accustomed to?'

'Is that a proposal or just a fact-finding mission?' she asked.

'It's a proposal.'

Daisy giggled. 'Yes, I would marry a poor copper. I'd even live in his dirty little ex-council flat. That's if he asks me properly.'

'Not the bended knee bit?' he said in mock horror.

'Oh yes, the full issue or not at all.'

Joel rolled off the swing on to the grass and crawled away from her. He selected a rose from a bush and crawled back with it in his teeth.

'Will you marry me, Daisy?' he said.

'I will,' she replied, and leaned forward to kiss him. But the swing moved back and she fell off it on top of him on the grass.

They made love again there, prolonging it even when they'd grown cold and the ground felt damp beneath them. 'We have to hang on to this memory,' she whispered. 'And when our silver wedding comes along, we'll do it again, just to remind ourselves what it was like.'

'But I'll be over sixty,' he whispered back.

'I'll keep you fit, don't you worry,' she laughed. 'I want your bum to be as firm as it is now, or I'll trade you in.'

Chapter Twenty-five

A week after her night with Joel, the postman called on Saturday morning with a parcel for Daisy. As it was around eighteen inches long and nine inches thick, she didn't for one moment think it was Josie's book. She had expected that to fit in a large envelope.

But as she tore off the outer brown paper and discovered two box-files inside, her heart began to flutter with excitement. She'd expected a few notebooks filled with scrawl, but this was a neatly typed manuscript.

There was a covering letter enclosed from the solicitor in Chancery Lane. It stated that he had been asked to pass the manuscript over to her, and it was hers to do whatever she wished with, but he hoped that if she decided to attempt to get it published, she would come to him first to discuss it. He also added that in the absence of a will, once probate had been settled, and Josie's flat and business sold, Daisy was likely to be the main beneficiary.

It was frustrating that she couldn't sit down and read the manuscript immediately, but her father was due back in time for lunch the following day, and as Joel had stayed almost the whole week, there was very little food left in the house.

When she returned with the shopping, she hastily put it away, then sat down at the dining-room table to read the manuscript.

Josie had said that a journalist had helped her with it, but almost immediately Daisy realized that was unlikely. Maybe a journalist had sparked off the idea to write it, and he or she might have wanted to do it as that way they'd make money out of it. But the work was all Josie's; Daisy could hear her voice on every page.

Josie had said too that it was badly written, but there she was mistaken. Maybe it was nowhere near publishable standard, but she had a flair for description and characterization.

She had begun the work in 1980, for the date was at the top of the page, and it was written in the main as if she were Ellen. But Daisy got the impression it wasn't only because Josie was supposed to be dead, but because she had found that by using Ellen as the narrator she could stand back from herself to recount her story honestly.

Yet she lapsed in this at times. In parts of the story Ellen couldn't have known about, or when something had clearly distressed her, she became Josie again.

The story began when Ellen was eight and discovered that her real mother had flung herself off the cliff with her baby. As Ellen she was able to show that Josie felt hurt too at finding that they were only half-sisters, that her conception was out of wedlock and her parents' subsequent marriage one of propriety rather than love.

This early part was hugely overwritten and repetitive, with lengthy descriptions of how close the sisters were, their games together, going to school and life for them both on the farm. It came across as if Ellen had the harder time, being burdened with a great many chores and bullied and humiliated by Violet, yet Josie had her own set of problems even then.

She wasn't as clever as Ellen, her father ignored her, and Violet was constantly trying to make her outshine Ellen. The picture she painted of herself was of a bewildered little girl, her loyalties divided between her mother and her sister and unable to satisfy either of them.

Yet despite continuing and often ruthless attempts from Violet to create animosity between the two girls, Daisy could feel their love for one another. In the descriptions of their games, swimming in the cove, and play-acting in the barn, Daisy could almost hear their laughter, and she didn't think it was just because they were thrown together and isolated from any other playmates.

Mavis had told Daisy about how Violet took Josie off to Helston in the summer when she was fourteen, but only by reading Josie's account of it could she see that this was the start of her rebellion.

She described in detail her uncle's luxurious house, the discovery of how good it was to watch television, play tennis, join a drama club, to be bought nice clothes and treated as if she was important. She met her first sweetheart there too, and bitterly resented Violet taking her home. Her account of Ellen falling for Pierre was very moving, and proved that although Josie no longer wanted to be at the farm, she still cared deeply for her sister. Daisy could almost see the two girls huddled down in the cove, confiding their innermost secrets, promising they would always look out for one another, no matter what their parents did.

In the next section, just before Ellen found the job in Bristol, Josie found it hard to be Ellen narrating the story. She switched from 'she' to 'me' all the time, trying to show how frightened Ellen was at being pregnant, yet at the same time revealing her own distress because her sister suddenly stopped confiding in her and appeared aloof and indifferent.

Daisy sighed deeply when she got to the part about the misunderstandings created by the girls' letters to each other when Ellen first left home. She could understand why Ellen didn't dare write frankly about her condition, and equally well see why Josie came to the conclusion she had been fooled and that Ellen only faked a pregnancy to escape from home and have some fun.

Looking back at herself at fifteen, Daisy could understand completely, too, why Josie left for London with the two young men. She was just as silly and wilful herself at that age. She ached for Josie being forced to take that awful room in Westbourne Grove, yet she also admired her courage in not running home.

The account of the glamour photography, the meeting with Mark Kinsale and his subsequent seduction of her, was written so well. Daisy knew that had she been in Josie's shoes she would have been just as naive, frightened and yet hopeful.

Josie thought when Mark wanted to make love to her that he must love her. She believed everything would change if he were her lover, that he'd be kinder, gentler. She was also afraid to refuse in case he abandoned her.

It was never good for her, even in the beginning, he was rough and said crude things, he belittled her and said she wasn't sexy. So she tried to be what he wanted, allowing him to do whatever he wanted, however perverted, acting as if she loved it. What else could she do? It seemed to be the only way through the doorway to fame and fortune.

For Daisy that brought back the first time she had sex, and the memory of it made her cry with shame. It couldn't be called making love, for that boy had forced himself upon her on the couch while his parents were out. She had submitted to it because he was something of a heart-throb at school, and she foolishly imagined he must be in love with her. It was like giving him a present for stooping even to notice her. She recalled the hurt when he didn't even walk her home later, but hurried her out of the door, saying, 'See you around.'

Daisy broke off from reading at five in the afternoon to make herself a snack, then returned to the section about Josie's meteoric rise to fame. She skipped a great deal of it, because it was all stuff she knew, but began again as Mark Kinsale introduced Josie to speed.

She needed something to give her a lift, because he kept her working for such long hours. Those little pills seemed so harmless; they made her laugh and chatter, banished weariness. But she didn't know until it was too late what they were doing to her. Or that by giving her drugs he was gaining complete and utter control over her and the money she earned.

Josie described that first couple of years of fame as like being in a Technicolor dream, complete with a soundtrack from the Beatles and the Rolling Stones. It was clear to Daisy that while Josie had some nostalgia for being dressed in fabulous clothes, meeting famous people and receiving adulation from the press, she was still very bitter that she'd never been anything more than a money-making scheme to Mark.

She wrote of her loneliness, for the high life of wild parties and night-clubs was a sham too. Mark would take her to these places, make sure the press noticed her, then whisk her away. In reality she spent most nights alone in her flat. The speed kept her awake, so Mark gave her sleeping pills. Then she needed more speed the following day to wake up.

Daisy was particularly shocked by one paragraph at this point:

Josie felt she was like a doll. Taken out of the toy box, dressed up and paraded. Then she would be stripped of her finery and abused by Mark before being flung back naked into the toy box in the dark.

She had been thrown abruptly into an adult world without any preparation, and there was no one there to help, love or advise her.

Daisy could see that Mark must have planned his strategy right from his first meeting with Josie. Paying her rent, luring her into a sexual relationship, feeding her drugs and withholding money prevented her even thinking of escape.

Josie described how she once begged Mark to let her have enough money to buy an armchair or settee, some pictures for the walls and a television, for her flat held only a bed. He laughed at her and said that was all she needed. This theme of wanting to create a real home for herself came in many times later on in the book, and it made sense of the luxury and comfort of her place in Askwith Court.

Ellen made a surprise visit to Chelsea and was shocked to find her sister living in bare rooms.

I was scared for her. Josie's face is in the papers almost every day, I thought she was making a fortune and I expected to find her living like a queen. But the sheets on the bed were filthy, piles of dirty clothes and underwear everywhere. She didn't even have enough money to take them to the laundrette, and she was so ashamed I had to see it.

Ellen, it appeared, questioned Josie closely about her earnings, and said that Mark was ripping her off. She even offered to go to him and have it out with him. Yet for some reason, and Josie didn't explain this, she didn't allow Ellen to do that.

It was during the same visit that Ellen had tried to tell her sister about her feelings at giving up her baby. Josie had obviously realized at some later time that she'd hurt her sister very deeply by taking no real interest, for there was a note of deep regret in her statement.

Josie was too wrapped up in herself, to be concerned at what I'd been through, or how much it had changed me. I made allowances for her then because she was so young, I didn't know at that time that she was taking drugs, neither did I know anything about them, that came later. But it was so hurtful that she wouldn't let me talk it out, that she laughed at me for taking a job with handicapped children, for wanting to rebuild my life by doing something worthwhile.

It was here, in just a few short paragraphs, that Daisy really began to see her birth mother. Josie was frank – at that time she had resented her sister attempting to do what she saw as 'spoiling her fun'. Yet, perhaps because she written this so long after, and had come to see that Ellen's warnings were given out of love for her, she had graciously described Ellen's character and personality.

Ellen liked fun too, but for her this was dressing up and going out to a club, shopping in the Chelsea boutiques, or going for a meal in one of the new American hamburger places. She wasn't averse to drink, but drugs frightened her. She liked men too, but it was the gentler, more thoughtful ones she was attracted to, not the outrageous show-offs who strutted down the King's Road in velvet jackets and knee-high boots, as though they were rock stars.

It was Ellen who adopted the hippie style and philosophy, not Josie. She loved Bob Dylan, Steppenwolf, Jimi Hendrix and the Doors. She would sit on the floor in her long, flowing dresses, flowers pinned into her hair, and talk about poetry, books and alternative religions. She cared, she wanted to put the world to rights, and in her own small way, through her work at the school and in her day-to-day contact with people, she put her beliefs into practice.

Later on in the second file, Daisy became immersed in the roller-coaster life Josie led – trips to Paris and Rome, staying in the best hotels, invitations to rich men's yachts in the South of France. She had beautiful clothes, a hairdresser and makeup artist on hand, but she never got to see the Eiffel Tower or the Coliseum, or had fun like everyone who read about her in the papers supposed.

In one poignant passage she described how Mark took her to the beach at St-Tropez. He took pictures of her sunbathing, posing in a minuscule bikini and doing handstands in the sand. But when he'd finished and she asked if she could swim, he refused to let her and took her back to the hotel room.

Daisy read too in horror of how Mark forced Josie to have kinky sex with a man introduced as the Duke, while he watched. There were many more accounts of three-somes in the same vein. It wasn't clear whether these were before or after the one with the Duke, as Josie had said her affair with Mark ended after that point. But it appeared to be afterwards, as if he'd blackmailed her into further trysts in return for more work.

Josie had already made it quite clear that she had never enjoyed sex, but now Daisy could see it truly disgusted her. She went along with Mark's fetishes because she was afraid not to. At one point she said she thought she might just as well become a hooker, then at least she'd get paid for it.

Ellen's joyful love life clearly both mystified her and made her jealous, for she had written one section at this point as if it were comments made by Josie while visiting her sister.

You're at it all the time like a bloody rabbit. I can't see what you get out of it. All your men are such earnest drips too. I'm surprised they've got it in them.

With Ellen's voice she'd written her view on the subject:

Josie was so screwed up, she couldn't see that if she was only to find a gentle, loving man, one that respected her, she might have found why I enjoyed sex. But she seemed, and perhaps this was conditioning by Mark or Violet, to be unable to look beyond a man's bank balance and status. I have certainly never found that a fat wallet alone makes a satisfactory lover.

The mystery of exactly why Josie's modelling career came to such an abrupt end was also explained.

It seemed Mark had been having an affair with Penelope

Cartwright, a married woman who for some years ran the biggest model agency in London, even before he'd met Josie. When Penelope finally felt ready to leave her husband for Mark, Josie had to be dispensed with.

Mark's ruthlessness had been apparent throughout the story, but he was clearly vicious too, for if he wasn't going to make any further money from Josie, he didn't intend to let anyone else either. He used his considerable influence to make sure no other photographer or agency would book her for work. He even sold salacious stories about her to the newspapers, so she lost all credibility.

The little money she had soon ran out. When she couldn't pay her rent, she moved to cheaper and cheaper places. Only Ellen was there for her.

Daisy found herself weeping as she read passages which showed so clearly that Ellen was the one person who truly cared, who never rejected her however badly she behaved. She wondered how after so much care and love Josie could even think of killing Ellen.

Perhaps as Josie had written this she was filled with remorse, and even believed herself to have been mad at the time she did it, for she recounted things most people wouldn't want to admit to. She stole money from Ellen several times, often landed herself on her in the middle of the night, and stayed for days, then left without saying goodbye. She contracted a venereal disease; Ellen took her for treatment. The police raided a flat in Knightsbridge and found Josie to be the only woman in the company of five men. She made some blue films and posed naked for several magazines, and still Ellen stuck by her.

Yet interspersed with running back to Ellen, Josie also frequently returned to Cornwall.

She had this terrible need to be accepted and approved of by our parents. Maybe if she'd just gone home quietly, she might have won them over, but she wouldn't do that. She always had to wear something sensational, she'd even pawn something to buy it if she had no money. Once she was there she behaved like a visiting film star, demanding special food from Violet, staying in bed half the day. Then she'd go off to Falmouth to show off to her old schoolfriends, and she always made sure the local press knew she was there. But then that was part of the lure of her home town, because there at least she was still a celebrity.

Daisy puzzled over that last section. It seemed to her that Josie felt as strongly about the farm as Ellen did, but for very different reasons. While Ellen loved the land, the animals and nature, for Josie the farm stood for security and perhaps the status which she'd failed to find anywhere else.

Nothing changed there, not the view, the lack of comfort, or her parents' disapproval. But living in a world where everything else changed faster than she could change her clothes, Josie found this comforting.

Daisy saw that the farm was almost like a character in itself, and its power had run through the whole story. Josie had learned at an early age that her mother had married her father for it. Even before that her father and his brother fought over it. All through her growing-up years she had observed people were impressed by it. Her mother had urged her to help her persuade her father to sell it. She even wanted rid of Ellen to make it easier. Ellen loved it and would have liked nothing better than to stay and work on it.

Daisy thought Josie must have eventually begun to wish it were hers, just because everyone else seemed to value it. Maybe she began to fantasize about how it would be if it became hers? Did she find out it was willed to Ellen when Albert died?

Sadly Josie gave no hint of any of that. But she did show that anger and resentment were building up in her, and got Ellen to relate it.

Mum told Josie she was stupid for not finding a rich old sugar daddy to keep her. She said if she'd had her looks she wouldn't be stuck on a miserable farm in the middle of nowhere. She took all Josie's clothes away on one occasion when she'd come home drunk from Falmouth. She beat her with a cane, and locked her in the shed all night as a punishment.

But Josie was hurt even worse by Dad. He didn't hit her, but he acted like she wasn't there. One night she pleaded with him to talk to her, and he said, 'I've only got one daughter now, I disowned you when you told lies about me.' She tried to explain how it was Mark who said all those things, not her, but he wouldn't listen. He just turned his back on her and said that in his eyes she was already dead.

There was a litany of such incidents, and Daisy found she couldn't read them all, for the harshness of Josie's parents astounded her. Yet the perverse thing was that on every visit, Violet kept urging her to find a rich man, and get him to keep her.

Daisy could see why Josie had lost all sense of right and wrong. The press had fêted her when she was under Mark's protection, then vilified her when he cast her aside. She had her father on one hand refusing to even acknowledge she was still alive, and her mother urging her into being an old man's plaything.

Drugs, drink, sex, and men. They were the things which drove Josie. She needed the first two to cope with the second two. She went with anyone who was prepared to keep her drugged or drunk. I knew she'd reached the absolute bottom when she turned up early one morning after being robbed and raped by two men. That time I refused her any further help. I let her have a bath, cooked her a meal and then I said she had to go. I hoped if I were tough with her she'd pull herself together. She went home to Cornwall, and it seemed it had worked. She got a job, even talked about buying a house.

Daisy turned the page eagerly, realizing she was now close to the part where Josie set the fire. But to her acute disappointment, the work ended there. A blank page followed it.

She sat for a while, thinking about what she'd read. She wanted to cry, yet she wasn't sure who for. She felt she now knew the whole family intimately, and each one of them was tragic in some way.

To close the file up, she had to manipulate the pages back on to the arched binder as many of them had come out, and as she got to the end, to her surprise she found another page sandwiched between some blank ones.

It was different to the rest, typed on what looked like an old manual machine. The page was dated 1 November 1978.

Daisy fell on it gleefully, knowing Josie must have written it right after the fire. She hoped it would shed some light on how she felt about what she'd done.

It wasn't a confession. She'd written it as Ellen, and it had a very melodramatic ring to it, as if she was experimenting with the part.

I am totally alone now. My entire family is gone, and I'm sitting here in my flat looking back at all the sadness, bitterness, hatred and envy, and trying to find some explanation within myself why my family members were all so damaged.

I cannot. They each had perhaps a little more than a fair share of disappointment and heartache, but many others have worse and carry their burdens lightly.

My beautiful, troubled sister is dead, and I grieve for her.

Yet I can't say I'm entirely sorry, for at least now her suffering is over. They say the phoenix rises out of a fire, and I shall strive to do likewise. In time I plan to move to London, and lead the kind of life Josie could have had if she'd just been wiser.

*

Daisy sat there for quite some time, reading and re-reading it. Was Josie mad then, deluding herself that she was Ellen? Or was it just part of the act, like putting on her sister's clothes, driving her car and living in her flat? She wondered too if Josie had really wanted to write a confession about what she'd done, but was afraid to commit it to paper.

As she picked up the page to put it back in the file, she saw there was handwriting on the back of it.

It was dated the end of April, and Daisy realized it was the day she went into the shop and spoke to her for the first time.

I don't know what to think or do. A girl came into the shop today and announced herself as my daughter.

For the first time since I became Ellen, the shock made me forget how she'd react. It came to me later, once I'd had time to think about it. Ellen would have cried, hugged the girl, closed the shop, told the whole world who this pretty, vibrant young woman was. She would have been filled with joy.

But all I felt was fear, even if I did manage to hide it.

I've been happy as Ellen. By taking on her character and values I found not only success in the business world but the peace I longed for, the kind of harmonious way of living I always envied her for.

But this girl threatens all that. If I let her into my life I will need to be on my guard constantly. Yet if I tell her I don't want her, what then?

I know I really don't have a choice, I have to do what Ellen would have done, and I have to trust that she will guide me, as I feel she has so often done before when I've been troubled. But is it possible for her to guide me through the correct emotions of being a mother?

If only I'd let her tell me about her baby. I don't know how long her labour was, if she had stitches, what the baby weighed, if she was fat, thin, bald or red-haired from the start.

I never asked. I turned away from her every time she tried to speak of it. Why did I? I always loved her, we shared so much.

Tonight I'm very ashamed, for suddenly I can see that being compelled to give away her baby was right at the centre of what she was.

It was her one sorrow, the quiet part of her I could never understand, and that deep well of understanding she had came from it too.

How ironic it is that I thought I knew everything about her, yet I had to be confronted with her child before I saw the part which was invisible to me before.

I was always so self-centred. I never truly considered another person's feelings, or why they reacted to certain situations in a certain manner. I certainly never held myself accountable for anything.

Ellen was so different. She was born with an instinct for nurturing, she forgave people, bore her troubles without blaming anyone else. Yet at the same time she could always find good reasons for everyone else's bad behaviour. She even managed to get Violet loving her in the end.

Maybe that's what set me against her finally. I was born to that woman, yet she only ever used me as a tool to get what she wanted. I can't mourn her or Dad, they were hateful to me, and made me what I became. But I do mourn for Ellen, and when I was confronted with her daughter, the terrible loss came back to me.

Everything Ellen did was right. She had a kind of purity that left no one untouched by it.

I think I saw some of that in Daisy too. I hope I did. And for Ellen's sake I can't turn her away.

This is going to be the ultimate test.

Daisy let the sheet fall to the table and wept. For Ellen, whom she could now see, feel and hear, and for troubled Josie.

There was still no way she could condone what Josie had done, but she now had a better understanding of why. It seemed to her the money Josie made from murder was secondary to getting a kind of revenge. She found a way to be reborn, and wicked as it was, it made a kind of sense.

That night Daisy was unable to sleep, her mind still in the pages of the book. Strangely, she wished Lucy were here, so she could discuss it with her. It was after all a story about sisters, and they could both find a few parallels to their own relationship in it.

She wondered too what Lorna would have thought about it. She was an Ellen type, a carer, a doer. Had she had a wayward sister she would have looked after her no matter what happened.

She could imagine Lorna pointing out the pluses that had come from looking for her birth mother. She would have said Daisy had learned to look beyond herself, found understanding of others' weaknesses, learned to value her own family, to forgive, and to recognize the true value of honesty. She wasn't dizzy any more.

On Sunday morning, as Daisy cleaned the house and prepared the lunch, ready for her father's return from his holiday, Joel was still in the sitting-room, reading the book. He had come straight from the night shift at six that morning, let himself in, and started on it.

It was torment watching him immersed in it. Daisy wanted to ask where he had got to, or what he thought of it so far. Yet she resisted the temptation, for it was important to get his rounded view of the whole story, not just parts of it.

When she heard his step coming down the hall towards the kitchen, she wheeled round. 'Have you finished it?' she asked.

He nodded gravely.

'Well, what do you think?' she said impatiently.

'As a policeman I'd say she had more than a few screws missing. But as a man, I feel like crying for her.'

'Do you?' Daisy gasped. She hadn't expected that reaction.

'Yes, very much so.' He reached out for Daisy and hugged her tightly, leaning his face down into her neck. 'If only there had been someone strong there for her when she first met that Mark Kinsale. What an evil bastard he was!' he said with feeling.

'But that doesn't excuse her!'

'No, it doesn't,' Joel said, straightening up and trying to smile. 'But it's a lesson to all of us about what can happen to kids when their parents fail them.'

That had been the last thing Daisy had thought before she finally fell asleep after reading the book, and she'd remembered how her mother and father had never given up on her, no matter what she did. She was glad Joel had seen it that way too, and she hoped one day they would be good parents.

'I know it's a weird question. But did you get to like Josie?' she asked. 'I mean, despite everything.'

'Yeah, I did,' he nodded. 'Troubled, mad, vengeful, whatever, there was something. But it was that note she wrote after you found her that got me. She was admitting then what she was. She could have saved herself by telling you to piss off, but she was trying so hard to do what she saw as the right thing, for Ellen.'

'She made a pretty good job of it too,' Daisy said wistfully. 'She was so interested in me, so admiring and generous too. Of course now, with hindsight, I can see that it wasn't really right between us. I always wondered why she didn't talk about when she had me, didn't shed a few tears, or even tell me about her work at the school. But I believed that she'd cut all that out of her mind after the fire.'

'Lots of adopted kids can't really bond with their birth mothers, even when they are both totally truthful,' Joel said, and his eyes were sad. 'That's why I was never enthusiastic about you searching for her in the first place.

408

I was afraid you were trying desperately to replace Lorna.'

'I never wanted that,' Daisy said, and stroked his concerned face. 'If I'm absolutely frank, I didn't want another mother. It was just the unravelling, the mystery that appealed to me. What a mystery too.' She sighed. 'And what do I do with that book now?'

'Sit on it for a few years,' he said with a grin. 'It's a ripping story in so many ways, it could make a fortune for you. But I guess you'll have to think what Ellen would have wanted you to do with it. Do you think you know her well enough now to judge?'

'She'd want it burned,' Daisy said firmly. 'She wouldn't want all that let loose on a sensation-seeking public.'

'What if it would buy us a nice house like this one?' he asked, reaching out and caressing her neck.

'Get thee behind me, Satan!' she laughed. 'Besides, it looks as though I might get a few bob when the estate's wound up anyway.'

All at once she realized she didn't want to discuss Josie or her book any more. Her troubled soul was laid to rest, that had to be the end of it.

She glanced at Joel, and wondered if he felt the same, for he was just standing leaning against the wall watching her make the gravy with a distant look in his eyes.

'What is it?' she said.

'Father's still unknown,' he said suddenly. 'Any thoughts about searching him out?'

She knew he was probably joking. A joke in bad taste under the circumstances, but she guessed he'd only made it to try to lighten the mood.

'No,' she said, and stamped loudly on the floor. 'I know I'm still pretty dizzy, but not crazy. Knowing that being able to do acrobatics came from him is quite enough. I don't want to know anything more.'

'You disappoint me,' he said in mock seriousness. 'I always thought you were the most curious girl I'd ever met.'

'I'm cured,' she said. 'I've been reborn totally lacking in curiosity.'

'I thought you might say that,' he said with a grin. 'So you don't want to know what I've got in my pocket then?' He patted his hip temptingly.

'No,' she said, but her eyes were glinting. 'I will not be tempted to ask.'

She went over to him and began kissing him until his arms went round her tightly. Slowly, without him noticing, she lowered her hand to his pocket and she could tell by the hard lump with a curve to the top that it was a small jewellery box. She slid her hand in, grabbed it and pulled it out, breaking away from him and running into the sitting-room.

Joel chased after her. 'Stop thief!' he yelled at the top of his voice.

Giggling, Daisy opened the box. As she half expected, it was an engagement ring, a single diamond surrounded by tiny sapphires. 'Oh, Joel,' she gasped. 'How wonderfully old-fashioned and romantic. But you shouldn't have! We should save our money for getting married.'

Joel took the ring from her and slipped it on to her finger. It fitted perfectly. 'See what a good detective I'd make,' he said smugly. 'Even found out your ring size without you knowing! And I can't boast you are going to marry me, not without some evidence of intent on your finger.'

'How did you find out my ring size?' she asked.

'You said you'd been reborn without curiosity.'

She heard the sound of her father's car outside in the street.

'I lied,' she laughed. 'But that still doesn't mean I want to dig out my trapeze-swinging father. The only dad I want or need is just coming in for his lunch.'